a
mother's
goodbye

a mother's goodbye

KATE HEWITT

Bookouture

Published by Bookouture in 2018

An imprint of StoryFire Ltd.

Carmelite House
50 Victoria Embankment
London EC4Y 0DZ

www.bookouture.com

ISBN: 978-1-78681-422-7
eBook ISBN: 978-1-78681-421-0

Dedicated to my father, George Berry,
who caught his train on December 23, 2015,
and to my wonderful husband, Cliff,
for always holding my hand.

PROLOGUE

Morning light slants through the hospital window as slowly I come through the door of the nursery, my body aching with both fatigue and fear. My heart is beating in a painful staccato as I approach the plastic bassinet. I am swathed in scrubs and latex, due to the possibility of infection, but my arms ache with the need to reach and hold, and then to never let go. But I can't; I know I can't.

A nurse smiles at me sympathetically and gestures to the bassinet, as if granting me permission to approach, or perhaps simply pointing out the right baby. But of course I know you, my child.

My child. The words buoy me inside as if I am filled with lightness, with air, so I feel as if I am floating. *My child.* How could I not know it? How could I not feel it? It inhabits every fiber of my being, every cell. I pulse with the knowledge, the fragile joy. Incredulously, I smile.

And there you are – small, so small, swathed in a white flannel blanket, a tuft of light brown hair under a little knitted cap, your fists by your face like flowers, your lips pursed like a tiny rosebud, cheeks soft and round. *Perfect.* I know every mother thinks the same, of course she does, but no one feels it like me. *No one.*

I stand in front of your bassinet, battling both tears and euphoria, because it's too soon to feel this way, or maybe it's too late. I reach out one hand and rest it on the plastic crib, longing to touch your soft, pink skin, your round cheek, already knowing how smooth it will feel. *I love you. I will do anything for you.*

I didn't expect to feel it so strongly, flooding me with both need and purpose. I'd separated myself somehow, over the last few harrowing months, because I had to. Because it felt safer and stronger, a necessary element of this whole torturous process, to keep myself a little bit distant. But now…

Now everything has changed. *Everything.* I lean forward, willing your tiny eyes with their sparse, golden lashes to open. To see me for myself, a mother.

And then they do, and I fall into their deep blue depths. I fall and fall, everything in me swelling with love as my heart starts to break.

PART ONE

CHAPTER ONE

HEATHER

Six months earlier

'Kev… I'm pregnant.'

Maybe I shouldn't have said it like that. Maybe I shouldn't have said it at all. But it's his problem too. And I know that's what it is – a problem. As much as I wish it was something else, something that it should be. A surprise, a blessing, a miracle. The normal things. The right ones.

'What?' Kevin stares at me blankly, slumped in the La-z-Boy with the threadbare arms and the stuffing come out of the bottom. I hate that thing. Especially since Kev's been sitting in it for the last three years.

I know it's not his fault. It was an accident. Hurting his back at work and now this baby. Two problems, two *accidents* that have torpedoed our little lives, exploding right into the middle of them so everything feels wrecked.

'Do you mind if I turn off the TV?' I reach for the remote resting on the arm of the chair. Kev grabs it instinctively, and I fold my arms and wait. He hesitates, and then, with a big drawn-out sigh, he puts the TV on mute.

Now maybe we can finally have a conversation, except I don't know what to say besides what I already have. Kev's gaze keeps flicking toward the screen. Doesn't he realize how important this is? We're going to have a *baby*. Another one.

'How can you be pregnant?' he finally demands. This probably wasn't the best time to talk, at the end of a long, pain-filled day, one spent in front of the TV, and then a tense phone call from the union lawyer. There's a hearing coming up but Kev didn't tell me about the call. I just heard his low voice, like a growl, and I knew it couldn't be great news.

But I think I'm at least twelve weeks along and we need to talk. I hadn't paid attention to the signs that now suddenly seem obvious. The sore breasts, the tiredness, the nausea, the nasty taste in my mouth. I told myself it was the usual PMS, but this morning I looked in the mirror and saw my thickened waist, my rounded belly, and realization clanged through me, an almighty alarm bell. I had to tell Kevin.

It had to be when the girls were in bed, because the last thing I need is Lucy demanding in her high, piping voice what I'm talking about, or Amy triumphantly informing her how babies are made – something she learned on the playground a few weeks ago – in terms I would never use or want her to hear. I also needed to tell Kev before he took his pain meds, since he's out for the count about twenty minutes after he pops them. Although maybe this conversation won't even take twenty minutes. What else is there to say?

'I think you know how it happened. The usual way.' I slump onto the sofa, too tired to stay on my feet. Last night I worked the night shift, cleaning an office building in Newark until three in the morning, and then grabbing a few hours of sleep before getting up for the girls, seeing them off to school through a haze of exhaustion. The thought of another baby, another need, makes everything in me churn with fear because I don't know how I can do it.

This is the thought that keeps blaring through me like a car horn, palm flat on it, since I finally acknowledged to myself that I was pregnant: *I can't have this baby.* We can't afford it, not the space, not the time, and of course not the money. I need to start work full-time; that was the plan when Lucy went to kindergarten. We can't make it without that money. I can't have this baby. But I can't see any way not to.

'But…' Kev narrows his eyes. His hair is rumpled, his face unshaven. He doesn't see the point any more, and I understand why. He's been out of work for two years and nine months. Lucy doesn't even remember when Daddy had a job. When life was normal, when the electricity didn't get cut off on a regular basis, when my bank card didn't get rejected at Stop & Shop and I fumbled through an excuse about changed pins while the cashier looked on in either pity or impatience. When Kevin wasn't sprawled in that chair every hour of the day, staring bleary-eyed at the TV, the life sucked out of him. This is Lucy's normal, and I hate that.

As for a baby… 'It's not like we do it that often,' Kevin grumbles, and I don't know whether to laugh or groan. What is this, a tenth grade sex-ed lesson? Or did he miss that, because we were busy cutting classes and making out behind the storage sheds, two shy quiet kids who broke the rules for each other? And look how that went. Pregnant at seventeen, Kev a year older, married three months later, happy for a while, and here we are.

I remember those hungry, hopeful kisses, pressed up against the concrete block of the shed wall, my hands fisted in Kev's shirt. Feeling so excited, so happy, like anything was possible as long as I had him. I'd never had a boyfriend before Kev. I'd drifted through high school, keeping my head down, trying not to get noticed, and he was the same. We lit each other up, like we had candles inside. Fireworks. I can't remember the last time I felt like that, all fizzy inside. It was a long, long time ago.

'It only takes one time, Kev,' I say, trying for a smile. 'Remember?' Emma was a one-time baby, both of us too shy and uncertain to attempt the mess of it again until we were married. We fumbled through everything, a hurried half hour in Kev's basement, zippers sticking, noses bumping, soft laughter in the dark, embarrassment rushing through us along with the dizzying lust.

As for more recently… not so different, really. A drunken fumble on the sofa, wanting to feel just a little bit of that connection again. And now this.

'Yeah, I know, but…' Kev shakes his head again, making me think of a sleepy bear. One who's thinking about getting angry. Because since the accident, I never know when Kevin is going to get angry. He can be so sweet sometimes, playing Guess Who or Connect Four with Amy, listening to Emma read her silly pony books, slipping his arm around my waist, surprising me.

Then all of a sudden he'll lash out, pushing the book or game away, demanding dark and quiet, which usually means beer and TV and sometimes cigarettes, the smoke snaking through the rooms of our little house, staining the ceiling.

I try to be patient. I do. I take deep breaths, I keep my voice mild, I let it all roll over me. But this? A baby? This is meant to be our problem, even though I hate that it's a problem in the first place. It's a baby. *Our* baby, already curled up inside me, heart beating hard. I'm not seventeen anymore, tearful and uncertain, except that's how I feel a little bit, inside. Like I'm not sure how this is going to turn out, or if Kev's going to be there for me. For us. For this baby.

Kevin runs a hand through his already-messed hair and lets out a sound I don't like. It's part groan, part sigh, and it sounds like despair. 'We can't have another kid, Heather,' he says in a low voice. He won't look at me, his stubbly chin tucked toward his chest. 'Things are tight enough as it is.'

He thinks I don't know that? That I don't realize we're two months behind on the rent, and we have all of two hundred bucks in the bank account? We're one teetering step away from destitution, and have been for so long that I've almost got used to living on that knife-edge. But you can only keep your balance for so long.

It wasn't always like this. When Kevin worked our lives were completely different then. I try to remember the people we used to be. I try to hang on to the woman I was, because sometimes I don't recognize this person I've become; this tired, stringy-haired, stressed-out woman who screeches and shrieks and bites her nails, whose pregnancy is a looming disaster rather than the joy I wish it could be.

Back then, before his accident, Kevin smiled and laughed and tossed the girls up in the air. He kissed me in the kitchen, and we walked around the block on a summer evening, the girls on their rusty trikes in front of us. Small, simple pleasures, but that's what happiness is, isn't it?

We had money – not a lot, we've never had that, but enough for birthday presents and take-out on Fridays and the occasional splurge – a trip to a theme park, a dinner out. I didn't hold my breath when I paid for the groceries, or wince when I checked the bank balance on the ATM, at least not often. Life didn't feel like a minefield, and now I've just stepped on one, everything exploding around us.

I can't have this baby.

I can't have an abortion, either. That might seem obvious to some, and sometimes it does to me, but I've felt my babies kick, I've seen them curled up tight or wriggling like crazy on the ultrasound screen. What makes this one so different? Just a little bit of money, or even a lot? Besides, we're Catholic. Not so much with the church going, not every Sunday, but still… It's the way I grew up; it's what I know.

And then of course there are other people to think about: Kev, my family, my neighbors, my friends. What if someone found out? What if I was seen? The gossip would never stop, along with the pity and judgment. I don't know which would feel worse.

This part of North Elizabeth, New Jersey, is like a small town where everybody knows everybody else's business. We gossip on our cracked front steps and out on the sagging back porches. Kids whisper in the schoolyard. Women lean across grocery carts. Men talk in bars. Someone would know. Someone would figure it out, and then what?

But am I tempted? Yes. I've looked up the number of the local Planned Parenthood clinic and sat there with the phone in my hand while Lucy played around me, chattering to herself, with no idea what was going on in Mommy's mind. I've told myself to call. No one would need to know, no one would find out, and it would solve *everything*.

'So what are you going to do?' Kevin asks, and I blink, stung by the 'you'. We've been married for eleven years, we have three kids, he's the only man I've ever kissed or done anything with, but it's my problem. Of course it is.

'What do you mean, what am *I* going to do?' I ask, and for once I let him hear my irritation. I'm always so careful with Kevin, but right now I don't have it in me. 'What are you saying, Kev?' I ask, and I know I'm daring him to say what he means, even as I realize he won't.

He's a good man, Kev. Underneath the pain and the bitterness, that good man is still there. He's still the one who stammered when he asked me out, who asked if he could kiss me that first time, and then bumped my nose with his. We both laughed, and it was okay. It's always been okay, until the accident. Until a fall from a forklift turned Kev into a man I don't feel I know and sometimes I don't even like.

Kev stares me in the face for a full minute. I hadn't realized how faded his eyes have become. They used to be such a warm hazel, glinting with gold, but now they just look muddy. He's thirty years old and he looks more than forty, but then so do I. Three babies, no sleep, no money. It adds up – and then it takes away.

'My workman comp ends in six weeks,' Kev says, and for a few seconds I just stare back at him.

'You mean you have the hearing.' That's what the lawyer called about this morning. Three years of disability payments and then it comes up for review. But Kev will keep getting it – he was injured on the job, something went wrong with the controls of his forklift and he ended up flat on his back on the concrete floor, a fall from fifteen feet.

I got a call at home, someone from work, and then the union, telling me the company would cover the hospital costs; that the company owed us. I could barely take it in; my mind was buzzing and blank, and everything in me felt gray and numb. I didn't know if Kev had hurt his brain along with his back, if our lives were changed forever. And it turned out they were.

He was in the hospital for three weeks and nearly three years later he's still on heavy meds. He can't lift anything more than ten pounds. He certainly can't go back to his old job. Of course he'll get the disability payments renewed.

But Kevin is shaking his head. He won't look at me. He picks at a threadbare patch on the chair with a ragged fingernail. 'The lawyer said today that they won't renew it. They're saying I've had *maximum medical improvement* – he sneers at the words – 'and that I can resume light duty, the dicks.'

I stare at him, hardly able to take it in. 'So you mean there will be no more money…?'

'The lawyer says I can get permanent partial disability, but it won't be much. And the company doesn't have any light duty for me. What a fucking surprise.' He sounds so bitter, and I can't blame him. But we have to have more money coming in, baby or not. We can't survive otherwise. We'll lose the house, we won't be able to eat, never mind another baby.

I swallow hard, blinking back the dizziness. 'But can't you appeal…?'

'The lawyer says it's not worth it. This is the best I'm going to get.'

The lawyer, the lawyer... I don't even know his name. Someone the union sent, someone with a loud voice, shiny shoes, buttons straining against his belly, a smell of sweat. I never liked him. I didn't trust him. I don't think he once looked me in the eye.

'So there's nothing we can do?' My voice is a squeak. Even after all the crap we've had thrown at us, I can't believe it. I make two hundred and twenty dollars a week maximum, and doing that many nights just about kills me. Our rent is eight hundred, never mind all the other expenses.

I didn't think we could sink much lower, but now I see a whole new pit opening underneath us. Losing the house. Going on welfare. Food stamps, public housing, the government paying our way, just barely. You never get out of that pit. You get lost in it, lost and forgotten and ashamed.

And I know it would just about kill Kev, to admit that much failure. Kev always has been proud how we've made it on our own. When we were first starting out, we didn't accept a single handout from my parents, not that they had much to give, and even less now. His parents didn't have anything – his father's a drunk, his mother just as bad. Kev doesn't even want the girls seeing them.

'That's it,' Kev says dully, and he reaches for the little orange canister that holds his nightly medication and pops the lid. 'Not much more I can do.'

'And this baby?' I ask in little more than a whisper. I feel sick inside, like that pit that just opened up beneath us is really inside of me. Everything is sinking into it until there's nothing left but fear and despair. 'What are we going to do, Kev? How are we going to manage?'

He looks up at me, bleary-eyed, as he shakes the pills into his hand. 'You tell me, Heather.'

CHAPTER TWO

GRACE

The day of my father's funeral one of the partners, Bruce Felson, calls to tell me I've made Harrow and Heath seven million dollars in a single hour after I set the share price yesterday for a new social media company.

'You're on fire, Grace,' he says with a laugh into the phone, that comfortable, jocular chuckle of an amused uncle, a forbearing father. I'm so tired even my teeth ache, and I've been wearing a pair of four-inch Louboutins for eleven hours.

'Thanks,' I say, my tone lacking its usual brisk vigor. I wonder why I even answered the call. I'd been in the elevator up to my apartment after attending my father's funeral service, burial, and an interminable two hours at the country club in Connecticut where I'd held the reception, making chitchat with strangers, old business acquaintances of my dad's, some of my parents' old couple friends I hadn't seen in about twenty years.

When I'd seen Bruce's name flash onto my screen I'd answered as a matter of habit, a Pavlovian response to the pressures of work, because in venture capital you've always got to be on the ball, looking for the next opportunity before anyone else finds it. And I want to make partner before I'm forty, which is in seven months. I've been a principal for four years, and I'm ready. I'm so ready.

'Oh,' Bruce says, as if he'd just thought of it, which I'm sure he has. 'Is today your father's…?'

'Yes,' I say simply, and his chuckle peters out.

'Sorry,' he says, all stiff politeness now. 'Did it go, ah, well?'

Do funerals ever go well? Can I even judge such a thing at this moment? People came. A priest spoke. There were a lot of murmured words and wilted sandwiches. 'It was lovely, thank you,' I say, and Bruce gives a pleased grunt.

'Good, good.' An awkward pause. 'Well, then. See you tomorrow.'

I disconnect the call and step out of the elevator to unlock the door to my apartment, my hands nearly shaking with the effort. I'm so tired I feel like I could cry, and that is something I haven't done since my father died a week ago. Behind me my neighbor's door, the only other one on the floor, opens.

'Oh, hello.' The woman's voice is cheerful, inviting conversation. I've been living here for four years and I should know her and her husband's names, but I don't. I turn back with a distracted half-smile and my key clatters onto the marble floor. 'Been somewhere exciting?' the woman asks brightly, and all I can do is stare.

I've shared minimal, meaningless chitchat with my neighbors over the years; I think our longest conversation has been about when the recycling is going to be collected after Christmas. They pushed me a Christmas card under the door several times, and I've forgotten to give one back. How on earth can I tell this woman with her squinting, near-sighted smile what I've been doing today? So I don't.

'Nothing terribly exciting.' I try to smile but my face feels funny. The woman nods, clearly waiting for more, but I don't have anything and so I turn my smile into something more of a farewell and stoop down for my key. She stays in her own doorway, waiting, while I fumble with the lock and finally, thankfully, close my door behind me.

My heels click across the marble foyer, echoing in the emptiness. Ahead of me floor-to-ceiling windows overlook Central

Park, twilight already settling over it, the shadows lengthening between the clusters of trees, the traffic emptying out, a few cabs gliding down Fifth Avenue.

The air smells of lavender and lemon, the organic furniture polish my cleaner uses. Everything is still and quiet and perfect, my oasis in a full, frenetic life.

My father is dead.

I feel like I should cry, but I can't. The tears have gathered into a cold, hard lump in my chest. I feel it every time I swallow. I picture it ossifying, getting harder and bigger, choking me, taking me over. But still the tears won't come. They came after my mother died; hot tears pouring down my cheeks while my father held me. A grief shared is one divided, lessened; I bear the weight of this one all alone, and it's crippling me. I am bowed beneath it.

I walk to the window, kicking off my heels, flexing my cramped toes, but even that small thing feels like an indulgence I shouldn't enjoy, not now. Not when my father is no longer alive. How can I enjoy anything any more?

One hand rests on the cool glass, connecting me to the world. Ten stories below two women walk along the cobbled pavement by the park, deep in conversation, gesturing widely. Behind them a mother, or perhaps a nanny, hurries her child along. He's holding a soccer ball and dragging his feet; the woman is steering him by the shoulder.

When the reception after the funeral ended, I went to the club's bar and drank two Scotches, neat, my father's drink, while the bartender polished glasses and the club emptied out. The alcohol seethes in my stomach now; I didn't used to like whisky, but I learned to drink it. When you work on Wall Street, whether it's investment banking or venture capital, and just about everyone other than the secretaries is male, you need to do that kind of pseudo-masculine stuff. Drink whisky. Laugh at the titty jokes. Play golf, or at least be interested in it. I've even smoked a cigar.

But now I'm home, and the apartment is as empty as it ever was, and I feel like I can't stand it for a second longer. The silence screams at me, hurting my ears.

On a normal night I'd change out of my suit, pour myself a glass of wine from the expensive bottle I keep chilling in the fridge, and settle down in front of the TV to watch the news on CNN. After about five minutes, if that, I'd switch to Bloomberg to keep up with the financial markets, because I can't stay away. Then I'd do thirty minutes on my elliptical trainer before getting ready for bed. And I'd feel happy, damn it. I'd feel happy and satisfied, and just a little bit smug, but in a good way. I had it all, I really did. Now I feel as if I have nothing.

I'm alone. The words rattle around like marbles in the emptiness of my mind. Of course, I've known I'm alone for a long time. I've been single for my entire adult life, save a few forays into relationships that never went all that far, mostly because I didn't see the point.

My work has precluded a lot of things: lots of good women friends, serious boyfriends, long vacations, any semblance of what most people call normal life. But it's made me a lot of money, including a cut of the seven million today, and I've enjoyed the chase, the discovery, the benefits. I never felt like I was missing out. I never wished for more than I had.

But right now I have a deep, primal need not to be so alone. I need someone here with me, someone to shoulder something of what I feel, and the sad and glaring truth is that there just isn't anyone to do that.

Friends, fine. I've managed with casual acquaintances and office chitchat, meeting my colleague Jill to work out, the occasional after-work drink with someone from my MBA days. One summer I shared a rental in the Hamptons with my friend Joanne and a bunch of her friends; it was fine. I could have taken or left it all, I've never been that bothered. I've never needed lots of friends.

As for boyfriends, lovers? I've had a few, some more serious than others, but I've never really wanted to go down that whole marriage and kids route that so many women seem to think is inevitable, and that's been fine. *Fine.*

But my dad? My *daddy?* The man who gave me twenty dollars to invest when I was seven? Who sat with me poring over the business section of the *New York Times*, who told me about getting in on Microsoft before it went big – never mind that he didn't, he just thought about it.

My dad was so proud of me. He didn't like me going into venture capital, true; he felt it was too risky. He played it safe, lived a middle-class life out in Newtown, Connecticut, and retired at sixty-five. But he was proud of me, even with the risks. When I found that first tech investment that went big, six years ago – All Natural, a company that sourced organic products from different stores to present the whole healthy living/wellness package to subscribers – he pumped his fist in the air and said, '*Gracie*, you did it. You damn well did it!'

My dad was everything to me: mother, father, family. When my mom was diagnosed with breast cancer when I was seven, he stepped right up. He came to my ballet recitals; he made spaghetti and meatballs for dinner; he sat with me at bedtime. He bought me pads for my first period and stammered through a talk about birth control right before I went to college. He took me out for my first legal drink on my twenty-first birthday; we shared a very good bottle of wine. He *can't* be gone.

But he is.

The lump of tears and grief is growing, taking me over like the cancer that ate away at my father's insides. Kidney, diagnosis to death took six weeks. *Six weeks.* Barely enough time to understand what was happening, never mind accept it. The impossibility of it is like slamming into a brick wall, leaving me not just breathless, but reeling.

Slowly, I walk from the window to the enormous kitchen I barely use, all marble counters and stainless steel appliances – a cliché, I know, the professional woman who doesn't even make use of the apartment she paid a fortune for, and certainly not the kitchen. You think I want to spend hours making some gourmet meal I'm going to eat alone in front of the TV?

The enormous sub-zero fridge holds very little – milk, some nice Brie that's probably gone bad, and the bottle of wine I opened last night and that is already half-empty. I pour myself a fishbowl-sized glass and for good measure I take another bottle from the wine rack and stick it in the fridge. I'm going to need a lot of alcohol to get through tonight. To get through the rest of my life.

I wriggle out of my pantyhose and black crêpe dress, leaving them crumpled on the floor of my bedroom before I slip into yoga pants and a t-shirt and curl up on my king-sized bed, cradling my wine.

I feel so lonely. It eats at me, like some physical attack from an invisible monster. I want to claw at my own skin, pull my hair, *scream*, anything to alleviate this moment. To change it. Instead I drink more wine.

It slips down nicely, and soon the glass is empty. I've only nibbled a couple of soggy sandwiches all day, and so I have a nice buzz going on as I walk back to the kitchen and pour a second glass. I think about turning on some music – I paid a fortune for a voice-activated system – but I'm afraid music, any music, will tip me over the emotional edge. I'm not ready to cry. Not yet, and maybe not ever. I don't know if I'd ever be able to come back from that.

So I drink and I watch darkness settle on the park and the lights of cabs stream by. The apartment is so quiet. I liked that about it, when I toured the place four years ago, after I got the big bonus that provided me with the deposit. I liked that I couldn't hear anything – not neighbors, not traffic, not the creak of the elevator or the blare of a car horn. But right now I feel like I'm in an isolation chamber. I *am* in one.

The second glass of wine goes down easier than the first, even though my empty stomach is starting to churn. Blearily, the world going fuzzy, I reach for my phone and start scrolling through contacts. I'm not so drunk that I don't realize this is a bad idea, but I need to talk to someone. I feel like if I don't, I might explode – or die.

I call Joanne, my friend from business school, first. She works in Chicago now, managing a hedge fund, and I haven't seen her in over a year. Her phone flips over to voicemail and I open my mouth to leave a message, except no words come out. What can I say that would make sense? I haven't talked to her in months. She doesn't even know my dad was sick. I swipe to disconnect the phone and toss it on the bed. I drink more wine.

I'm not sure what time it is, but it feels late. After a little while, I'm not sure how long, I pick up my phone again. I swipe through my contacts and then, sober enough to know I'm being stupid, I press call on a certain number.

Ben answers after a couple of rings, sounding uncertain. 'Grace?'

'You still have me in your contacts.' I let out a hiccuppy laugh and then close my eyes. What am I doing? This is so not me, I do not make drunken phone calls. I don't even get drunk. And yet here I am.

'Yes, I do.' A pause and I can hear him moving, maybe getting up from a chair or a bed. Was he with someone? Does it matter? 'Grace, are you… are you all right? Because you sound…'

'My father died.' The words are stark and abrupt. 'His funeral was today.'

A pause. 'I'm sorry,' Ben says quietly, and I know he means it. Ben is the closest thing I have to a great, lost love, and the funny or maybe the sad thing is, we only dated for a little more than a year. We met years ago at a party thrown by one of my MBA colleagues, and we just clicked. He was as ambitious as I was, but also funny and fairly laid-back. I had fun with him, and the thought of forever flitted through my mind.

'Thanks,' I say, and I sniff. My eyes are closed and my stomach and head are both spinning. 'Sorry, I know I shouldn't have called.' We broke up five years ago, when Ben, a corporate lawyer, got headhunted to San Francisco.

We had an awkward, stilted conversation about keeping it going long distance, and Ben suggested, rather hesitantly, that I consider moving to San Francisco. I remember looking at him in disbelief; I couldn't leave my job, or my father. I did fly out once, about three months after he moved. We had a nice if awkward dinner, and then a discussion about how we might as well break up because our relationship was clearly not going to last an East Coast/West Coast divide.

'It's okay,' Ben says after a moment. 'I know you were close to him.'

'Do you?' I sound almost childishly eager. Does he have some story, some recollection that I've forgotten? He feels like a link to my father, a precious thread I want to unravel and see where it leads.

'You met him for brunch just about every weekend,' Ben remarks dryly. 'Not many thirty-five-year-olds have that kind of relationship with their dad.'

'No.' I loved those brunches. Father-daughter time, an institution he insisted upon every Saturday morning since my mother died when I was fourteen. Our last one was seven weeks ago, before all this happened. I've gone over every second of that brunch, trying to remember if I missed some clue. My father had white chocolate waffles, but he left a lot on his plate, saying they were too rich.

We had the *New York Times* spread out on the table, as we often did, and as we sipped coffee and nibbled toast we'd read out bits to each other, commenting on various news stories or investment snippets like an old married couple. If I'd known that was the last time we'd do that... what would I have done differently? I torment myself with that question, with remembering how I checked my watch at the end, how I turned down a third cup of coffee because I had some errands to run. *Errands.*

I do remember how he talked about my mother; how he said he missed her but he was glad he'd been able to be both mom and dad to me. I didn't pay much attention; my dad liked to get sentimental sometimes. Later, I tried to remember every word. I even wrote it down, a transcript that was half remembered, half wishful thinking.

Sometimes I wish we'd been able to give you a sibling. He'd definitely said that, and I'd simply shrugged, because what else could I do? Now I wonder how much easier this grief would be if someone else were bearing it with me. If there was anyone, absolutely anyone, to put their arms around me and say they understood; that they were sad too, as sad as I am. Because I know no one is.

I try to remember if my father seemed tired or in pain. Was he hiding it from me? He swore he hadn't but *six weeks*, and at diagnosis the doctors said the cancer had already spread to his stomach and lymph nodes. He must have known. He must have at least suspected. And I know he never would have wanted to worry me. He would have waited until the last possible moment to say anything, and while I understand that protective impulse, it doesn't feel completely fair. I didn't have enough time to adjust, to accept; to begin to grieve. I'm still half-expecting him to call, to hear his message on my voicemail. *Hey, Gracie. I'm coming into the city. Want to grab a bite to eat?* Never again.

In the background of Ben's home, wherever it is these days, a baby cries. I stiffen.

'Is that...?'

'My daughter.' Ben almost sounds apologetic. 'I got married a year ago.'

'You did?' The words burst out of me, high, bright, and false, like the sudden squawk of a parrot. 'That's great. Congratulations.' This call now feels like a huge mistake. 'Congratulations,' I say again, because I'm drunk and I can't think of what else to say, but even so I'm not ready to get off the phone.

'I'm sorry, Grace, but I should go. Lauren's visiting her mother and Isabella sounds like she needs me…'

Lauren. Isabella. I'm picturing warm-hued scenes of cozy domesticity, a king-sized bed, a baby kicking chubby legs and blowing bubbles.

I'm not maternal, never have been. I threw that biological clock right out the window when I started at Harrow and Heath, pulling sixty- and seventy-hour weeks. But in this moment, when loneliness is eating me from the inside out, I crave a connection with someone. I think of my dad, telling me how he was never lonely as long as he had me. I think of how we were a team, how even when I missed my mom, I never felt as if I were missing out. Dad and I were enough.

I want that closeness with someone; I want to bring someone into the world and show them how it works. I want to love and be loved, and I crave it so badly I feel breathless with longing. A gasp escapes me, a noise that sounds ragged and needy, so unlike me, and yet completely encapsulating me in this moment.

'Sorry,' Ben says again, and I realize he is saying goodbye.

'No, please don't worry.' I'm trying to sound brisk, and clearly failing. Even drunk I know that. 'Please, it's fine. It's fine. I shouldn't have called.'

'If you need to talk…' Ben begins, and I soften at the thought that he still might want to talk to me. Help me. Perhaps I'm not quite as alone as I thought I was. 'There are counselors,' he finishes, and my heart hardens right back up.

Counselors. Right. Because if I need a sympathetic ear, a friendly face, I'd better pay someone for the pleasure. I disconnect the call without saying goodbye.

And then I stare at the ceiling, my eyes dry and gritty, the wine swirling in my stomach, and I ache. *I ache.*

CHAPTER THREE

HEATHER

'I never thought I'd be here.' I didn't mean to say it out loud, but the words pop out anyway. It's been two weeks since I talked to Kev about the baby, and we haven't spoken about it since. If he's waiting for me to do something, I don't know what it is. I'd think he'd forgotten, but I see him look at me sideways sometimes, with a combination of guilt and accusation. I have to bite my tongue not to remind him that it takes two.

In the last two weeks I've called Planned Parenthood twice, and I got as far as making the appointment before I got scared. I called back to cancel, my hand shaking on the phone, afraid I might get some awful follow-up call that Kev would answer, and then what?

Nobody but Kev knows I'm pregnant. I pretend I don't know; I don't want to think about this baby. I can't bear to, because then it's real and what I'm doing, what I'm thinking of doing, feels awful. Unforgiveable. Worse, in some bizarre way, than an abortion.

'Most women don't expect to be in this position.' The woman behind the desk – Tina, she said her name was – smiles at me. I don't like her smile, kind as I know it's meant to be. It's too full of sympathy, of pity, and right now that's the last thing I need. I wouldn't be here if I wasn't poor and desperate. We both know that.

I take a deep breath, my fingernails digging into the padded armrests as my stomach churns. I'm afraid I might actually be sick. 'So how does this whole thing work, anyway?' I ask. I sound belligerent, and so I take a deep breath and expel it, willing my stomach to settle. 'Adoption, I mean.' The words falls into the room like something heavy dropped on the floor. *Thud.*

The possibility came to me a week ago, when I was at my parents'. Mom's MS had flared up and my dad needed a trip out to the bar or Meadowlands Racing Track, it didn't matter which. He goes, and either my sister Stacy or I pick up the slack. That's how it has always been.

I started cleaning up, taking half-drunk cups of cold coffee and overflowing ashtrays to the kitchen, while Mom positioned her wheelchair in front of the TV and changed the channel from Fox News, my dad's favorite, to QVC – hers.

'Come sit beside me, Lucy,' she ordered, and Lucy obeyed, perching on the edge of the wheelchair, my mom's arm around her little shoulders. 'It's time for *Mary Beth's Kitchen.*'

While they listened to Mary Beth's instructions on how to make a lemon meringue pie, I started on the kitchen, which was a mess – yesterday's dishes piled in the sink; that morning's on the table. Everything felt sticky, and the air smelled stale, of fried food and cigarette smoke, making my stomach heave.

I dumped a bunch of grease-splattered plates in the sink and that's when I caught sight of the free newspaper my mom always kept around in stacks, mainly to clip the coupons she never remembered to use. It was turned to the classifieds, a list of pathetic personals and overpriced offers for used furniture, and then—

Are You Pregnant?

I pushed some more dirty dishes aside and picked up the paper. The ad had a photo of a heavily pregnant woman cradling her belly, smiling down at her baby bump, all in hazy soft focus.

Are You Pregnant? Confused?

She didn't look confused, but I knew I was. My mind kept going in circles, wondering how we could make it work, where the money would come from to keep this baby. To keep our house, the kids fed, everything.

I looked down at the newspaper and read some more, squinting at the small type. *Open Heart Adoptions. Make a family happy today.*

I felt as if a fist had reached inside and squeezed my heart. It *hurt*. And yet with that pain was something I hadn't felt in so long I barely remembered the sensation: a treacherous little flicker of hope, even as I cringed with guilt. I couldn't really be thinking about this.

'Sweetie?' my mother called from the living room. 'Could you get me a Crystal Light?' My mother drank the stuff by the gallon, peach iced tea, double-strength.

'Sure, Mom.' I put the paper back on the table, so the classified ads were face down. I felt dirty, as if I'd been looking at porn.

I made up a pitcher of Crystal Light and poured my mother a glass, my heart beating hard. I told myself to forget about that stupid ad, even if it felt like someone had thrown open a window and I was suddenly breathing fresh air, taking it in by the glorious lungful.

Because the last sentence on the little ad was the one I remembered, the one I can still see now, dancing in my head, bold-faced, black type: *All Maternity Costs Covered.*

And so now I'm here, sitting in this overheated, pastel-decorated office, wearing a dress I last wore at my cousin's wedding. It strains across my belly and under my armpits. Bad choice, but this feels like an interview and I don't have anything else.

'What has led you to consider this avenue, Heather?' Tina looks maternal, a little overweight; comfortable in herself, dressed in loose clothing in various shades of beige. Her eyes and smile are soft but it feels like an act, her persona for the poor women who have been driven to come here. Women like me. I decide to talk straight.

'I'm married and I have three kids already. Girls. My husband injured himself at work and the workman's comp ends in a couple of weeks. We can't afford another baby.' I blurt out each sentence like a bullet, machine-gunning her with the facts. But then my tough act disintegrates and my stomach heaves.

'Sorry,' I mutter as I double over, cold sweat prickling my back. 'Is there a bathroom…?'

'Of course.' For a large woman Tina springs up from her chair pretty fast. 'Right down the hall.'

Somehow I make it down the hall and into the bathroom stall, where I throw up my breakfast. I kneel on the cold, tiled floor, my cheek resting on the rim of the toilet bowl, feeling awful in all sorts of ways.

I shouldn't have come. I was desperate, and I tried to convince myself this could work, but it can't. Of course it can't. I can't just give away my baby like something extra I don't need or want, especially when I have three girls already to watch me do it. What on earth would they think? What on earth could I tell them that would make any sort of sense?

And yet what else can I do?

Yesterday morning we got our first eviction warning. We have to pay the rent in the next week or they'll start proceedings. We could be out of the house by the end of the month. And where would we go? My parents don't have space for us, and neither does my sister. The social housing has a waiting list longer than my arm, and it would be months if not years before we could get a place big enough for us. I picture us huddled in a homeless shelter, barely surviving, and the worst thing is, I know it could happen. It could happen soon. Is that what I want to bring a baby into, someone innocent and trusting, with only me and Kev to depend on? I close my eyes as another wave of nausea rolls through me.

'Heather?' Tina opens the door to the bathroom, her voice full of concern. 'Are you okay?'

'Yeah, sorry.' I ease up from the floor, my head still spinning, trying to recover from this moment even though I know I can't. 'Sorry, morning sickness.'

'Of course.' She is standing behind me, and I wish she'd leave. I don't want her to see me like this. I don't want anyone to see me like this. But she doesn't move, and so I get up and go to the sink, wash my face and hands and rinse out my mouth, all while Tina watches. Judging, maybe, although she must have seen this before.

'You know,' she says as I'm drying my hands, 'there are other options.'

'I know.' Although I wonder if Tina really gets how few options there are for someone like me. How this feels like the best one, despite all my doubts, the endless guilt. If I'm able to give all four of my children better lives, then surely I can live with a little guilt? Or even a lot of it.

'Do you want to continue talking, or would you like to come back another time?'

I don't want to have to come back. It was hard enough to get here in the first place. I dry my hands with a paper towel. 'I'll keep talking.'

Back in the room Tina waits while I sit down and smooth my crumpled skirt. I catch a whiff of vomit and I wince.

'How does your husband feel about this possibility, Heather?'

I think of Kev's seeming indifference over the last few weeks. It's like he doesn't care, and yet I know instinctively how angry he would feel about this, how hurt. But like me I hope he'd realize there aren't any better options. 'He's on board with it,' I say as firmly as I can.

Tina nods slowly. 'We'd need to see both of you before we moved ahead. If the father is involved, he needs to sign all the documentation as well, make sure we're all in this together. It's a big, difficult decision to make, and of course you need to take your time with it.'

'Right.' Does she think I don't know that? That I haven't held my girls as we all cuddle on the sofa, stroked their fine hair, felt Lucy's petal-soft baby skin, and wondered what the hell I'm doing? How I can even think of doing it?

Last night I sat in the girls' bedroom while they slept – Emma curled up in a tight little ball, Amy flung out, arms and legs sprawled in a star shape, and Lucy all twisted in the sheets. My girls. I thought of the baby inside me: girl or boy, tiny and waiting. I pictured myself holding it, bringing it to my breast. And then I stopped, because I was just torturing myself, and what was the point?

I looked at my girls again, all three of them, all depending on me for just about everything. They were the ones I needed to think about now. Emma, eleven years old, shy and quiet; eight-year-old Amy, always getting into trouble; Lucy, who seems clingier than most four-year-olds. They need me. This baby just needs a mother. That's the way I have to think, no matter how much it hurts.

'So why don't I talk you through the process?' Tina suggests, and when I give a quick nod she launches into a long description of everything that is going to happen; lots of meetings and appointments, how much choice I'll have, how all my costs will be covered, including some living expenses if needed, which I latch onto like the life preserver it is. I hate that it comes down to money, but it just does. Then Tina assures me that I can back out at any time, even after the baby is born.

'After?' I feel suspicious. 'That doesn't seem fair, if some couple think they're getting my baby and then I change my mind at the last minute?'

Tina smiles and nods. 'It's the birth mother's right, up until seventy-two hours after you give birth.'

'Oh.' I don't want to have that choice. How could I possibly give my baby away if I still have a choice to keep it, even then? It feels worse, twice the loss, a double betrayal. If I'm able to give my baby away after I've held him or her, after I've watched them come squalling into the world, what kind of person am I? What kind of mother could I possibly be? That's a choice I feel like I could never be strong enough to make.

'Have you considered what kind of adoption you want to have?' Tina asks kindly. I feel as if she's asking me what flavor ice cream I like. 'Some people prefer an entirely closed adoption, where the child is placed with an adoptive family and has no contact with the birth parents at all. Others are more open, with a certain amount of ongoing contact, decided by both parties, of course. This can be beneficial—'

'Closed.' Ongoing contact? Ongoing torture. How could I keep looking at my baby, my child, knowing he or she would never be mine? It would be a constant reminder, a never-ending taunt. 'I want it to be closed.' I picture something snapping shut, a key turning in a lock. I need finality. 'So what happens next?' I ask. I shift, the dress sticking to my back. The room feels stifling and airless. It's hard to breathe.

'If you still feel you wish to move forward, then we can make an appointment for you and your husband to come here together, discuss the details, sign the paperwork.' Tina smiles. 'Then you can start looking at some prospective parent profiles.'

She makes it sound as if we'd be looking at wallpaper samples. Choosing parents for my child. How on earth can I be entrusted with such a decision? I feel dizzy, as well as sick again. I'm not ready for this, but I'm not sure I ever will be – who is?

'The profiles are all on our website,' she continues. 'We have pictures, biographies, even videos and blog updates. It's important that you feel entirely happy and comfortable with who you're placing your baby with.'

'I need to think some more,' I blurt. My hands are clammy and I clench them into fists. 'I'm sorry, but I'm still not sure.'

'Of course. Take as much time as you need. It's important you feel comfortable with every stage of this process.'

Which is a joke, because I can't ever imagine feeling comfortable with any of this. This is about necessity, nothing else. I glance at the clock and realize I have to pick up Lucy from preschool. 'I need to go,' I say, lurching upright. Tina nods and rises from her seat, extending her hand for me to shake. I don't want to, because my own is damp and clammy, but to refuse would be rude and she probably would think I didn't know better. *I'm not stupid*, I feel like saying. *I'm not some dumb high schooler who got knocked up.* I once was, fine, but not now. *Not now.*

'Call me if you have any questions,' Tina says as she escorts me out of the office. 'Anything at all. We're here to help, Heather.'

'Sure,' I say, unable to look at her, and then I hurry outside, blinking in the bitter November wind that stings my cheeks, my stomach heaving once again.

I get in the car and sit there for a moment, fighting the urges either to throw up or cry. It feels so unfair, but I know that's a stupid thought, a pointless one. No one ever said life was fair, certainly not me.

I take a deep breath, force it all back. There's nothing I can do about any of this except keep moving forward, and right now I need to pick up Lucy, because Kevin isn't going to do it.

That night, when the girls are in bed and Kev is parked in front of the TV, I fire up our five-year-old desktop computer, given to us by my sister Stacy when they bought a new one, that sits on a card table in the corner of the dining room, along with a pile of unfolded laundry and some junk mail I've never bothered to throw out just in case it might be important.

Open Hearts Adoption Agency. I gaze at the pink curlicue heart and the picture of the smiling family, the pregnant lady cradling her bump, everything soft and hazy and perfect. As if life is really like that, a movie montage of cute moments, with a blissed-out soundtrack playing in the background.

I click on the family profiles page that I didn't bother to look at the last time I was on this site, before I made the appointment. Now I blink at the pictures of loved-up couples: arms around each other, wide, cheesy grins in place. They're all standing in front of some mountain or tree, looking so happy and perfect with their whitened-teeth smiles and fake tans.

I read about Lisa and Drew; he's a financial analyst and she's a physical therapist. They like hiking and camping and cooking ethnic food. There's a picture of them cheek-to-cheek in front of Mount Rushmore, and another one flexing their muscles by a huge pool, and yet another in a gorgeous kitchen. Every image makes me seethe because this smug couple want to buy a baby off me. Why do they get it so easy, and we don't?

I click on another profile and then another, and they're all the same. Cute, adoring couples, living in huge houses with plenty of money and no problems except, ha ha, they can't get pregnant. I wish I had that problem.

'Mommy, I can't sleep.'

I turn to see Amy standing in the doorway of the dining room, her eyes narrowed as she gives me a calculating look. My middle child, too smart and sassy for her own good, always looking to her own advantage. I love her drive, her stubbornness, but sometimes –most of the time – it can be exhausting.

'Go back to bed, Amy.'

'I can't sleep.' She stands there, arms folded, chin raised, challenging me, and I know she won't move until I tuck her in. With a sigh, I heave myself up from the chair.

'What are you looking at?'

She peers around me to look at the screen, and as quick as I can I click the mouse to minimize the browser window. 'Nothing.'

Back in the girls' bedroom I weave through the piles of dirty clothes and battered teddy bears heaped on the floor to Amy's bed, pushed up against the window. The bedroom is small, and it's made even smaller by the three beds crammed into it with barely enough space for one dresser for them to share. We live in a two-bedroom house, and a fourth bed will never fit in here. If we kept this baby, we'd have to turn the dining room into a bedroom, or have one of the kids share with us. If we even hold onto this house.

I'm thinking of the impossible practicalities even as my mind skims back to that web page: Lisa and Drew and their sushi.

'Mommy, my shoe broke today.' Amy is snuggled in bed, eyes wide over the covers as she delivers this news.

'What?' I stare at her, my mind still on sushi, and she nods toward the shoes by her bed. New school shoes, bought from Payless less than two months ago for the start of third grade, and not all that cheap. 'It should be called Paymore,' Kevin joked when he saw the receipt.

'My strap broke.'

I bend down to look at her shoes. Just as she'd said, the strap has snapped on one, because she pulls them so tight. The other one, I see, is wearing thin.

'We'll use duct tape to fix it.' Amy nods sullenly, knowing better than to argue even though I know she doesn't want to limp to school with a duct-taped shoe. But as I stare at the strap I feel something harden inside me. Amy knows we can't afford another pair of shoes, and I hate that. I hate that she knows not to ask. Not to expect. My smart-mouthed, sassy girl, accepting this silently, knowing there's no point to protest, because the money simply isn't there.

I look at Emma curled up in her bed, and Lucy sprawled in hers, and my heart aches with fierce love for my three girls, girls who already have had a hard start in life thanks to Kev's accident, who know not to expect new shoes or special treats, who don't even ask for them any more. I want more for my girls. I want to be able to give them more, not less. And there is only one way I can do that.

After I've tucked Amy in I head back to the computer. Kevin has dozed off and the TV blares a replay of a football game. If I turn it off, he might wake up, so I leave it on and click on another profile. And another. All these happy families. Except of course they're not families. Not yet. I don't want to give my baby to any of them.

Then I see a photo of a woman by herself. She looks sharp and sleek, wearing a navy-blue skirt suit, arms folded, hair back, barely smiling. Her gaze is direct and a little challenging, and somehow I like that.

I read her profile, which is full of business stuff I don't understand, but there's a picture of her apartment in Manhattan, with floor-to-ceiling views of Central Park. Grace Thomas is sitting on her sofa, looking stiff, legs folded to one side, her mouth curled in a faint smile as if she's thinking of something else.

I don't know why I keep staring at her photograph. Maybe because she's so different from me. Maybe because those lovey-dovey couples feel like such a slap in the face. They have everything I don't, and I'm meant to give them more? I'm meant to hand over everything they've ever wanted, put the icing on their triple-layer cake?

This woman, this Grace, has a lot. She's obviously super-rich, and she could provide for this child way, way more than we could. But she's not part of a smarmy couple; she's not flaunting her happiness in my face. She's clearly driven and independent, and I imagine how she's made her way on her own, how she's climbed to the top with her own two hands. My hands creep to my belly.

I could give my baby to someone like this. Someone different and driven, someone smart and ambitious. Someone who will give this little one everything I can't.

I could do it, even if it would kill something inside me, even if I had to live with the guilt and the grief every day of my life. I could do it… and it might be the best thing for my baby, never mind me or my girls.

CHAPTER FOUR

GRACE

'Grace, we might have a match.'

In one quick movement, I rise from my desk and twitch closed the blinds on the floor-to-ceiling window that overlooks the rest of the office floor. I take a deep breath and turn to the two other floor-to-ceiling windows, the ones overlooking the Hudson River. My corner office. Finally. A perk of that social media deal back in November, although it ended up not doing quite as well as I'd hoped.

'We do?' I say carefully. My heart is beating hard and I feel that tingle of excitement, a flare inside, like I do when I sense a good investment no one else has spotted. And this... this is the biggest investment of all.

It's been two months since my father's funeral and the loneliness hasn't let up. If anything, it's become worse. And along with it has grown a need, a craving I feel with every fiber of my being, that I need someone to love. Maybe it's my biological clock, maybe simply the human urge to live for something greater than myself. In any case, six weeks ago, I decided to begin the process to adopt a baby.

I didn't have time to find a man, marry, and start trying the old-fashioned way. That would take months, years, and it was sure to be complicated and messy. I'm thirty-nine; it's already getting late. Besides, adoption felt right: a baby without a mother, a mother without a child. We'd fit, two interlocking puzzle pieces, holding tight together. We'd be a team, the two of us, just like my father and I used to be, needing nothing but each other.

When I decide something, I do it, and that's how it was with this. I bought the books, I found an agency, I went through all the loops and hoops, the home study and assessments, with single-minded determination. It gave me a focus, something I desperately needed after my father's death, and more importantly, gave me hope.

Even now, two months later, I'll suddenly remember he's gone and it's startling, like I've heard it for the first time, the wave of grief breaking over me as fresh and cold as ever. The phone will ring, and I think it's him. The words *Hey, Dad* are almost out of my mouth when I hear the telemarketer's drone.

So thinking about a baby, my baby, my family, has helped me. Grounded me. And now I might be taking the next step to making that a reality.

'Yes, a couple have come forward to express interest,' Tina, the woman who handles my case at the adoption agency, says, and my heart turns right over. 'They specifically requested a closed adoption, just as you wanted. She's due in the middle of May.'

It's early January now; the city is covered in dirty snow and the air is frigid, sharp and metallic. Christmas might as well not have happened. Dad and I always had Christmas together, over at his place, exchanging a gift each and sharing a bottle of wine. It was low-key but I loved it, because we weren't trying to oversell the holiday or pretend everything was normal, without my mom, without the extended family most people take for granted. We just were, and that was always enough. It always had been.

This year I simply pretended it wasn't Christmas at all. I worked pretty much the whole time and on the actual day I holed up with a bottle of wine, takeout Chinese food, and Netflix.

'And she – they – picked me?' I can't help but sound disbelieving. Me, the single, driven career woman who, I'm secretly afraid, doesn't even look maternal?

'Yes, they did.' I hear a smile in Tina's voice. 'It does happen.'

And yet I didn't expect it to happen quite *this* quickly. Everyone yammers on about how adoption takes forever, at least on the internet forums I ventured onto one drunken night. The desperation seeped out of my laptop like some toxic gas, and the worst part was, I felt it too, like something being carved out of me. I clicked and clicked on message after message, read stories of adoptions that fell through, sometimes heartbreakingly late, and then of course the ones that never even happened. Couples waiting years, decades, longing only for a child to love. Just like me.

'So who is she?' I ask Tina.

'Her name is Heather, and her husband is Kevin. They live in Elizabeth, New Jersey. He's got a permanent injury and they have three children already. They're not prepared to have a fourth. Grace…' Tina pauses, and my fingers tighten on the phone.

'Yes?'

'This might not be as simple as it first sounds.'

I tense, because I don't like the sound of that. But is any adoption simple? We're talking about a human being, not a business transaction, as much as I sometimes would like this to resemble one. 'What do you mean, Tina?'

'It's just… a fourth child, a couple that's together. It's not the usual adoptive scenario.'

'So you think there's a risk of her changing her mind?' I'm in finance mode, analyzing, assessing; deciding if this investment is worth the potential loss, even though I know it doesn't work like that. It can't.

'There's always a risk.' Tina hesitates. 'And, to tell you the truth, Heather has shown some definite uncertainty about the situation.'

Definite uncertainty. Talk about an oxymoron, and yet this whole situation feels like one. Two mothers. One baby. Someone is losing out. 'How much uncertainty?' I ask, as if Tina can give me a percentage.

'She says she's decided, and she and her husband have both signed the paperwork, so I can't really say. I just feel I have to warn you. It's… a delicate situation.'

'Why didn't she get an abortion?' As soon as the words are out of my mouth I realize they sound callous, cold, but in this day and age, it seems like the obvious solution.

'I'm not really sure. Maybe she realized later than she felt comfortable with for terminating a pregnancy, or there might be a… faith element. I believe she's Catholic.'

'Huh.' I haven't known any real Catholics. I know people who grew up Catholic, but they talk about it the way you talk about being Italian or from the Midwest. A part of you, yes, but not really relevant to who you are now or the decisions you make.

'And,' Tina adds, 'it's not an easy decision to make in the best of circumstances… every woman feels differently about these things.'

'Of course.' The last thing I want is for this Heather to get an abortion, which I suppose she could still get, legally anyway, if she's due in May. This situation might be delicate, but it's the only one I've got. I don't want to be one of those tragic people on the internet forums, waiting years, the nursery gathering dust and mildew like something out of a horror film. 'So what happens now?'

'Heather and Kevin want to meet you. Soon, if possible.'

'Okay.' My mind races. I can squeeze in a lunch appointment this week, but evening would be better. Yet as I'm thinking this, I know I'm being utterly ridiculous. A baby is not an accessory to add to my life, or an appointment to squeeze in my calendar. I *know* this, and yet…

'My schedule's a little crazy this week. Could they do next week?'

There is a tiny pause, and I know I've said the wrong thing. I feel it, along with a rush of shame. What am I *thinking*? This is the most important decision of my life, the most important deal

I'll ever make. Who cares if I annoy Bruce Felson or one of the other partners by taking a sudden personal day? 'Of course I can meet them whenever it suits,' I say quickly. 'Any time at all. Do they want to come here, or should I go there? Wherever…' I'm babbling, because whatever it takes, I'll do it. I have to.

'I'm not sure what they'd prefer, but I'll call you back when I've spoken to them,' Tina promises. After we've said our goodbyes I stand there, my phone in my hand, my heart beating hard as I stare out at the city.

For the first time since I decided to go down this route I feel a tiny, treacherous flicker of doubt. Of fear. It surprises me, because I've moved forward with such decisiveness, such certainty, and yet now that it's all happening, I I feel a little lost. I want to feel excited, and I do, of course I do, but I also feel afraid.

I swallow and feel the stirrings of true panic. I've been having panic attacks since my dad's funeral, usually at night, when I'm trying to go to sleep. I'll be lying there about to drift into much-needed unconsciousness when all of a sudden it's like a gun has gone off in the room, and every muscle tenses as my heart starts beating wildly and there is a metallic taste in my mouth.

I feel so alone in those moments, the loneliness like a weight bearing down on me, and the more I think about it the worse it gets, until I feel as if the dark is suffocating me, strangling me, and my breath bursts out of me in ragged gasps that echo through the room.

It stops after about an hour or so, usually with the help of alcohol or work or both, but it leaves me sweat-soaked, shaking and exhausted. I can't have a panic attack now, at the office. I can't lose it like that in the one place where I am most in control.

'Grace?' My assistant Sara knocks on my door. 'You've got a meeting with Starling Corp in five.'

'Right, thanks.' I'm almost tempted to cancel the meeting, because they're a tech company that looks good on paper but I suspect has some pretty big holes they're trying to hide. Less than one percent of companies looking for venture capital get it, and at my level I still have to weed out the ones that won't work. When I'm partner, something I'm hoping is very soon, I'll be signing off on the deals, not searching through the dross looking for dubious gold.

When I started at Harrow and Heath I hit the jackpot in my first year, finding All Natural, the organic everything company that went big at the start of the tech boom. It was lucky but it also set me up for an impossible task, to try to beat my record from the start. I got funneled into tech and emerging social media right away, the ultimate boys' club, although Bruce Felson still keeps trying to steer me toward the make-up and style companies, because I'm the firm's only female principal.

In reality I don't actually like either the tech or the style all that much. I pass a lot of the glamour companies on to Jill Martin, the only other woman who is near my level. I don't think she likes them either, but I pull rank when I have to, and she started a year after me. We pretend to have a female solidarity thing going but we both know it's pretty fake.

I pinch the bridge of my nose and close my eyes, willing my heart rate to slow. I cannot have a panic attack now; I simply cannot. And I don't want to back out of the adoption process because I've committed to it. This fear I feel right now will fade. And at the end I'll have a baby. A family.

I open my eyes and drop my hand to stare out at the choppy river, the steel-gray sky. When I make partner, I won't have to work so hard. I'll have stopped needing to prove myself, and so I will be able to take weekends off like Bruce does. I can go on vacation more than ten days a year; I can go home at seven and not ten or later. I can have a life.

I can have a baby.

For a second I let myself picture it – sitting on the sand at Cape Cod, where my dad and I always went for two wonderful weeks in summer, a chubby toddler with a bucket and shovel by my side. Strolling through the cobbled streets of Paris, my smart, switched-on son or daughter next to me, chattering a mile a minute. I picture Christmas in my apartment – presents and a tree, laughter and voices. We'll start traditions, the two of us; we'll cocoon ourselves with love. I want that. I want that so very much.

Tina calls back that afternoon and says Heather and Kevin will meet me at my apartment tomorrow at ten in the morning. I decide to act as if I'm going out to scout a new contact. Venture capital can be a lonely business – often I'm working on my own, researching, networking, finding opportunities and leads. It doesn't have the cut-throat camaraderie of investment banking, but it's also less pressurizing. Supposedly.

So at nine-thirty the next morning, on the pretext of meeting a mysterious new contact in midtown, I'm running around my apartment, tweaking the fresh flowers, which now seem ostentatious and showy. I've also bought some macaroons from a bakery on Madison, and they sit on a plate on the coffee table, looking too elegant to eat.

I probably should have baked, had a plate of warm oatmeal cookies at the ready, but that's just not who I am. I have herbal tea and fennel apple juice, both of which look and taste disgusting, but All Natural keeps shipping me free samples of their new products. It's healthy, anyway, and that's what moms are supposed to want, right? Except I don't feel anything like a mom. Yet.

The intercom buzzes at ten minutes after ten, and my nerves leap and jangle. 'Tina and Heather to see you, Miss Thomas,' Sergei the doorman's voice comes through the speaker, and I tell him to let them up.

Two minutes later the doorbell rings, a discreet, melodious chime. I take a deep breath, check my reflection – I've worn my hair down, unusually for me, and have paired a crisp white blouse with tailored trousers. I thought about going more casual but I didn't want to seem like I wasn't taking this seriously. So here I am, Grace Thomas, venture capitalist, mother-to-be. Maybe.

I take another deep breath and open the door.

The first thing I think is that Heather is not at all what I expected, and yet at the same time she completely is. Her hair is stringy and limp, her eyes faded, like life has worn her right out. I know from Tina that she's only twenty-nine.

Yet she's also not how I thought she'd be, because there's something in her expression that is alert and intelligent, although she is clearly nervous – as nervous as I am, although I think I hide it better. She's dressed neatly, in jeans and a loose button-down shirt, and what really gets me is her smile, both hesitant and sincere. It transforms her face, makes her eyes crinkle, wiping the strain of years away for a breathtaking second.

I don't know how to feel about that smile, because it makes her seem so genuine and nice, but, meanly, I'm not actually sure if I want her to be either of those. I realize I don't want her to be anything, beyond someone anonymous I can forget about later, which sounds awful but I can't help it, it's true. She's an extra to my story, my family, and yet she's also the most integral part. Yet another oxymoron about this *delicate situation*.

'Heather. Hi, I'm Grace.' I hold my hand out for her to shake, which she does rather limply. Then I step inside and usher her in, chatting about how nice it is to meet her, and was there traffic? I laugh lightly at something Tina says that isn't all that funny, but ice breaking is something I know how to do, putting people at their ease even as I make a snap judgment. Right now I need to feel like I'm good at something.

Yet Heather doesn't seem at ease as she walks toward my living room and then stops on the threshold, staring down at the thick cream plush carpet.

'Should I take my shoes off?'

She's wearing a pair of dirty knock-off Keds, no socks. 'It's fine,' I say. 'Honestly. Would you like something to drink? Herbal tea? Green juice?'

'Green juice?' Heather stares at me blankly.

'This is great,' Tina assures me. 'Thank you so much for having us.'

'I have sparkling water,' I tell Heather. 'Or just tap water. Whatever you like.'

'Um, sparkling water, I guess. Please.'

'I'll have the green juice,' Tina says, and she gives me a reassuring smile before I get the drinks. When I come back to the living room Heather is strolling around, leaving gentle indentations in the plush carpet as she gazes at the artwork on the walls, which is all abstract and, now that I look at it, kind of ugly.

I don't have any personal photographs in here; I keep those in my bedroom and study, mostly of me and my dad through the years, as well as one arty black and white of my mom when she was in college. They're too private for strangers to look at, not that I have strangers in my apartment all that often, or ever. Except for now.

'So.' My voice comes out too loud and Heather jumps a little as she turns around. 'Was Kevin not able to come today?'

In the ensuing silence, the air practically crackles. Heather stills. I am instantly regretting my question, an attempt at small talk that has obviously failed. 'He has a chronic injury to his back,' Heather says, 'and he isn't able to leave the house very much.' Her tone makes me think it's her standard excuse for Kevin's no-shows.

'I'm so sorry.' She doesn't reply and I gesture toward the two sofas upholstered in soft, gray leather. 'Shall we sit down?'

Heather moves obediently to the sofa and sits, her head slightly bowed. I feel a sadness emanating from her that makes me feel sad myself, sad for her, for whatever shitty circumstances brought her to this decision, but her sadness also alarms me. Tina said Heather had decided to go ahead, but I'm not feeling that right now. I take in the tired lines and faded eyes, the sense of both acceptance and despair that hangs about her like a shroud. I don't want to feel sorry for her, I don't have space for it, and yet I do. I really do.

'You have a nice apartment,' Heather says rather dutifully, and I murmur my thanks. I can see how she's taking everything in, from the paintings on the wall to the modern sculpture to the pile of expensive coffee table books I never even open, and I feel nervous about what she might think.

This house was an interior decorator's blank canvas, and yet right now it seems to reveal too much about me. A lack in me, because it's so impersonal, like an upscale hotel. I should have personal photos around, and well-thumbed paperbacks, a cookbook left open somewhere.

Oh, this? I was just thinking about whipping up a quinoa and chickpea salad. Although maybe Heather doesn't even know what quinoa is. I'm not sure I do, no matter that I'm supposed to be some organic expert now, thanks to All Natural.

'So, Heather, maybe you could tell Grace why you liked the look of her profile,' Tina says. She sounds as if she's instructing two four-year-olds to share.

Heather swings her glance between Tina and me and still doesn't say anything. Is she overwhelmed? Unsure? Is she wishing she hadn't come at all? Her skin is pale and freckly, and there are violet circles under her eyes. I smile encouragingly, waiting for her to begin.

'I guess I picked you,' Heather begins slowly, choosing each word with care, her hands clasping her fake leather bag in her lap, 'because you are – I mean, you want to be – a single mom. And I… I admire that.'

She admires me? I want to feel pleased but I'm not sure I believe her. And, I realize, I'm kind of a weird choice for her, aren't

I? I would expect someone like Heather – although I realize I'm making assumptions – to want the typical family, complete with white picket fence and slobbery dog. I wonder why she doesn't.

'I'm glad you admire that, Heather,' I say. 'I know a lot of people might be taken aback by a single mom, even in this day and age, which is sad.' I'm going into talk show mode, all fake intimacy and forced cheer, making me cringe inwardly, but I can't stop it.

'Well, I'm not.' She sounds stubborn, like she's fighting against the tide, and maybe she is. Maybe in her world a single mom, or at least choosing to be a single mom, is a strange and suspect thing. But it still doesn't feel like a completely credible reason to choose me for her child's mother.

'And what about Kevin?' I ask carefully. 'How does he feel about this?'

Tina and Heather share a quick, worried look, and I tense. More uncertainty, it seems. How much is too much? When do I decide it's not worth the risk, the pain? To come so close and then have it all snatched away? To love and lose? That definitely is worse than never loving at all. I know.

But of course it's worth it, it has to be, because I still want this so much. And I'll take just about any risk to find my family.

Heather turns back to me, her expression resolute. 'Kevin,' she says flatly, 'doesn't care.'

CHAPTER FIVE

HEATHER

Tina and I don't speak on the way down in the elevator, which looks almost as luxurious as Grace Thomas's apartment. There's a table and a chair in it, as well as a CCTV camera in the corner. I wonder how many people pick their nose or their wedgie in here and are caught on camera by a bored doorman.

Once I might have giggled at the thought, and Kevin would have joked around about it, got right up in the camera and wiggled his thumb in his nose. I can picture it, but it's like looking through the wrong end of a telescope, because he hasn't been funny like that or even happy for months. Years. The knowledge is like a dragging weight inside of me, pulling everything down.

'I'm sorry Kevin wasn't able to make it today,' Tina says, not for the first time. She pursed her lips when I first told her he wasn't coming.

Now I shrug and look away. Tina has met Kevin just once, two weeks ago, to go over the initial paperwork. He didn't say a single word the whole time we were there, didn't even ask who we might be giving this baby to. I'm the one who has got us this far, pushing and dragging all the dead weight. It hasn't been easy, and the only way I've done it is because I don't have any other choice.

After looking at those parent profiles online, I got spooked and I started to backtrack. I couldn't just give my child away. I wasn't some pregnant teenager or heroin junkie; I was a married woman with three children, a respectable person in a small, close-knit community. Other people had hard times and they didn't go and give up their kid. I wouldn't either.

And so I convinced myself I could make it work. I swallowed my pride, went online and applied for food stamps, even though I knew Kevin would hate the thought of us accepting a handout from the government. I also took out a loan from one of those shady sharks on the street corner, the kind of guy who murmurs in sympathy as he cracks his knuckles. I knew it was crazy but when the alternative is losing your house, what are you going to do?

I paid it back two days later when Kev's last disability check came in, plus the huge interest, which meant we had absolutely no money at all; I'd even gone through the sofa cushions and coat pockets for loose change, all eight dollars and forty-eight cents of it, which I used for gas. Kevin never questioned any of it, never even noticed.

We had the food stamps, so at least we'd eat. Although they aren't food stamps anymore; we got an EBT card, and it looks like just a credit card, except I wouldn't have to pay it back. After it came, I took the girls to the grocery store, feeling generous, almost hopeful. We were eligible for nearly four hundred dollars a month for food. I could feed my girls. So I let them toss things into the cart, a few treats, nothing too big, and when Amy asked if we could buy one of those rotisserie chickens for dinner, because they smelled so good, I said sure, why not? We had the money, for once. They deserved it.

Then we got to the checkout, the food already packed in bags, and I went to pay. I tried to be subtle about it, just sticking the card into the machine like it was no big deal, but the cashier saw and shook her head.

'Sorry, but not everything here is eligible for food stamps.'

I went still and cold inside, the card, with BENEFITS written in big, black letters on it, suddenly seeming obvious, still clutched in my hand. Then the cashier started taking stuff out of the bags and stacking it on the side. A bottle of economy-brand shampoo, some toothpaste, a six-pack of beer for Kevin, that damned chicken. Amy let out a little cry of protest and Emma looked at me in confusion. Lucy pressed close to my side, her thumb in her mouth.

From behind me someone let out a loud, drawn-out sigh, and the cashier gave me a smile of tired sympathy.

'Sorry, hon, but it's the law. You'll have to pay cash for those.'

But I didn't have any cash. I thought that was the point of an EBT card, of the whole system. You didn't *need* any cash. I saw a woman I recognized from school waiting in line behind the guy who had sighed and was now tapping his foot, craning her neck to see what was going on.

'Mommy,' Lucy said, tugging on my sleeve. 'Why can't we buy the chicken?'

'What do you want to do, hon?' the cashier asked. She was trying to be nice but I could tell she was impatient too. The line was growing longer. I felt my face flush, my whole body, with hot, prickly shame. The mom from school caught my eye, and without even thinking through what I was doing I grabbed Amy and Lucy's hands and walked right out of the store, Emma hurrying behind, leaving all the food in the bags, the chicken and shampoo and beer piled on the side.

'Mommy, what are you *doing*?'

'What about our chicken?'

'Quiet,' I hissed, and I marched, my head held high, my whole body trembling, all the way to our car, dragging Amy and Lucy with me. I buckled Lucy into her car seat while Amy flung herself into the front seat even though she knew it wasn't allowed, and Emma climbed quietly into the back.

'What are we going to eat?' Amy demanded.

'Be quiet, Amy,' I snapped. 'Be *quiet*. I need to think.' I rested my hands on the steering wheel and stared straight ahead, my heart still pounding hard from the whole horrible scene. I had no money. No food. Less than a quarter tank of gas in the car. Kev's disability was gone, my income only covered our rent, and if I had this baby, we wouldn't even have that. I laid my head on the steering wheel and closed my eyes.

I knew I could go back in, get the stuff the EBT card would pay for at least, but at that moment I couldn't manage it. Not emotionally. Not even physically.

'Mom...' Emma sounded scared. 'Mom, what's wrong? Are you okay?'

'I'm just tired.' I ached with fatigue, with hopelessness. I couldn't see a way through the darkness. I felt too tired even to try.

'Mommy...' Amy now, her defiance gone, and that made me feel even sadder. 'Mommy, look up.'

And so I did, dredging up a smile with what felt like the very last of my strength. 'It's okay,' I told my girls, trying to mean it. Something hardened inside me, and my voice came out stronger. 'It's going to be okay.'

That night I told Kev about the adoption idea, and he gave me that dead-eyed stare of his and shook his head.

'Are you fucking kidding me?'

'Don't swear.' He didn't normally, not since we'd had kids. Amy was probably still awake; she was always the last one to drift off, and the whole shopping trip had unsettled her. We'd ended up eating plain spaghetti; Lucy had whined about wanting sauce. Amy and Emma had both eaten in silence, wide-eyed and frightened, and the misery I'd been feeling hardened all the more into resolve.

'Adoption?' Kevin hissed at me. 'Our own *child*?'

'I know.' I bunched my fists, fighting tears. 'I *know*. But you tell me what to do then, Kevin. You tell me how to fix this.' I wanted to feel sorry for him. I always tried, but he made it so hard sometimes, parking himself in that chair and staring at the

TV for hours on end, never offering a suggestion, a solution. I knew he was hurting and frustrated, maybe even depressed. I knew, and yet sometimes that wasn't enough.

'If we give this baby up for adoption,' I continued in a low, steady voice, 'the adoptive couple will pay all the costs. Contribute to our living expenses, too, at least a little.' Although I wasn't thinking of a couple. I recalled Grace Thomas's profile, that faint, sure smile. In my mind she was already the adoptive mother, not one of those smug couples who already had everything.

Kev shook his head. 'What the hell are we supposed to tell people?'

'The truth: that we can't afford another baby and we want to give someone else a chance to be a parent.' Saying the words felt like swallowing bits of broken glass, but I was determined now. I couldn't put my girls through another day like today; I couldn't put myself through it. Kevin made a sound of disgust.

'What else am I supposed to do?' I demanded in a low voice. He couldn't have it both ways. He couldn't act like I had to deal with it on my own and then get mad when I did. 'Do you want me to have an abortion? Is that it? I'm already fifteen weeks. I'll feel the baby kick any day now.' My voice choked, and I sucked in a hard breath. Those little flutters would just about kill me.

'An abortion?' Kevin looked genuinely horrified, and then he shook his head. 'Heather, no. *No!* I'd never want that. Our own kid…'

'I know you wouldn't.' I was relieved that he'd said it, because even though this felt like the hardest thing I'd ever done, I knew that would be harder. 'But what then, Kev? Tell me what to do.' For a second I let myself remember the way he was when I told him I was pregnant with Emma, seventeen and scared. He'd pulled me into a hug, my head tucked under his chin. 'Then we'll just have to get married,' he'd said, making it sound so wonderfully simple. I felt so safe in that moment, safe and happy, sure of my future. *Our* future.

But now, fourth time around, Kevin just stared at me for a long moment and then he dropped his head into his hands with a sound like a moan. It was the opposite of everything I hoped for, and it brought me near to tears.

'Kevin…'

'I fucking hate this.' His voice was low but not angry. Angry I was used to, angry I took on the chin and soldiered on with slumped shoulders, and right then I'd have preferred it to the despair I heard in his voice, the despair he usually tried to hide. 'I fucking hate that I'm stuck in this stupid chair, that I can't even provide for my fucking *family*.' He raised his head and then he took the remote control resting on the arm of the chair and hurled it at the TV.

Thankfully it missed, causing a dent in the wall rather than one in our TV. He winced and sagged against the chair, and I knew he'd strained his back just by that one movement.

'This isn't your fault, Kevin.' I picked up the remote control and put it back on the arm of the chair. 'You had an accident and you can't work…' Even if sometimes I wish he'd just *try*.

'Tell that to the fucking lawyers.'

'Please don't swear.'

He looked away and I continued steadily, 'This doesn't have to be a bad thing.' I knew I was speaking to myself as much as to him. 'We'd be making someone happy. This child would have a great life, and we could give our girls the lives they deserve too. Everybody wins.'

'Sure as hell doesn't feel like winning to me.'

'Breaking even, maybe. I don't see any other way, Kev. I really don't. And the truth is…' It hurt to say it, but I knew I needed to. 'We need the money. All the costs would be covered, plus some living expenses.'

His lip curled. 'So you want to sell our kid?'

'It's not like that.' Why did he have to act like I was happy about this? Didn't he realize how it was tearing me up inside so I didn't know if I'd ever put myself together again? I'd just be bits and broken pieces. 'There's a limit to how much you can take from the adoptive parents. Usually it's just the basics covered – hospital costs, maternity clothes, that kind of stuff, plus help with bills if you need it. And we do.'

Kevin shrugged like it didn't matter, but we both knew it did. 'And this baby would have a really good life,' I pressed on. 'We could be happy about that.'

'Better than I could provide, you mean.'

'Well, yes.' How could I not admit that? 'But it doesn't have to be a bad thing. It just… is. Wouldn't it be nice to know this baby is having a good life?' A better life, maybe, than the three girls we'd kept, although I didn't say that. I tried not to think it.

Kevin didn't speak for a long moment and then he picked up the remote control. 'Do whatever you want,' he said, and clicked the power button. A second later the room was filled with the sound of football. I stood there for a few seconds, fighting both fury and despair, wanting to say something to get him out of his sorry-for-himself stupor, even if it was something mean, but I stayed silent. It wasn't worth it, even if I felt like screaming at him that I couldn't keep everything going. I couldn't keep doing this all on my own.

I walked into the dining room and I emailed Open Hearts to ask Tina for an appointment. When I told Kevin he had to go in with me, he just nodded. In the office, a few days later, he stayed sullenly silent, and didn't even look at Tina or me, just scrawled his name. Later, when he'd left the room, Tina said something about needing to make sure he was okay with this, and I shook my head.

'We're having a hard time with a lot of stuff,' I told her, trying to keep my voice firm and sure. 'But this is what we need to do. Kevin knows that.'

'Do you know that, Heather?' Tina's voice sounded too gentle, and I forced myself to meet her compassionate gaze without flinching, or worse, falling apart.

'Yes, I do. It's a hard decision, of course it is, but…' My voice wobbled and I took a quick, steadying breath. 'I've come to terms with it. I have.'

At least, I thought I had. I'd told myself I had. But now that I've met Grace Thomas, seen her apartment, heard her talk? She was so elegant and self-assured, everything I've never been able to be, not that I'd even know how to try. How do her clothes look so smooth, like they've never seen a wrinkle? And her hair is so shiny.

But she also seemed untouchable and a little brittle, and I wonder how she'll be as a mom. Will she love my baby? Will she be able to handle the nighttime feeds and all the poop and puke and whining, the way it never, ever stops, even when they get older? Especially when they get older. I can't picture it, but maybe I just don't want to.

'So are you happy to proceed?' Tina asks as we step out onto Fifth Avenue, a freezing wind funneling down the sidewalk. 'You can think about it, of course, and talk to Kevin. And if you'd like to meet with Grace again…'

Suddenly I am filled with panic. I didn't ask Grace *anything*. I don't even know why she wants to adopt, or what kind of mother she'll be. Will she have a nanny? Is she good at hugs? Does she have a boyfriend? I am completely, utterly ignorant. And I'm meant to hand her my baby in a couple of months?

'Heather?' Tina looks at me, her face filled with concern. I whirl around, some desperate part of me intent on going back into Grace's building, marching right up to her front door. But then I see her coming out, an expensive-looking leather bag over one shoulder. She is cradling her cell phone between her shoulder and ear as she waves down a taxi with her free arm. Before I even know what I am doing, I stride up to her.

'Heather—' Tina calls, sounding alarmed, but I don't listen.

'Grace.' My voice comes out loud and hard. She looks up, her eyes widening. She drops her arm and says something into the phone, ending the call, before sliding the phone into her blazer pocket.

'Heather.'

We stare at each other, two women, both wanting something. Grace's expression is calm and steady, almost as if she expected this. I know I must look wild.

'You never told me why you want to adopt. Why you want a baby.' I'm breathing hard, ragged gasps tearing through me as I practically glare at her.

Grace hesitates, as if she's thinking through her options, and then she settles on the truth. I see it in the way her shoulders square, her jaw sets. 'Because my father died a few months ago and I realized how alone I was. Am. I work a lot, I don't have any family and not even that many friends. My dad was everything to me, the best dad I could have asked for. And now I want a chance to be the best mom.' She lifts her chin a little. 'I know I probably don't seem very maternal to you, and the truth is I've barely even held a baby before. But I know I'll love this child with everything I have. Every breath, every heartbeat.'

The air rushes out of me; I feel relieved, because I believe her, and I needed her to say that, as much as it hurts.

'Now it's your turn,' Grace says, surprising me. 'Why, really, did you choose me, a single career woman, to be the adoptive mother?' She eyes me appraisingly and I decide on honesty, just as she did. Maybe it will draw us together in some strange way.

'Because I didn't want to give my baby to a couple who already has everything, who would be like Kev and me, only a better version. It's hard enough as it is.' I meet her gaze unflinchingly. 'You're different. I won't… I won't compare myself to you all the time. And you might have a lot, I know that, but you don't have something that I have.' I realize how petty that makes me sound, and I bite my lip. 'It makes it easier somehow, and I need this to be easier. Otherwise I don't think I can do it at all.'

Grace nods slowly, accepting. Understanding. 'Okay,' she says, and waits. Another tense second passes; I feel as if we're both standing on a set of teetering scales.

'Okay,' I finally reply, a farewell, and then I turn back to Tina, who is waiting a few yards back, looking uncertain. I nod at her; I feel strangely satisfied, even though the pain is still there. It always will be.

'I want to go ahead,' I tell her, and keep walking.

'You know,' Tina says once we're at the car, 'it would be a really nice gesture to invite Grace to your ultrasound. Isn't it next week?'

'Okay,' I say as I hunch my shoulders against that unforgiving wind. 'Can you ask her?'

Back at home Kevin flicks a glance my way and then back at the TV. 'How did it go?' he asks after a second, his voice low, and my jaw practically drops because he's acknowledging that this is happening. Sort of.

'Pretty good, I guess.'

I told Kev I was meeting a prospective parent, but I left Grace's single status out of it, and he didn't ask. He certainly didn't volunteer to go with me. I would have told him if he'd asked, if he'd shown any interest at all, but he has always refused and so I've refused to beg or plead. I knew he wouldn't be thrilled about Grace being single. He'd probably make some comment about lesbians and turkey basters. In any case, he'll find out soon enough.

I haven't told Stacy or my parents that I'm pregnant yet, either. Loose clothing and winter coats let me get away with it so far, but I know I'll have to tell them soon. And what about Emma and Amy and Lucy? None of them have noticed, but they will one day, especially Amy. And I'm still not sure how I'm going to make it all seem okay. But I will. Somehow, I will.

Kevin clicks off the TV and turns to me. I still, surprised. 'I'm sorry,' he says, his voice a rasp I strain to hear. 'I should have been there today.'

Now my jaw really does drop. 'It's okay.'

He shakes his head. 'I'm letting you down, Heather. I'm letting you all down.' He stares at the wall, his jaw clenched. 'I know that.'

I hate to see his despair; it feels worse than my own. 'It's not your fault, Kev.'

'Doesn't matter.' He struggles to sit upright. 'I'm going to look for a job.'

'Okay,' I say cautiously. In three years this is the first time he's ever said that, and it fills me with wary hope. I know Kev isn't qualified for much, and what he is qualified for, he can't do. But surely there's something out there. There's got to be, because I need a glimmer of light in the midst of all this darkness.

A couple of days later I'm in the kitchen making dinner when Stacy stops by to ask if I can check in on Mom and Dad tomorrow. It feels like an okay moment for once – the TV is off, and Kevin is sitting on the sofa with Amy and Emma, listening to Emma read a pony book she got from the school library. Lucy is on the floor, playing with her Paw Patrol set from Christmas – five bucks at Walgreens – and half-listening to Emma read.

The smell of meat and onion frying makes my stomach turn but it's a good smell. A homely, family smell. I look around and I feel a flicker of contentment. This is what we used to have, what we took for granted, and now it feels so precious, simple as it is. Dinner, a home. Warmth and family. I yearn to hold onto it all.

Then Stacy comes in, says hello to all the girls, calling to me about needing me to help out with Mom and Dad. She stops in the doorway of the kitchen.

'*Heather.*'

'What?' I turn, instantly self-conscious, because I'm over halfway through now and while the girls have managed not to notice, it's getting kind of obvious when I'm not wearing a coat.

Stacy steps toward me and lowers her voice. 'Are you *pregnant*?' she whispers, with a glance back at Kevin and the girls in the other room.

I turn to the stove and prod the hamburger. 'Yes. Obviously.' Or not so obviously, to most people. Yet.

'How far along are you? And why didn't you say anything?'

'I'm nineteen weeks. And I didn't say anything because…' I hesitate, glancing through the dining room to where Kev and the girls are all piled together on the sofa. Amy is starting to get bored and Lucy is throwing her Paw Patrol figures at the TV. 'It's not exactly great news, is it?'

Stacy swallows and looks at me seriously. 'I know you guys have been having a hard time of it…'

I prod the hamburger some more. Stacy has no idea. She did everything in the right order – school, marriage, then babies. She works part-time at Stop & Shop and her husband Mike works in a garage. They have two kids, Jake and Kerryn, and they live a pretty middle-class kind of life, at least compared to us. Last year they even went to Disney World for a whole week.

'We can't afford it,' I tell Stacy in a low voice. I stare at the hamburger, not wanting to see the pity on her face. She didn't get knocked up by accident. She doesn't have a husband who barely gets out of his La-z-Boy. Kev said he was going to look for a job, but he hasn't yet. I try not to feel bitter, but it's there, eating away at my insides, turning everything to acid. 'We just can't.'

Stacy is silent and I don't look at her. I'm afraid she's going to offer money she doesn't have, money I can't take because while she and Mike are doing better than us, they're not doing that well. They can't bail us out again and again, not the way we'd need.

'I wish we could help,' Stacy says at last. 'If it really is just a question of money. But Mike…' She pauses, biting her lip, and I turn to her.

'Stace…?'

'Mike's been laid off. He'll get another job, I know he will, but in the meantime…' She shrugs.

'I'm sorry.' We're not the only ones struggling. Of course we're not. I always knew that, but it still surprises me to hear Stacy say it so starkly.

'What are you going to do?' she asks after a moment.

I take a quick breath. I didn't want to tell her or anyone like this, with the kids and Kevin around, when things were happy for one beautiful second, but there's no point pretending I haven't decided when I know I have. 'I'm not keeping it.'

'*Heather.*' My name is a gasp. 'What…?'

'Not that,' I say quickly. 'I'm – we're – giving it up for adoption.' I don't like saying *it*, but speaking that way makes everything easier. It. A thing, a problem. And I'm solving it.

Stacy is silent, and I can feel her shocked disapproval crackling like a force field around her. She's so quick to judge, and she's my *sister*. What are other people going to say? Think?

'Are you… are you sure that's what you want to do?'

'It's not like we have a lot of choice, Stacy.'

'But surely, if it's just money…?'

It's never *just* money. 'It's everything,' I say. 'It's Kevin's back, and me needing to work, and the size of our house.' My words start to come faster and faster. 'It's Amy's shoe and a stupid chicken and life feeling like an avalanche, things always toppling on top of us so we never have the chance to get out from under it.' I blink rapidly. 'I wish to God I could keep this baby somehow, that I could make it all work, but I've been trying and trying and nothing's ever enough. And I know in my heart this is what I need to do, even if it tears me apart. Even if everyone I know thinks I'm a terrible person for giving away my baby.'

'Heather—'

'People will judge. You know that.'

She nods soberly, not pretending otherwise.

'I don't care,' I say with a sniff. The hamburger is burning and I prod it again, poking the blackened bits. 'This baby is going to have a good life, and my girls are going to have good lives. Isn't that what matters, in the end?'

Stacy is silent, arms folded, shifting from foot to foot, clearly itching to tell me what to do, and what not to do. Typical older sister, she wants to boss me around. She marched me to school when we were little; she gave me her maternity clothes when I got pregnant with Amy. She has been my maid of honor, my best friend, and sometimes my enemy. She feels like all three right now.

'Maybe,' Stacy says at last, 'but what are you going to tell people, Heather? Mom and Dad? Your kids?'

I swallow and stare at the browning meat. 'The truth. That we can't afford to give this baby the life it deserves.' I turn around and fold my arms so we are having a staring standoff. 'And someone else can. Someone who can't have a baby and wants one very much.' I believed Grace when she said that she did. I saw the intensity in her face, the sincerity.

Stacy blows out a breath, shaking her head. 'So you just give the kid away.'

I blink, absorbing her harshness.

'Sorry,' she says, 'but that's how people are going to see it. You'd be better off telling people you're being someone's surrogate or something.'

'Which I would do for money,' I point out, and Stacy shrugs.

'It's different, though. And if you don't make up some story like that, you're right, people around here are going to judge you. They're going to think you're heartless, giving away your own baby.'

'Or maybe just desperate.'

'That, too.' Stacy softens. 'Heather, I know things have been tough but there's got to be some way…'

'Does there?' The bitterness spills through, splashing over both of us. 'I've stopped believing that.' I pause, glancing at Kevin in the other room but he's watching football. The girls are arguing over the Paw Patrol figures; even Emma wants them now. Typical. 'Kev lost his workman's comp a couple of weeks ago,' I say quietly. 'He had his hearing and they said he's had maximum medical improvement.'

Stacy absorbs this for a moment. 'So are they offering him a job?'

'They don't have anything for him. He's been cleared for light duty, but they say there isn't anything like that. He's going on to permanent partial disability.' Which is all of eighty-five dollars a week. 'He's looking for a job,' I add, because I know what Stacy is thinking. Mike thinks it too, which is why we don't see them all that much. They never say it, not exactly, but it's there, pulsing between us, an accusation, a judgment. Kev is just lazy. He needs to get off his ass and find a job he can do with a bad back.

I know they're thinking it because sometimes, when I let myself, I think it too. I'm trying not to think it now. 'But it's hard,' I insist, before Stacy can say something I don't want to hear. 'There's not much out there for someone like him.'

'And if he gets a job? You guys could afford...'

'No, we couldn't,' I cut across her. 'And he doesn't have a job yet.' I don't want to tell her about the eviction notice, the EBT card, how close we still are to losing everything. 'Trust me on this, okay? I think I know my life better than you do.'

Stacy blows out a breath, looking exasperated. 'You could use birth control, you know.'

I almost laugh. 'Yeah, sure. A little late, but thanks for the tip.'

'I'm sorry, Heather, it's just...' She stops, and I turn to face her, something hardening inside me.

'It's just what?'

'You're both such victims,' Stacy bursts out. Out of the corner of my eye I see Amy look up, eyes narrowing as she strains to listen. 'Everything bad happens to you because you let it. I'm not trying to be harsh, but you've got to help yourselves. Kevin needs to work. He should have gone back to work years ago, Heather. And you could retrain, get your high school diploma, whatever. You just stand in the road and let yourselves be run over by life, and I'm telling you, it doesn't have to be that way.'

For a second I can't speak, I'm so angry. *I'm* a victim? Me, who has been holding this family together for three years, clinging by my fingernails, a breath away from losing my grip, falling forever? Stacy has no idea.

'I'm sorry,' she says quietly, and I know she means it, that she regrets being so harsh, but it's not enough. I turn away from her, focus on our dinner. That flicker of contentment I felt? I can't even remember what it feels like now.

Later, after Stacy has left and we've eaten dinner, I am cleaning up in the kitchen and Kevin comes in, moving slowly, a shuffling step I've got used to over the last three years.

'You told Stacy.'

I glance toward the living room, but the girls are all in the tub. Kevin is supposed to be washing their hair and keeping an eye on Lucy.

'She noticed. It's getting obvious.'

'I mean about this whole adoption thing.'

'Yes.'

Kevin is silent and I scrub at a scorch mark on the pan. I can hear the girls splashing and laughing, and I picture all three of them crammed in our little olive-green tub, knees up by their elbows, blonde hair piled on top of their heads. Three little soapy angels.

'So you're really doing this.'

'*We're* doing it. You signed the paperwork, Kevin.' I glance at him, trying not to look as accusing as I feel. As desperate. I want just one person in my life to give me a hug and say, 'You know what? I get it. I understand why you're doing this. I know how hard it must be, that it's tearing you apart, but it will be okay eventually. I promise.' But there's no one. Not Kevin, not Stacy, not even Tina, who must see this situation ten times a day, and not my neighbors and friends when they find out.

I'm alone in this, and there's nothing I can do about it. Maybe I am standing in the middle of the road like Stacy said, but I'm too tired to move. Does she know how that feels? To have everything ache all the time, so even the basics of life – cooking, laundry, loving my girls – feels like it sucks all my energy, all my being, down into a dark hole and there's no way to climb out?

It feels like no one knows how alone I feel, and then I think of Grace. I remember the pain that flashed across her face as she told me about her dad, the lack of friends or family, her loneliness. A sudden wave of empathy washes over me. She really is alone, even more than I am.

From the bathroom someone screeches, and I tense, but then they erupt into laughter.

'You're right,' Kevin says quietly. 'We're doing this. Together.' He reaches for my hand and I twine my fingers through his. We stay that way silently, hands linked, as close as we've been in a long time, and the pressure building in my chest eases. I may feel alone, but I'm not. Not like Grace.

CHAPTER SIX

GRACE

When Tina called to invite me to attend Heather's ultrasound with her, I felt a ripple of pleasure, a dart of alarm. It felt like an invasion of Heather's privacy, and I wasn't sure what role I'd have there, but I wanted to see some concrete evidence of this baby. My child.

I still couldn't quite believe Heather had decided to go with me after all. I'd thought I'd botched that whole first meeting, seeming prissy and business-like because I was so nervous. And then that surreal confrontation in the street, both of us laying our cards down right there. It felt good, a chance to reveal something I knew I couldn't hide forever. And Heather's admission about why she chose me didn't faze me, not after I'd thought about it. She was being honest too, and it felt as if we'd found equal terms, ones we could both live with.

And so now we're going ahead, signing more forms, making it real. Tina asked me to cover the maternity costs plus some basic living expenses, which I was more than happy to do. Money is easy.

I arranged to have two hundred dollars a week put into Heather's account, which seemed like little enough but Tina was strict about the whole financial side of things. There were rules about that, formulas to follow, spreadsheets to fill out. No one should be buying a baby. If only it were that simple.

I rent a car to drive to the hospital in New Jersey where Heather is having the ultrasound. As I'm stepping out of my apartment, already running five minutes late, my neighbor opens her door. I brace myself for the usual opening gambit of bright questions. At least I know her name now – Eileen. At least I think it is. It was hard to make out the writing on the Christmas card she slid under my door.

'Hello,' she says cheerfully. 'Going somewhere nice?'

'Not particularly.' That feels a bit rude so I temper it with a smile as I press the button for the elevator. 'How about you?' I don't feel quite confident enough to call her Eileen.

'Oh no, dear, not with my eyesight.' She shakes her head ruefully. 'Can't go much anywhere these days.'

Surprise jolts through me; I hadn't realized her eyesight was that bad, but then why would I? I know nothing about her or her husband, who I realize I haven't seen in a while. I can't think of what to say and then the elevator door opens and I step inside. My neighbor is still standing there watching me and I blurt suddenly, 'I'm sorry, but I'm not actually sure of your name. Is it… is it Eileen?' I give an embarrassed laugh.

She smiles, wide and easy. 'Yes, and you're Grace.'

The doors of the elevator close with her still smiling. I feel a twinge of both guilt and regret that I've been so indifferent, so focused on other things. I'm going to be better about that kind of thing from now on. Now that I'm going to be a mother.

As I pull into the parking lot of Trinitas Medical Center tension begins to twang through me. I haven't been to a hospital since my father died. When I step through the automatic doors and breathe in that awful smell of antiseptic and illness, it all comes back in a sickening rush: the evenings I spent by his bed, watching the sun sink slowly outside as the room became lost in shadows; the persistent beep of all the monitors he was hooked up to, and the way people were always coming in and out – nurses, cleaners, aides to deliver the meals he never ate. The trays stacked up on the side, with their little plastic-covered dishes of canned peaches or chicken noodle soup, everything untouched.

Doctors hardly ever came; once a day, if that, managing to seem both important and disinterested. My father stirring occasionally, his eyelids fluttering as he smiled at me, saying something nonsensical because of the morphine he was getting through an IV. Or coming out with something astonishingly lucid that stole my breath before I could speak, because I knew it was all slipping away and I absolutely could not stand it.

It felt as if his life was being played out reel by reel in his mind, for he'd mention things from all over – his first job, when I was a baby, meeting Mom at UConn, the last movie we saw together, just two months earlier. Garbled snapshots that faded before I could look at them properly, and I longed to hold onto them. He was imparting his history to me, giving it like a final gift, offered in fragments and sighs, and I couldn't even keep it.

It went on that way for a week and then the doctor told me quite matter-of-factly that Dad had no more than twenty-four hours; his body was shutting down, his organs starting to fail. It felt as if the doctor had slapped me in the face and then smiled. In reality he'd given me a sorrowful look and then left before I could ask him any questions, before I could even think.

I spent all those hours – it turned out to be sixteen – sitting by my father's bed, holding his hand, my fingers sliding over the loose skin and frail bones, savoring that last connection even as I tensed with both hope and fear every time his eyes flickered open. Holding his hand was all I had to offer, my final gift to him.

The morning of the day he died, my father opened his eyes and looked around, blinking slowly, and then he focused on me and, in a croaky voice, asked what time it was.

'Why?' I asked lightly, my throat aching with the knowledge that I'd already lost so much, and there was only more to lose. 'Do you have somewhere to be, Dad?'

My father smiled faintly, and his fingers squeezed mine. I wanted to cling to him, but I was afraid of hurting him. 'I have a train to catch,' he joked, and then his eyes closed again. Those were the last words he spoke.

The next few hours were an endless agony, both painful and profound. Doctors say it's painless, the gentle slip into death, and maybe it was, for him. It wasn't for me. I didn't know how much he could feel, how much he could think, and that ignorance tortured me. Was he hurting? Was he scared? Could he hear me, when I spoke in a wavering voice, and told him I loved him, that I was there? How much of him was actually *left*? No doctor can tell you any of those answers.

Those hours stretched on and on, while he sunk deeper into unconsciousness and his breathing became more and more labored, the slow, ragged draw and tear making me tense every time. I lost more of him with each passing moment and I almost wished that he would just die, simply to end the misery for both of us, but then when he took that last, shuddering breath, when his body went totally still and everything was suddenly, totally silent, I realized I hadn't wanted that at all. *At all.*

I sat there for a full minute, holding his hand, feeling how it was already becoming cool.

A dead body looks dead very quickly, so don't give me any of this 'He looked as if he was asleep' shit. My father was *gone*. All it had taken was a second; he was there, and then he wasn't. He absolutely wasn't, and I realized that even lying in a bed with his eyes closed and his hand limp in mine, his every breath so painfully labored, he'd been *there*. He'd been alive, and I wanted that back so much it felt as if I would not be able to get through the next minute, never mind the rest of my life.

I went to get the nurse, walking as if I were outside my body, observing everything from a distance that had opened up in myself, a gaping sinkhole that was sucking everything in – my breath, my thoughts, my very self. I watched while they draped a sheet over his body and unplugged all the machines and somehow that made it so much worse, like packing up after a show or a vacation, the nurses so brisk and efficient, just another dead body to them. I didn't even like their sympathetic smiles, because they had no idea. Tonight they were going to go home and watch *The X Factor*.

And so I walked out of the room; I signed the paperwork, avoiding everyone's compassionate yet impersonal gazes, and then I left the hospital. I don't even remember the next few days; I went to work because to stay home felt like torture, but I can't remember what I did or said or felt. Eventually I felt myself come back into focus, but I knew I'd never be the same. I'm missing something, I always will be, and a baby won't plug that hole in my heart. I'm not looking for that. If anything, I'm looking for a way to pay my father's love forward.

Now I'm in a hospital again, and I feel sick. As I walk through the lobby an aide rolls a stretcher past, and I hear the *beep beep beep* of some kind of monitor and a visceral reaction goes through me, a full body shudder. I'm not sure I can do this.

But I keep walking, one foot in front of the other, because I want to find Heather. I want to see my baby on that screen. And then I come to the maternity unit with its ultrasound ward and the expectant mothers with their hands laced across their big bellies, and the room is so cheerful, I almost forget I'm in a hospital at all.

Heather is already there, clutching her bag on her lap. She looks tired and a bit forlorn, but she smiles hesitantly when she sees me. 'Grace. Hi.'

'Hi.' I sit down next to her, give her a quick smile although I'm already feeling awkward.

'How are you feeling?' I ask, which feels like a fairly safe opener.

'Like I really have to pee.' Heather gives an embarrassed grimace.

'Oh?' I glance around for a bathroom sign. Surely there has to be one? 'Do you want to go to the ladies'? I'll listen out if they call your name.'

'Oh, no.' Heather lets out a little laugh. 'I can't. I mean, you have to have a full bladder for the ultrasound. So they can see the baby on the screen.'

'Oh. Right.' I think I knew that, somewhere in my subconscious stores of trivia. I feel like I should have known that, considering. I should have done more research.

Heather looks at me curiously, obviously wondering at my ignorance. 'Did you try to get pregnant yourself? Before you decided to adopt?'

'No, I didn't.' I decide to be honest, just as we were out in the street. I think that's what Heather wants, too.

'Why not?'

'Well, as you know, there's no potential father in the picture,' I say with a little, awkward laugh. 'And I didn't really feel like going the whole turkey-baster route.' Which is true. Plus I couldn't take the time off work, which sounds heartless, so I decide to keep that part to myself.

Heather smiles a little. 'That sounds like something Kevin would say.'

'Oh?' I'm surprised by the mention of her husband. I don't know anything about him besides his injury but I get the sense that he can be difficult and unpleasant. 'He didn't want to come today?'

Heather's expression closes right up. 'No, he didn't. Why would he?' There is something dignified about her response, about her lack of pretending. 'Since we're not keeping this baby. The less he knows, the better. Otherwise it just hurts.'

'I'm sorry,' I murmur, although I'm not exactly sure what I'm apologizing for.

'No, I'm the one who should be sorry.' Heather blows out a breath. 'I shouldn't have said that. I didn't mean… it's just this has been difficult for us, but I know we're doing the right thing.' She tries to give me a reassuring smile, but it wobbles. 'For us and for you. I really do know that. So…' With determination she injects a false note of brightness in her voice. 'What would you rather have? A boy or a girl?'

'Oh, um…' I am thrown by the sudden change, Heather's willingness to ask a question I've been too hesitant to ask myself, much less answer. 'I've been picturing a girl,' I admit almost shyly. 'Boys are so different, I'm not sure what I'd do with one.'

She laughs a little. 'Me neither, although Kev would like a boy, I think. A son.' Then, realizing how that sounds, she backtracks quickly. 'I mean, he would have, you know, if…' She starts again. 'We have three girls and we love them. Of course.' She shakes her head, annoyed with her babbling, and I smile.

'I know you do.' Of all the things I might wonder about Heather, her love for her family is not one of them. She wouldn't be doing this if she didn't love them all with the same, heart-stopping love I already feel for this unknown little person. That much I get.

'It's probably a girl, anyway,' she says. 'Seems like that's all we make.' She shakes her head again. 'This is so weird. I don't know what to say that sounds right.'

'I know, I don't either.' And then, because for a second we feel close, bound by our shared confusion, I touch her hand lightly. She smiles at me, and I see gratitude in her eyes, and I release the breath I hadn't realized I was holding.

'So do you want to find out?' Heather asks. 'The sex?'

'It might be fun. Make it more real.' I try for a laugh. 'This feels pretty surreal to me. I can't believe I'm actually going to be a mother in a few months.' Just saying the words sends an uneasy thrill rippling through me. A *mother*.

'At least you won't have to deal with the recovery while you have a newborn. Milk coming in, sore down there…' She shakes her head, frowning, and I realize she's thinking how she'll have to deal with it. Without the newborn.

'A bonus of adoption, I guess,' I say lightly, and she nods, not looking at me. I want to get back to that brief moment of solidarity, but it feels like it's already gone.

'Heather McCleary?' A nurse in hot pink scrubs appears at the doorway, smiling and holding a clipboard.

Heather struggles up from her seat and after a second I take her arm, and she gives me a quick, uncertain smile.

The nurse's gaze moves questioningly between me and Heather, although she doesn't ask who I am. Friend? *Customer?* What if she thinks I'm Heather's partner, her wife, a clear case of opposites attracting? She's probably seen it all.

We're led into a room with a lot of beeping machines and an examining table. It's surprisingly dark, the lights dimmed, everything hushed, and I stand in the doorway as that same visceral reaction I experienced in the lobby takes hold of me once more, even stronger this time. *This is where death happens.*

'Ms. McCleary?'

'Mrs.,' Heather corrects, sounding strident. She turns to look at me. 'Grace?'

'Yes.' I draw a deep breath into my lungs and will myself to take a step into the room.

Heather is already clambering up onto the table, and the technician sits on a stool next to her, both clearly waiting for me.

'Sorry.' My voice sounds tinny, and I clear my throat. 'Sorry, I…' There's nothing I can say. I sit down in the chair on the other side of the examining table, and breathe in deeply.

Heather lifts up her shirt to reveal her baby bump, which looks flaccid and fish-belly white, and for some reason I recoil a bit at the sight. It's so… intimate, so *other.* I think of my own flat, toned stomach and I don't know whether to feel glad or sorry for it.

The technician squirts clear gel on Heather's belly and then prods it quite forcefully with a metal wand. That can't be comfortable; I see Heather wince. I want to ask if it could hurt the baby, but it must not or the technician wouldn't be doing it. I stay silent.

'Let's have a look at Baby,' the woman murmurs, and Heather and I both turn to the blurry, blobby image that has suddenly appeared on the black screen. 'There's the head,' the woman continues, and Heather smiles faintly and nods. I squint, trying to see what they both see, but all I can make out is a moving Rorschach test. 'And heart, stomach, kidney, liver…' Nope and nope, nope and nope again. I feel completely unqualified. How am I going to take care of this baby, if I can't even see it on the screen?

'Arms and legs… fingers and toes…' The technician spares me what I fear is a withering glance and then leans over to point out all the digits on the screen.

And then, all of a sudden, I see it. It's like the optical illusion where you blink and suddenly the old crone becomes a young woman. You see something that was definitely not there before at all. Right in front of me on that screen is an honest-to-God baby; he or she is sucking his thumb. I *see* it, and I feel a leap of excitement inside, a sensation like the turn of a kaleidoscope, the sudden burst of colors.

'Do you see it, Grace?' Heather asks softly, and I sniff and nod. I am feeling far more emotional than I expected, but that's my baby on the screen.

'It's amazing.'

'It is, isn't it?' She turns her head toward the technician. 'Grace is going to adopt this baby.'

'How wonderful,' the technician murmurs, eyes on the screen, face carefully neutral.

The technician continues with her measurements and calculations, talking about the nuchal fold, the distance between the eyes, and I tune out a bit, intent on focusing on the way the baby on the screen is moving around, scrunching up its legs, waving its arms. It's a person. A child. And it's mine.

I feel that with such a sudden, solid certainty that it takes my breath away. I've had a lot of doubts, about me, about Heather, a lot of worries and fears, but right now I *know*. I might not be the most maternal woman out there, God knows I can admit that, but my arms are empty and my child is *there*.

'Do you want to know the sex?' the technician asks in a carefully diffident voice, and Heather gives me a quick, questioning glance, waiting for me to speak.

'Yes, please,' I say, and Heather confirms this with a quick nod.

'Well…' The technician leans forward, peering at the screen. 'It's hard to tell because Baby is moving around so much, but if I had to call it, I'd say you're having a girl.'

'Great.' I hear relief in Heather's voice, strong enough to surprise me. What if it had been a boy? Would that have changed anything, having Kevin's son? Surely not. But in any case, it isn't a boy, it's a girl. My little girl. I can see her already, her pale blonde hair, her rosebud mouth.

I glance at Heather; she is sitting up, wiping the gel off with a rough paper towel. 'I told you,' she says with an attempt at a laugh, 'Kev and I only make girls.'

'I like girls.' I have an urge to hug her, to thank her, but the words feel jumbled in my throat, a pressure in my chest. 'Heather…'

'Everyone tells me girls are terrible when they're teenagers,' she continues determinedly, 'but we're not there yet.' She glances at the technician, a proud tilt to her chin. 'I have three girls already.'

'How nice.' I wonder how many complicated situations the technician encounters in this darkened room; families made of disparate parts, jammed together any which way, trying so hard to fit.

Heather stands up, struggling a bit, and I take her arm again. She accepts it with a grateful smile, and I feel that sense of solidarity that I didn't expect now but which we both need. For better or worse, we're in this together.

Heather turns to me with a smile. 'Now you can start shopping for baby clothes.'

'Yes, that will be fun.' I haven't bought anything yet, haven't dared. Now I think of all the wonderful things I can buy, the nursery I can decorate, the life I can plan. It's really happening. I'm going to have a baby, a family. Finally, finally, I'm going to feel part of something – someone – again. I'm going to have everything I've wanted.

CHAPTER SEVEN

HEATHER

A week after the ultrasound Grace calls me and asks if I'd like to go shopping.

'Shopping?' I repeat, as if she'd spoken in a foreign language. These days the only shopping I do is with a fistful of coupons and my EBT card. I know the rules now. No hot food, no beer, no toiletries or paper products. I'm never going to make that kind of mistake again.

We're managing so far, but only just. Less than one hundred dollars in our bank account, and Kev hasn't found a job, not even a hint or hope of one. Lucy's eczema has flared up again, all over her elbows and knees, red and sore and angry-looking. The only cream that helps isn't covered by insurance, and so I spent twenty-six dollars on a tiny tube of cream, and then Emma mistook it for regular lotion and slathered it all over her hands. I actually had the desperate gall to wipe it off her and then try to force it back in the tube.

'I'm sorry, Mom,' Emma gulped, fighting tears.

'It was a mistake, sweetie. Not your fault.' Easy to say, not so easy to feel. We can't afford another tube, and Lucy's preschool sent home a note because her elbows were bleeding.

Yet even though money is as tight as ever, things feel good, or at least a little more settled, in my own mind and heart, and also between Kevin and me. I don't feel like I'm fighting everyone any more, pushing against the tide that felt so relentless. We've given in, and sometimes that feels like a good thing. A relief.

When I got back from the ultrasound appointment, I told Kev it was a girl, and he nodded. We didn't say anything else, but I think he felt the treacherous flicker of relief that I did, although I don't know if either of us would admit it.

It feels wrong, but how could I hand over our only son? The boy I think every father must secretly long for? I picture Kevin playing football in the yard, wrestling in the living room while I look on, smiling. The two McCleary men. At least I'm not giving away that dream, although that's all it would ever be, anyway. Kev can't wrestle or play football, not with his back.

Still, seeing that screen made me remember with an ache what a newborn is like. The snuffling noises they make, the way they curl into you, the sweet, sleepy smell of them. The knowledge slammed into me that this baby is a part of me, a part of Kevin; a sister to my girls.

But then I watched Grace watch the screen, and I knew this little girl also belonged to her. I saw it in the way her eyes lit up, the tremulous smile that spread across her face. She's so excited, and despite all the pain and regret and sadness I still feel, I'm happy for her, and I'm happy that I'm happy. It feels good, to want that. To feel it, even if just a little.

Grace will love this baby. She already does. I picture them hand in hand walking through Central Park, or playing together on that plush rug in Grace's living room. *Mother and daughter.*

Now Grace wants to meet me at some swanky store on the Upper East Side of Manhattan, which will take me an hour on the PATH train plus the bus. I can't make it there and back during the three government-paid hours of Lucy's preschool, so I call Stacy and ask for a favor.

'You want me to pick Lucy up? Why?' She sounds suspicious, which she has since she found out I was pregnant.

Suspicious and disapproving, even when she doesn't say anything. After her blistering life-running-you-over comment, we've talked less than usual. I certainly haven't asked her for any favors, because I don't want the lecture that I know will come with them. I know Stacy means well, she always does, but I can't handle her brand of sisterly advice right now. I just need some help.

'I'm going into the city, to meet Grace, the adoptive mother.'

'The dad's not going to be there?'

I bite my lip, cursing myself for the slip. 'There is no dad.'

'What—'

'Can you just do it, Stace?' I'd wanted to keep Grace's single status quiet, because the last thing I need is more judgment. Single motherhood is common enough in my town, but it's hardly ever chosen.

Stacy sighs. 'Yes, okay. Of course I can. I'll always help you, Heather. But I really don't like this.'

'Trust me, I know.'

'Not for my sake, but for yours.' She pauses. 'I'm sorry for what I said before, about you being a victim. I know that wasn't totally fair, but… I'm afraid you're going to regret this later, when you can't go back.'

I feel a pressure in my chest and I close my eyes. 'Stacy, if we could keep this baby, we would.'

She is silent.

'Do you believe me?' I ask, my voice turning a little ragged. 'Do you honestly believe that if I could see a way to make it happen, I would do it? Whatever it took, if it really were possible?' The words throb through me.

Stacy doesn't answer and I suck in a hard breath. 'Do you?' My voice rings out, filled with pain.

'Yes, Heather.' My sister's voice is quiet and sad. 'Yes, I believe you.'

I sag in relief.

'Whatever I can do to help, I will.' She let out a shuddery breath. 'Of course I will.'

I take the train to Penn Station, and then walk to Thirty-Second Street and Seventh Avenue to get the M4 bus uptown. I've only come into the city a handful of times, even though we live so close. We went to see The Rockettes once, and we took the older girls to the Empire State Building when they were little, peering through those old-fashioned viewfinders to see the city up close.

New Jersey feels like a different world from the Upper East Side. It's a sparkling, sunny day in February, and everything seems cold and shiny and bright, little flecks in the sidewalk glittering like silver.

Everyone walking by me seems purposeful and important, smartphones clamped to their ears as they hurry along, sipping their fancy Starbucks coffees, or mothers pushing strollers that remind me of race cars, their hair expertly highlighted, looking chic and skinny and so not like me. For a second I want to go home, back to the familiar, but I also don't. This is my one day out, my one chance at something different. I keep walking.

The store where Grace asked me to meet her looks just as expensive all the other boutiques on the block, with the name spelled out in big gold letters. Inside it's all crystal chandeliers and white velvety sofas, and when the sales assistant catches my eye I immediately feel like Julia Roberts in *Pretty Woman*.

I'm wearing my best maternity dress, but it's an old sack compared to the stuff in here. I try for a smile and look around for Grace, but I don't see her anywhere.

'May I help you?' The sales assistant has exactly the skeptical sort of tone I'd expect her to. My smile freezes. I am not going to let her intimidate me. At least, I'm not going to let her see it.

'I'm waiting for someone.'

'All right.' Her expression is cool as she nods to the racks of clothes placed artfully around the room that only have about two or three items on each one. 'Feel free to take a look around.'

'Thanks.' I walk over to a rack of t-shirts in different pastel colors and randomly glance at the price tag of a white one. It's a plain short-sleeved t-shirt and it costs *one hundred and twenty-eight dollars.* My wedding dress didn't cost that much. I back away from the shirt, afraid I might have stained it or something. What if I have to pay for it? What am I *doing* here?

'Heather.' Grace's voice comes out like the peal of a bell and I turn around.

'Hi.'

'I'm so glad you made it.' She looks smart and sleek in a navy skirt suit like in the photo on the Open Hearts website, everything crisp and tailored, a black leather messenger bag slung over one shoulder. She's carrying a smartphone that looks top of the range and she slides it into the inside pocket of her suit jacket as she stands in front of me and looks me over. 'You got here okay? Great.'

'Yeah.' I glance around, shifting from foot to foot. 'The stuff here is really expensive.' As soon as the words are out of my mouth I wish I hadn't said them. They're obviously not expensive for Grace.

'You don't need to worry about that,' she says with a smile, and for a second I resent how easy she has it. Does she even realize? Then I tell myself to relax, that this is the point of being here, of doing it this way.

'Why don't we get settled, have a drink, and see what the sales assistant can rustle up for us?' Grace nods at the frosty woman behind the cash register, who comes forward, all beaming smiles now.

'We need a full set of maternity clothes,' Grace says briskly. 'Everything you've got. My friend is—' She glanced at me, perfectly plucked eyebrows raised. 'Five months now, right, Heather?'

'Yes, just about.'

'And we'd like some mocktails as well,' Grace says as she sits down on one of the velvety sofas and crosses her legs. 'How about some virgin strawberry daiquiris?'

She glances at me for confirmation and I smile and nod, trying to relax.

Another assistant joins the first and they scurry about, now eager to serve us. The place is empty except for us, so we have their full attention. Grace has taken her phone out of her blazer and is scrolling through E-mails or texts or whatever. After a minute or two she looks up with a guilty, distracted smile. 'Sorry, hazard of work.'

'What exactly is it you do?' It was something important and financial, but beyond that I can't remember and never really understood anyway.

'I work for a venture capital firm.'

I stare and Grace laughs lightly. 'It's a type of private equity, a form of financing that provides funds to emerging start-up firms with maximum growth potential.'

I still don't get it, and it must show in my face.

'Basically, we invest in companies that we think will succeed, and when they do we get a percentage of the profits.'

'You must be busy.'

'Yes—' Grace stops suddenly, and it takes me a second to figure out why.

'Will you take time off when… when the baby is born?'

'Of course,' she says, a little too quickly. I'm guessing not much.

'And then what?' I ask. 'A nanny?'

'Well, yes.' Her gaze assesses me, checking to see if I'm going to judge her. Am I? I don't know. I've been a stay-at-home mom since Emma was born. I only started working nights cleaning offices after Kev got hurt, and even then I was at home all day with Lucy. I've wiped so many noses and butts, watched endless hours of *Barney* and sung 'The Wheels on the Bus', fetched milk and juice and cut PB&J into countless squares and triangles. It all blurs together, and some days I wonder if any of it means much. As long as a nanny does the same thing, does it matter?

Or am I just trying to make myself feel better for choosing Grace and not one of those smug couples, where the woman would plan to stay at home until the kid's eighteen, making organic lunches and volunteering as class mom every year? Being a better mother than I ever could be?

Is *that* why I really chose Grace – because I know she won't? Because I feel like I'm one up on her, however much she might have? I'd told her I wouldn't compare myself to her, but now I feel confused. Everything feels complicated.

The assistant starts bringing out clothes: jeans and t-shirts and dresses and underwear, everything. She lays it all out for Grace to inspect, even though I'm the pregnant one.

Grace looks at it all, choosing some things and sending away others without even asking my opinion, which annoys me a little, because I would have liked to pick out something pretty, and a lot of the clothes she's choosing are totally impractical for my life… but I'm guessing they work for hers. A slinky black cocktail dress? Where on earth am I going to wear that? To work in Newark, cleaning the piss off the men's toilets?

'Why don't you try some of this stuff on?' Grace asks, and then belatedly she adds, 'Sorry, I should have asked your opinion. Do you like this?' She gestures to a pale blue button-down blouse with a side tie to accommodate a baby bump.

'Yeah, sure,' I say, although it's not really my style, if I even have a style. One of the assistants arrives with two virgin strawberry daiquiris garnished with fresh mint leaves and fancy straws. I take one sip of the fruity drink before Grace ushers me toward the dressing rooms, fancy ones with thick velvet curtains and gold ropes. The assistant follows me, carrying all the clothes.

With the curtains closed I slip off my clothes, avoiding study-ing the pale, doughy body I see in the mirror, and reach for the first piece of clothing.

It's a t-shirt top with lacy sleeves that Lucy would use it as a Kleenex in about two seconds. There is a pair of skinny jeans to go with it with the tiniest stretch of elastic band for my belly, and I marvel at these new, trendy maternity clothes that certainly never made it into my wardrobe back in the day.

'Heather?' Grace calls. 'What do you think? Will you show me?'

Shyly I part the curtain and step out. I feel self-conscious, but Grace's wide smile is worth it. 'Heather,' she exclaims, 'you look fantastic! Oh, we're definitely getting those. Those jeans are great.' She looks at me anxiously. 'Do you like them? Am I being too bossy? Tell me if I am.'

'Well…' I laugh a little. 'Sort of.'

She slaps her forehead, and I laugh again. 'Sorry, sorry. I'm an idiot. You pick the clothes, okay? Whatever you want. Whatever looks and feels good.'

'I wouldn't mind a pair of sweatpants.' A few seconds later the assistant bustles toward me with a pair of slinky black yoga pants. Not quite what I had in mind, but I'll take them.

As I'm changing into them, Grace pokes her hand through the curtains, holding out the black cocktail dress.

'Why don't you try this?' she suggests. I peek out and see that she looks flushed, happy. 'I know it might not be the most practical thing, but…' She shrugs and laughs. 'It could be fun.'

Fun. I feel like I haven't had fun in I don't even know how long. And this is meant to be fun, isn't it? No matter how we got here.

'Okay.' I take the dress, which feels like spun spider webs, thin and silky. 'Thanks.'

Grace insists on seeing me in the dress, and so, with a self-conscious smile, I sashay out into the store. The dress is ridiculous and sexy – low-cut, swishy around my legs. I've never worn anything like it.

'Oh, *wow*.' Grace claps her hands together. 'You look amazing! One hot mama.'

I laugh, a little bubble of pure happiness rising inside me. I didn't expect to have fun here, but I am. And Grace seems to be happy too – asking me to try on other stuff, insisting on seeing me in each outfit, exclaiming over everything.

'We'll take it all,' she announces at the end, and I boggle. All of it? I've tried on a dozen outfits at least. She sees my surprise, and shrugs, smiling. 'Why not? You look great in everything. I can't remember the last time I've had so much fun shopping.'

'Me, neither,' I admit. I have had a lot of fun, something I never expected.

Back in the dressing room, when I am taking a top and jeans off, I notice the price tags. One hundred and thirty dollars for the shirt, two hundred for the jeans. It's like a bucket of ice tipped down my back. How can I buy this stuff, how can I let Grace buy this stuff, when Amy is still going to school with a duct-taped shoe, and Lucy's elbows are covered in scabs? *How?*

I sink onto the plush stool in the dressing room, the clothes crumpled around me, my fragile happiness burst like the soap bubble it was. I feel guilty for having fun, and yet helpless too. What can I do, besides accept the clothes as the gift they are? Then Grace pokes her head in, her eyes sparkling.

'Do you have time for lunch?'

CHAPTER EIGHT

GRACE

I'm still buzzing slightly as I pay for the clothes, surprised at how much I've enjoyed myself. Today was meant to be simply something to tick off my list, but watching Heather come out of her shell, shy and hesitant, and then start to enjoy parading around in the clothes… it was nice, to see that. To know I made it happen. And the truth is I don't get out with friends much, or even at all. Can I call Heather my friend? In this moment, yes.

'I hope you enjoy these,' I say as I take the six gold-corded shopping bags and loop them around my wrists. Heather seems a bit quieter since she came out of the dressing room. 'What about lunch? There's a cute little place around the corner that does salads and soups. Why don't we go there?' I don't really have the time, but I'm also weirdly reluctant to have the morning come to an end.

Heather blinks me into focus, smiling uncertainly. 'Okay,' she says. 'Thanks.'

A few minutes later we're settled in a plush booth with large menus hiding our faces. While Heather is studying hers with a rather endearing intensity, I scroll through the messages on my phone. Nothing too urgent, thank God. I can spare another half an hour, at least.

'So,' I say, once we've ordered and the waitress has taken the menus. 'How are you finding all this?' I give her a frank look, determined to be honest, maintain the tone we set before. 'Is it… is it very hard?'

Heather stirs her iced tea slowly, her gaze lowered. 'I haven't told my kids yet. Or my friends. Only Kev and my sister know I'm pregnant.'

That surprises me. She *looks* pregnant, at least to me. 'You're going to tell them sometime, though,' I remark, not quite making it a question. 'Sometime soon.'

'I know.' She smiles wryly. 'You'd think they'd guess, right? But it's winter, and when I'm outside, I wear a big coat.' She sighs and pushes her drink a little bit away. 'I don't know, I just don't want to deal with the fallout, you know? Everyone's going to have an opinion.'

'Yes.' I can only imagine. Although actually, I can't. Her life, her family, her friends are all outside my realm of experience. And now that I think about it, I haven't told anyone I'm adopting, so we're basically in the same boat.

'But let's not talk about all that.' Heather waves a hand. 'Sometimes I feel like it's all I think about. This baby. Giving it away.'

Her confession alarms and moves me in equal measures. I picture Heather lying in bed, unable to sleep, wondering what the right thing to do is, and whether she's strong enough to do it.

'Okay. Let's talk about something else.'

Cue silence as we struggle to think of what to say, how to unite our experiences. Heather laughs, the sound bubbling up, and then I'm laughing too, although I'm not sure about what. Maybe just the oddity of the situation, the awkward intimacy of it.

'Have you seen any good movies?' I finally ask, and she shakes her head.

'We never go out.' A pause as she slurps from her straw. 'Have you?'

'Nope.'

And then we start laughing again, and something inside me lightens. It seems we do have something in common, however small.

Our salads arrive then, and I watch as Heather picks through hers, taking out all the walnuts and bits of blue cheese. 'Sorry,' she mutters. 'I didn't think it would be so fancy.'

I wave her apology aside. 'I'm not a fan of blue cheese, either. And it's not supposed to be good for pregnant women.' I feel proud of my little trivia.

'It's not?' Heather looks blanks as she shrugs. 'Have you thought of names?' And so we're back to talking about babies.

'A few.' I haven't quite wanted to dare that far. To hope that much.

'And have you told your family?'

I shake my head, my throat turning tight even after all these months. 'I don't have any family.'

Heather's expression softens. 'You told me about your dad, but...'

'There's no one.'

Heather looks surprised; she's probably surrounded by family; aunts and uncles and cousins, sisters and brothers. A big, happy Irish Catholic family, with massive Thanksgivings, the table bowed under the weight of the food, the conversation lively and boisterous, everyone vying to get a word in edgewise. For a second I am envious, utterly envious, of what she has and I never will, even with this baby. *My daughter.*

'My mother died when I was a teenager,' I explain. 'And you know about my dad. My mother was an only child, and my dad's brother died five years ago. He never had children, so it really is just me.'

'When did your dad die?' Heather asks quietly.

'Three months ago.' I stare down at my salad. Why does this have to be so hard, *still?*

'I'm sorry.' I feel Heather's hand skim my own, the lightest of touches. 'You said you were close.'

'Really close. Maybe too close.'

'What do you mean?'

I shrug, my throat still tight. 'Maybe if I hadn't depended on my dad so much, I would have made time for other people. A boyfriend or a best friend, someone who could be here for me now.' Too late I realize how revealing this all is, how pathetic I must sound. I try to rally. 'I'm a solitary kind of person, mostly. I'm not…' I can't finish that sentence. 'What about you? You've got Kevin and your girls, I know…'

'My parents live in Elizabeth too, and my sister Stacy and her husband and their two kids. Plus cousins, aunts, uncles.' She smiles, shrugs. 'I can't get away from them.' It's just as I imagined, and again I feel that painful pang of envy.

'That must be nice.'

'Sometimes it is. Sometimes it's a pain.'

'Yes.' The weight of my loneliness suddenly hits me again, full force, as I try to envision a life where I am surrounded by family – brothers, sisters, cousins. Parents and grandparents. It seems like an inconceivable luxury. Heather must see some of that in my face because she hurries on,

'But I am grateful. For everyone, all of it. They've been there for me. My sister, especially. And Kev,' she adds quickly.

'I'm glad you've had the support,' I say, even as I wonder where my support will come from. Yes, I'll have a nanny, and a baby nurse, and whomever else I hire to help. But what about people I don't have to employ? What about the network of family and friends so many people take for granted, everyone pulling together when life gets tough, offering help, hugs, a meal, a listening ear? Where are those people? Will I find them after my baby's born? Or will I still be alone?

I think of my father in his hospital bed, how I held his hand, the fragile bones beneath my fingers; that last, vital connection that linked us together bound me to the only family I've known.

Who will hold my hand in the hospital, when the doctor says my body is shutting down? Who will offer me that desperate comfort, hear my last words, and speak into that awful silence?

Heather touches my hand, letting her fingers rest on mine for a moment. 'It will be okay,' she says, and I feel as if I've voiced my fears out loud.

'You're lucky,' I say, and despite or perhaps because of everything, I truly mean it.

Heather lets out a soft laugh. 'Yeah,' she says, her voice full of wonder. 'I guess I am.'

After lunch I insist on putting Heather in a cab, and as I peel off a couple of twenties to pay for it, I slip in another few hundred bucks. 'For expenses,' I say firmly. 'Treat yourself.'

She looks surprised, but she takes the money. I stand on the sidewalk and watch as the cab cruises forward, joining a sea of others. I have a pang of something almost like homesickness; I realize I miss her. I had fun today, and more than that, I had companionship.

That evening after work I stop by the Barnes & Noble on Eighty-Sixth and Lexington and stock up on baby books, feeling both furtive and excited, hoping I don't bump into anyone I know, even as part of me wishes I would, so I could share some of my excitement. My joy.

I don't see anyone, though, and the multi-pierced teen at the checkout looks bored by my book choices. I clutch them to my chest all the way home, and then back at my apartment I curl up on the sofa with a large glass of wine and an order of sushi, the books scattered all around me. I feel as if I'm about to open Christmas presents. I want to learn all this stuff; I want to become an expert in this new, unexpected field.

I pick up the first book, *First Days with Your Newborn*. I study the pictures of the babies on the front; they are wide-eyed and skinny-limbed, and they remind me a little bit of humanoid aliens. I haven't held a baby since I was a teenager, babysitting for some neighbors. I haven't talked to a toddler in twenty years. I'm entering a whole new universe, going where no woman has gone before, at least none I know, and I am determined to do it.

I take a sip of wine and flip to the opening chapter, skipping the cutesy intro for the factual details I need. Like, how do you actually *hold* a newborn baby? Or put on a diaper? Or feed them a bottle?

As I read more of the book, and then skim through the others, I realize how completely unprepared I am. Cradle cap, colic, night feeds, RSV, gas, fever, baby acne… I never even knew such things existed. But I'll learn.

Restless now, I rise from the sofa and take my wine to my study. When the baby comes, she'll have this room and I'll have to move my study to the little maid's room off the kitchen, which is currently filled with boxes of stuff from my dad's condo. Going through the photos, the mementoes, the sweaters that still smelled of him, holding his reading glasses and breathing in his aftershave… it was one of the hardest things I've ever done. I boxed up what mattered and brought it back here.

I walk slowly around my study, looking at all the photos. Dad and me when I was a gap-toothed seven-year-old, grinning wildly at the camera on a fishing trip. My mother had been diagnosed with breast cancer the year before, and Dad stepped right up, taking over all the little duties as well as the big ones. Doing everything for me, being everyone to me.

I pause in front of a photo of my mom from her college days, her hair a dark cloud around her face, her expression dreamy. Sometimes I feel like the cancer kept me from getting to know her properly. I loved my mom, but I think I miss the idea of her more than the real person, because I can't remember a time when she wasn't sick.

Throughout my childhood, she was always in and out of the hospital, pale and sick, needing chemo treatments, wanting to hug me, too tired to talk. Her death wasn't the devastation my father's was, and that makes me feel both sad and guilty.

I look at another picture, this one of Dad and me at my graduation from Tufts. My cap is at a rakish angle, and my smile is a little smug. I'd already been accepted into a two-year competitive internship in the city, with a deferred entry to Harvard's MBA program. Next to me Dad looks proud and happy, with his salt and pepper buzz-cut, his bright blue eyes, his slight paunch that he used to joke about. My beer belly, he'd say, even though he never drank beer.

I picture myself telling my daughter about my dad, sharing the stories that now only matter to me. It can be lonely, being an only child, especially when your parents die. No one else feels the way you do. Absolutely no one else is bearing the grief you feel in that moment.

Of course, this daughter of mine will be an only child too. It will be the two of us against the world, just like Dad and me. A team, a partnership, an unbreakable bond. I'll just have to do a better job of preparing her for when I'm gone.

A week later, Joanne, my best friend from my MBA days, calls to tell me she's in the city for work and asks if I'm free for dinner. We meet at Ocean Prime on West Fifty-Second, near her hotel. Joanne looks just as sharp and savvy as she did a year or so ago, when I last saw her. We do a quick air kiss and sit down, reaching for menus. Even this feels like a business meeting, as we prepare to exchange the relevant data about our lives.

'So, how are you?' she asks, her gaze sweeping down the list of seafood appetizers. 'Are we doing three courses?'

'Why not?' I feel expansive. I want to tell her about my adoption plans, but I don't know how she'll react. We order our drinks and then Joanne sits back, her eyes narrowed as she inspects me.

'You look different.'

'Older.' I roll my eyes and take a sip of the restaurant's signature cocktail, whiskey, honey water, and lemon and orange. My dad would tell me it was a waste of Gentleman Jack; he liked his neat.

'Well, yes, we both are,' Joanne says as she sips her wine. 'But you look… I don't know. Are you seeing someone?'

'No.' I'm amazed that she can sense something is different, and yet of course something huge has happened. In the last week, I've cleared out my study and bought paint samples. Paint samples, *me*. No pink for this baby girl. I picked a fresh, minty green with an antique white trim.

I could have hired someone to paint the room, to decorate the whole thing, and I admit, I was a little bit tempted, because time is something I don't have a lot of. But I decided to do it myself because I want to own this. And with every dab of paint, every throw pillow or sleepsuit I buy, I feel like I am putting down a deposit to make this more real.

'What, then?' Joanne asks. 'Because you look like you're dying to tell me something.'

'Not dying… but something has changed.' I take a deep breath, plunge. 'I'm adopting a baby. A little girl.'

Joanne's eyebrows arc toward her hairline. 'Seriously? What about work?'

I take a sip of my cocktail, trying to mask my hurt. Couldn't she have just said congratulations? 'What about it?'

'You're going to be Mommy-tracked.' She shakes her head. 'Don't you want to make partner?'

'Yes, and I think it's going to happen soon.' There's a meeting of all the partners in mid-April, and I'm fully expecting Bruce to tell me the good news afterward. 'Besides, I haven't actually told anyone at work about this.' Suddenly that seems absurd. I'm adopting a child and I'm going to keep it from everyone at work, which is basically everyone I know? Why should I keep something so exciting, so important, a secret?

Joanne stares at me for a good thirty seconds. 'I understand why you haven't,' she says finally. 'But you're going to have to sometime, aren't you? I mean, kids always mean time off. They're sick, the nanny cancels, they have some show at school you've got to attend. Parent meetings...'

'I won't have to go to those for a while.'

'But you know what I mean.'

'Yes.' I take a sip of my drink. 'I'll tell them after I make partner.' Once I have that security, everything will feel simpler. I'll celebrate, then. I'll bring in a cake.

Joanne sits back. 'I'm surprised,' she says after a moment. 'I thought you didn't have that biological clock.'

'I'm not sure I do.'

'Then...?'

'It's deeper than that. Bigger. You know about my dad...' I'd texted her after the funeral, and Joanne had sent flowers, a beautiful, big bouquet.

'I know. I'm sorry, Grace.'

'I want a family. I want to give a child something of what my dad gave to me.'

'That's very noble.'

'Not really.' I try for a laugh. 'It just feels... compelling. And right. I *need* to do this.'

She sighs, the sound of someone washing their hands after having given their advice. 'If this is what you really want, then I say go for it. But *is* it what you want? Because, to me, you just sound lonely.'

I am lonely, but that isn't the whole story.

'Maybe you just want a boyfriend?' Joanne suggests. 'Or a dog?'

I try for another laugh; they're hard to come by. 'Those are two very different things.'

'But they serve the same purpose,' she answers with a smile. 'It's just that a kid is a big investment, you know? Lifetime commitment, and all that. And if you decide in a couple of months or a year or whatever that you weren't actually up for this parenting thing...'

'I wouldn't.' My face burns; does she think I'm that shallow, that selfish? That I'd hand my child *back*? 'Look, I'm being honest here. I know I'm not maternal, not really. I barely remember my own mom, at least before she got sick.' My throat is tight again and I take a long swallow of whiskey, savoring the burn of alcohol at the back of my throat. 'But I've thought a lot about this. I don't want to just live for my work any more, or even just for myself. And I've done the research. I want this baby.'

Joanne nods slowly. 'So you have one in mind? How does it even work?'

I explain to her about Open Hearts and Heather. 'The baby's due in May,' I finish, my voice filled with pride. 'A little girl.'

'And she can't change her mind? You read about that, you know? It's so sad for the adoptive parents. They just get this baby they've loved and cared for yanked away from them without, like, a second's warning.'

'She can change her mind,' I say, 'but she won't.' I think of Tina warning me about this delicate situation, of Heather at the ultrasound, trying on clothes, the sad, pensive look she gets on her face sometimes. 'She won't,' I say again and this time I sound like I am trying to convince myself.

CHAPTER NINE

HEATHER

In the middle of February, when I am twenty-four weeks pregnant, I decide it's time to tell everybody. My belly has started to pop, and I can feel the baby move, real kicks that I savor even though I feel like I shouldn't, each little flutter a reminder. *I'm here. I'm yours.* Except she's not, and everybody needs to realize that, including me.

That afternoon at that swanky boutique felt like a turning point, from the what-if to the inevitable. When Grace handed me three hundred dollars in cash, it felt as if we'd shaken hands on a business deal. There was no going back, even if, somewhere in the foggy reaches of my mind, I had imagined there was. If Kev got a job. If we found a new house, or a pot of gold, *something.* That tempting, treacherous *if.*

Taking that money stomped it right out, which was a good thing. There's no point thinking in ifs. Not anymore.

When I got back home Kevin was out for once, at a meeting with the union lawyer, to see if he could claim unemployment while he looked for a job. I laid out all the fancy maternity clothes on the bed, making sure their price tags were showing, and then I took photos. Within an hour, before the girls had got home from school and with Lucy tuned into PBS Kids, I had them up on eBay and the bidding had already started. In the end I got nine hundred dollars for everything but the jeans and lacy top that I kept, just in case Grace expected to see me in something she'd bought. I also kept the yoga pants, because of all the stuff, I might actually wear them. And I tried not to feel guilty, because nine hundred dollars will pay our rent for another month. I need that a lot more than I need a fancy shirt with a big bow on it.

I'd just bundled the clothes away when Emma and Amy came running in from the bus, complaining they were hungry, as always, and Amy whining that the strap on her other shoe had broken. I stared at those battered, duct-taped shoes and for once I smiled.

'You know what we're going to do, Amy?'

Amy looked at me warily. 'What?'

'We're going to get you a new pair from Payless.'

Emma looked up, surprised and a little bit indignant. 'Can I get a new pair, too?'

'You got a new pair in September. But you can have an ice cream at the mall.'

Both girls looked at me suspiciously, because since when did I offer ice cream? My smile got bigger, spreading across my face. I wasn't going to blow through this cash, no way, but my girls needed a little treat. And watching them enjoy their ice creams, licking the last drops from their cones, faces covered in chocolate, would be a big treat for me.

Kev didn't even question the new shoes or the ice creams; the girls swarmed him the minute they came through the door with chocolate-smeared faces, hyped up on sugar. He patted their backs and half-listened to their excited gibbering before turning back to the TV, not asking about any of it – the shoes, the ice cream, the rent being paid.

I wiped each of their faces in turn, smiling as they squirmed and resisted the firm swipe of the wet cloth. I felt like I had a double dose of patience and goodwill, thanks to the money in my sock drawer. I also had a surprising measure of peace that I hadn't expected; I truly felt, deep down, like I was doing the right thing, for the baby, for my girls. For me and Kevin.

And so that's why I'm here, sitting on my parents' saggy sofa while my father reluctantly mutes the television and my mother twitches in her wheelchair, looking both concerned and impatient. The air is thick with cigarette smoke and air freshener, and even though I'm past those awful days of morning sickness, my stomach churns from both the smell and sheer nerves at telling them what I'm planning to do. Disappointing them again.

I've never shaken the feeling that I'm the daughter who messed up. Pregnant before I graduated high school – my father never said anything, but I felt his disapproval, and worse, his disappointment. A lot can be communicated with a sigh or a silence.

When my mother was adjusting my veil right before my rushed wedding, and I was five months pregnant and definitely starting to show, she said sadly, 'This wasn't what I imagined for you.' It hurt worse than anything else she could have said.

But Kev and I worked hard to be a family, to get by. When we started out, Kev at the container company on little more than a minimum wage and me cleaning part-time until I got too big, we managed. Only just, in a two-room apartment with stained ceilings and carpets, barely money for groceries, but still. We survived.

And then I had Emma a month early. She was in NICU for a week and after that I didn't work any more. We struggled on, but we were happy. Happier, perhaps, than we are now.

'What is it you've got to say, Heather?' my mother asks. 'You look awfully serious. You're not sick, are you? It's not cancer?'

'No, it's not cancer, Mom.' That has always been my mom's biggest fear, although I don't know why since nobody in the family has died of cancer. My grandfather had a heart attack when he was sixty-five, and my grandmother had Alzheimer's. Mom has MS, Dad high blood pressure. But for some reason cancer is the big fear she has, the bogeyman she's always afraid is going to jump out of the closet.

'Actually…' I feel like I'm about to take a flying leap onto jagged rocks. Who hurls themselves out like that, bracing for the fall? But I know I have no choice. So I say the words. 'I'm pregnant.'

The silence stretches on. My father is glancing back at the TV, drawn in by the news presenter babes on Fox News, with their shellacked hair and tight shift dresses. I'm not sure he's heard me, but my mother obviously has. Her mouth drops open a little, and her eyes widen.

'Oh, Heather…' Her voice is full of sympathy and sorrow. Everybody knows this isn't good news for us and even now, after everything, that stings.

'It's okay,' I say quickly, because I need to get this part over with, knowing they won't understand. Not enough, anyway. 'As you probably know, we can't afford another baby, not with Kevin…' I stop, because I don't want to make this just about Kevin. 'With everything the way it is. So we've decided the best thing to do, for this baby and for us, is to give it – her – up for adoption.'

My dad jerks back from the TV. My mother's mouth drops open fully. They both stare at me for a long, shocked moment, looking horrified, and then, as the news sinks in, they look sad. That, I discover, is even worse than disappointment. I look away.

'Heather,' my mom says again. My dad just shakes his head.

'I know it sounds strange,' I say steadily. 'And… I don't know… heartless, maybe, like we don't care about this baby.' I feel a lump forming in my throat but I push past it. 'But it's not like that. I know this baby is a part of me, of us, and I've given this a lot of thought. Kev and I aren't making this decision lightly, I promise.'

'I know you aren't.' My mom sniffs and then reaches for her cane. She relies on her wheelchair most of the time but she'll walk when she can, and now she struggles up to standing while

I watch her miserably. 'I'm going to get us a drink. Who wants a drink?' It's as if she can't bear to look at me.

'Mom…'

She doesn't answer me, just hobbles into the kitchen. My dad looks at me, and then at the TV. I have no idea what he's thinking. He was a plumber before he retired, the kind of man who is happy working or kicking back and having a beer, and doesn't ask for much else in life. We never doubted he loved us, but we never thought he loved us the way Mom did.

'You sure about this, Heather?' he asks gruffly, not looking at me.

'Yes,' I say, and I really am. There's no going back, and it feels like a relief.

Mom comes back in, leaning heavily on her cane, looking older than when she went out. 'I made a pitcher of Crystal Light,' she says as she sinks heavily into her chair. 'If you don't mind getting it.'

'Of course not.' I fetch the plastic pitcher of double-strength peach iced tea and a couple of glasses. I pour us a glass each, even though I can't stand the stuff.

'If it's a question of money…' Mom begins when the silence has stretched to breaking point. My dad stiffens, looking tense. I know they don't have a lot of money, or even enough for themselves. Dad lost most of his pension when the stock market went bust in 2008, and Mom's never been able to work. What little they have left over Dad spends at Meadowlands. I can't blame him, not really, not when so much of life is so hard.

'Mom, it isn't. Not just that, anyway. And you can't afford to prop us up.'

'Kevin wouldn't want that, Janice,' Dad says. 'You know that.'

'No, but a baby…' My mom looks agonized. 'Our own flesh and blood.'

I suppress the stab of hurt, as if she's thinking something I haven't. As if I haven't agonized over this, again and again. 'I know,

Mom.' I take a deep breath. 'But we've made this decision and we're sticking to it. I didn't come over here to ask you for anything, or think about possibilities, I'm telling you what we're doing.'

My mom blinks, looking like I've slapped her. I almost apologize, but then I don't. No one's walked in my faded, worn-out shoes. No one knows what it's like to feel this trapped and cornered, fighting your way out. And no one can make this decision but me and Kevin.

'All I'm asking,' I say, my voice thickening a little, 'is that you support us. Emotionally. Because I know there will be people – neighbors, friends – who won't understand what we're doing. Who will judge. And we're going to need our family around us.'

'Oh, Heather. Oh, honey.' My mother holds out her arms and with a sniff I walk over to her. She smells like cigarette smoke and artificial sweetener and her arms are thin and ropey as they wrap around me. I press my cheek against her shoulder and breathe her in.

'You know we'll be there for you, Heather,' my dad says gruffly, his gaze still on the TV, after I've returned to the sofa. 'You've sure as hell been there for us.'

Later that night, buoyed by my parents' acceptance, I sit the girls down to tell them. They look at me so innocently, eyes wide, lined up on the sofa, their hair damp from the bath, wearing their matching pink nighties. Kevin is in the La-z-Boy as usual, but at least he's turned the TV off and he's half-turned toward us.

'So,' I begin, trying to frame the words in my mind, 'Daddy and I wanted to tell you about something that's happened, a decision we've made.' Blink. Blink. Blink. I can see Emma starting to look worried, chewing a strand of her hair. Amy is intrigued, eyes narrowed, and Lucy is picking her nose.

My love for them surges up, squeezing me, making it hard to speak. How can I explain this so they understand? So they're not afraid?

'I'm going to have a baby,' I continue, gazing at each of them in turn, 'but we're not going to keep this baby even though we love her. We're going to let someone else adopt her, a very nice lady who would like to have a child of her own.'

More blinking. Lucy kicks her legs, bored now. Amy's eyes narrow to slits. Emma just stares.

'What do you mean,' Amy asks, 'you're not keeping a baby? Why wouldn't you keep it? How can you just give it *away*?'

'Well…' I glance at Kevin, whose gaze is fixed beyond us, on the wall, 'because it wouldn't be… fair to the baby. Or to any of you.'

'*Fair?*' Amy looks incredulous. Not fair is someone getting two scoops of ice cream when she only gets one.

'What Mommy is trying to say,' Kevin interjects, surprising me with his steady tone, 'is that we love you all so much and we want to give you the best opportunities that we can. And we won't be able to do that if we have another baby.'

Emma's eyes go even rounder. 'Why not?'

'I have a baby,' Lucy announces. 'I have a pink baby named Susie.'

'Yes, you do, Lucy, and she's very nice.' A doll that cries and burps, a present from my parents a couple of years ago that makes me tense every time I hear its shrill bleat.

Amy makes a sound of disgust. 'They're not talking about that kind of baby, stupid.'

'Amy—'

'You mean a real baby, don't you?' Emma asks. She sounds so confused, and it makes me ache. Even though she's two years older she's far less streetwise than Amy. 'You mean you have one in your tummy.'

'Babies aren't actually in tummies,' Amy informs her. 'They're in ut-er-usses. I learned that at school.'

'Yes, I do have a baby.' I rest one hand on my bump and all three girls stare at it, noticing it for the first time.

'I thought you were just getting fat,' Amy says, and from the steely glint in her eyes I know she's trying to hurt me, because she's hurt. That's how Amy works, and the news that we're giving up her little sister for adoption is hurtful. Of course it is. I can't take away the pain, maybe only blunt it a little.

'Your mom is beautiful,' Kevin says, and my heart swells with love. Despite the pain-glazed eyes and set jaw, he seems more like he used to be right now than he has in a long time, and I need that reminder. I crave it, this hint of who we once were, who we could be again. 'She'll always be beautiful. And we're doing this, Amy and all of you, because we love you so much. The truth is since my back got hurt there hasn't been a lot of money.' Kev presses his lips together, and I know how hard, how shaming, it is for him to admit this to his own children, his little girls. 'And we can't afford to have another baby, not if we want to provide for you the way we do. So that's why we're doing this. For you, and for all of us, even though it seems strange and it's hard.'

'Would you ever give *me* away?' Amy asks, jutting her lip out, and even though it's totally unfair, I feel like shaking her. She *knows* we wouldn't give her away. I can tell by the calculating look on her face, the angry challenge in her eyes. She's acting up, and of course it stirs up Emma and Lucy.

'Give us *away*?' Emma cries, her lower lip wobbling, and Lucy launches herself at me and burrows herself into my belly, making me wince.

'No one's giving anyone away,' Kev says, and he picks up the remote control, done with being sensitive. 'Now go get ready for bed.'

'We *are* ready for bed,' Amy says, but he isn't listening.

'Come on, girls.' I rise from the sofa, taking them with me. 'We'll have stories on my bed.'

The next few days are just as hard. I go to Stop & Shop and run into a mom of a girl in Amy's class. She looks at my belly and then at my face, uncertainty flashing across hers, and then she keeps walking.

We're not friends, so I don't need to feel offended, but before all this I would have expected a hello, maybe a few minutes of chitchat. Not now, obviously. Now no one knows what to say to me, and so they choose to pretend I'm invisible.

And it continues with just about everyone I meet – the mailman, the lady across the street, Lucy's preschool teacher. The news has filtered out just as I knew it would, and I can't avoid the stares, the whispers.

'People aren't judging you,' one of my friends, Annie, says when I work up the courage to ask her what people are saying. 'Not exactly.'

'Oh, great.'

'It's just no one knows what to say. To think.'

Even you? I want to ask, but I don't. Annie gave birth to her son Jaden a year after I had Emma, and when they were little we were a lot closer. We'd hang out at each other's houses, with *Teletubbies* blaring in the background and plenty of coffee to get us through those endless days and sleepless nights. But then the kids started school, and Jaden turned out to be a rough boy's boy and Emma was a dreamy girl, and it was obvious they were never going to be anything close to friends. Annie and I drifted apart, although I still see her around, and I usually make the guest list if she's having a girls' night out or something like that, even if I don't go because of work or not having the money or just plain tiredness.

But right now, as I stand in Annie's kitchen, my hands cradled around a cup of coffee, I don't know what she thinks, and I'm not brave enough to ask. I don't want to hear the truth, and I can't stand the thought of seeing through her lies.

'I guess it's too much to ask people to mind their own business,' I say, and Annie shrugs.

'Probably.'

'Do you think they will get used to it?'

'They'll have to, won't they?' Annie smiles. 'And after all, you won't be pregnant forever.'

I nod slowly. Yes, people will forget once I'm not pregnant any more, or at least not remember quite so much. But will I?

As my belly grows and this baby kicks I am confronted by that question every day, every moment – by my round reflection in the mirror when I step out of the shower; by my hand on my belly as I lie in bed and feel her squirm. When I walk past the baby aisle in Stop & Shop, and then go back and stand in front of the packs of newborn diapers, simply staring. The stack of baby albums in the hall closet, photos peeling at the corners. One afternoon I take them all out and look at them, torturing myself with images of Emma's drooly smile, Amy's frizzy hair, wondering about this little one, trying not to, unable to keep myself from it.

One rainy afternoon in March, I'm waiting outside St Timothy's for Amy to come out of her first communion class and a woman I only sort of recognize from school comes over. She doesn't say anything, just grabs my hand and squeezes hard. Her eyes are full of compassion, and suddenly my chest feels tight. I don't know who she is, but I know she realizes my situation and understands.

We stare at each other for a few heartrending seconds and then with a final squeeze and smile she moves on. I feel energized by the strange, silent exchange, like someone injected me with hope, with courage. In that moment I believe I can do this. I can get through it, because I am not alone.

CHAPTER TEN

GRACE

The invitation from Heather in early April surprises me. Dinner? At her house? I feel an uncertain wariness, a flicker of curiosity and even pleasure. I want to meet her family, and yet at the same time I don't.

'Sure,' I say brightly when she calls my cell while I'm at work. I forgot I gave her my number. 'That's so kind of you. When were you thinking?'

'Friday?' Heather suggests hesitantly. 'At six?'

'Great.' I'll have to leave work hours early to make that, but I don't feel I can suggest an alternative. I haven't seen or talked to Heather in six weeks, which feels like a long time, especially after the fun we had shopping, but Tina has kept me updated and I suppose a little distance might be a good thing.

But it's getting close now, and I've gone ahead with my plans: decorating the nursery, hiring the nanny, a Jamaican woman named Dorothy who has had six grown-up kids herself and seems so wonderfully relaxed and self-assured compared to my own high-octane brand of crazy that after I hired her, I wanted to hug her.

I've booked two weeks off at the end of May, and am praying that the baby comes on time. I've bought clothes, white and mint-green and some pink, fuzzy sleepsuits and tiny onesies and booties.

Most of all, I'm getting excited; it's a freight train of feeling that makes me want to jump out of its way, because it's so intense and I'm not used to feeling this much. Wanting this much. It leaves you vulnerable, open to disappointment and pain. And I know that one of the reasons I've been avoiding Heather is because the more we've come to know each other, the more complicated our relationship has felt.

And this already feels like a pretty complicated situation, never mind *delicate*.

I drive to Heather's house bearing gifts; I've put some thought into what to bring – a bottle of wine, although I don't know if Heather or Kevin drink it, and some Godiva chocolates in their shiny gold box. Then presents for her three girls, because I want them to feel included.

I asked Tina about them, because Heather hasn't said much about her daughters, and she told me their names are Emma, Amy, and Lucy. They are eleven, eight, and four. I buy sparkly lip balm for Emma, a glittery hairband for Amy, and a plush toy for Lucy. Nothing too outrageous or overwhelming, just a gesture of my goodwill and gratitude.

Heather lives in a tiny box-like ranch house on a semi-suburban street of similar houses, all of them weathered, shabby, and small, plenty with weed-filled yards and broken-down cars in their driveways, but others with neatly tended yards, flowers in the window boxes, flags on the front stoop. Somehow those houses make me feel sadder.

I ring the doorbell and try not to peer through the diamond-shaped window at the top of the door, knowing I'll look nosy and anxious. Then a girl opens the door, hard and fast, and stands there with her hands on her hips, her eyes narrowed.

'You must be Grace Thomas.' She sounds accusing.

'And you must be… Emma.'

'No,' she said in a *well-duh* voice. 'I'm Amy.'

'Oh, right—' She's already flounced away. I stand there uncertainly, feeling like a teenager on a first date.

Then Heather appears, looking flushed and flustered. Her hair is back in a ponytail, secured by a big pink scrunchie. She's wearing the maternity jeans and t-shirt I bought her on our shopping trip, and her belly has really popped. I stare at it, amazed by its fecund roundness. *My baby.*

'Grace, hi. Come in, come in.'

'I brought some things. Chocolate, wine—'

'Oh, you shouldn't have.' I can't tell if she means it or not. I hand her the bottle, which she holds by the neck, like it's a dead chicken.

'Wow, fancy chocolates. The girls will love those.'

I have the individual presents for the girls in my bag, but now I'm not sure if I should break them out. Maybe it will seem like overkill, like I'm bragging with my generosity, bribing them somehow.

I follow Heather into the living room. A heavy smell of stale cigarette smoke, old beer, and the overlying scent of synthetic floral air freshener permeates the room, which is dominated by a large flat-screen TV and a sectional sofa upholstered in fake suede. There is also a La-z-Boy placed prominently in front of the TV, and Heather's husband Kevin is sitting in it.

I think I've been most nervous about meeting Kevin, and yet looking at him now I think how small he is. He's a slight man, with thinning brown hair and muddy eyes. He looks like he's been beaten down by life and he's not getting up anytime soon. He doesn't get up from the La-z-Boy when I come into the room. He doesn't even mute the television.

'Kev, this is Grace.' Heather stands there, looking between us, twisting her hands together. Kev nods at me.

'Hi,' he says, and turns back to the TV.

Well, he's rude. I expected that. But I was also expecting some beefy tattooed guy who'd crack his knuckles and grunt.

Put Kevin McCleary in a suit and a pair of glasses and he'd look like a mediocre accountant.

'Nice to meet you, Kevin,' I say, and I can't help it, I sound like a schoolteacher. Then I let out a startled '*oof*' as a small, solid body barrels into my legs. I step back instinctively, but grubby little hands clutch at my thighs and a chubby, snot-nosed face looks up at me, blinking.

'This is Lucy,' Heather says, and her voice is full of affection. I try to smile.

'Hey, Lucy. I've got a little present for you.' I fumble in my bag for the plush toy, a little white seal. Kevin shifts in his chair, maybe mutters something. I hand the seal to Lucy, who coos over it for approximately three seconds and then throws it to the floor.

'Lucy,' Heather says, so half-heartedly I grit my teeth. I'm being touchy about everything, but only because I feel so insecure. Lucy runs off and Heather turns toward the kitchen.

'Thanks for having me over,' I say to no one in particular. 'It was so kind of you.'

I follow Heather through a dark little dining room crowded with furniture and junk to a tiny kitchen with ancient linoleum and even older appliances. She bends down to peer into the oven.

'I think it'll be ready soon.'

'Great. It smells delicious.'

Heather straightens and gives me a nervous smile.

'How are you doing, Heather?' I ask. 'How are you feeling?'

'Oh, you know. Good.' She pats her bump self-consciously. 'I'm thirty-two weeks now. Not too much longer.'

'I know, I'm so excited. I can't wait to meet her.' The words feel forced, even though I mean them utterly. But this crazy dance we're doing together makes me so dizzy. We're dodging minefields at every moment, the awkwardness of a relationship that really isn't there even though we're trying to act like it is, and sometimes it has felt like it's real. But it's not going to last.

In about eight weeks I'm hoping never to see Heather or her family again.

'Have you started getting ready?' she asks brightly, her voice a little too loud. 'You know, clothes, a nursery…?'

'Well, yes.' Suddenly I feel shy, almost embarrassed. 'I've decorated the nursery. I'm doing an elephant theme.' Does it sound silly? I can't tell. 'I used to love elephants when I was a little girl.'

'That sounds really cute.'

'And… I found this.' Before I can stop myself, I'm taking out the fuzzy gray sleepsuit I saw in one of the baby boutiques on Madison Avenue before picking up the rental car. It's got elephants' ears lined with pink velveteen. I couldn't resist.

'Oh, wow.' Heather has a slightly funny look on her face as she takes the sleepsuit from me and examines it, her fingers stroking the soft velveteen. I feel like I shouldn't have brought it out and I fight the urge to snatch it back. Then she looks up and smiles. 'It's so sweet.'

'Thanks.'

She hands it back to me and we stand there awkwardly, both of us trying to smile.

'Kev's got a new job,' Heather says after a few seconds, and by her tone I can tell this is big news.

'Wonderful. What is it?'

'He's selling cellphones. It's not too bad on his back, working in a store.'

'That's fantastic.' I glance back at Kevin, still slouched in his chair, watching the TV with an avidity that suggests stubbornness or perhaps just determination. 'Really good news.'

'It's been a long time coming,' she admits in a low voice, so Kevin can't hear. 'He was on disability for three years, and then it got cut but he couldn't go back to his old job, not with his back the way it is. But I guess you know all that, from Tina.'

'A bit…'

Her eyes sparkle with unshed tears and she blinks them back as she lifts her chin. 'It's been really hard, but we're doing better now. We really are.'

'Great,' I say slowly, but a big, gaping hole of dread is opening inside me. What is she telling me? That since they're doing better they can keep this baby? Surely not? Surely that's not what this dinner is about?

'It doesn't change anything,' Heather says, as if she can guess my thoughts. She presses her lips together, something shuttering behind her eyes. 'It's only part-time. I still need to work.' She turns to check on the oven yet again. I can't think of anything to say. To express relief seems cruel, and yet what else am I supposed to feel?

Eventually we eat, the girls all crowded together on one side of the table – dreamy Emma, bossy Amy, baby Lucy. Heather smiles at them all, encouraging Emma to talk, Amy to be quiet, Lucy to eat her dinner. Kevin is mostly silent at the end of the table, and Heather glances anxiously at him from time to time. In the middle of dinner the phone rings; it's her sister, and while Heather tries to hurry the call, I can tell they're close. When she gets off the phone, she apologizes to me and tells Kevin she's going to stop in to see her parents tomorrow.

It's all chaotic and crazy and depressingly small, from the ready-made lasagna straight from the freezer section of Stop & Shop to Lucy's incessant whining and Kevin's oppressive silence. And yet. And yet, as I pick at my lasagna and listen to the chatter, I realize I am feeling envious of Heather, just as I did before, when I imagined exactly this kind of lovable crazy.

I'm envious of her life, of all the people in it; of the love she so obviously has bubbling up for her family, the love that sustains her through the billows and gales of this stormy season.

And Heather's daughters clearly adore her, even difficult Amy. Lucy climbs into her lap during dessert and Heather absently strokes her hair. Amy makes a big fuss over not being able to have Sprite instead of milk, but at one point in the evening she leans her head up against Heather's shoulder and Heather puts her arm around her, the gesture unthinkingly affectionate. Even Kevin puts his arm around her at the end of the meal, murmurs thanks into her ear and Heather smiles, closing her eyes briefly.

Yes, I am envious. I am terribly, chokingly envious. Who is the wealthy woman now? The privileged one, who takes the blessings of her life for granted? Right now it doesn't feel like it's me.

Then Kevin retreats to his La-z-Boy and the girls disappear into the bedroom, and Heather and I are left alone. Heather starts clearing the table, and I rise to help her. 'You don't have to…' she protests, and then stops. What else am I going to do? Sit and watch her wait on me?

'You must be feeling tired,' I say as I scrape plates into an overflowing trash bin. 'Are you still working?'

'Oh yeah. I can't afford to take any time off. If the baby comes at a good time, I won't even have to miss a day.'

I am appalled and silent. Not one *day*? And I thought I worked hard. 'Do you need anything?' I ask. 'Maternity-wise?' I nod at her outfit. 'The clothes working out okay?'

'Oh, yeah. Thanks.' Heather looks strangely guilty, and I wonder how many of the clothes she's worn. The black cocktail dress, fun and sexy as it was, was not the most practical purchase for her, and now it makes me feel both stupid and ashamed. I should have let her pick the clothes herself, instead of getting carried away on my own.

'But do you need anything else?' I press. I have an urge to give her something. To ease her life, at least a little bit. Money, sadly, is the only thing I have to offer. 'Some more clothes?' I suggest. 'Or… toiletries? Something…?'

Heather hesitates, and I can tell she wants to say yes to something, but she's too proud.

'Look, why don't I just write a check? For whatever extra expenses you might have? It's easier that way.'

She frowns. 'I don't think you're supposed to do that, not on top of everything else…'

'It's fine,' I assure her, even though I suspect it probably isn't. But Tina doesn't need to know. 'I want to make sure you're comfortable, that's all.' I take out my checkbook, grateful to have something to do.

When Heather takes the check, her eyes widen. 'Five thousand dollars…'

Maybe it's too much, but it will make me feel better, and hopefully it will make her feel better too. 'For whatever you need,' I say firmly. 'Treat yourself.'

'Grace…' Heather looks at me, and for a second she almost looks angry. I feel guilty, as if I'm trying to buy her off, but that isn't what this is about. At least, I don't think it is. Then Heather nods and presses her lips together. 'Thank you,' she says, and we leave it at that.

I make my excuses a little while later. Heather has her three girls line up and say goodbye to me; Emma whispers it, Amy just scowls, and Lucy picks her nose. I tell them all how great it was to meet them, and Kevin says goodbye from his chair.

Heather walks me out to my car. 'I'm sorry about Kev,' she says in a low voice. 'I know he seems grumpy, but it's just he's so tired in the evenings. His back really hurts him.'

'Of course,' I say. 'Completely understandable. I'm sorry about his back.'

'I just wanted you to know us,' she continues in a halting voice. 'And for us to know you. Especially the girls. I… I want them to know who their sister is going to. So they have an image in their head, you know, later…'

'Of course.' I feel a lump forming in my throat as I picture it. Will they remember this baby, memorialize her as if she's died?

It feels so sad, and yet it's hopeful for me. 'That's a good idea. It makes a lot of sense.'

'People around here think it's weird, that I'm giving this one away.' Heather rests a hand lightly on top of her bump. 'And I guess it is weird. Most people don't do this kind of thing, do they?' She glances at me uncertainly. 'They make it work somehow, you know?'

I have no idea what to say. The last thing I want is for Heather to figure out a way to make it work, and yet... if I were in her position... I swallow hard. 'Do you think you could make it work, Heather?' I ask, each word tenuous, painful.

She jerks a little, startled, and we are both silent, waiting for her answer. 'I doubt myself,' she admits in a low voice, not looking at me. 'I think I'm chickening out somehow, or that I'm not strong enough.'

'Heather, you're very strong. The strongest person I know, in fact.' And I realize I mean it. 'Look,' I blurt, my heart racing and my palms slick, hardly able to believe what I'm about to say. 'If you think there's a way this could work for you guys, to... to keep it – her – then you should make that happen. I don't want you to live with that kind of regret.'

She turns toward me, her eyes wide. 'Do you mean that?'

No, no, a thousand times no. I struggle not to scream the words. But much better now than later, right? No matter how much it hurts. And maybe Heather needs this from me. Maybe I need to be the kind of person who would say it. Mean it. 'Yes,' I say as steadily as I can. 'I do. If you think there is a way you can keep this baby, then I think you should. If you want to, I mean. If you...' I can't finish.

Heather is silent for another long moment. A car horn sounds in the distance, and a dog barks. Then she lets out a long, shuddery sigh.

'Grace, I appreciate you saying that. So much. More, I think, than you could know... but I can't. I know I can't, deep down.

Not with… everything the way it is.' She sighs again, the sound coming from deep within her, and then she straightens, shooting me a quick, tremulous smile. 'This baby belongs to you. I know that. I think you know that. At least, I hope you do.'

My heart leaps at her words and relief rushes through me, making me feel weak, my limbs watery. 'Thank you,' I whisper. 'I will take such good care of this little girl.' I hear the throb of emotion in my voice; feel the force of it in my chest. 'I already love her so much.' I've never meant anything more.

Tears sparkle in Heather's eyes and she blinks them back. 'I know you do.' She takes a quick breath, 'Do you want to feel her kick?'

'You mean… now? Is she kicking now?'

Wordlessly, Heather reaches for my hand and places it on her bump, which is harder and tighter than I expected, like she's got a basketball stuck under her shirt. We stand like that for a moment, my hand on her belly, her hand on top of mine, and then I feel it: a kick, surprisingly hard, right into my palm, like a promise. I laugh out loud, and Heather does too, although the sound is shaky.

'Amazing,' I say, and we stand there for another few moments, our hands on top of one another, forever connected by the tiny, persistent kick of the baby that binds us together.

CHAPTER ELEVEN

HEATHER

Five thousand dollars. After Grace leaves I sit on the toilet – the only place I can get any privacy – and stare at that check. Part of me wants to rip it up, which is crazy. I feel angry, which doesn't make any sense, because Grace has been so generous. But it's not about her generosity, which is so easy for her. It's about me taking this money. It feels like I just sold my baby, like there's a big, glowing dollar sign above my bump. Tears crowd my eyes and I press the heels of my hands to the sockets, willing them back.

Tonight was harder than I expected. Things have been going pretty well. Kev finally got a job, a favor from a friend, even if it's only ten hours a week and he's paid on commission, which ends up being hardly anything at all. Still, he's going out, bringing something in, and that's important for him as well as for me. We've turned a corner that we hadn't even had in our sight for a long time.

Things had started to seem better with my parents and Stacy too, the whole neighborhood. People still stepped around us but it didn't feel so hostile. A few moms at the school have asked how I'm feeling, even if they don't always look me in the eye, or at my bump. Stacy has been a rock, bringing over meals, arranging babysitting so I can get out. One afternoon she brought over a bag of pregnancy stuff she'd held onto – disposable underwear, maternity pads, the kind of stuff I'll still need even without a baby.

I got a little teary as I looked at it all and she didn't say anything, just gave me a hug. I burrowed into her for a few seconds, and after that I was okay. I've been okay. So why do I feel so shaky now?

If you think there's a way this could work for you guys…

But there isn't. I know there isn't. And I'm angry that she gave me an out, because I can't take it and that makes me feel guiltier than ever. I should have taken it. I should have been able to.

'Mommy, are you in there?' It's Amy, pressed up to the bathroom door by the sounds of it, her lips against the keyhole.

I take a quick breath and slip the folded check into my pocket. 'Yes, sweetheart.'

'Can I come in?'

I flush the toilet to make it seem like I was peeing instead of staring at my blood money and then I unlock the door. Amy stands there, looking surprisingly tearful. She doesn't like to cry. 'What's wrong, baby?'

'I didn't like her.' She hurls herself at me, throwing herself into my arms, and I hold her close, stroking her hair, my chin resting on top of her head.

'Why not?'

'Because she didn't like us.'

A chill steals through me at that stark statement. She sounds so certain. 'Why do you say that, Amy?'

'Because.' Amy burrows closer, making me wince. 'She just didn't. She kept looking like she thought everything was yucky.'

Tears blur my eyes and I clench them shut. I think of Grace's luxurious apartment, the carpet that was so deep I sank into it up to my ankles. It even smelled expensive, like lemon and leather. She must have thought our house was the crappiest of crap. And even Amy noticed. How come I didn't? Or did I just not want to see?

'It doesn't matter, Amy,' I say, wanting to mean it. This is our home, and we're a family. That's what matters. 'Grace is going to take good care of the baby, and I know she already loves her so much.' I think of Grace's hand on my belly, the little kick into her palm. She loves this little girl, but so do I. 'That's all that matters, sweetheart.'

Amy twists away from me, angry again. Of all the girls, she's taken this the hardest: fighting it, fighting me. Emma's just been silent and Lucy doesn't really understand. But Amy... Amy has tested me, taunted me. She's either hurling an insult or trying my patience, saying the cruelest things because she knows they cut the deepest.

Yesterday she called Lucy retarded, just because she doesn't know her letters yet. I yanked Amy over to the sink and threatened to squirt dish soap into her mouth.

'Don't use words like that,' I snapped, surprised and shamed by my own sudden rage, 'or I'll make you drink this whole bottle.'

'I hate you,' Amy screamed, twisting away from me, and I let her go. I knew where her anger came from, but where was mine boiling up from? I had to control it. I might have been hurting, but her pain mattered more.

'I don't want her to have the baby,' Amy yells now, and then she runs into her bedroom and slams the door so hard it feels as if the whole house shakes.

I start running the bath for the girls, trying not to let her words hurt, even though they've already cut me to the quick, so I am raw and bleeding. I want to savor these children I do have, because I love them so much, even when they're angry. I want to absorb their confusion and grief and anger, because I understand why they feel it. I feel it too.

And so I pour half a bottle of shampoo into the running water for a bubbly treat, and then call the girls for their bath.

Lucy fights me as I take off her clothes, but the sight of her toddler belly with its sticky-out belly button makes me smile. Amy, her anger forgotten for the moment, struts around our tiny bathroom, doing rock star poses stark naked, which probably should alarm me, but doesn't. She's got so much confidence, and I just hope she's able to hang onto it, make her way in this world in a way I never did.

Emma, I notice with a pang, is getting too old to take shared baths with her sisters —there is a fuzz of hair between her legs and she crosses her arms protectively over her barely-there breasts. How can my big girl be growing up?

I feel the baby kick, and I place one hand on my belly as I hold a wet and squirming Lucy with the other, trying to wash her hair.

Half an hour later the girls are all clean, their hair in damp, dark blonde ringlets, their faces freshly scrubbed, dressed in their pajamas, my favorite time of day. They run into the living room in search of Daddy, and Kevin pretends to be surprised by the sight of them and then gives them all a tickle so they scream with laughter, which makes my heart swell with love and gratitude. I have so much. Far too often I feel like I have too little, but right now I think of Grace, alone in her big, empty apartment, and I know I'm lucky. I'm blessed.

Of course it doesn't last. Amy knocks Lucy over by accident and she starts wailing, and then Amy flounces off, refusing to apologize because that's just how she is. Emma slips away like a shadow and gets her library book, burying her nose in it. I give in to Lucy's wailing and put on a *Paw Patrol* DVD, which Kevin complains about because he was, he says, about to watch the baseball game, even though it isn't an important one.

'Just for five minutes, before bed,' I plead, wondering why I have to beg for something like this, and then I go into the kitchen and see all the dirty dishes piled up in the sink from dinner. The baby kicks again, hard, right into my pelvis, a flash of pain. I turn on the tap. At least I had that moment.

The next few weeks slide by in a tired haze. Now that I'm firmly in the third trimester I'm uncomfortable and emotional, and I'm also very, very pregnant. My bump precedes me into a room, and it feels so overwhelming, so obvious, like the biggest thing about me.

Normally around this time I'd be getting excited. I'd have brought out the baby clothes, washed and ironed them, put them in a drawer. Kev would have found the old infant car seat in the basement, probably covered in mildew because we wouldn't have cleaned it properly before putting it away. I always mean to, but I never do. I would have washed it in the backyard with the hose, spraying the girls as they played around me. Everyone would have been excited, hopeful.

Now this baby feels like a ticking time bomb that everyone can hear. No one talks about when it will come, but I think about it all the time. Will I hold her, or will I just ask the nurse to take her away? Will I look into her face? Do I want to? Can I bear not to?

When I am thirty-four weeks Tina calls me to discuss the birth plan. 'Would you like Grace to be there?'

I picture Grace standing by my bed, her arms folded, tapping her foot as I writhe and scream and push. Or will she be leaning forward, eager for that first glimpse of my baby, her daughter? Which possibility feels worse?

'I don't know. Does she want to be there?'

'I haven't asked her yet, because I wanted to talk to you first. Will Kevin be with you?' The question sounds careful, and that annoys me.

'Yes,' I say firmly. 'He will be.' He was there for the other three, but that was before he hurt his back. Stacy can watch the girls, and yet… I can't quite picture Kev there. Will he find it harder to give this baby up if he sees her? Some guilty impulse in me feels like I should do this alone, hand this baby off to Grace and then go home as if nothing has happened. Nothing has changed. My secret sin, my scarlet letter, to bear alone.

But it doesn't need to be like that. I've read the stories on the internet – the parties in the hospital room, popping open the champagne, birth and adoptive parents all celebrating. I've read about the birth mother being the godmother, the adoptive parents keeping a blog of photos and updates, family dinners and Christmases because it really does take a village, or at least more than one family. I don't want all that, I don't think I could stand it, but why can't this be just a little easier? Why does it always feel like a fight, even when we're getting along?

'Well, in terms of Grace being there,' Tina says, 'there's still time to decide. You can think about it.'

'Okay,' I say, and my voice wobbles a little.

'Heather…' Tina pauses. 'If you're not sure about this…' She lets it hang there, waiting for me to what? Admit that I'm not? Assure her I am? I stay silent, because I have no idea what to say, what to feel, and I don't want to start blubbering on the phone. 'It would be okay,' she finishes quietly.

I wonder if it's in her job description, to give me an out, just as Grace did. 'I'm fine,' I say. 'I'm just ready for this to be over. Move on, you know?'

'Yes,' Tina says gently. 'I know.'

A couple of nights later I wake up in the middle of the night, hot and uncomfortable, the baby kicking at my insides like she's desperate to leave me. Kevin isn't lying next to me, and so I slip out of bed, and pad quietly into the living room. He's not there either, to my surprise. I thought he would have fallen asleep in his chair. I look around our tiny house but I can't see him anywhere, and then I notice the front door is ajar. My heart lurches and I walk to the door. Kevin is sitting on our front stoop, elbows braced on his knees as he stares into the darkness.

'Kev,' I speak softly, not wanting to startle him or wake the girls, 'what are you doing out here?' It's a warm night for early

April, but not that warm, and he's in only a t-shirt and boxers. I shiver, my arms wrapped around me, goosebumps rising.

'I couldn't sleep.'

'Is it your back...?'

'No.'

The definitive answer pulls me up short. Cautiously, I open the door wider and slip outside. Everything is eerily silent – no cars, no barking dogs, no doors slamming or the tinny sound of our neighbors' TV on constant ESPN. 'Why, then?' I ask.

He shrugs. 'Don't know. Just thinking about stuff.'

I ease down next to him, one hand on my ever-growing belly. 'Stuff?'

'Remember when Emma was born? You screamed the whole way down the hallway. I'd never heard you so loud.'

I smile at the memory. Emma was born a month early, and she came fast. They were still prepping the room as I pushed her out on the stretcher in the hall, and looked down at her, a red, screaming scrap of a baby.

'Yes, I remember. I think the other patients thought I was being killed.'

'I thought you were.' He lets out a little huff of laughter. 'It was amazing, though.' He shakes his head. 'I was scared shitless. No idea what I was supposed to be doing.'

'We were little more than kids ourselves.'

'I know.' A faint smile curves his mouth as he stares into the night. 'And then Amy came late, didn't she?'

'Two weeks late and thirty-six hours of labor. It didn't seem fair, after Emma.'

'Typical Amy, making an entrance.' We both laugh, the sound soft in the darkness. 'And little Lucy, right on time,' Kev continues. 'I felt like I had some experience, then.' He pauses, his gaze fixed ahead. 'What do you think it will be like this time?'

'I don't know.' We are both silent, but it doesn't feel tense. It rolls out between us, like a stretch of still water. 'I can't imagine it,' I whisper. 'How it's all going to happen.'

'Me neither.' Kev reaches for my hand and laces his fingers through mine. 'I don't know what I'm going to feel, when the time comes,' he says in a low voice, a confession.

'I don't, either.' A lump is forming in my throat and I have to speak around it. I squeeze his hand, finding strength in his grip. 'Do you want to be there?'

He glances at me sharply. 'I've always been there.'

'I know, but...' The lump is getting bigger. 'It might be harder, you know...'

'I'm not letting you go through this alone.' He lets out a ragged breath and rakes a hand through his hair. 'I know I haven't been great about this so far.'

A tear trickles down my cheek; I can't speak, for love and grief.

'I just felt so guilty, Heather. I still do. Like this is all my fault.'

'It isn't, Kev—'

'But if I'd kept my job, if I'd found another one—'

'You have found another one.'

He lets out a hard huff of breath. 'And I make piss all. You know that. This isn't what you agreed to when you married me.'

'I agreed to better or worse, Kevin McCleary.' Now my voice is strong, despite the tears. 'No matter what.'

He's silent, struggling, because he knows I'm right but it doesn't make much difference. 'Still,' he says finally.

'Yes, still.' I lean over and rest my head on his shoulder. 'I love you, Kev.' It's been a long time since I've said it. Since I've felt it.

'I love you, too.' Kev's voice is gruff and he squeezes my hand. 'It's going to get better for us,' he says, his voice a little louder now, more sure. 'We'll get over this. Grace will give this baby a good life, and we'll give our girls good lives. I'll get more work.

Maybe we can rent a bigger house. We'll take the girls to Disney World when Lucy's bigger.'

He's painting a picture I desperately want to be real, to make it all worthwhile, but right now it's enough that he's saying it. 'Yes,' I say, clinging to him, nestling into him. 'Yes, that's exactly how it's going to be.'

The next day I call Tina to tell her Grace can be at the birth. It feels like the right thing to do, even though part of me, a large, frightened part, resists. I don't really want her to see me in the bloody throes of labor. And I don't want to see her hold my baby when she is tiny and new, fresh from my womb. But I agree to it because it seems unfair to Grace to keep her from it. Tina is warmly approving when I tell her.

'I know Grace will be thrilled.'

I don't reply.

A few days later I am on one of the night shifts at an office in Newark, heaving a bucket of dirty water onto my cleaning trolley, having finished the worst part of the evening, the men's bathroom, when I feel a pop low down, and then a gush of water.

I stare in shock at the fluid darkening the industrial carpet around my feet. It's way too early, well over the month it was with Emma. I stand there, my mind going blank with shock and then panic as I feel the tightening bands of a contraction around my stomach. A real contraction, not just the Braxton Hicks I've become used to. I'm in labor. I'm thirty-four weeks and *I'm in labor*.

I fumble for my cell phone to call Kev, but the phone just rings and rings. Maybe He's left his cell somewhere, or maybe he's just that dead asleep. I disconnect the call without leaving a message, and call Stacy instead. The phone rings and rings and I remember that it's three o'clock in the morning and she keeps her phone charging in the kitchen.

My belly tightens again, and it *hurts*. I take a deep breath, trying to keep calm, to figure out what to do. I need to go to the hospital, but I want Kevin, or at least Stacy, *someone* there with me. It wasn't supposed to happen this way. Not even in my worst imaginings was it like this, me alone in an empty office building in the middle of the night.

'Okay?' Aneta, one of the Polish women I work with, stands in front of me and gestures to the puddle at my feet: 'Baby?'

I nod, biting my lip. 'It's too soon, though,' I say, and my voice sounds strained and high. 'It's too soon to have the baby.' Emma was a month early, and that was scary. It's six weeks until my due date this time.

Aneta nods, although I'm not sure she understands. 'I drive?' she asks, miming holding a steering wheel. 'To…'

She frowns and I fill in shakily, 'The hospital.'

Aneta brightens and nods. 'Yes. That.'

'Okay,' I say, and as she gives me a reassuring smile I try to keep the panic back. I didn't want it to be like this, on my own, panicked and scared. Aneta reaches for my hand, and I try to smile back at her. I tell myself it's going to be okay. That this baby – *my baby* – is going to be fine. It isn't until we're on our way to the hospital that I even think about Grace, and then only for a second.

CHAPTER TWELVE

GRACE

The new partnerships are due to be announced in mid-April. Bruce has as good as told me I made partner. So I celebrate before the partners are set to meet by buying a five-hundred-dollar bottle of champagne and drinking it all myself, while sitting in the glider in my daughter's pristine nursery.

Everything is ready and waiting and perfect – the white Stokke crib, the matching changing table. The walls are a fresh, minty green with stenciled elephants cavorting along the picture rail. White gauzy curtains frame the window overlooking the park, with gray velvet sashes. A green polka-dot cushion rests behind me in the chair, and there is one framed print on the wall, a watercolor of a young girl in a field of daisies. A photo of my father holding me as a baby smiles from a sterling silver frame on top of the dresser.

I've sat in this room a lot lately. I find it very calming, because when I go in this room the baby feels real to me, as if I could scoop her up from the crib and hold her to my chest. When I'm in this room, I'm happy.

Right now I am more than a little bit drunk. My head lolls back and I reach for my phone to check for messages. Bruce hasn't called yet but I know he will. I've given my lifeblood to this company. I've given them my time, my energy, my passion. I'm forty next month and I deserve to be made partner. *I will be.*

Lying there in a bit of a drunken doze, I picture myself in this room, with my baby girl, in less than two months' time. I picture myself holding her, cradling her into my chest, inhaling her warm baby smell. I scrunch my eyes shut, willing it to become real. To feel it.

But reality intrudes – I need to pee, and I am remembering a recent conversation with Jill, after one of our workouts, when she discovered I was planning to adopt. It happened stupidly; we'd finished working out and we were checking our phones as we waited for our protein shakes. When they came, I laid my phone on the counter, and it was open to MetroMom, a website for urban mothers that has an adoption forum. I'd taken to reading the posts rather obsessively, gobbling up stories of bringing home newborns, the bottle feeds and bonding, the wonderful reality of it, the incredulous joy other parents felt contagious. I hadn't yet dared to post anything myself.

Eagle-eyed Jill, of course, saw what was on there before I'd managed to swipe the screen.

'*Grace*,' she said, her eyes wide with shock and, I feared, a kind of awful fascination. 'Are you thinking of *adopting*?'

I hesitated, my instinct to deny it, because Jill and I didn't share much personal stuff, and I still hadn't told anyone at work. But denying it felt wrong, like denying myself, my baby. And so I lifted my chin and tried for an insouciant shrug.

'Yes, actually, I am.'

'You're adopting a *baby*?' Her eyes were like dinner plates.

'The time feels right,' I said, shrugging again, as if I wasn't taking this life-or-death seriously.

'But… but…' Jill practically spluttered. 'You're about to make partner. This could derail everything.'

'Why?' I challenged. I felt defiant then, as if I could take on the world, or at least Harrow and Heath. I'd just ordered two boxes of newborn diapers off Amazon, and had even dared to subscribe to a box a month. Every step I took, whether buying diapers or folding a onesie, made me feel more hopeful, more certain. This was what I wanted, and it was happening. 'They can't keep me from being partner just because I have a child,' I told Jill firmly, determined to believe it. 'That's sexual discrimination.'

She rolled her eyes. 'They wouldn't say it was because of that, but they'd still do it. You know how this business works, Grace. It's still a boys' club no matter what PR they try to spin.'

'Well, I'm not telling anyone at work,' I said, already regretting that she'd found out and that I'd admitted to it. 'Anyone else, anyway.'

Remembering it all now, I think I should have lied to Jill, but what can she do? Tell Bruce? I feel cold at the thought. She wouldn't, I tell myself, but I know she would, if she could just find a way to do it that didn't make her look like a tattle. The real question is, would Bruce keep me from being made partner because of it? After all my work, the years I've put in, I can't believe he'd be so cavalier about a piece of gossip from someone who he must know is envious of me.

I force myself to dismiss my worries about Jill and scroll through my contacts, deciding I am not too drunk for an impromptu phone call. I ring Ben. He answers on the fourth ring, which makes me think he was debating whether to take the call.

'Grace?' He sounds cautious.

'Hi, Ben.' I do my best to sound sober. 'How are you?'

'Um, fine.'

'I know this is kind of out of the blue, but I just wanted to share some news.' I slur a little, and I realize I'm drunker than I thought. I also shouldn't have called Ben. He's got to be wondering why on earth I did.

'Oh?' I hear him moving, shutting a door. 'Yeah? What?'

'Two things, actually.' I try to enunciate. 'I'm about to be made partner at Harrow and Heath and…' I take a deep breath, my chest bursting with pride and happiness. 'I'm adopting a little girl.'

'Oh. Wow.' Ben sounds pleased. At least I think he does. 'Grace, that's really good news. I'm so happy for you.'

'Thanks.' I feel the sloppy grin spreading across my face, but with it comes a sudden, piercing sadness. I don't want to be sharing this news with Ben Foley, of all people, a person I haven't seen in years; someone who I *know* doesn't care about me any more. I want to be sharing it with someone who loves me. I want to be sharing it with my dad.

'I've got to go,' I say abruptly, and I disconnect the call without waiting for his reply. Then I throw the phone across the room; it lands on the soft, cream-colored area rug and bounces harmlessly, which is less than satisfying. Part of me wanted the screen to shatter.

I miss my father. He'd have been so happy for me. I picture him cuddling my little girl, how he'd drape her over his shoulder while she burped, rubbing her back in slow, rhythmic circles, an expert grandfather from the get-go. I can see it so clearly that I can't believe it isn't going to happen, that it isn't going to be real.

He'd have been such a great grandad. He would have taught her Pinochle, slipped her sweets, always been patient and ready to listen. He'd have taken her fishing, the way he did with me; the three of us on Cape Cod, Dad building the world's biggest sandcastle, having barbecues on the beach, toasting marshmallows. Arms around each other, proud, cheesy grins in place, for the photos of those key moments – first day of school, piano recitals, graduation.

I can see it all, and I want it so badly, it's like a physical ache reverberating through every part of me. I don't want to be alone in this, and yet I am. I always am.

I sit there, drunk, half-dozing, trying to fight the tidal wave of sadness that threatens to drown me. I don't want to feel sad now. I'm about to be made partner, to meet my daughter. I'm about to finally have everything I want. Why do I have to feel so lonely now?

Because happiness hurts when there is no one to share it with. I picture that on some inspirational poster with a picture of a kitten in a wine glass, or on a paperweight or a mug. Not exactly words to inspire.

Eventually I fall asleep; I feel myself slip into unconsciousness, like being tugged underwater, and it's a relief. I don't want to think any more. I awake suddenly, minutes or hours later, to my phone buzzing on the carpet where I threw it.

My mouth tastes horrible and my eyes feel glued together. I stumble out of the chair and fumble for the phone. When I glance blearily at the screen I see it's 6 a.m. and Tina is calling me. My heart feels frozen, a block of ice in my chest. My fingers tremble as I swipe to take the call.

'Tina?' My voice comes out in a croak.

'Sorry to call you so early.' She sounds tense and grim. 'It's Heather. I just got a call from the hospital. She's gone into labor.'

'Labor… but she's only…'

'Thirty-four weeks. It's early. Very early.'

'Dangerously early?' My stomach plunges.

'That's impossible to say. But I thought you might want to go to the hospital.'

'Does Heather still want me there?' I know she said yes to me being there for the delivery, but this feels different.

'She asked them to call me.' Which isn't exactly a yes. And if I don't show up at work today, the day I'm meant to make partner… I push that thought aside. The choice is obvious, overwhelming.

'I'll be there in an hour.'

I yank on jeans and a top, brush my teeth because that is a must, and run a comb through my hair before I hurry downstairs.

I don't have time to rent a Zipcar, and I curse myself for not having bought a car yet – I thought I had time.

I end up taking a cab to the hospital, which costs a fortune, not that it matters. I thrust a bunch of bills at the driver and jump out, my heart racing as I search for the maternity ward. Hospitals still remind me of death. But not this time. Please God, not this time.

At the reception desk a nurse calmly tells me that she can't give out information about a patient, thanks to the HIPAA laws. I try to explain who I am, but she's not having it. She points to a plastic chair and, like a schoolteacher, tells me to sit down and wait. I obey, and then I call Tina.

'No one's telling me anything.' My voice is shaking. 'And they won't let me see Heather. Do you know what's going on?'

'No,' Tina says, her voice calm and soothing. I wonder if she ever gets upset. 'But I'm coming over right now.'

I spend an hour on a plastic chair, my hands tucked between my knees, rocking back and forth. People must think I'm strung out on something, but I can't keep still. I can't focus. I listen to the blood roar in my ears and my heart thud, thud, thud. That's all I can manage. My mind is a numb blank, which is better than the terrible fears seething just below the surface. I know they're there, swirling and swarming, but I won't give into them. *I can't.*

Tina comes at eight o'clock, and she gives me a quick hug that I desperately need. Then she talks to the receptionist, and somehow she works magic I don't have, because she comes back to tell me that Heather's waters broke, and she went into labor early this morning.

They tried to keep it from progressing but the baby was in distress and so they're doing an emergency caesarean section right now. Every word feels like a thrown punch. I blink, too dazed to process it all.

'But the baby, she'll be all right?' My teeth are chattering. I'm so terrified I feel sick, as if I might actually throw up right there on Tina's Easy Spirit clogs.

'Neonatal care is amazing, Grace,' she says steadily. 'And thirty-four weeks is still a good gestation. I'm sure she'll be fine.'

'You're sure?' I hang onto it like a promise.

'As sure as I can be. Of course there are risks—'

But I don't want to hear about risks. I can't handle more fear.

We wait. An hour later my phone buzzes, and I see that it's Bruce. Dimly, I realize I never called in sick. Dully, I take the call, moving out to the hallway so I'm not told off for being on my phone.

'Bruce?'

'Grace.' He sounds serious. I take a deep breath.

'I'm sorry that I'm not—'

'Grace, look. I'll cut to the chase. You didn't make partner.'

I blink, absorbing this coolly stated fact, his tone touched with impatience, as if this is nothing more than an irritation to deal with before getting on with his day.

'Just because of today…?'

'Today?' Bruce sounds confused and even more impatient, and I realize he probably doesn't even know I'm not at work. It's only a little after nine. So this has nothing to do with me not showing up. 'It was a hard decision, but the partners feel you haven't discovered any truly substantial investments since All Natural, and that was six years ago now.'

Damn All Natural. I knew having a big hit when I was new would bite me in the ass one day. I just didn't expect it to be this hard.

'That's not exactly true,' I begin, wanting to mention the social media deal from six months ago, but I know there's no point fighting it. When the partners decide, they decide. It's over. 'Was there any other reason?' I ask woodenly.

'Well…' Bruce blows out a breath. 'We did feel that you've been a bit distracted lately… it seems you have a lot on your mind?' He pauses, as if he's waiting for me to confess. I feel cold.

'No,' I say. 'I'm not distracted. Why would you think that?'

'I don't know.' Bruce backs off hastily. 'It's just a feeling. Personal issues maybe…' He trails off, again waiting for me to fill the silence.

A suspicion is growing in me, an awful, sickening suspicion. 'Did anyone else make partner?'

Bruce hesitates, and then I know. I can't believe it, but I know.

'Jill,' I say, even though it seems unbelievable. She's not even a principal yet. 'Was it Jill Martin?'

'Yes.' Bruce sounds guilty, and he damn well should.

Jill. Jill stabbed me in the back. She must have told, or at least hinted, that I was planning to adopt. I was Mommy-tracked and I don't even have a baby yet. Harrow and Heath have wanted a female partner for a while now, to look more PC, and they picked fucking Jill.

I disconnect the call without saying goodbye, even though I know it's unprofessional. *I didn't make partner.* I see my future with awful clarity; I'm going to be shunted to the sidelines, down-graded to the grunt work of searching through companies that will never so much as break even. I'll either stay at that depressing mid-level or I'll have to leave and start all over somewhere else, put in my time, my blood and sweat, prove myself again and again and again and still maybe never make the grade. I'm swamped by disappointment, and yet another part of me doesn't even care. What's my job compared to my daughter?

'Grace?'

I turn to see Tina coming down the hall, and she doesn't have a good look on her face. It's a sympathy face, and my fingers go slack and my phone falls to the floor. This time the screen shatters.

'No…'

'The baby's healthy,' she says quickly. 'Jaundiced and the lungs are underdeveloped, but a good weight. Four pounds, six ounces.'

'And Heather…?'

'She's fine. Tired, I'm sure.'

'Have you seen her? Have you seen the baby?' *My little girl.* Somehow I can't say the words, as if I'll jinx it.

'No, not yet.' Tina hesitates, and I resist the urge to grab her by the shoulders and shake her.

'What? What is it? What are you not saying?'

'It's only… the baby's a boy.'

'A boy…' I blink, trying to get my head around this new reality.

'And Heather… Heather is saying she's not sure any more.'

I stare, uncomprehending, refusing to believe. So Tina clarifies it for me.

'She's saying she might want to keep the baby.'

PART TWO

CHAPTER ONE

GRACE

Seven years later

'Come on, Isaac.' I try to smile, my voice as upbeat as I can make it as I stand by the front door, a pair of sneakers in my hand. 'Put your shoes on. We're going to be late.'

Isaac drags his feet along the carpet and lets out a theatrical sigh, his bangs sliding into his face. I keep meaning to take him for a haircut, but somehow I've never got around to it.

'Do I have to go?'

'You know you do, bud.' I try to pitch my voice between sympathy and cheerfulness, but it's hard. I dread these visits as much as Isaac does, although I try not to show it. 'Come on.' I ruffle his hair and he ducks his head away from me, something that's only started recently. My little boy doesn't want cuddles anymore. 'Maybe we'll stop for ice cream on the way back.' I've resorted to bribery, but that happened a while ago when it comes to dealing with Saturday afternoons.

'Okay.' He takes the sneakers and I try to relax. I'm always tense on the fourth Saturday of the month: the day we visit Aunt Heather.

It wasn't supposed to be this way. Seven years later I can't help but still think it. A closed adoption, we both agreed on it, way back when. Easier, cleaner, safer, simpler, no matter what anyone might spout about making an open adoption work, how everybody wins.

When Tina told me that awful first morning that Heather might have changed her mind I felt both winded with shock and yet also completely unsurprised. Hadn't a dark, frightened part of me been waiting for this, bracing for it? My response was to go into action mode, treating it like a work crisis because that was the only way I could deal with my fear.

'I need a lawyer,' I snapped at Tina.

'I can recommend someone, of course, but I'd suggest you give Heather a little time. This is a fairly normal reaction…'

I shook my head, scrabbling for my phone after I'd dropped it on the hospital floor. The screen was badly cracked but it still worked. 'I've got someone already.' I'd engaged a lawyer when I'd started this whole process, but I'd hoped I wouldn't need her until the official adoption took place, until I was in court, my daughter in my arms, everything needing only to be signed and sealed.

'Grace…' Tina placed a hand on my arm, but I shook her off. I felt like she'd become the enemy. Maybe she'd been that all along, and I just hadn't realized. She would be telling Heather her rights, reminding her she could change her mind whenever she wanted. I was done with Tina.

'Why do we have to go?' Isaac asks as he fumbles with his shoelaces. He asks the same question every time.

'You know why, Isaac.' Years ago, I explained who Heather was, but I'm not sure Isaac really understood. I still don't think he understands; the McClearys are so different from him. From us. And I admit, I haven't pressed the point too much. Going to Heather's house once a month is all the blood money I'm willing to pay.

Seven years of visits, barely missing one, because I felt I owed it to Heather. I made her a promise when Isaac was only three days old, when we were both strung out on emotion and fatigue, everything feeling fragile. I promised, and Heather had a lawyer seal the deal.

As we wait for the elevator my neighbor Eileen opens her door and gives us a smile. I swear she waits by her door for the sound of ours opening. Her eyesight's nearly completely gone now and her husband is bedridden.

Sometimes Isaac visits with them, plays Chinese checkers and comes home with old-fashioned, boiled sweets in sticky wrappers. Sometimes, when I remember, I try to drop off something, some cookies or one of the gossip magazines that I know are Eileen's guilty pleasure, even though she can barely see the pictures now. We've come a long way from the days when I didn't know her name. As for Eileen, Isaac is almost like the grandchild she never had.

'Going out?' she asks, as usual, and Isaac looks away from her without saying anything. Gently I put a hand on his shoulder and steer him back to face her. He's an introvert, always has been, quiet and shy, like I was when I was young.

'Yes, we're going to visit some friends in New Jersey,' I say. Although Eileen knows Isaac is adopted, I haven't explained about Heather to her, or anyone. It's too complicated, too unwelcome, and I know I'd just moan and bitch about it anyway, which doesn't feel fair.

'Have fun,' Eileen chirps. 'Come see me when you get back, okay, Isaac?'

Isaac nods and we step into the elevator. He lets out a gusty sigh and slumps against the wall, scuffing his sneakers on the floor. He's shot up this year, and I notice that his jeans are about an inch too short. When did that happen?

Last week we had his seventh birthday party at The Gaga Center. I hadn't even known about gaga, a form of dodgeball, before Isaac became interested in it at school. He went to a Hebrew Montessori until this year, when he started at the all-boys

Buckley. The party was with boys from his old school and just one from Buckley, Will, who is Isaac's new best friend. His mom Stella is mine; Will and Isaac clicked on the first day of school, and so did Stella and I.

With work, I don't see her as much as I'd like to, but we keep in touch via WhatsApp and texts, and occasionally we even manage a night out – girly cocktails, or a sappy movie. It's been a long time since I've had a good girlfriend, someone who I'm not in competition with, because truth be told there's no way I could beat Stella in the mommy stakes and so I don't even try. I just soak up her cheerful energy and humor. She is a stay-at-home mom with a husband who makes millions, two sweet boys and a list of charities she volunteers for as long as my arm. I don't even feel envious, because Stella's too nice for that. At least, I don't feel it that often.

The doors ping open directly onto the underground parking garage and Isaac races out.

'Isaac,' I call. 'Cars.'

He slows down for a millisecond, and then keeps on skipping ahead. Testing me, another new development, and one I don't feel emotionally prepared for.

That first morning I left Tina to call my lawyer, Eleanor. She was calm, no-nonsense, and I felt my heart rate start to slow when I heard her speak so practically.

'In agency adoptions the birth mother can't surrender the child until seventy-two hours after the birth,' she told me. 'It won't be considered valid beforehand.'

'So she has time to bond.' I pictured Heather, cradling my son. My son, whom I hadn't even seen yet, wasn't allowed to see. A ragged gasp escaped me.

'Not necessarily,' Eleanor answered calmly. 'The baby is in ICU at the moment, correct? So the birth mother can't see him easily.

That could work in your favor, especially if you don't cover any medical expenses once she changes her mind.' She sounded so cold but in that moment it was what I needed. 'If you feel you have the relationship,' Eleanor suggested, 'and she wants to see you, you could talk to Heather. See what she's thinking. But be careful.'

'And after the seventy-two hours? If she doesn't… surrender?' I pictured Heather waving a white flag from her hospital bed, a war being waged. Why did it have to be like that? The soft-focus stories I read online made everything seem so amicable, and she and I had reached a certain kind of friendliness, hadn't we? Now it seemed like so much fakery, even though I felt it at the time. I'm sure I did.

'There's not much you can do then,' Eleanor admitted.

'But I gave her money,' I said, even though it wasn't remotely about the money.

'You mean you paid for her expenses, I hope,' Eleanor returned sharply. 'Any compensation should have gone through the proper channels, Grace. The laws are very strict about how you give money to a birth mother. Trust me, you do not want to look as if you were trying to buy a baby.'

'I know.' Guilt and fear prickled through me as I thought about that five grand I'd given Heather. I hadn't thought it mattered, but what if it jeopardized my case? What if she used my generosity against me, made me seem unfit or even criminal? Everything felt like a minefield, explosions all around me.

'And what if she does sign the papers after seventy-two hours?' I asked, trying to focus on the what-ifs, the ones I wanted. 'Can she still change her mind, even then?'

'She has forty-five days to reconsider her decision after executing the form. But she'd have to take you to court, and it wouldn't be a certain outcome for her.'

Or for me. Still, I felt the tiniest bit better. I didn't think Heather wanted the expense and drama of going to court. But the next three days were critical.

*

I click my keys to unlock the door to the SUV I bought after Isaac was born. He clambers in the back and I slip into the driver's seat, steeling myself for what lies ahead. Four excruciating hours of Heather's overt neediness, her family's tense silence, my son's heart-wrenching discomfort. Every month. But that's going to change. Finally, that's going to change. Isaac buckles up, and then asks if he can play his iPad, as usual.

'Why don't we play the alphabet game?' I suggest. It's something we've started doing in the last two years, since Isaac learned to read. 'You go first.'

'A on Avenue!'

I meet his eyes, the same hazel as Kevin's, in the rearview mirror. 'Good one, bud.'

'Your turn, Mom.'

I never tire of that word. *Mom.* Me. 'Hmm, let's see,' I say as I turn onto Eighty-Sixth Street. 'Where am I going to find a B?'

'Columbus!' he crows as we drive through the park, toward Columbus Avenue. 'And C too!'

We've finished the game – Z in Zappos on a billboard by the GW Bridge – by the time I turn onto I95, and I relent and let Isaac play on his iPad. I'm used to this hour-long drive to Elizabeth. I've made it eighty-two times in the last seven years, eighty-two visits, excruciating for everyone. But maybe this one will be the last, or at least close to it. I can hope.

Seven years ago it was twenty-four endless hours before Heather agreed to see me. I'd gone home, then gone to work because I didn't know what else to do and I needed to face the partners and Jill, who wouldn't even meet my eye. I went back to the hospital in the evening, feeling as if I were on an awful loop I was desperate to get off, and yet I still dreaded seeing Heather. Reading the truth in her face, hearing it from her own mouth. Facing the end of everything.

When Heather finally said she would see me, and I cracked open the door to her hospital room and saw her struggling to sit up in bed, I had no idea what to expect. My mouth felt dry and my heart thudded. I ached to see my son, but I didn't even know if he would be mine. But he *felt* mine.

'Don't sit up, not with your stitches,' I said, waving her back down with one hand and putting the huge bouquet of flowers that now seemed showy and completely inappropriate on a side table with the other. I'd debated getting the flowers, but it had felt wrong to come empty-handed. 'How are you feeling?'

Heather's lips trembled and she pressed them together. 'I've felt better.'

'I'm sure you have.' I sat on the edge of the chair near her bed. 'Have you seen Kevin?'

She nodded jerkily. 'He was here earlier. My sister watched the girls.'

'How is… how is the baby?' The words felt incendiary, but I had to ask. I needed to know.

'He's going to be fine.' Heather turned toward the window, away from me. 'They're going to have to keep him in the hospital for a couple of weeks, because of his lungs. And they'd like him to be over five pounds before he… before he goes home.' Her voice wobbled and she sucked in a hard breath. Tears pricked my eyes and I realized, with a ripple of shock, that they were for Heather.

Underneath my fear and selfish desperation, I ached for her. I knew I couldn't even begin to imagine what she was feeling, and I was humbled by that knowledge. No matter what I was facing, Heather faced more. And yet maybe it was still all going to be okay for her. Maybe I was the one going home with empty arms and an aching heart.

'He's beautiful, you know,' she said, her voice thick. 'Tiny but beautiful.'

'I'm sure he is.' Now I was the one who sounded like I was going to cry. The two of us broken over this little baby boy we didn't even know yet but we both loved.

'I'm not going to change my mind,' she said, her voice hardening, the threat of tears gone now, her face still turned toward the window. 'When I first saw him…' She draws in a quick breath. 'Well… All you need to know is I'm not going to change my mind. So don't worry.' I couldn't mistake her bitterness, and yet everything in me pulsed with painful relief.

I released my breath in a slow, quiet rush. 'Thank you.' I had no other words.

'But things are going to have to be different,' Heather continued.

I wanted her to look at me, so I could see her face. She took a deep breath.

'I want an open adoption.'

Her tone was so non-negotiable that I almost wished my lawyer were there. 'What… what exactly do you mean by that?'

'One visit every month.' She turned to me, suddenly fierce, furious. 'Every month. Saturday afternoon. That will be mine.' *Forever.* She didn't say it, but I heard it all the same, felt it, and everything in me recoiled. I pictured Heather's and my lives forever intertwined, hopelessly tangled, this baby boy at the center, tugged in different directions.

'I'm not going to back down on this,' Heather said, and she sounded tougher than I'd ever heard her sound before. 'I know it's different from what I said before, but I didn't know how I'd feel, seeing him. Holding him.' Her voice broke and she sucked in a hard breath. 'And it's not just because it's a boy, if you're thinking that. That jolted me, maybe, but it was bigger than that, Grace. My own *child…* I'd forgotten how it felt, to hold them in your arms. To know they came out of you. He was so tiny.' Another breath, this one ragged. 'And he knew me, right off. He knew my voice, he turned to me when I spoke. He tried to nurse, but he was too small. But he *tried*.'

She was torturing me with her words, and I knew I just had to take it, punch after punch. 'I'm sure he did,' I manage.

She sniffed and dashed a tear from her cheek. 'So that's how it's got to be. I'll give him to you, Grace, I swear I will, but I'm not backing down on this. I want it drawn up, legal. You can pay the lawyer like you have everything else.' She spat the last words. It felt as if she hated me, and I wasn't even sure I could blame her.

I stayed silent, not wanting to commit to anything. I didn't want either to put her off or make promises. 'I'll contact a lawyer,' I finally said, and Heather nodded, her jaw set.

'Fine.'

It felt like I should leave, so I got up from the chair. I stopped, hesitant but also determined. 'Heather... can I see him?'

A long, tense silence. 'Fine,' she said finally. 'I'll tell the nurse.' Before I'd made it to the door Heather had curled up onto her side. I heard her gasping, tearing sobs, and I started to turn again.

'Go away,' she choked. It sounded as if she were being rent apart. 'Please, go *away*.'

It felt wrong to leave her like that, yet I could hardly force myself on her. And so I went, and a little while later, the nurse came and took me to the NICU nursery, all the plastic bassinets in a row, the babies tiny and swaddled and red. I knew him right away. I don't know how, I just did. And when he opened his eyes I felt myself fall. *My child. My son.* It seemed so simple, then. So right. Like it would all fall into place, just because it had to.

Isaac is bored with his iPad and so he starts drumming his legs against the back of my seat.

'Isaac,' I say, keeping my voice mild, 'easy.'

These visits are always so tense; they have been since that first, aching one, when I, exhausted and emotionally overwhelmed, both afraid and euphoric, brought a four-week-old Isaac to Heather's house. When he'd cried, which he'd done a lot of in those first fatigue-fogged weeks, her shirt grew damp patches and she'd laughed in embarrassment, but also in a sort of pleasure and pride.

'They gave me pills to dry up my milk, but I guess they don't work so good.' She held out her arms for Isaac; he was still in his car seat, dressed in a pale blue onesie, his scrawny, red legs akimbo, his little face screwed up for another one of his bleating shrieks. He couldn't take the bottle easily yet; I'd only had him at home for five days.

'Let me take him,' Heather said.

For a single, frozen second the words registered with both of us, and then, wordlessly, I handed her the car seat. I've gone back over that moment, which felt like stepping off a ledge into thin air. What if I'd refused? What if I'd said no, this won't work, I can't? I won't? But I couldn't have. Isaac was only twenty-eight days old. Heather still had seventeen days to change her mind, and we both knew that. I saw it in the steely glint of her eye, felt it in the tremble of my soul.

Of course, there have been many times since then that I could have refused. Those first few months, when she took him from me so possessively the second I came in the door, and told me all the things I was doing wrong? Laughed as she watched me fumble and said I couldn't hold a baby like a briefcase?

His first birthday, when Heather made a gooey chocolate cake and insisted on feeding it to him, smearing it all over his face? When he was two, and she gave him Sprite in a bottle? When he was five, and her little demon daughter Amy cut off all his hair and Heather just laughed and said he'd needed a haircut, he looked like a girl? They'd been his baby curls.

Or maybe after the ill-conceived vacation I was forced into last year, when Heather booked tickets for Disney World, including one for Isaac, without asking me. A week with her family, and she'd never even asked me if I minded, or checked if we were free. I'd struggled with what to do, how to respond, because I could see she was absolutely counting on this trip. Refusing to let Isaac go would destroy her, and no matter how resentful I felt, I couldn't make myself do that. So I decided on an awkward compromise; I went too, and ended up paying for a lot of it. Worst seven days of all our lives, or at least mine.

No one knew how to act with me and Isaac there; Kevin simmered with resentment, the girls kept shrieking and asking me for money for candy or games while they ignored Isaac. Heather clung to him, holding his hand when he obviously didn't want her to, insisting on going on all the rides with him, even when Isaac asked to go with me. Everything about it was awful, but I thought, stupidly of course, that maybe after that Heather would back off, be satisfied for once, but she only came closer, clinging, always clinging, always wanting more.

And now finally, it's been seven years. Seven *years*. And I've talked to a lawyer; a judge can legally enforce open adoption agreements but she thinks I have a strong, solid case to terminate, or at least limit, contact. I can show that the visits aren't beneficial to Isaac, because they're not. He doesn't like Heather, or her family, and that is not my fault.

'Almost there, Isaac,' I call back, and he groans and kicks my seat again. I don't mind. It's almost over. It has to be, because I really don't think I can take any more.

CHAPTER TWO

HEATHER

I am icing the cake in Minecraft green when Kevin comes into the kitchen.

'What is that?'

'A cake,' I answer, although it's obvious. 'For Isaac.' Minecraft is his favorite game. I managed to track down a little figurine of the character Steve from the game and placed it on top, along with the glittery candle in the shape of a seven.

Kevin looks at the cake for another moment and then looks away, saying nothing. I'm used to this by now, the silences that I've stopped trying to analyze. Is he angry? Bitter? Bored? Or maybe, after all these years, Kevin is just indifferent to our son. I really have stopped trying to guess.

'We're having pizza too,' I tell him as I squeeze another blob of green onto the cake. Last month all Isaac could talk about was Minecraft. That is, when he was talking. He tends to be pretty quiet during these visits, shy like Emma, but I always try to get him to open up, and sometimes I succeed. 'Can you get the sodas and put them on the table?'

I don't really need Kevin to do anything, but I want him to be involved. So often during these visits he just sits in his chair, sullen and silent, the way he used to be when his back was really bad.

I don't remember exactly when his back started getting a little better; it happened gradually, in small, hopeful increments. After

Lucy started school, he got another job, full-time, working the counter of a UPS store, and financially, after a couple of years, we just about managed to get ourselves on an even keel.

When Lucy was seven I got my high school diploma at night school and then took a course in computing at the community college.

It was a big step, and one I still feel proud of. Stacy supported me through it, picking up the girls when needed, taking up the slack with my mom, whose health has continued to flag and fail. She doesn't leave the house most days, and my dad can't manage on his own. We take it in turns, but Stacy did more for her – and me – then.

Kev supported me too, in his own way. The classes weren't cheap, but he never said a word. And he put his fair share of frozen pizzas in the oven when I was going out to one of them at night.

For the last three years I've worked as a receptionist for a small company that owns a couple of greeting card stores in the area. It's not much, just answering phones and doing some data entry, but the pay is much better than cleaning and I like wearing nice clothes to work: low heels and button-down blouses. It makes me feel like I've come up in the world a little bit, like I've managed to hold onto a dream amidst all the lost and broken ones.

Kevin grabs the two-liter bottle of Coke and puts it down on the dining room table with more force than necessary, not quite a slam. Again with the Mountain Dew. I focus on the cake. A few seconds later Lucy skips in, her angelic smile telling me that she's up to no good.

'Amy's left,' she announces proudly, always glad to be the bearer of grim news, and I can't keep from letting out a sigh.

'Left? What do you mean?'

'She's gone to meet her friends.' Lucy's eleven now, and she and Amy, who's fifteen, are usually bickering. Amy gets into trouble and Lucy tattles.

I squint as I try to finish the green piping on the cake. My fingers ache from kneading and squeezing the icing bag so hard. Lucy leans forward and takes a big swipe of icing with her finger.

'*Lucy.*'

'Is Amy going to get in trouble?'

'Maybe, but so are you for messing up the cake.'

'It's a gross color.'

'Thanks.' It *is* a gross color, but I know how much Isaac loves Minecraft. Every month I try to find something for him to like, to enjoy while he's here. Every month I try not to doubt myself and the decision I made seven years ago.

His birth was a blur, right from the moment my waters broke all over the carpet, and Aneta drove me to the hospital. A rush of doctors, tests, tubes, the pain squeezing the breath out of me, and I feared, the very life. The insistent *beep beep beep* of some monitor, and then how the beeps suddenly got faster and doctors began talking urgently, telling me I needed an emergency C-section. I felt as if I were seeing everything from afar, from behind a gauzy curtain. I wanted Kevin.

And then the next thing I knew they were putting up a little curtain so I couldn't see the mound of my own pregnant belly, and someone, a stranger, was holding my hand. I felt a weird, tugging sensation, everything moving too fast, and then the words I'll never forget: *You have a little boy.*

It jolted me, because I'd been expecting a girl, but then it didn't matter, boy or girl, because all I saw, all I thought, was *mine.* They laid him on my chest and he blinked up at me with those deep blue eyes and I saw myself in him. Of course he was mine. I didn't even think about Grace once. Not once, not even for a second. I just looked at my son and smiled and then I fell in love.

Maybe from that moment it should have been simple. Forget Grace. This was my *child*. He'd been ripped out of my body. I was never going to hand him over like something the mailman had delivered that I needed to pass on.

But then they took him to NICU and they wheeled me away, and my body throbbed and ached and I still hadn't talked to Kevin, and I remembered that I'd deposited that check for five grand, and some of it was already gone. Nothing seemed simple any more.

Kevin came later that morning, unshaven, his shirt buttoned wrong.

'Did you hear?' I gasped out and he nodded. Then I started to cry. I didn't mean to; I'd wanted to be strong, but I couldn't help it. I was so tired and absolutely everything hurt.

'Babe,' Kev said softly. He sounded torn, hurting the same way I was. 'Babe.' And then he climbed into the bed right next to me, gently, and even more gently, he took me into his arms. I cried into his shirt and Kev just held me.

We didn't talk much, even after my tears had subsided. I may have slept a little, and when I woke, Kev was still holding me. My stitches throbbed and I was so very tired, but I also felt just a little bit better, although I couldn't even say why.

'I didn't expect to feel like this,' I whispered.

Kev stroked my hair. 'I know.'

'I thought it would have been easier to give it up, if it was a girl, but I don't think it matters. Either way it's our baby, Kev.'

'I know.'

'What are we going to do?' I asked, and his fingers stilled on my hair.

'The same as we always were.'

That seemed incomprehensible to me, even as the truth thudded through me. Nothing had changed, and yet everything had. For me.

'Do you want to see him?' I asked, and Kevin stiffened.

'No,' he said after a moment. 'No, I don't want to.'

And stupidly perhaps, that hurt. After he left I asked the nurse to bring my boy to me. She said she couldn't, he was too little; he had to stay in the incubator. But she could take me to him, and so I struggled into a wheelchair, my body sagging and aching in ways it never had before, and then let myself be pushed to the NICU.

I knew him right away, even though I'd only seen him for a second, lying there on my chest. He was tiny and wizened and red, squalling and perfect, raging against life already. He had a tuft of light brown hair, a miniature cowlick, just like Kevin. And when he opened his eyes, I felt myself fall. *My child. My son.* It felt so simple, then. So right.

Later, the doctor came and told me he was doing well, but his lungs were weak and he was jaundiced. He'd have to stay in the hospital for a couple of weeks, and he might suffer from some complications later in life.

'Complications?' I stared at him fearfully.

'Premature babies often have a few health issues as they grow up,' he explained, his expression kind. 'But for the most part they can be managed, with the proper care and attention.'

Care and attention I doubt we could afford. He left me alone, and I lay in bed and stared at the wall and thought about my baby boy, and my three girls, and Kev and Grace. Everyone jumbled up together, but beyond the tight burn in my chest and the empty ache in my arms, I knew. I knew that just like Kevin had said, nothing had changed. I knew that Grace could provide this little boy with so much more than I could, including the medical care he might need. I knew that she would love him, and that if I kept him from her, I'd break her heart. I knew, even as I railed and raged against it, that he was hers, at least as much as he was mine. And I was the one who had made it that way.

So when Tina came and asked if Grace could see me, I said yes even though I didn't want to see her at all. I wasn't ready, but I needed to be. And that was when I thought of it, how Grace owed me something. Life owed me something. Maybe not a lot, not everything, but something, damn it. One afternoon a month. That felt reasonable to me. It felt fair.

The front door opens and I look up from the cake, my heart lifting, but of course it isn't Grace and Isaac. They always ring the doorbell, even though I've told them they don't have to.

'It's me,' Emma calls, sounding tired. She works every weekend at CVS, eight-hour shifts on both Saturday and Sunday. She comes into the kitchen, still quiet and shy at eighteen years old, and just finishing high school. In the fall she's planning to train as a nursing assistant, something I'm proud of although I was secretly hoping she might try for college. No one in my family has gone to college. No one's even thought of it. Who has that kind of money? That kind of drive?

'Oh.' Emma notices the cake. 'I forgot it was that Saturday.'

'How could you forget?' I ask, keeping my voice light. 'What do you think of my cake?' I stand back and survey the gray and green gloopy mess. The only thing to show it's Minecraft-themed is the figure of Steve on the top.

'Um... interesting?'

'Yeah, sure.' I sigh, wishing I could get it right sometimes. For the last seven years I've always felt like I'm just a little bit off with these visits. It was easy at the beginning, even though it hurt. Isaac was a baby, and I knew what to do with babies.

The first time I held him he curled right into me. I swear he smelled me as his mother. He knew me, no matter that it had been almost a month. He'd only been out of the hospital a week, and Grace was awkward with him. She hadn't got the hang of him; she held him as if he was going to break, as if he were one of her expensive pieces of crystal.

She watched as I rocked him, my hand curving around his back, my fingers tracing the tiny knobs of his spine. He snuffled against my neck and I breathed him in. I turned away from Grace and sang a lullaby to him, love swelling inside me as he relaxed against me, tiny eyelids fluttering closed.

I knew I was hurting Grace, and part of me was glad. I didn't care if it made me petty or wrong. Grace had her money and her job and her apartment; she had her son. At least I had this.

The next few visits I always played the expert, even though I knew it annoyed her. I told her when he was getting a tooth, when to start baby food, how to get him to sleep through the night. She was so uncertain, always doubting herself but never wanting my advice. Once I changed his diaper and made more fuss than I needed to about his diaper rash; she fought tears as I found the cream and applied it, clucking my tongue.

But then Isaac got a little older, and he went through a phase of being not just shy but terrified of us. Of me. I'd go to cuddle him and he'd back away, burying his head in Grace's knees, refusing even to look at me. Then she was the one who was smug, although she tried to hide it, at least a little. Not enough, though. Never enough. I could tell, and I wondered if it would always be a silent competition between us, a standoff over our son. I'd made it this way by insisting on these visits, and seven years later, I can't even be sorry.

Everyone else always seemed to fade into the background during these Saturday afternoons. Lucy, Amy, Emma, Kev. They're in the room, but I don't remember them. I remember Isaac, commando crawling toward the TV; then later, running around hyped-up on sugar, touching everything. I remember him playing Connect Four with me and how I'd slide the pieces in so slowly because I wanted the game to go on forever. By the next month he'd forgotten about Connect Four; I'd been waiting to play it with him again, counting on it, and he wouldn't even open the box.

And as he's got older, it's continued to be that way. I buy caramel popcorn only to find out he doesn't like it any more. The new *Cars* movie is has-been by the time he comes over to watch it, never mind that the DVD cost twenty bucks. I ask about the school play, his piano lessons, the trip to California, but by the time I catch up he's already moved on, losing interest, slipping out of my grasp. Still I try to hold on, even though it's hard. Even though part of me whispers one day I'll have to let go.

I don't think he's grown out of Minecraft, though. I've asked Lucy and she said kids still play it, like it. It was all he wanted to do the last time he was here; Grace let him have his iPad – he has his own – in the house, which annoyed me because I could barely get him to look up from the screen. The cake is starting to topple forwards, the icing sliding off in a gloopy avalanche, and I hurry to right it, before I turn to the oven to get the frozen pizzas ready.

'Emma, can you get the paper cups out?' I call, but she's already drifted away, probably hiding in her room. Two years ago we could finally afford to move from the two-bedroom house that was so tiny for us. We now rent a three-bedroom duplex on First Avenue, a little bit away from the old neighborhood, new schools for the kids. We needed the change, and the space is great. I'm proud to have Grace and Isaac in this home, with its wood floors and fresh paint – well, once, anyway – and the back porch with the swing. It's a nice house, a good home, even if Grace's is far better.

The doorbell rings, and as always my heart tumbles inside my chest. I'm so nervous and excited for these visits, every single time. It never gets old; it never feels familiar.

I hurry to the door, past Kevin, who is sitting in his chair, the same old La-z-Boy I wanted to throw out when we moved, but he wouldn't let me. It was good for his back, he said.

'Grace, Isaac!' I give them both big smiles; Isaac is standing a little bit behind Grace, who is holding a gold carrier bag with rope handles. She always comes with gifts – wine or chocolate or cheese, things that are too expensive to taste good. She brought artisanal chocolates once that the girls all spat out, right in front of her, brown drool dripping down their chins. I apologized for them, but the chocolates did taste bad, like dirt. It almost feels as if she is showing us up, pointing out again and again how we're different.

'Hi, Heather.' As always, Grace sounds dutiful. She puts a hand on Isaac's shoulder and steers him forward. 'Say hello, Isaac.'

'Hi,' he mutters, hanging his head, his hair sliding into his face, and I act like he's just given me a big hug. What else can I do?

'Hey, Isaac. I'm so happy to see you.' And then, because I can't not do it, I lean forward and gently put my arms around his skinny shoulders. He's so like Kev, with the same floppy brown hair and hazel eyes, the slight build – although he might muscle up later. Kev did, at least a little bit.

I wonder if Kev has noticed the likeness; he hardly ever looks directly at Isaac, except when I urge them to do something together, like play a board game or go outside and throw a ball. I flap my hands, pushing them toward each other, and they obey, hesitantly, silently, but my heart still sings.

And it nearly bursts when, on rare occasions, Kevin and Isaac relax into a game of catch or checkers, and I catch Kev's slow smile, the flash of pleasure in Isaac's eyes. I feel then that I almost have everything I've ever wanted, and yet I know it's nothing more than a moment. Amy, in a spate of fury, once demanded what I wanted from these visits with Isaac. 'Do you want him back?' she asked. 'Or do you just want us gone?'

Typical of Amy, to make it about her. Of course she'd feel slighted when this has never been about my girls. I've given my whole life to them; Isaac only gets a couple of hours. Such a small amount of time; I just want it to feel like enough.

Grace hands me the gold-corded bag and Isaac shuffles inside, head ducked low.

'Amy's gone out, but Lucy and Emma are here,' I say brightly. Too brightly. 'And Kevin, of course.' Early on, I tried to get Isaac

to call me Aunt Heather and Kev Uncle Kevin, and while Grace
didn't refuse, she never insisted or introduced us that way, and
somehow it's fallen by the wayside, like a thousand other things.
It doesn't feel right to try for it now.

'Emma,' I call. I peek in the gold bag and see a bottle of sparkling wine, something Kev will never drink. I tell myself Grace
means well, but sometimes I wonder. After seven years, has she
not noticed that Kev only drinks beer and I barely drink at all?

Lucy skids into the room and gives Isaac a challenging look.
Nearly five years apart, they've had an on-again, off-again friendship over the years. When Isaac was a cute baby, a chubby toddler,
the girls couldn't get enough of him. They'd plop him down on
the living room carpet and lie on their bellies all around him,
handing him toys, enraptured by his cuteness.

Then he got older, and older still, and everything started to
get more and more awkward. The girls drifted away. I tried too
hard. And Grace continues to endure.

'Let me get you a drink,' I say in the same too-bright tone I can't
seem to ever switch off when they visit. 'Coke? Mountain Dew?'

'I'm sorry, Isaac's off soda,' Grace says firmly. 'He needed a
filling at the dentist a couple of weeks ago, so we're really trying
to limit the sugar.'

'Okay.' How many moments like this have I endured, having
to bow down to Grace's over-the-top dictates? No sugar. No soda.
No peanut butter, *just in case* he had a nut allergy. He didn't.
No screen time, except when she brings in his iPad. No violent
games, never mind it was only a couple of water pistols on a hot
summer's day. No PG movies, even though I'd checked, and there
was nothing too bad in it.

I grit my teeth and go along with it, because I know I don't
have much choice. I don't have any choice. 'Would you like
something else, Isaac?' Of course I don't have anything else.
'Water or milk?'

Isaac shakes his head. He's kicking his feet in his hundred-dollar Nikes, head still bent, refusing to look at me. I try not to mind. He's still little, still so small. I suppress the ache to slide my fingers through his hair, his bangs out of his eyes.

'The pizzas are in the oven so dinner shouldn't be too long.' He's been here five minutes and I'm already feeling like I need to fill up the time. 'Lucy, why don't you get some games out?'

Lucy shrugs and then goes to the living room cupboard that's stuffed with board games, most of them in tattered boxes, missing pieces or dice, or both. 'You wanna play Monopoly?' she asks Isaac, who shrugs right back at her.

I turn to Grace, determined to remain upbeat. 'Grace? Something to drink?'

'I'm fine.' She never has anything to drink. Whatever food I make, she barely nibbles. It's like she can't get out of here fast enough, and while I accept that, she could try a little harder. Pretend, at least, for Isaac's sake if not for mine.

'So, how are you?' I ask as I move into the kitchen, one eye on Lucy and Isaac, who are setting up a battered Monopoly board on the living room coffee table.

'I'm fine.' Something about Grace's tone makes me turn to look at her, waiting for more. 'Actually, Heather, there is something I want to talk to you about.'

'Oh?' Already I don't like the sound of this. Her voice has gone all officious, like she's at a board meeting. She glances back at Isaac and Lucy playing their game, Kev in his chair, then she moves closer to me and lowers her voice.

'The truth is, I've been thinking about our visits here, mine and Isaac's, and how… productive they are, and I think perhaps it's time to… disengage a bit.'

'Disengage?' My heart thumps in my chest. 'What do you mean, exactly?'

'It's just…' Grace takes a quick breath, stepping even closer to me and lowering her voice to little more than a whisper. 'It's been seven years, Heather. That's a long time. And I think now it would be better for Isaac, for me, and even for you, if we visited… less.'

'Less.' I feel the first flare of rage, masking a far worse hurt. It's one afternoon a month, I'm hardly dominating their lives.

'Yes, less.' Grace sounds strident now. 'Maybe every three months, for a little while? And then, maybe every six?'

'And then what?' I snap. 'Never?'

'This isn't sustainable, Heather. I'm sorry, but it isn't.' Grace folds her arms, looking stubborn and mutinous, and suddenly I hate her with a viciousness that curls my hands into claws, makes me itch to slap her. She has everything, and she still wants more. This was how I felt seven years ago, and it's how I feel now. Nothing ever changes, no matter how hard I try.

Looking at Grace, I realize she's been waiting for this moment, and in a totally different, awful way, so have I.

CHAPTER THREE

GRACE

Three interminable hours later I climb into my SUV, Isaac scrambling into the back. I rest my forehead on the steering wheel, feeling too exhausted even to start the car.

'Mom.' Isaac huffs out an impatient breath. 'Let's *go*.'

'Okay.' I raise my head and turn the ignition, pulling away from the curb and the McClearys' house with a sigh of relief. As always, I'm happy to leave, but tonight I feel an uncomfortable prickling of guilt along with the vast relief. When I told Heather I wanted to curtail our visits, she looked, for a second, as if I'd just ripped her heart out. And the truth is, I knew I had.

I pretended to myself that she would be expecting it, maybe she'd even agree. But I knew I'd blindsided her with my request. She's been deceiving herself so desperately all along, that these visits work, that Isaac enjoys them. And, to be fair, he has had some good moments through the years. It hasn't all been an endurance test for him. Just for me. After I told Heather my intention we didn't talk about it at all. She just lifted her chin and went on her merry, determined way, chirping to Isaac about the pizza and the cake, which looked like a complete disaster. When Heather brought it in so proudly, icing the color of cement sliding off the top, Isaac looked horrified, although he tried to hide it.

'Minecraft,' she explained proudly, because I'm sorry, it wasn't obvious.

Isaac glanced at me uncertainly; it was clear he didn't want to eat it.

'It looks delicious,' I said, giving him a pointed look. We'd all have to try a piece. That's how these visits always went.

'You still play Minecraft, don't you?' Heather asked in that same chirpy voice. She'd started cutting the pieces and they were falling apart, gray icing oozing everywhere like glutinous cement.

'Umm…' Isaac glanced at me, looking for instruction, but I wasn't sure what was wrong this time. 'I play Clash of Clans now,' he admitted in a low voice, a hint of apology in his tone.

'Oh.' Heather's face fell. I would have felt more sorry for her if she hadn't basically shut down my request for limiting visits.

Isaac pushed his cake around on his plate and didn't eat more than a bite, despite Heather's repeated urgings.

'Sorry, Mom,' Lucy said as she pushed her own plate away. 'But it does look kind of gross.'

Kevin, who hardly utters a syllable during these visits, gave his daughter a glower. 'It's delicious, Lucy.' He glanced at me, just as pointedly, and I looked away. I'd eaten the damn cake, or at least most of it.

Heather rose from the table, her lips trembling. 'I'll get some ice cream.'

On and on it went, everything stilted and awkward and wrong. Emma came out after we'd finished eating and gave Isaac an awkward wave; it was clear she'd been hiding in her bedroom the whole time. Right as we were leaving, Amy swanned in, fifteen years old and smelling of cigarettes and beer. I've watched her get wilder and wilder over the years, and Kev and Heather don't seem to notice. Maybe they don't care.

'Hey, Isaac,' she smirked, ignoring me, and then flounced past us into the kitchen, where she took a carton of juice from the fridge and swigged from it. Eventually we were able to scuttle out, breathe silent sighs of relief. Another month down.

Neither of us talk on the way home; we're always subdued on this drive, exhausted by the emotional energy Heather drains from us both. Isaac reminds me of my promise for ice cream, but since he had some at Heather's I tell him he can have frozen yogurt instead. He accepts, and I pick up some from the Pinkberry on the corner before we head thankfully home.

After our frozen yogurt, Isaac disappears into his room with his iPad and I try to think of my next steps – refuse a visit? Contact my lawyer? – but I already feel defeated. This is one battle I know I will have to fight, just as I know it will be painful and exhausting, and not just for me. I feel almost as badly for Heather, knowing the pain I will cause her. Knowing I will have to cause it. And what about Isaac? The last thing I want him to feel is as if he's in the middle being pulled in two directions, and yet of course he is.

I go to the kitchen and pour myself a glass of wine. I close my eyes and take a long sip, savoring the cool crispness. I finish the glass and pour myself another one. I deserve it, at least today: the one day a month I always dread and somehow survive.

I wander into my study, the little cramped maid's room that used to house the boxes of my father's stuff, and sit in front of my laptop. I can't quite summon the energy to turn it on, check my emails, find out how the markets are doing. I've come a long way since those days when I was so driven and determined to be at the top. A long way down, but it's a price I've always been willing to pay.

After I lost the partnership to Jill, I was, predictably, shunted to the sidelines, condemned to a lifetime of searching out the next big deal so someone higher up could take credit. It was a demotion, no question, and Bruce and all the other partners were just waiting for me to leave. The trouble was, I couldn't. Not with Isaac. No way could I start over, log all the hours again, fight my way back up.

So I stayed mid-level, just as my dad did, and I told myself it was fine. I still made enough money to keep my apartment, pay for a nanny, and then later the outrageous school tuition – over forty grand a year for Buckley. But it's not a given; it's not *easy*. The life I'd wanted for both of us never quite materialized, but that's okay. We still have more than most. We still have plenty. And I have the most important thing, the best thing: my son.

When I think back to what I expected, what I hoped for all those years ago, I almost want to laugh. Either that or cry, or maybe just sigh and shake my head over my total naïve stupidity. I intended to take two weeks off when Isaac was born. Two *weeks*. Was I crazy? Or just completely deluded?

Losing the partnership was a mixed blessing, because at least without that tempting and expensive carrot dangling in front of me I didn't feel too guilty about taking another two weeks off after the first two, and thanks to Jill, I let everyone know I'd adopted a son.

I'll never forget the exhausted craziness of those first few weeks, even though the moments have all merged together, a blur of wonder and fear and intense joy. Isaac was in the hospital for three weeks, while I attempted to work, going to and from the hospital to visit him, trying to bond from behind a plate glass window. When he was eight days old they let me hold him.

Heather had signed the surrender papers five days before, and then she'd been discharged from the hospital. It was as if she'd vanished, and I was so relieved. I even convinced myself that the whole open adoption plan she'd come up with wouldn't materialize; she'd think better of it.

Then I took Isaac home, needing one of the NICU nurses to buckle him into the car seat because I couldn't figure out the straps. I felt totally unequipped in every possible way. I'd never changed a diaper. I'd barely held a baby before him, and I'd only held Isaac a handful of times, with nurses looking on, gently correcting me, reminding me to support his tiny head, fragile as a robin's egg, his pulse throbbing through his skull.

I'd once imagined that when I brought Isaac home there would be an army to support me – baby nurse, nanny, competent officials to surround me and keep us both safe, guide me through it all. It didn't happen that way. The baby nurse, who had postponed to start with, backed out completely when she learned that Isaac had health issues – a heart murmur that needed monitoring and weak lungs that haven't given him any trouble except a touch of asthma over the years.

Dorothy was visiting her grandchildren in Chicago until the last week of May, when she was meant to have been starting, so for those first two weeks I was entirely on my own, and it felt like being launched into outer space. I wanted to bond with my boy but when I took him out of the car seat into the yawning emptiness of my apartment, I felt as if I were holding a cross between a Ming vase and a stick of dynamite.

I held him against my chest, so scrawny and small, and tiptoed into the nursery, everything feeling fragile, like the moment was a bubble – beautiful, translucent, and easily broken. I eased into the rocking chair as I cradled him like a football, terrified I was going to break him; that he was going to cry, that I wouldn't know what to do.

Then I looked down into his face and saw how he blinked up at me, studying me so seriously, and my heart ached with love and thankfulness and a deep, abiding joy. I'd learn. This would become familiar, easy. He was mine. Of course he was mine.

I'd already decided on his name, unorthodox as it might have seemed: Isaac, the Hebrew name meaning laughter. It was a nod to my father's Jewish mother, despite my completely privileged, Protestant upbringing. I wanted to give my son some of his history, ground him in the truth of my family, my lineage. Heather made a face when she heard his name, not the good Irish name she'd probably wanted, but I wasn't going to back down. He was my son now.

Still, she played on my early fears during those first visits. Every laughing criticism made me flinch, doubt myself even more. Wonder if I'd ever get this right, if I'd ever be a good mom, no matter how much I tried.

It's been a long time since I've struggled with how to open a stroller, or had to have Heather help me give Isaac some antibiotics one visit when I couldn't get him to take a spoonful, but I feel like at each visit with Heather still takes a little something from me. And more importantly, she takes something from Isaac. He feels torn, uncertain; as he's grown older he's sensed the tension and sometimes the downright hostility between us, and it worries him. More and more he's asked why we have to go, and my answers don't satisfy him. I'm doing this for his sake as much as my own. If these visits worked for Isaac, I'd keep them going. At least, I hope I'd be a strong and good enough person to do that.

Outside twilight is falling on Central Park in full bloom – daffodils waving their yellow-orange heads in neatly tended flower beds, cherry buds in full, blowsy blossom. I try to summon a pleasure in the sight, but I'm still feeling on edge from my conversation with Heather. I don't want to go the way of lawsuits and acrimony, but I know I will if I have to. The knowledge lodges like a stone in my stomach.

I go to find Isaac; he's lying on his stomach on his bed, the iPad propped in front of him, chin in his hands.

'Time for bed, bud,' I say gently. He looks up, blinking me into focus, and then he smiles, a grin that steals my heart every time. I'll never get tired of it.

'Can we have a story?'

'Of course. *Wimpy Kid* or *Captain Underpants*?'

'Both?' he asks hopefully and I smile, that edginess starting to fade. It's a whole month until the next visit, and maybe it won't happen at all.

'Sure,' I say, and I toss Isaac his pajamas before reaching for a book. 'Why not?'

Monday begins with the usual chaotic crazy of my working week, navigating school drop-off and getting to work, leaving a note for Dorothy outlining Isaac's many afterschool activities. Since he started school two years ago, I had to reduce Dorothy's hours; I couldn't justify paying her for a full working week when she picks him from school at half past three. I'm not making that kind of money, not really. I made it up to her by finding a working mom from Isaac's old school who needed daytime care for her baby. We nanny share and so far it's worked out well, thank God, because I don't know what I'd do without Dorothy.

As soon as I get to the office I try to put all mom thoughts to the back of my mind – the science project due next week; the yellow belt Isaac's working toward in Taekwondo; the reciprocal play date I should have scheduled last week. So often I think of Joanne's warning when we had dinner together all those years ago – *Kids always mean time off.* I didn't believe her; I chose not to, but of course she was right.

Before Isaac was three months old I had taken four extra personal days. One for that first pediatrician's appointment I didn't want to miss, then when he had a febrile seizure and had to go to ER before he was six weeks old; again when Dorothy had a stomach bug and couldn't come in, and finally because I was just so exhausted.

Even now there's always something – sick days, doctor's appointments, teacher's meetings. I don't begrudge any of it, of course I don't, but sometimes it's hard. There are only so many favors you can call in, so many people you can ask.

And the truth is, there aren't that many people in our lives. Single parenthood and a demanding job make maintaining a social life a challenge. When Isaac was little I took one morning off a week for a while to join a baby group, and I met some nice moms, but our lives were so different – they all stayed at home – that in the end I stopped going.

When he started preschool, it got better. At the Hebrew Montessori I made a couple of friends; there were play dates, and moms' nights out, and organized trips to the Central Park Zoo or the Children's Museum. Having a child feels like an automatic entry into a club; I share knowing smiles with other moms at the playground, I catch someone's eye as I swing hand in hand with Isaac when we walk down the street, and feel the gratitude expand in my chest that I'm finally part of something bigger than myself. Something wonderful. And now, with Isaac starting at Buckley, there are new friends. I've only known Stella for the better part of a year but she and her family already feel integral to my life.

There might not be a lot of people in my life, but there are enough. There's Isaac.

I make it to the office at quarter to nine, which is late by Bruce Felson's standards, never mind that he often breezes in at ten, only to take a two-hour lunch at noon and come back smelling like booze. That's the partner's life, not mine.

My corner office is gone; they claimed it was because of the full-floor renovation a couple of years back, but I knew the truth. Everyone did. I wasn't going anywhere, not up and not out, and so I stagnated in the smallest office I'd ever been in since I started at Harrow and Heath, crouched over my computer, researching start-ups that, just like me, were destined for nowhere.

It was so much less than what I once hoped for, and yet in a bittersweet way it made me think of my dad. Did he give up a promising career to put me first, when my mother got sick when I was so little? I don't actually know. He never said, and to my shame I never asked. But now I wonder, and if it is true, I know he would say it was worth it, in an instant. Just as I would. I don't have that old ambition any more. Most days I don't miss it.

Occasionally I torment myself with the what-ifs. Never for more than a second or two, and those seconds shame me. But yes, I have them, just as I believe every working mother does. How can we not? You give up everything – baking cookies, being promoted. No woman can have it all, and so essentially you end up with two halves of nothing, always feeling inadequate even as you know you wouldn't change a thing.

I push such pointless thoughts away as I sit at my desk on Monday morning, pry open the lid of my daily skim latte and breathe in the comforting steam. I have two start-ups to research – a personal stylist app that's probably no different than a dozen others that have sprouted up in recent years, except perhaps a bit flashier, and a company started by a woman in her mid-fifties in Indiana, selling child-friendly kitchen gadgets out of her garage.

I'm particularly taken with the self-heating knife to cut butter and the no-blade fruit slicer, all the quirky tools in fun, bright colors that appeal to kids.

It's the kind of company that Harrow and Heath wouldn't look at for a moment –grassroots, woman-led, family-oriented. I'm amazed it's even appeared on my radar, but Betty Mills has got a lot of good press lately – just local and indie stuff, but still. I sip my latte and wonder if presenting this kind of company to the partners would tank my career even more. Do I have any lower to fall? Do I care?

Sara is still with me at least; she stayed even when it was obvious I was being sidelined, and then demoted. She pokes her head into my office to tell me my meeting with a hopeful start-up tech company, a dime a dozen these days, is waiting.

At lunch my cell rings and I see it's Dorothy. A tightness starts in my chest – a sign of my rising blood pressure. Please, please let her not be calling in sick. Not last minute.

She isn't, I find out seconds later. She's quitting.

'I'm sorry,' Dorothy says, and she does sound genuinely regretful, a hint of tears in her voice. She's been with Isaac his whole life. 'But my daughter's getting divorced. She needs all the help she can get.'

'You're moving,' I state numbly, even though it's obvious. My mind spins. I've always counted on Dorothy, the one constant in our lives.

'Yes. I have to move to Chicago.'

'Chicago…'

'I'm sorry,' Dorothy says again. 'She called me this morning. I didn't realize how bad it had become, with—well…' Dorothy sighs heavily. She's told me a bit about her daughter over the years; the husband's a drinker, three little kids, a history of depression. 'She needs me, Grace. I'm sorry. I'm flying out on Thursday.'

'I understand, Dorothy, of course I do…' But *Thursday*? That's in three days. What on earth am I going to do?

'I know it's not much warning,' Dorothy says hurriedly. 'But I have to. My daughter… she's not doing well, Grace. I really am sorry. I wish I could give you more notice.'

After the call I sit there, my phone in my hand, reeling. Dorothy, gone. Just like that, after seven years. She taught Isaac to walk, she took him to toddler groups, she sat by his bedside through childhood fevers and a frightening bout of pneumonia when his lungs took a serious beating. She's been there as much as I have and, if I'm torturously honest, sometimes more. And now, just like that, she's gone.

I can't even think how Isaac will react, and more urgently, what's going to happen after Thursday. Hiring a nanny takes weeks, if not months. I'm in serious trouble.

I don't have time to think about it, though, because work has to take priority if I want to keep the job I do have, never mind any chance of upward mobility. That night I get home by six thirty, early for me, already exhausted even though it's only Monday.

Dorothy meets me at the door the moment she hears my key in the lock. 'Everything all right?' I ask, and she nods.

'Yes, I've just got to leave on time tonight, with my trip to plan.'

I lower my voice. 'Have you told Isaac?'

Dorothy shakes her head. 'No, I wanted to wait. You let me know what you want to do.' She smiles comfortingly, the way she has when I've felt clueless and panicked, when I looked to her the way I would have to my mom, to tell me what to do, or at least to tell me I'm doing okay.

'Right. Okay. I'll tell him tonight.' I gulp at the thought. I need to get Dorothy a parting gift, and make Isaac write a card, and right then it all feels like too much. I haven't ever really wanted a husband, a full-time partner, but occasionally I'd like to be able to say to someone 'You do it'.

I haven't dated once since having Isaac. There hasn't been the time, and I've never felt the need. I'm used to being alone in that way, and I have Isaac. But occasionally I feel the absence, and I wish things had turned out a little differently. That there had been someone, that I'd found him. But mostly I tell myself it doesn't matter, because Isaac and I are a team.

As it turns out Isaac doesn't seem to mind Dorothy leaving all that much. He blinks and nods, and I gaze into his serious, little face, wanting him to understand the import.

'Isaac, do you understand what I'm saying? Dorothy's moving away to be with her daughter. We're not going to see her any more.'

'I know.' He stares at me, wide-eyed and accepting, utterly unruffled, and it bothers me a little. I would have preferred tears, even a tantrum. At moments like this I have to keep myself from being reminded of Kevin, that blank-eyed stare, the hint of surly impatience in the set of his mouth. I hate those reminders, that his genes aren't mine, that someone else's blood flows through him, that maybe I can't shape him the way I want to.

'Okay. I thought maybe you could make her a card.'

'Okay.'

I put one hand on his shoulder, wanting to anchor him in place, in the importance of this moment. 'Why don't I get out the markers and some cardstock? You can make it in the kitchen.'

In the end the card is only half-made, and I do the kind of thing I once thought I'd never do – I finish it, sloppily, so it looks like Isaac's work. I don't even feel guilty.

On Thursday I arrange a dinner for the three of us, but Dorothy's flight leaves at eight and so we end up bolting through it, everything feeling rushed instead of important.

I give her Isaac's card, and a card from me, and a gift card as a going away present, but what I really want to do is hug her, cling to her, beg her not to go. Losing her feels like being cut away from my anchor so I'm free-floating in a foreign sea.

She's the closest thing I have to a mom, someone whose calm, comfortable capability has soothed me over the last seven years. She has talked me down from the ledge of helicopter parenting more than once, boomed out her big belly laugh when I've stressed about things that definitely don't need stressing about, like whether Isaac is getting enough Omega-3 in his diet or if he should learn a second musical instrument.

'Child,' she'd say, clapping a great big hand on my shoulder, 'you don't need to worry about a thing like that.'

I'll miss her so much. I'm scared to be a mother without her in the background, my safety net for sick days or sudden, panicked requests for advice or reassurance.

'Keep in touch,' I tell her as she heaves herself up from the sofa. 'Please. And if you do decide to come back to New York…'

'You'll have someone by then,' Dorothy says with one of her easy smiles. 'You'll be fine, you and Isaac. Right, my little man?' She puts her arms around him and Isaac gives her a quick hug, still looking unfazed. And in that moment I realize he doesn't remind me of Kevin; he reminds me of me I was around Isaac's age, when my mother went into the hospital for the first bout of intensive chemo. I remember my father telling me to hug her, and I did quickly, squirming away before she'd let go because I was afraid and it all felt so strange. Maybe that's what Isaac is feeling.

He catches my eye and I give him a reassuring smile. It's going to be okay. The two of us, a team, against the world. Just like me and my dad. That's how it's been; that's how it will be now.

Moments later Dorothy is gone, and I stand in the doorway after the elevator doors have closed, unwilling even now to accept that she has left for good. I've made a call to the agency I used to hire her but I haven't even seen any applications yet. Tomorrow Isaac is going to Stella's after school, but after that I don't know what I'll do. I can't depend on Stella every day; in any case, Will and his brother have about a billion after-school activities. I suppose it will have to be after-school club for Isaac, although that always feels like the garbage can of childcare solutions, a bunch of lonely-looking boys stuck in a classroom until seven at night.

Then my phone rings, and with a wave of trepidation I see that it's Heather.

'Heather?' I try to keep my voice light and bright, as if I didn't give her a pretty devastating ultimatum four days ago. 'What's up?'

'Grace.' She sounds serious, even grim. 'We need to talk.'

CHAPTER FOUR

HEATHER

I don't tell Kevin or the girls about Grace's request to halt Isaac's visits. Not right away, at least, mainly because I'm just trying to absorb it myself, but also because I'm scared. I don't want to hear what they think. Not, at least, until I know what I'm going to do.

I end up telling Stacy, because while it's not always easy to hear her plain-speaking advice, she's sensible and she's on my side. At least, she's not on Grace's side. She's never been bowled over by Grace's glamour, not like the girls were when they were little, trying on her lipsticks and touching the buttery-soft leather of her bag. Kevin, of course, has never liked Grace; in fact, he's liked her less and less as the years have gone on.

As for me… every time she talked about my son in those first few weeks, it took everything I had not to ball my hands into fists and scream at her to give him back to me. I certainly thought about it many times. I envisioned it, almost relished the look of shock and despair I knew I'd see on her face. I pictured plucking my baby out of her arms, as easy as that. It was my right. For six whole weeks, it was my right.

Of course nothing is ever that simple. The night before I signed the papers, I asked the nurse to bring Isaac to me. She resisted, because he was still in the NICU, but I just wanted a few minutes with my child, and she knew about the adoption.

So she wheeled him in, and I held my son for the first and last time. I cradled him like a football, his head resting against my knees. He blinked up at me, scrawny and frog-like and so very beautiful. I stroked his petal-soft skin, I traced his faint eyebrows, the bow curve of his little lips. I memorized him, imprinted him on me.

'I love you,' I whispered, so only he could hear. 'I love you. That's why I am doing this. I hope you realize that one day. I hope you understand it.' He began to squirm, and I hefted him gently; he was so very light. 'You're going to have a good life,' I told him. 'A happy life. And I'll still see you. You won't forget me.' I kissed him then, and I put him back in the bassinet, and the nurse wheeled him away while my cracked heart broke in pieces all around me.

The next morning I signed the papers, and then I left the hospital, and it felt as if someone had just snipped the strings that had been holding me up. I went back home, surrounded by Kev and the girls, everyone needing me in different ways; I wanted to fill up my hours taking care of them, but I was so tired and I felt as if I were viewing the world through a cloudy haze. I stayed in bed, letting the world unravel around me, for as long as I could.

After a few days Kev's patience and goodwill ran out, and Lucy started wetting the bed again, and Amy was suspended from school for two days for hitting some kid. I didn't have time to indulge my grief. I put it away, and I soldiered on, waiting for that first visit, counting on it to sustain me. And it almost did.

Now, sitting across from Stacy in her pretty kitchen with the fake granite countertops and colorful stencils on the walls, I tell her about the conversation with Grace. She raises her eyebrows but I can tell she's not surprised.

'So she finally worked up the courage to say something,' she says when I'm finished, and I flinch. Even Stacy didn't have to be that blunt. She's supported me since I was pregnant, even though her kind of love has been tough sometimes. She babysat the girls when I was sore and aching, recovering from the Caesarean; she accepted it when I insisted on the open adoption, although I could tell she felt cautious. She's even met Isaac a couple of times, and been cheerful and friendly, easy-going in a way that helped everyone else. But I can tell she's going to give me a dose of her older sister know-it-allness now, and I'm not sure I'm ready for it.

'You think she's wanted this all along?' I ask.

Stacy sighs and shakes her head. 'Oh, Heather. Of course she has. Why wouldn't she?'

'Plenty of people have open adoptions, and the relationships are all positive and healthy.' I read that in a book, but still.

Stacy shrugs. 'Maybe somewhere that's true,' she says, but she sounds doubtful.

I sip my coffee, squinting outside at her yard with its trampoline and above-ground swimming pool. Mike got a new job six years ago, and he and Stacy moved to a bigger house, better neighborhood. Up and up.

'I'm just surprised it took her this long,' Stacy says. 'I mean, seven years. She's been bringing Isaac to you for a long time, Heather.'

'You sound as if it's been so terrible for her.'

'Don't most birth parents lose touch after a little while, even in those so-called open adoptions? I mean, a couple of phone calls and photos, whatever. But, Heather…' Stacy looks at me seriously, the same look she gave me when she told me I was going to regret all this. And I did. How I did. Still I'm not ready to hear whatever it is she has to say. 'I think this could actually be a good thing, if you let it be.' Her voice is gentle, and that makes it worse.

'A *good* thing?' I swallow hard, trying not to show how hurt I am. 'How on earth could it be a good thing?'

'Heather…' Stacy leans forward, coffee cup forgotten, her elbows on the table. 'I'm not trying to hurt you, but you know, you've been kind of… obsessed with Isaac. Since you gave him up.'

'Obsessed? I have not been *obsessed*.'

'A little bit,' Stacy persists. 'Come on, even you can admit it.'

'How can you be a little bit obsessed?'

'I just mean, these visits. Every single month. Didn't Grace once call and ask to skip because Isaac was sick?'

'No, because he was tired.' I press my lips together. It had been such a lame excuse. He'd had a science fair on Friday night, and then a soccer match on the Saturday morning. He was worn out, Grace said. He couldn't take much more. She made it sound as if visiting us –me – would be this great big burden he had to bear. And maybe it was for Grace. But it didn't have to be for Isaac. So I played hardball and said they still had to come. That *tired* wasn't a good enough reason.

It was dangerous, playing that game, because I was playing a trump card I didn't actually have. What if Grace called my bluff? What if she said no, they still weren't coming? What would I do? What am I going to do now? My head hurts thinking about it all. My heart hurts.

'But, Heather…' There is far too much sympathy in my sister's eyes. 'Did you honestly think this was going to carry on forever?'

Forever? No, of course not. Nothing lasts forever. I know that, and yet… I hadn't let myself imagine an endpoint to this. To Isaac and me. A time when I would see him less, and then not at all. Just the thought of it gives my heart a wrench, like a giant hand has reached into my chest. I picture him on my chest, bloody and new. The first time I held him, and he snuffled into my neck. When he was a chubby, complacent baby, balanced on my hip. And then later, five, six, now seven years old. The tentative strides I've made, playing Connect Four, talking about Minecraft. I know how little it seems. How little it is. And yet it matters so very much to me. How can I let it go now?

'Heather,' Stacy says, and now she sounds stern, 'you have three beautiful girls who need you as their mother.'

'They have me as their mother,' I snap. 'And if you're going to, for one second, tell me I'm not a good mom because of one Saturday afternoon a month…'

'It's not just the Saturday afternoons.'

'Yes, it is.' The words are ripped from me, savagely. 'Trust me, it is.'

'But it isn't,' Stacy says in that awful, gentle voice. 'I'm not even there and I feel it. The week before he visits you're hyped up on plans, rushing out to buy special ingredients or presents, whatever. And the week after you're down in the dumps, moping around—'

'I'm not *moping*—'

'That's how it feels, Heather. Mom's said the same thing—'

'*Mom?* Mom's met Isaac once.' A couple of years ago, for his fourth birthday. I had all my family over, and Grace wasn't pleased. She didn't say anything, acted like it was so nice for Isaac to meet his birth relatives, but I could tell. I can always tell when I've pissed her off.

'This isn't about Isaac so much as it's about you, and how you are. How everyone around you feels you are. Ask Kevin if you don't believe me.'

'You've talked to Kevin about this?'

'No.' Stacy sighs. 'But ask him and see what he says.'

But I don't want to do that, not yet.

When I get back home, the kitchen is a mess, music is blaring from Emma and Amy's room, and Lucy is in tears.

'Amy called me a little fucker,' she wails, and I briefly close my eyes.

'Amy!' I bawl, knowing my daughter can hear me even over the blaring rock music with its pulsing techno beat. No answer. 'Get out here!' Still nothing. '*Now!*'

After several taut seconds Amy wrenches open her door and slouches out of her room, her expression managing to be both indifferent and defiant. 'What?'

I stare at her face. 'Were you wearing that much make-up at school?' Because she definitely wasn't when she left for school this morning.

Amy just shrugs. She's wearing heavy pancake foundation and thick dark eyeliner, blood-red lipstick. She looks like a slutty vampire.

'You know you're not allowed to wear that much make-up,' I say, although I don't know why I bother. Amy won't bother replying, and what am I going to do about it? I ball my fists. 'Don't call your sister names, especially swear words.'

Amy flicks a scornful glance at Lucy and folds her arms, still saying nothing. Silence is her best weapon, and suddenly it enrages me.

'You speak respectfully,' I shriek, and for once I get a response. Amy's eyes widen a fraction and her lip curls.

'Fine,' she says. 'What do you want me to say?'

'Why did you call Lucy such a rude name?' Except that isn't the question I wanted to ask, because it doesn't matter why. There's no reason good enough.

'Because she's so annoying.'

Lucy lets out a little shriek of protest and fury floods through me again. '*Amy*! You can't – you can't say things like that.'

Amy arches an eyebrow that is too dark and sculpted to look remotely real. Where does she get all this make-up, anyway? She doesn't have the money, and no one else in the house wears this kind of stuff. I certainly don't. 'Why not?' she challenges me, sounding almost smug. 'It's true.'

'That's it.' My temper snaps with an almost audible sound; I feel it thrumming through my head. 'I'm taking away your phone.'

Amy looks furious for a second, as furious as I am, and then she shrugs. She slips her hand into her pocket and takes out the Nokia brick that is all we can afford. 'Fine. Take it. It's a crap phone, anyway.' She throws it at me, right at my face, and I dodge, too surprised to attempt to catch it. The phone clatters to the floor as Amy disappears back into her bedroom, slamming the door behind her loud enough that I feel it vibrate through my body.

'Mommy,' Lucy says, her voice a whine in my ear. 'She didn't say sorry.'

As I start making dinner, Lucy moping, Amy silent, and Emma doing her homework as quietly as she can in the living room, I feel guilt start to sour my stomach and worse, doubt fogs my mind. Is Stacy right? Have I been obsessed? Has it hurt my girls?

I reject the thought instinctively, thrust it away from me like it's something dirty and wrong – because it is. I gave up Isaac *because of* the girls, for their sakes, so they could have a better life, more opportunities. So Amy wouldn't have to wear broken shoes, and Emma could dream of college, and Lucy could get braces. All of it, everything – it was for them. The idea that it might have hurt them in the end is inconceivable. I won't let myself think of it; I can't.

Later, after dinner, when the girls have drifted to their bedrooms and Kevin is parked in front of the TV, I log onto the computer that sits on a desk in the corner of the living room, then I wait as it hums to life.

I type *open adoption legal options* into the search box and hold my breath. It takes me a while to wade through all the legalese I don't understand. I may have got my GED but this stuff is dense, and I'm biased, skimming paragraphs, looking only for reassurance. I want something in print to promise me that I can call the law on Grace and make her stick to the agreement we outlined seven years ago, when my body was still aching and empty.

I think of that afternoon now; I remember the sunlight streaming through the window, the perfect spring day outside, the papers in front of me. Three days after Isaac's birth, I still could barely get out of bed.

Grace was wearing a business suit, as was her lawyer, a silver-haired woman who used official terms and made me feel like a thing, not a person. *Biological mother.* As if my connection to my son was only biological, not emotional or intimate or real. Just a matter of nature or science, something easily severed and dismissed.

Kevin stood behind me, hands in his pockets, gaze distant, the only way I knew he could get through it. When I'd told him I wanted an open adoption, he'd stared at me.

'Do you really think that's a good idea, Heather?' He sounded tired.

'Why not?' I was rebellious, restless, fingers picking at the cotton sheet, wanting to move, to act. 'This is our son, Kevin. I know we can't care for him the way we want to but we can still have some part, some small part, in his life. And I think it would be good for him. Good for us. We're not just signing off, forever.'

Kev shook his head. 'I kind of thought that's what adoption was.'

'It doesn't have to be.' I heard my voice getting stronger, more sure. I could picture how it would work, feel it. 'Not in this day and age. It can be different. Everything's more open these days. It's healthier.'

Kevin sighed and raked a hand through his hair. He'd been taking care of the girls around the clock for three days, while I was in the hospital, and he was tired and I knew his back hurt. Stacy hadn't been able to help as much as she'd wanted to; my mom had had one of her turns. 'Do whatever you want,' he said, and it sounded like defeat. 'I know you will, anyway.'

I didn't think that was fair but I didn't argue. I'd won, and that's all I'd wanted.

But now, as I sit in front of the computer, I wonder if I'd really won all those years ago. If I had, I didn't win much. I think of the vacation we took to Disney World last year, the huge, huge hopes I had for that week. I'd wanted Grace to let Isaac come on his own, but of course she didn't, and I understood that, even if I didn't want to. He was little, and he didn't know us all that well. But even with her there, especially with her there, I wanted us to bond. To get along in a way we never have been able to. I wanted Grace to understand and accept that I was a part of her son's life. An important part. That definitely didn't happen.

Kevin couldn't go on the rides because of his back, and Amy found it all boring and kept trying to lose us in the park so she could go flirt with boys, and Lucy whined and Isaac kept clinging to Grace. That was what hurt me the most. It was as if he was stuck in an elevator with strangers, just enduring the awkwardness. It was a relief to get home, away from the constant cycle of expectation and disappointment.

'Mom?' I look up from the computer to see Emma standing there, a textbook clutched to her chest. 'What are you doing?' Her eyes move to the screen and back to me, and I know she's read the search results. Probably figured it out faster than me.

'Nothing.' I click the mouse to minimize the browser, even though I know it's pointless. Emma's gaze moves over my face, searching for answers. Of all the girls, she looks the most like me – blonde hair that will turn mousy as she gets older, light blue eyes, pale skin, freckles. She's like me too in the way she moves quietly about, always working hard, keeping to herself. I was the same at her age.

No one expected me to get pregnant at seventeen and not even finish high school. No one ever noticed me, except Kevin, and that was only because we were assigned to work on a chemistry project together, two mousy misfits who bonded over our inability to operate a Bunsen burner. We used to laugh about it, but right now it makes me feel sad. I glance at Kevin, his gaze fixed determinedly on the TV. He's watching some mindless game show like it holds the answer to life.

'Is this about Isaac?' Emma asks in a low voice. 'Did Grace say something to you?'

Even Emma doesn't sound surprised, like she expected this. I push the keyboard away, restless. 'Maybe.'

'What are you going to do?'

'I don't know.' I don't know what I can do. I bet Grace is banking on me not contacting a lawyer, knowing a messy legal battle will hurt Isaac. When I consider that, I realize even I'm amazed at how long she's let Isaac visit. She could have pulled the plug at any moment, but she didn't. But if I'm supposed to feel grateful, I don't. I still want more.

'What do you think, Em?' I ask, trying to sound practical. Strong. 'Do you think I should give him up?'

'Mom,' Emma says softly, and she sounds sad, 'you did that seven years ago.'

I blink, startled. 'Is it hard, having him visit?' I ask, the words tearing my throat. 'Do you wish he didn't?'

Emma doesn't answer for a moment. 'I don't know,' she says finally. 'It's weird. I don't like thinking that he's my brother, so I don't.'

I jerk back a little at that admission. 'Why don't you like thinking it?'

Emma shrugs, her gaze sliding away. She doesn't want to hurt me with her answer, but suddenly I want to know. I need to.

'Tell me, Emma.'

'Because you gave him away.' Her voice is so small and soft I almost don't hear the words. 'And it feels wrong somehow, that you were able to just *do* that, so I just pretend he's some distant relative or an old friend. Nobody who matters. Or at least no one who matters that much.'

I try to keep my face neutral, try not to show how devastating her words are, how they cut to my heart and tear it right open. I'm bleeding out, right there, and I don't want to show it. Emma must see something of it in my face because she says, 'Mom, I'm sorry…'

'No.' The word is ragged but sure. 'No. You have nothing to be sorry for, Emma.' But I can't look at her; I'm afraid I'll break down.

'Okay.' Emma stands there for a moment and then uncertain, she drifts away. I stay where I am, my heart like a stone within me. I don't know how long I sit there, staring straight ahead, but eventually I take a deep breath and then I pick up the phone.

CHAPTER FIVE

GRACE

We need to talk. Heather sounds grim, but I am determined to remain hopeful. At least we have something to talk about, and I'm praying she isn't going to tell me she's consulted some pro bono lawyer who is going to go apeshit on me. That's the last thing I need.

'Okay, Heather.' I try to pitch my voice somewhere between friendly and practical, but I think my tone is a little off. 'Do you want to talk now?'

'Not over the phone.' She sounds hard, almost angry. I feel a tremor of fear. With Dorothy leaving, I am not up for a big legal battle. I am just not.

'Okay, then,' I say, and I am really trying to hold onto my accommodating tone. 'When is a good time for you?'

She's silent for a long moment. 'I can't get time off work easily…'

No kidding. 'On the weekend?' I suggest, although I really don't want Isaac there for whatever she's going to say. The trouble is, I no longer have the childcare for him.

'Not the weekend,' she says decisively, and I hold onto my temper.

'So when are you thinking?' I ask as pleasantly as I can. I'm bending over ass-backwards but she doesn't see it. She never does.

'Next week, I guess,' she says finally. 'I get off early on Fridays. How about next Friday, around… two?'

Two o'clock in Elizabeth, New Jersey. Like that will be easy for me. 'Sure,' I say. 'That sounds great.'

I try not to think about Heather for the rest of the evening. Instead I go into Isaac's bedroom, lie next to him on the floor where he's playing his iPad, his precious hour of screen time. Outside it's starting to get dark, and I know I should tell him to get ready for bed, but I don't want to go into good-mother mode. I just want to be.

Eventually Isaac puts the iPad aside and flips over onto his back. The glow-in-the-dark planets and stars we stuck to his ceiling a year or so ago are coming out as twilight settles outside, fluorescent, yellowish-green twinkles above us.

Isaac's room has changed a lot from the pristine elephant-themed nursery of seven years ago. He grew out of the elephants by age four, asking for race cars, and then a year ago I redid his room in a more age-neutral scheme that I hope will last through the teen years – varying shades of blue with red accents and a fairly subtle solar system theme with a lava lamp that has stars showering through its glass base and a framed, antique map of the solar system on the wall. And of course the stars above us.

'Where's the Big Dipper?' Isaac asks as we look up at the stars together.

'I'm not sure.' I tried to follow a pattern of constellations when I put them up, but some have peeled off and it's hard to tell now. 'Where do you think it is?'

'There.' Isaac points straight above us, and I can make out the vague dipper-esque shape.

'I see it, Isaac.'

He shoots me a grin, and my heart expands with love. I feel so grateful for this moment, for every tender, little, unimportant exchange that matters more than anything in the world. And for a second my mind flicks to Heather, to how few moments like this she has, and I feel a pang of guilt. Am I being cruel, taking

Isaac from her? Am I being selfish, demanding more when I know she has so little?

And yet I know, I absolutely know, I can't go on the way we have been. Isaac can't. Maybe if Heather wasn't so needy, or I wasn't so paranoid, but the way we are, the way it's been... I can't do it any more, and I don't want Isaac to suffer through it, either. Something has got to give.

The next evening I pick Isaac up from Stella's apartment on Eighty-Sixth and Park. Close enough, I've thought more than once, for them to walk to each other's apartments when they're a bit older. I picture him riding his scooter down Park Avenue, kindly doormen casting a benevolent, watchful eye, and it makes me smile.

'*Grace.*' Stella throws open the door with an expansive gesture as soon as the elevator doors open onto her floor. She lives in huge, sprawling apartment with her husband, Eric, who works in corporate litigation, and her two boys – Will and his younger brother, Jamie, who is a lovable terror.

'I'm making cocktails,' she says as she ushers me into their hallway, which is a welcoming mix of clutter and style. 'Since it's Friday. And you *must* need one, since you've had this childcare *nightmare.*' Stella has a tendency to talk in italics, but I love her warm-hearted enthusiasm, so different from my own cool containment. Perhaps that's why we work as friends, why we hit it off from that first play date in early September, spending forty minutes chatting by the elevator, exchanging our life details along with knowing smiles, while Will and Isaac raced around us.

Now I follow her into the huge kitchen, which is a happy mess in a way my kitchen will never be. Mixing bowls are out, and kids' artwork is papered all over the walls, and Justin Timberlake is singing about the sunshine in his pocket, blaring from her phone stuck into a set of speakers.

Stella dances around to it as she fetches a large glass and salts the rim with a flourish. 'Margaritas,' she says, 'because it's so warm out.' She takes a sip from her own as she pours mine from a pitcher she's made up, and then garnishes it with a wedge of lime. 'Ta da!' She dances over to me to hand me my drink, and I laugh, heartened by her exuberance.

I take a sip. 'Oh, this is fantastic. Thanks.'

'Come sit down.' She pats one of the high bar stools around the huge marble island. 'Tell me about it. So she just *quit*?'

'Yes, but she kind of had to.' I slip onto the stool and take another sip of the margarita, which is delicious, and heavy on the Patron.

'Had to?' Stella wrinkles her nose. 'Couldn't she have given you some notice?'

'I guess it came up kind of suddenly.' I don't want to be disloyal to Dorothy, whom I still miss and love, but a tiny dart of bitterness fires through me all the same. She knew how difficult leaving so quickly would be for me.

'So have you found anyone else yet?' Stella slips onto the stool next to mine, her half-started dinner preparations forgotten. It looks like she was making some kind of paella, with pink, unpeeled shrimp lying in a fat pile on the island, along with a bag of Arborio rice.

Since having Isaac I have tried to cook a little more. A couple of times a week I manage to make something healthy and fun – homemade pizza with a whole-wheat crust, a colorful stir fry. But the other nights I'm late home from work or I'm too tired, and so we have take-out or something simple, pasta and sauce from a jar. I try not to feel guilty about that, but inevitably I do. Motherhood feels like constant tug-of-war between guilt and love, fear and joy.

'No, I haven't found anyone yet.' I take another sip of my margarita, which is going down nicely. 'I was thinking about putting him in the after-school club, actually.' We both grimace, as if I've said I want to stick him in a Romanian orphanage.

'Surely you can get someone. You used the same agency as I did, didn't you?'

I nod. I used the same elite agency just about every mother on the Upper East Side uses. Not that Stella has a nanny any more; after ten years as a human rights lawyer, she quit work after Jamie was born, and is a happy and satisfied stay-at-home mom.

'It just takes such a long time. Reading the applications, figuring out the ones I want to interview. It's such an important decision.' I think of Dorothy with a pang. I miss her so much – her comfortable confidence, the way she filled my apartment with her presence, her belly laugh, her easy manner. I'd interviewed six prospective applicants before I found her, and when I found her, I knew. It felt like coming home.

'You were lucky to hold on to Dorothy for so long,' Stella says with a knowledgeable nod. 'So many nannies quit when the kids start school, don't they? I'm lucky I never had to go down that route.'

'Do you miss work?' I ask impulsively, and Stella pauses to seriously consider her answer.

'Yes, of course I do,' she says at last. 'How could I not? But I still wouldn't change a thing.'

'And when Jamie starts kindergarten?' It's always the million-dollar question for the moms who were lucky enough to be able to stay at home. When do you go back to work? What kind of job do you get? Back into the eight-to-six slog (nine-to-five doesn't exist in the corporate world) or do you let yourself be shunted into part-time purgatory? It's a choice I've never had to make, and never will. If I want to stay in New York and see Isaac through school, I'll be working full-time until I retire.

'I'm not rushing into anything,' Stella says after a moment. 'We don't need the money, and I'm enjoying everything.' She wrinkles her nose. 'To tell you the truth, I actually like being class mom.' Which makes me laugh. 'And we couldn't go to France in the summer if I had to work.'

Stella and her family rent a villa in the south of France every year for three whole months while her husband Eric telecommutes. It makes Isaac's and my one week on Cape Cod look a little pathetic in comparison. We go to the same weather-beaten cottage my dad and I used to go to, and in truth I wouldn't change it for anything.

Those seven days on the Cape are the pinnacle of my year – lazy days on the beach, games of Pinochle by the little woodstove, a week of relaxation and remembering how much I love my son, how grateful I am for my life. I remember how I'd imagined those vacations before Isaac was born. Before I even knew he was a boy I saw us there, lying on the beach, looking up at the stars. Toasting marshmallows, building sandcastles, and savoring every single moment.

'You know I'll have Isaac over here,' Stella says. 'We have karate on Monday and swimming on Wednesday, music lessons on Friday…' She grimaces, acknowledging, at least a little bit, how crazy and ridiculous the Manhattan child's overscheduled life is. 'But Tuesdays and Thursday, it's no problem. At all.'

'That's really kind.' I'm hesitant to take her up on such a generous offer, even though I know she means it. There's absolutely no way I could repay her in kind, ever. 'I might take you up on it.'

'I mean it, Grace.' Stella leans forward, her expression turning intent, her voice urgent. 'Look, I know how easy I have it. How lucky I am.' Another grimace. 'I'm sure some people look at me and think I don't realize it, that I'm a spoiled princess of a Manhattan mother, and I probably am, but…' She sighs and spreads her hands. 'Let me help. I want to.'

I believe her, and so I smile and hoist my margarita. 'Trust me, I will.'

Sitting there, sipping my drink, I feel light with happiness despite the childcare worries. I am grateful for these simple moments – friendship, motherhood. No matter how difficult it all feels sometimes, I know I'm lucky, just as lucky as Stella, but in a different way. I have more than I ever thought I would. More than I ever thought was possible.

Stella looks like she's going to say something more; she pauses, her glass halfway to her mouth, and I tense, sensing something big. 'What?' I finally ask with a little laugh, and she gives me a slight abashed smile.

'It's just… I hate to seem nosy because I know how tricky these things are… but is Isaac's father involved in any way?'

The questioning smile freezes on my face. I haven't told Stella Isaac is adopted, and he obviously hasn't mentioned it either. I decided a long time ago to be completely open with Isaac about his adoption; even when he was a baby, I made it into a bedtime story, pointed to photos of him as a wrinkly newborn, explained how he was special, how I'd chosen him. And, in truth, I didn't have any other options really, with Aunt Heather in the picture from day one, although in those cozy stories I didn't always mention her. Mostly I didn't. And obviously I didn't advertise his adoption, either. It's always felt personal. Not a secret, but… private.

'Isaac's adopted,' I say now to Stella, keeping my tone easy and matter-of-fact. 'There never was a father in the picture.' Which feels a little unfair to Kevin McCleary.

'Oh. Wow. Sorry, I didn't know.' Stella absorbs this information as she sips her drink. 'That's wonderful, though. Did you go international?' she asks, which makes it sound as if we're talking about a shopping trip to Paris.

'No, domestic. Actually…' With Heather's phone call still in the forefront of my mind, I find myself admitting, 'His birth parents live in New Jersey. We see them once a month.'

'Once a *month*?' Stella looks incredulous, as well as both admiring and slightly horrified. 'Wow. That must be so… well, how is it? I mean, I can't even *imagine*.'

'It's a bit difficult.' I want to confess how completely awful I've found it, how I'm longing for it to end, but something holds me back, maybe even a weird loyalty to Heather.

'Why do you…? I mean, did the birth parents suggest it? They must have… and did you have to agree?' She shakes her head, still seeming disbelieving, and I feel a satisfying little pinprick of validation. Yes, it is weird and difficult and I've been enduring it for seven years. Thank you, Stella, for getting that.

'The birth mother did,' I say. 'Her name's Heather. She was pretty insistent about it, although beforehand she said she wanted a closed adoption, like I did.' I can't quite keep the bitterness from seeping into my voice like some poisonous gas. *Why, Heather? Why couldn't you have just stuck to the original agreement?*

'Oh, wow.' Stella's eyes are wide. 'That must be *so* incredibly difficult. I mean, *is* it?'

I laugh, the sound coming out a bit too hard. 'Yes, actually,' I say, and drain my margarita. 'It is, a bit.'

'Goodness.' Stella shakes her head slowly. 'Do you guys… I mean, do you get along?'

'Sort of.' It seems petty to admit we don't. Why *can't* I get along better with Heather? Why can't I just shrug my shoulders at her unending neediness, remind myself it's only one afternoon a month, and I'm the real winner, I have Isaac all the time? She gave him to me. Why can't I remember that instead of gritting my teeth, getting annoyed at every little thing? I'm not being fair to her, I know that, but she's not fair to me.

'How long do you think you'll have to keep the visits up?' Stella asks. 'Does Heather want to… you know, keep going? Forever? And what about Isaac?' She lowers her voice even though the boys are miles away in the TV den. 'How does he find the visits?'

'Tricky.' I hesitate, again feeling that weird sense of loyalty. 'He enjoys them sometimes, but it can feel… confusing.'

'I'm sure.' Stella nods vigorously. 'Of course it does.'

'Actually,' I say as she refills my empty glass, 'I've asked Heather if we can visit once every three months instead. Start to let things taper off naturally.' Although I know none of it will feel natural to Heather.

'And how did she take that?'

'Not very well.' I pause, searching for something that sounds diplomatic. 'She's a bit… clingy.'

'Oh, great.' Stella rolls her eyes in commiseration. 'Honestly, Grace, that sounds like a nightmare. The sooner you can cut things off, the better, if you ask me. Do you think it might get… messy?'

'I don't know. Open adoption agreements aren't automatically legally binding, but a sympathetic judge could enforce it, if he or she thought it was in Isaac's best interest.'

'But surely they wouldn't…?'

'I don't know.' I feel my stomach clench with the awful what-if. 'Someone might see Heather as the underdog in this situation…' And me as the merciless career woman, who employs nannies to take care of her son, who doesn't want to spare a single afternoon a month. If Heather got a good lawyer, it could go badly. Very badly.

'You can't let that happen,' Stella says with surprising fierceness. 'Look, if you need legal advice…'

'I've consulted an adoption lawyer, but thanks.' I smile, feeling better for having someone to offload to. 'I mean that. You've been great, listening to me moan. And Heather's not that bad, honestly.' I semi-regret what I said, fighting a prickling sense of shame at badmouthing Heather. 'She gave me Isaac, after all, and she's a good mom.' Although I remember Amy's smirk, the way she sashays about the house, and I wonder if Heather is completely in control of that situation. What would Isaac be like, in that household? I can hardly bear to think about it.

'Trust me, Grace, you're not moaning.' Stella rises from her stool and starts chucking some things onto a cutting board. 'Why don't you stay for dinner? It's just paella, but you're more than welcome…'

'Okay.' I smile, happiness unfurling inside me at the invitation. I've stayed for dinner a few times, but it always feels like a privilege. This is the world I live in now. The loneliness that once ate at me like a canker is finally, forever gone. I stand up, and my head swims a bit from the alcohol. 'Let me set the table.'

We have a wonderfully pleasant evening, the boys boisterous but not too much, Eric genial, opening a bottle of wine even though I really don't need anything more to drink. Stella is as bubbly as ever, managing to effortlessly whip up a delicious meal, keep the conversation sparkling and light, and also keep the boys – all three – in check. I'm in awe of how effortless she makes it seem, although when I say as much when we're clearing up in the kitchen, she rolls her eyes.

'Effortless? It's the margaritas.' She rests her elbows on the sink, her expression turning thoughtful. 'I know I'm lucky, like I said before. But no matter what, parenting is hard. It's completely full-time, isn't it? Even if you have a job. Especially if you do.'

'Relentless,' I agree, thinking of the worries always circulating in my mind like some ever-revolving in-tray of concern: what Isaac is eating, who his friends are, whether he's done his homework, the eczema on his elbow.

Stella nods in commiseration. 'Yes,' she says, 'relentless. And yet we wouldn't have it any other way, would we?'

Eventually Isaac and I leave, with promises of coming again soon, and also vague invitations to come to France one summer. Stella is even more expansive than usual, hugging me and kissing both my cheeks as I leave.

'This was so much fun. Please, please call me if you need anything. And I'll definitely take Isaac on Tuesday and Thursdays.'

'Thank you. You're amazing.' I feel mellow and happy as Isaac and I walk up Park Avenue. It's a warm spring night, and Isaac skips ahead while I stroll slowly, enjoying the cherry blossoms, the balmy evening air, letting the pleasantness of the evening linger like a fine wine.

My mellowness continues for the rest of the evening, as I sit with Isaac as he does his homework, correcting his spellings and helping him with his four times tables. Afterward we snuggle up in bed as I read him three chapters of *The Indian in the Cupboard*.

After he's tucked up in bed, I end up getting photos out that I've never managed to put into books, and organizing them by year. Isaac as a two-year-old, chubby and red-cheeked. Isaac as a preschooler, with a backpack bigger than he is and a pie-eating grin.

There are no photos of our visits to the McClearys, although I know Heather takes lots of pictures when we're there. There are a few up on her wall, above the TV. Her holding Isaac as a baby; a picture Kevin took of them playing Connect Four. For a second I picture us comparing our photo books, our different experiences of Isaac and his life, my play by play versus Heather's single snapshots.

Then I push the thought away. *It's almost over.* I honestly believe that. I'm feeling optimistic, humming in the shower I take before I go to bed, feeling almost happy, like for once I can see the future stretching ahead of me, shining and bright, without Heather in it. Isaac and I will have all our weekends back; we can go away, to Boston or Philadelphia, see the turning leaves in Vermont. It feels as if my whole life will be freed up, even though I know it's only one weekend a month. And yet it's been so much more than that, always hanging over me, always there. Without it, the horizon feels expansive, limitless.

I sing out loud as I rinse the shampoo from my hair, the soap from my body. 'I'm Walking on Sunshine'.

And that's when I find the lump.

CHAPTER SIX

HEATHER

A whole week until I have to talk to Grace. Until I have to start to give Isaac up. I've made my decision, I feel it in my leaden gut, but it weighs me down so much I start to doubt. To wonder if there is some way to make it work, a way that even Grace would be happy with.

What if Isaac came here by himself? I'd pick him up and drive him back, make it as easy as possible, but even as I'm thinking of it I know she'd never agree. She's always watching me during their visits, jumping in to correct or to limit or just to rain on my damn parade. That's one thing she wouldn't want to give up, the control she still gets to exert.

What if I met them in New York? But then Kevin and the girls wouldn't be part of the visits, and I don't like that. It would breed more resentment, greater hostility, and that's the last thing any of us needs.

So what if we had a visit every three months, but it was for longer? A whole day? A weekend? I can already picture Grace's pinched face, her thin lips. She's not going to agree to anything. I feel it. I know it. This is the beginning of the end, and deep down I can't even blame her.

That's what hurts the most; that despite the injustice that burns through me, as well as the longing, there is a feeling deep inside me that Grace's request is actually reasonable and worse, fair. That I gave Isaac up and she's kept coming for seven years, nearly every single month without complaint, and eventually, like Stacy said, there had to be an endpoint. And now it's here and I need to make my peace. I know that, I do, but it's so hard. So, so hard.

On Monday night, I talk to Kevin. I should have told him earlier. I should have involved him from the beginning, from the moment Grace talked to me about tapering off Isaac's visits, but I resisted because I was afraid of his response. I was afraid he might breathe a big sigh of relief and say *finally*, and that would just about break my heart.

I know Kevin doesn't enjoy the visits with Isaac the way I do. Of course I know. I crave them, I wait for them breathlessly, while he seems only to endure. Sometimes, once in a while, he seems to enjoy being with Isaac, but most of the time he's silent in that surly way that puts both me and Grace on edge; we're united in that, at least.

Now it's quiet; Emma is in her room, studying, and Amy is out. Where, I don't know. I've stopped asking, which I know is no good thing considering she's only fifteen. Lucy is in bed, although she's likely to wander out asking for a snack or a drink of water at least two or three times. But Kevin and I are as alone as we're ever going to be.

'It's a nice night,' I say. 'Do you want to sit outside?'

Kevin looks surprised; it's not something I'd normally suggest. But he follows me wordlessly outside, the screen door slapping against the weathered frame as we step onto the back porch with the swing I was once so proud of.

Now the chain is rusted, the wicker fraying, and the porch is filled with junk – an old plastic tricycle, weather-beaten and broken; a rusty bike; a hamster cage from a brief, unfortunate period of having a pet; a plastic tub of withered begonias. We should throw it all out, but somehow we never do.

I sit gingerly on the bench, just in case it breaks. It creaks in protest but holds my weight. I swing a little, enjoying the night air, the feeling of calm. Our yard is small and scrubby, with a rusted chain-link fence separating it from our neighbor's, who has a Great Dane that prowls alongside it all the time, meaning the girls never used to like to go out and play. Now they don't want to, anyway. But the dog, for once, is inside, and dusk cloaks the yard, making it look less bare.

'Join me,' I say, and Kev looks at the swing askance.

'I don't want to break that thing.'

'You won't,' I say, although our combined weight together might. He just shakes his head and lowers himself onto the weathered porch step, knees resting on his elbows.

'So,' he says, and I know he knows I asked him out here for a reason.

'Grace talked to me on Saturday. She... she wants to slow down Isaac's visits.'

'Slow down?'

'To once every three months. And after a while, once every six months. And after that...' I can't say it, even now.

'Never,' Kevin finishes flatly, and I nod.

'What do you think?' I ask quietly, my voice little more than a whisper, as he just sits there and stares out into the night.

'What do *you* think?' he asks eventually.

'We could get a lawyer...' I begin.

Kevin shakes his head. 'We can't do that to Isaac,' he says, and I love him for saying that. I also know he's right.

'I know. I wouldn't want it to end up in a big fight. I never wanted to fight with Grace.' Although I'm not sure that's even true. I haven't exactly been trying to get along with her all these years, have I? To make it easier for her? The realization both humbles and confuses me, because for so long I've been feeling sanctimoniously right, the only one who deserves to feel aggrieved.

I haven't thought that much about how Grace might feel. I haven't wanted to, because deep down, beneath the veneer of civility we share, I've always felt the burning injustice that she has my son. And that, I realize, is not fair to her... or to Isaac. *I* made the choice seven years ago. I made it, no matter how beaten into a corner I felt.

'So that's it, then?' Kev asks, and I nod slowly.

'She's coming over on Friday. I'll tell her then.' The knowledge rests inside of me, a weight that is both crippling and in a small, still way, oddly, almost peaceful. It will be over. I will mourn and grieve and wail, but it will finally be over.

We're both silent, the evening warm and still and quiet. 'Kev... will you miss him?' The words are an ache. I have to ask; I have to know.

Kev turns to look at me, but I can't make out his expression in the dark. 'Of course I will,' he says, his voice a low throb, and I believe him. For a second I have a glimpse into my husband's heart, and the pain he might be hiding. He doesn't love Isaac the way I do, perhaps, the way I've let myself, like a firestorm inside me, burning everything up. Kev has kept himself from that, and that's probably a good thing, a healthy thing, but he cares, and just like me, he knows this will hurt.

Friday comes all too soon. I get home from work and fly around, cleaning the house, putting out cookies, God only knows why. I want to impress Grace, when it's far too late for that. But it feels important somehow, to show her that I'm a good mother, a good person. Good enough for her son, even if she never thought so. I tell myself I'm going to be dignified and kind, that I'm not going to cry. Finish strong. End well. But I'm not sure I can.

Two o'clock comes and goes. I check my phone, but there are no voicemails, no texts. It's utterly unlike Grace to be a no-show;

with our monthly visits she's always confirmed, always texted if she was going to be even a few minutes late. Right now I realize how much I should have appreciated her reluctant thoughtfulness. All those visits. Dozens and dozens, and she showed up every time, gritting her teeth maybe, but still. She came. I never even thanked her, not really. But where is she now?

I call her cell phone, but it switches to voicemail. I leave a message, and then I wait some more. It's getting near three o'clock, and the girls will be coming off the bus soon. Grace and I can't have this conversation with them around, and then I realize we're not going to have this conversation at all. Grace stood me up, and I'm not sure whether to feel resentment or relief. I ping between the two, my emotions all over the place because I wasn't ready and yet somehow I want it all to be over.

The girls burst into the house, Amy flouncing in, wearing a full mask of make-up. Since I took away her phone she hasn't even hidden how much she makes herself up, and I haven't had the strength to protest. I haven't given her phone back, either. Sometimes parenting is nothing more than a ceasefire.

Emma slips in, dropping her backpack by the door before she slides by me with a quick smile and gets a glass of milk. Amy practically rips the hinges off her bedroom door as she disappears inside without a word. I think of following her, but then Lucy comes home, upset about some stupid boy in class who's teased her for reading 'a baby book', and I try to soothe her while I start dinner.

When Kev comes home from work he raises his eyebrows in silent question, and I shake my head. 'She didn't come.'

Later, when we're getting ready for bed, he asks, 'What do you think happened?'

'I don't know. It's not like her.' I fight a sense of dread. 'I hope she's not going to just leave it. I mean… I want to… to say goodbye.' My face starts to crumple.

'Oh, babe.' Kev pulls me into a hug and I bury my head in his shoulder.

'Has it been too hard, Kev? Having him visit every month?' I whisper the words against his chest, not sure I want to hear the answer. The truth.

'It's been hard,' he answers slowly. 'But it was always going to be hard, wasn't it? No matter which way it went.'

'I hate thinking that I made it worse.'

'Worse for who? Grace?'

'Us.' I let out an unruly sob, my fists bunching in his shirt. 'Have I made it worse for us?'

Kev eases back, his hands on my shoulders. 'Heather, you've done your best for this family. Nobody doubts that.' He gives me the glimmer of a smile. 'Not even Amy.'

I smile back through my tears, grateful for his words and yet still so uncertain.

The days pass and I still don't hear from Grace. A week, and nothing. I leave her a message, and then another. I ask her what happened, and then I ask her to call me back because I'm starting to worry. What if something bad has happened? What if Isaac has come down with meningitis, or has been hit by a car? My imagination goes into terrified hyper drive.

One night I slip out of bed and tiptoe to the computer. I turn it on, the screen casting an electric glow in the darkened room. I type an email. *Grace, what's going on? Why have you not been in touch? – Heather* Maybe it's too abrupt, but I'm feeling too strung out to moderate it. I push 'send' before I can have second thoughts. It's eleven o'clock at night, and it's not inconceivable that Grace is still up, still on her laptop, billing hours or whatever it is she does. I wait an entire hour, just staring at the screen, but no emails pop into my inbox.

A couple of days later, two weeks after Grace stood me up, she finally calls. I'm at work, and I'm not supposed to take personal calls, but when I see her name flash on the screen of my phone I slip into the office's one bathroom, little more than a broom closet with a toilet and a tiny sink.

'Grace?' I sound incredulous and a little accusing.

'Hi, Heather.' She sounds exhausted. 'I'm sorry I didn't call. And that I didn't come out there a few weeks ago.'

'What's wrong?' Because something clearly is, judging from the tone of her voice, the tiredness. 'Is Isaac…?'

'Isaac's fine.' A pause; it feels like she's debating what to say. 'Everything's fine,' she says, but I'm not sure whether I should believe her.

'Why didn't you come?'

'I'm sorry, it completely slipped my mind.' That seems unlikely, but I stay silent, waiting for more. 'It's been…' She lets out a rush of breath. 'Really busy.'

'So will you and Isaac come as usual next weekend?' His visit is less than two weeks away.

Grace lets out a shaky laugh that, shockingly, holds the threat of tears. 'Oh, Heather…'

I panic, because Grace never sounds like that. So emotional, so *weak*. 'Grace, what's going on?'

'I can't talk about it now,' she says on a shuddery breath. 'I'm sorry, I don't think we're going to be able to make it.'

For a few seconds I can't speak. 'Why not?' I finally manage, the two words squeezed from my throat.

'I…' Grace pauses. 'I haven't been feeling all that well.'

I don't know how to respond to that, how to feel. Is she lying? Is she really sick? What if she's just done, and she's making excuses to keep Isaac from me? 'Grace,' I choke out, 'I thought we were going to have a conversation about this first.'

'Oh, Heather, it's not that.' She sounds exasperated as well as exhausted, like I'm just too much work for her. 'Look, I've barely missed a visit in seven years. Just let me duck out of one, okay? Just one.' Her voice breaks, and I feel a mix of guilt and confusion. What is really going on here?

'Just one?' I press. 'You'll come next month?'

She lets out a ragged laugh. 'Oh, whatever. Fine. Yes. Although I have no idea what next month will be like.' And then she disconnects the call before I can ask anything else.

I'm left both fuming and uncertain, replaying the conversation in my mind, looking for answers I know I won't find. Someone knocks on the bathroom door, and sliding my phone in my pocket, I unlock the door and brush past Steve, my coworker with the sweet smile and sweat-stained shirt, and go back to my desk.

I don't have time to think too much about it, though, because when I get home everything feels chaotic. Emma and Amy are screeching at each other; Amy borrowed Emma's favorite jeans without asking, and then ripped holes in both knees, probably on purpose.

Emma is so rarely angry, but even so she's no match for Amy, who is fiery and scathing, while she, poor girl, just goes white and speaks in a breathy voice that is full of tears. She doesn't stand a chance.

Lucy adds her own brand of difficult to the mix, tearful and defiant, as she thrusts a note from school at me, right up into my face.

'What's this?' I ask, the words blurring before me.

'From my teacher.'

I start to read it, how she's failed her last three spelling tests. How did I not know that? The teacher, Mrs. Bryant, is asking for a meeting next week, after school. I'll have to take time off work.

'You *suck*!' Emma cries, her final thrust, which bounces off Amy, who just smirks. She's still holding the jeans.

I walk into the kitchen, just to get away from them. From all of it. I feel so tired by everything, the constant needs and demands. I open the fridge and stare into the near-empty depths. I forgot to go food shopping; in fact, this whole afternoon is a blur. What did I do? I left work and sat in my car for a while. I drove around. And I came back early, right after the girls got back. I could still go to Stop & Shop and do a quick runaround, but I can't face it now. I can't face anything.

'Mom, are you going to go to the meeting?' Lucy asks anxiously. 'Am I in trouble?'

'Mom, make her give back the jeans,' Emma cries. 'They're mine.'

'Just try to get them,' Amy calls defiantly, clutching her stolen treasure. 'You never wear them, anyway. They're too small for you.'

I ignore them all, and I can't even feel guilty about it. I walk into my bedroom and close the door, for once shocking all three of my daughters into silence. Then I lie on the bed and stare at the ceiling, my mind blanking out. Eventually I fall asleep.

I wake up a few hours later, blinking in the dusky light. Kev has come into the bedroom and is taking off his UPS uniform.

'What… what's going on?' I ask muzzily.

'What do you mean?' He tosses his shirt on the floor.

'I fell asleep… are the girls okay?' Guilt needles me. I'm a *mom* – I can't just check out like that.

Kevin shrugs. I roll onto my side, tuck my knees into my chest. 'What's up with you?' he asks after a moment.

'I was tired.'

'You sick?'

'No.'

He pauses, his hands on his belt buckle. 'Is this about Grace?' He sounds like he regrets asking the question.

'I had a weird phone call from her today.'

Kev shakes his head.

'I'm serious, Kev, it was weird.'

'So what?' he asks, and I am silent. 'So what?' he asks again, his voice louder, and I close my eyes. 'Heather, you've got to let this go.'

'Let Isaac go, you mean.'

'You already agreed to it, even if you hadn't told her yet.'

'I know that, but not like this. Not without… anything.'

'What was so weird about the phone call?' he asks on a sigh.

'She sounded tired and kind of upset.'

'So?'

I know nothing I will say will dent his determined indifference right now, and I don't want to try. 'Trust me, it was just weird.'

'So it was weird.' He pulls on a pair of sweatpants. 'What's for dinner?'

I keep thinking about Grace for the next few weeks, as the silence stretches on and on. The fourth Sunday of the month passes without comment; in a burst of manic energy, I pack a picnic and we walk to Phil Rizzuto Park, spread a blanket by the playground, although only Lucy goes on the swings, and even then only halfheartedly. But I got the whole family out, even Amy, which feels like a miracle.

As I lie on the blanket and nibble my soggy sandwich, I feel a flicker of happiness, like a fragile beam of light emerging from behind dark, dank clouds. This can be enough, surely – a sunny afternoon in May, my family around me, Kev's thigh pressed to mine. Do I really need more than this? Am I going to be so greedy?

Two days later, while I'm at work, Grace calls again. This time she sounds awful, her voice no more than a croak.

'Heather… I'm so sorry to ask you this… but please can you pick up Isaac from school?'

CHAPTER SEVEN

GRACE

I have cancer. Bad cancer, although is there any good kind? I think once upon a time, I might have thought so. I might have been so insensitive as to say it. *Isn't that a good kind of cancer?* My own mother died of cancer, my father too, and I had no clue. No idea what it feels like to have your body betray you, to know that your very cells are corrupted, multiplying their evil with every breath you draw.

After I found the lump, I called right away. With my mother's history I'd always been eagle-eyed for the signs, and yet the lump still seemed unbelievable, impossible. Dr. Stein did a biopsy, and then she called me in for the results. I knew right away, from the look on her face, the sad eyes, the droopy mouth, that it was bad news.

I just didn't know how bad.

The words kept coming. Stage four, metastatic, invasive, aggressive. Awful words. And then more words about treatment, which were nearly as bad. No quick blitz with the radiation gun for me, no easy pill, swallow and smile. No, the course of treatment she recommended was immediate chemotherapy, the kind that left you flattened, hair falling out, reduced to scrawny skin and bone, sleeping and sick. When the lump has shrunk I'll have a double mastectomy, and I'll need to have some lymph nodes removed because apparently the cancer is there, as well.

Afterward, when the numbness had worn off, Novocain of the heart, I twitched with impatience, the need to do something. Solve this before it got any worse. Act while I could. I hated the thought of the cancer growing inside me and I was just waiting, helpless, letting it take over.

Despite Dr. Stein's dire news, I had to wait a whole week before my first chemotherapy treatment, an endless week where my entire life spun out in a bittersweet reel, and each day that slipped past felt far too precious.

Then the chemo began and I realized even more how precious that waiting period had been, when I'd felt well, when all I had was one stupid lump and no real symptoms. When I went to work, I made dinner, I read to Isaac. I stroked his hair, I felt the sunshine on my face, I looked like anyone else, busy and happy. Soon it would all start slipping away.

I didn't tell anyone at work what was going on; I was naïve enough to think I might not need to. I'd read stories online, about how some people don't even have side effects from the chemo. I thought I could simply take a couple of days off work – I was only scheduled treatment for the first two days of each week, for three weeks – and then soldier on. Obviously it would raise a few eyebrows, and I might have to tell someone in HR the truth, but I would survive. So much of this was about survival.

I didn't tell Stella, either. I was tempted to, to have her exclaim and sympathize and enfold me in her arms, but at the same time I didn't want to because I was afraid of being defined by my cancer, my neediness. She was already taking Isaac two afternoons a week, but it still felt like we were equals: two moms, two sons. I didn't want to change that. And the truth was, I still thought I could control this, stay on top of it. Have my treatment and let no one be the wiser, not even Isaac, until I got the all-clear and life returned to the blissfully normal.

Yes, I was very naïve.

That first day I walked into New York Presbyterian feeling more alone than I ever had in my life. I wished I'd told Stella; I wanted her here with me now, holding my hand, telling me it was going to be okay. I think she would have done that for me, but of course it's a whole new level of friendship, of painful intimacy, to walk with someone through cancer. To hold their hand.

Of course, I have other friends than Stella. There's Alyssa, the mom of one of Isaac's friends at his Montessori school. We keep in touch mostly by text these days; she's hippyish and I'm uptight, and when our sons went to different schools, we drifted apart a little, although we manage to see each other once every couple of months. But I know she's having marriage troubles and asking her to support me through this feels a little over the top.

During Isaac's baby days I made friends with Lara, a High-powered lawyer, when we met in the pediatrician's office. We were both there one morning as soon as it opened at 8 a.m., both dressed in power suits, balancing our babies on our slim-skirted knees, both checking our phones compulsively. We caught each other's eye and each of us laughed shamefacedly; we started talking and for a couple of years we got together with some regularity. But then Lara's husband got a job in Los Angeles, and while we talked about Isaac and me flying out for a visit, it never happened.

And then there's been Dorothy, the one person I've really counted on, but she's in Chicago now, and she has her own family to look after. I can hardly ask her to come help, as much as I want her to. So I do it alone, the way I've done just about everything, because at the end of the day, as a single mom, that's so often how it happens.

I take Isaac to school and then I go to the hospital, my heart beating with heavy thuds, hands clammy and cold with nerves. I lay on a reclining chair, like the kind you'd lie in at the dentist, and am fitted with a cold cap, a strap-on helmet with gel coolant that could, just maybe, help prevent the worst of the hair loss. A kindly, smiling nurse hooks up the IV. 'This may pinch a little,' she says, as if a needle is the worst thing I am going to face this morning.

I watch the liquid, clear and viscous, going in. Drip, drip, drip. I tell myself it is mind over matter – how can I let this innocuous, watery-looking substance affect me at all? I breathe in and out slowly and tell myself to stay strong. I don't feel anything yet; I almost convince myself I am going to be fine. Chemo, surgery, boom. I'll be one of the survivors, pink ribbon and all. I'll do the charity run. I'll eat everything organic. Hell, I'll even give up alcohol. And I'll tell everyone my inspiring story.

Dr. Stein has assured me breast cancer has a high rate of survival. It has an eighty-five percent five-year survival rate of cases where it's spread to the lymph nodes. The trouble is, five years doesn't seem that long. Isaac would only be twelve. And where will I be?

The other knowledge that is lodging like a stone in my gut is that my mother survived five years, but only just, and those five years were a blur of struggle, treatment, and pain. Is that what I want the rest of my life to look like? Maybe I won't have any choice.

But I don't like to think like that, to spin this story to whatever end I'm going to have, because today, damn it, is plenty hard enough.

It only takes twenty minutes to finish the drip, and then I take a cab home. I walk around my apartment, feeling edgy and restless. And fine. I feel fine, mostly, although I am waiting for something, a looming disaster, as if thunderclouds are suddenly going to appear above my head as lightning strikes. After about an hour, when I still feel fine, I decide to go to work, log in a few hours at least, while I can.

I've gone so far as to start getting dressed, putting on discreet make-up, because the truth is, no matter how I feel, I look like shit.

I am just putting on my pantyhose when the side effects hit me, slamming into me with the force of a sledgehammer or a freight train. I barely have a chance to make it to the bathroom, stumbling in my half-put on tights, my stomach heaving so violently I feel as if I am being wrung inside out.

I hang over the toilet, my cheek resting on the rim, as I spit bright yellow bile and know this is merely the beginning.

Eventually my stomach has emptied itself out, and I half-walk, half-crawl to bed, where I doze on and off, still half-dressed. I wake suddenly, as if an alarm has gone off, and see from the clock that I need to pick Isaac up from after-school club in five minutes. I don't think I can get off the bed in five minutes.

But somehow I do, because I don't have any choice. Somehow I manage to change into more comfortable clothes, grab my house keys and phone, and get outside my building, feeling as if I am about a hundred years old, my body as worn out as a wet dish rag.

I hail a cab, my arm waving limply, and make it to Buckley twenty minutes late; Isaac has been sent to the office and is looking disconsolate as he kicks his legs against his chair and a secretary thins her lips in disapproval.

'Sorry,' I mutter, and reach for Isaac's hand.

'Mom, what's wrong with you?' He looks at me not with concern, but a kind of hurt impatience.

'I'm just a little under the weather, bud. I'll be okay.'

I know I am going to have to tell people at some point. Cancer is not exactly something you can keep secret, but I don't want to blare it from the rooftops, either. And the truth is, I don't know how to tell Isaac. Not yet, not until I know more. Until I can make him some promises I know I'll be able to keep.

So I muddle on, making Isaac dinner, helping him with his homework, putting him to bed, everything feeling as if I'm scaling a mountain, pushing that rock that just keeps rolling down again.

'Are you sure you're okay?' he asks as he blinks at me from under his duvet, eyes wide, his expression worried. My heart spasms with both love and fear.

'Yes, bud, I am. Just a little under the weather, like I said.' How can I tell him the truth? I'm all he has. He's all I have. We're a team, and I feel like I'm letting him down, as well as myself. My body is betraying me.

The next day is the same, the hours endless, my body wrung out, but while lying on my bed with a bowl by my head – although I'm pretty sure there's nothing left to throw up – I log onto the nanny agency website and look through some profiles. I manage to arrange an interview with two of the best candidates for later in the week, praying I'll be well enough to see them through.

Fortunately the next few days without the chemo treatment are a bit better, and I drag myself to work.

'Are you okay?' my assistant Sara asks with concern as she hands me a coffee I know I won't be able to drink. I've barely eaten anything in forty-eight hours.

Dr. Stein told me it was important to keep my strength and weight up, but it feels impossible. A few saltines and some canned chicken broth are all I've managed. I'd bought *The Chemotherapy Cookbook* at Barnes & Noble last week, trying to feel optimistic, but the recipes for warming soups and protein-rich smoothies seem like a joke. If it were realistic, *The Chemotherapy Cookbook* would be nothing but blank pages.

'I'm okay,' I say and sit down at my desk gingerly, every bone and muscle aching. I am dreading talking to HR. I did some research online and I know I am entitled, through FMLA, to twelve weeks of job-protected, unpaid leave, but to pull the trigger on that is to tank my job prospects in the long term. No one in this business takes that kind of leave, ever.

And yet since my job prospects are already pretty much in the basement, why shouldn't I? The kitchen gadget start-up I was excited about was shot down at the latest meeting with barely a blink, considered 'too home grown'. I've got nothing exciting or urgent on my desk, and I have two weeks of vacation left this year, as well as a couple of sick days. All told I could survive this from a career perspective, never mind my actual health. The trouble is, I don't know how much worse it's going to get. When should I cash in those days? When will I be at rock bottom, unable to keep coping?

I decide to leave things as they are, and I tell myself that next week I'll go into work after my chemo, since it's done by ten in the morning. I compose an email to HR saying that 'personal health issues' are going to make me an hour late to work on Mondays and Tuesdays for the next two weeks. I hold on to the desperate hope that I'll only need one round of chemo to shrink the tumor and move onto the next stage of my treatment and recovery.

And so the weeks drag on, and I survive. I manage. The effect of chemotherapy is cumulative, so I feel worse – sicker, achier, more tired – but somehow I still struggle on. It's amazing how quickly you can get used to feeling horrible.

It all becomes depressingly normal, and when my hair starts to thin in the third week, that almost feels normal too. My skin is pale with a strange, waxy feel, and I develop sores in my mouth, which feels unbelievably dry all the time. Dr. Stein prescribes what she calls 'a magic mouthwash' to help with the sores, and it does, but I still feel like a walking wreck. I'm just used to it. When I look in the mirror, I don't see myself any more; I feel as if I'm looking at a mannequin, and I just have to wait until she's replaced. This isn't going to last forever.

Isaac asks again and again if I'm sick, and each time I tell him in as matter-of-fact a way as I can that yes, I am sick, but I am going to get better. That, I tell both Isaac and myself, is non-negotiable. It's just going to take a little while.

He seems to accept it, but I can tell he's worried, and I spend as much time with him as I can, wanting to reassure him, as well as myself, of my constant presence. I sit next to him as he plays his iPad, listening to the clatter and ding of his game. I watch him do his homework, noticing the furrow in the middle of his forehead, the way he sticks his tongue out as he does his times tables. I read extra stories at bedtime, sometimes falling asleep next to him because I'm so tired, but I don't think he minds. We need each other. Now more than ever, we need each other.

One evening as I am coming in from work, all my focus on just getting into my apartment, Eileen opens her door. I haven't seen her in a while, and now is definitely not a good time for one of our chats. No time is good any more.

'Grace!' She sounds so happy to see me. Then she clocks how I look, and her forehead dissolves into wrinkles. 'Are you under the weather, my dear?'

'You could say that.' I feel too tired even to fish for my key in my bag. I turn to her, take a deep breath. 'Actually, I have cancer.' It feels good to say it. Liberating, in a way I didn't expect, and yet also horrible, because somehow saying it out loud to my well-meaning neighbor makes it even more real than it already is.

Eileen's mouth drops open and her eyes crinkle up. 'Oh, my dear. My love,' she says, and then, to my surprise, she opens her arms. Even more to my surprise, I walk into them.

Her bosom is soft and pillowy and she smells old, like lavender and mothballs. She pats my back and after a few seconds where I feel unbearably comforted, I step away and sniff.

'Thank you.'

Her smile is both sad and understanding. 'My dear, when did this happen?'

'I started chemo a few weeks ago.' It feels like a million years.

Eileen shakes her head sorrowfully. 'What kind of cancer is it?'

'Breast cancer. My mom had it. She died when she was forty-five.' I'm holding on to my matter-of-fact tone with effort. Eileen nods again, and I wonder if she knows that I'm forty-six.

A few days later Heather calls and leaves a voicemail, sounding accusing and annoyed, and I realize I completely forgot about our meeting, the all-important meeting that was going to determine whether Isaac and I kept visiting. I finally dredge up the courage to call her back, and my lack of excuse makes her even more irritated. When she asks about our visit next Sunday, I want to both laugh and scream: I can't face a trip to Elizabeth, not on top of everything else.

But I don't tell Heather I have cancer. I don't even know why; it feels like a self-protective instinct that doesn't make sense. But still I stay silent.

After three weeks of chemo, I go back to Dr. Stein for a re-evaluation and discover the tumor hasn't shrunk enough to operate. Disappointment drags through me in a leaden wave as she explains, with a cheerful optimism that I don't share, that for a tumor of this size, with this stage of cancer, she would expect two or three rounds of chemo before she was able to operate.

I keep from saying that she could have told me that before, because I know why she didn't. Hope is the single biggest factor in cancer treatment. There's no substitute for it. I'm trying to hold onto it, but it's hard when I face at least three more weeks of the drip, the vomiting, the feeling that I am nothing more than a bag of aching bones and screaming joints. And maybe another three weeks after that. Maybe this is what the rest of my life will look like. That's how it was for my mother, and there's no reason I should be any different.

I've thought a lot about my mom as I've lain in that stupid reclining chair and watched the poison enter my body. I feel sad and guilty that I don't have more memories of her, that for seven years she seemed to me nothing more than an inconvenient invalid, but I don't think she actually was. She drove me to school sometimes, I remember, and she came to some of my piano concerts, and she tested me on my French vocab.

No, the truth is, I realize now, I don't have many memories of her because I chose not to. Because as an eight- or ten- or twelve-year-old, her illness, her cancer, *bored* me. I didn't like how tired she got, the wan, apologetic smiles she'd give me, the endless naps she took. I hated the wigs she wore; my father bought her several, all in wildly different styles.

Looking back, I see how brave she was, picking me up at my swanky girls' school wearing a fire engine red bob, but at the time I was embarrassed and annoyed. I was so petty, focusing on such small, stupid things, and I didn't even realize it until now.

And so I find I can't be hurt by Isaac's occasional impatience with me when I have trouble getting off the sofa, or when I'm not up for another game of Hungry Hippos, as much as I wish I were. He doesn't understand. Illness is an irritant. Children are, by their very nature, selfish, and they're allowed to be. Sacrifice and self-restraint take time to develop and grow.

At least I've managed to hire a nanny – a twenty-four-year-old woman from Croatia named Yelena. She was friendly enough with Isaac, in an overly bright sort of way, but with me she had a bit of attitude, assuring me that she doesn't do any cooking, cleaning, or laundry.

Since I have a housekeeper, Maria, who comes in twice a week, whom I never actually see, I tell myself this doesn't matter, but Dorothy did do a fair bit of tidying, and all of Isaac's laundry. Still, I don't have much choice. I need someone to start now, someone with a driver's license, good references, and flexibility.

I don't tell Yelena I have cancer. Maybe that's unfair, bringing her into such a fraught and volatile situation, but I have a feeling it would be a dealbreaker for her and I'm too desperate to risk it.

The second round of chemo starts, and it feels twice as bad as the first. I thought I was prepared, but I soon discover I wasn't. The first day is manageable, just, but the second day feels like I've been felled and then flattened.

I take the day off work and lie in bed, groaning softly, while Yelena huffs around in the living room, clearly not pleased to have me at home, cramping her style. God knows what she gets up to when I'm not here. She works from two until seven even though Isaac doesn't need to be picked up until three thirty. It was the only way I was able to get her to agree, and as I lie on bed, I realize how weak I've become in every respect, to agree to pay this woman to mooch around my house for an hour, refusing to cook or clean.

I end up composing an email to Lenora in HR, invoking FMLA and taking two weeks off work. I don't say the C-word, just mention health issues. I don't know what the legality of the situation is; can she force my hand? Is she allowed to ask? Should I talk to an employment lawyer? I'm too tired to care.

Another week passes, in a blur of nausea and pain and exhaustion. Is chemo this hard on everyone? I read stories of people who kept working through their treatments but on a day like today, when I have eaten nothing, still thrown up twice, and wince every time I move, I can't imagine it.

Stella calls and texts a couple of times, and I fob her off, saying I have the flu. I don't know why I don't tell her; I know she'd help me in a shot. I know she'd hug me, which is something I feel like I desperately need. And I also know she'd look at me differently, that I would become a cause, a charity case. Maybe that's just in my own head, maybe it wouldn't be that way at all. And yet still I say nothing.

I do end up, out of necessity, confessing to Yelena that I'm undergoing some treatment. She stands by the sink, peeling an orange with brightly polished nails, her eyes narrowed, her hair pulled back into a high, tight ponytail.

'Treatment? What is this treatment?'

I look at her and feel a welling-over of dislike. She's so young and pretty and cold. She doesn't care about me at all, but why should she? I've known her for all of two weeks.

'Cancer,' I say flatly, and she recoils as if I'm contagious.

'You should have told me,' she says haughtily, and I have no reply because I know she's right.

'It doesn't affect anything,' I say, which is a joke. I can barely stand up straight. 'Your hours or...' I trail off as I feel tears gather in my eyes. I do not want to cry. I have never been a crier. And I certainly don't want to start bawling in front of pert-bottomed, Lycra-wearing Yelena, who will merely wrinkle her nose at me.

'I should have known,' Yelena insists darkly, and then she walks out of the room. I officially hate her.

Another week drags by, and then the inevitable happens: Yelena calls in to say she can't work on a Friday, because of some appointment or other. She gives me proper notice and agrees to take the day unpaid; there's nothing I can do. Stella is away for the weekend with her family and there's no after-school club, because it's the Memorial Day weekend, and the entire city is evacuating. I tell myself I can get in a cab and get Isaac from school. Surely I can manage that.

But at two o'clock I am hanging over the toilet, dry-heaving into its porcelain depths, utterly wretched. I can't get in a taxi. I can't even get up from where I'm half-lying.

And there is only one person I can think of in the whole world, who might be free to pick up Isaac, and more than willing to do it.

I call Heather.

CHAPTER EIGHT

HEATHER

My mind is spinning as I drive into the city. It's Memorial Day weekend, and thankfully the traffic is going entirely in the other direction. Getting home is going to be a pain, but I don't care. When Grace called me, sounding tired and desperate, of course I only had one answer to give.

The very fact that she called me when I know she wouldn't want to, that I'd be the last person she'd want to call, both alarms and pleases me. Something must be really wrong.

I find Buckley School easily enough, an impressive-looking building on East Seventy-Third Street, and then I not so easily find a parking space two blocks away. As I head up the school steps I feel underdressed in my black skirt and plain white blouse, both from Walmart.

Everyone here is in designer clothes, the kind where the labels are obvious. Mothers swan up and down the stairs, heavy handbags dangling from their skinny wrists, faces made up, hair expertly highlighted.

I push past them, practically rude in my desire to get to Isaac. To see him. I'm ten minutes late, and he's been taken to the office, sitting in a chair, kicking his legs, looking glum. He isn't surprised to see me, because Grace already called them, but he doesn't look happy, either. He's unsmiling, wary, and my heart lurches.

'Hi, Isaac.' I want to hug him but I don't.

'Identification, please?' The office secretary holds her hand out, snooty and authoritative. I blink.

'Identification…?'

'I need to confirm your identification. You are Heather McCleary?'

'Yes.' I am annoyed; she's acting like I'm some kind of criminal. Would a 'Hello, nice to meet you' be too much to ask? I fumble through my purse, my hands practically shaking in my nervousness. I don't even know why I'm nervous. Seven years on and I'm finally doing something for Isaac, for my son, other than seeing him on a strained Saturday afternoon. I should be excited. Thrilled.

I finally find my driver's license and thrust it at the sniffy woman; she inspects it thoroughly, as if checking it's real. I start to feel angry, and then she hands it back.

I turn to Isaac. 'I have my car.'

He nods silently and picks up his backpack, which looks huge for a boy his age and size. I realize he hasn't spoken since I've seen him. He remains silent as we walk out of the school and down the block. It's a beautiful spring afternoon, not too hot yet, and this block of elegant brownstones with flowerboxes and wrought-iron railings is serene and beautiful, unlike any street I know back in Elizabeth. I feel slightly awed by it all.

'Do you want me to take that?' I ask, and reach for Isaac's backpack. He shrugs it off without a word, and I hitch it over my shoulder. I shoot him curious, searching glances; he's wearing his school uniform, khaki pants and a blue polo shirt. Shiny shoes. He's had his hair cut, pretty short. He looks different.

'Are you taking me home?' he asks when we reach my car.

'Yes. Gr—your mom couldn't pick you up, so she asked me to.' I speak lightly, as if this is a totally normal event, as if I haven't dropped everything and driven an hour simply to do this one small favor – not for Grace, for my son.

I unlock the car and Isaac slips into the back seat. I toss his backpack on the passenger seat and then get in, wishing I could prolong this moment. Could I suggest we go out for ice cream? I wouldn't even know where. I glance back at Isaac; he's staring out the window, seeming uninterested in everything, including me.

'How have you been, Isaac?' I ask as I pull out into the traffic, which is getting heavy. He shrugs, not replying. My fingers tighten on the wheel. 'Well?' I press, keeping my voice playful.

'Okay.' His gaze remains on the window. I focus on driving, because the traffic is intense and I'm not used to driving in the city. Trying to force a conversation with Isaac now will just frustrate and hurt me.

It takes us thirty endless, silent minutes to get to Grace's apartment on Eighty-Sixth and Park Avenue. She told me there was a garage under the building, and that I could park in one of the visitors' spots.

Isaac slouches out of the car toward the entrance to the building; I don't have a key, obviously, but there is a video intercom and the doorman; after seeing Isaac and listening to my halting explanation, he buzzes us in. I follow Isaac into the elevator, clutching his backpack, again wanting to prolong these moments, wishing things could be different.

We're silent in the elevator, and Isaac steps out first, going ahead of me to open the door, which Grace has left unlocked. I follow, pausing to breathe in the expensive smell of her apartment; it smells just as it did the last time I was here, over seven years ago, of lemon polish and leather. It looks the same too; the same plush carpet and abstract art, the same leather sofas, although perhaps they're identical replacements, because they look pristine. Everything does.

There are differences too, of course; evidence of Isaac is everywhere. I run my hand along his various coats hanging by the door. I step into the hallway, noting the jumble of sneakers and boots in a wicker basket. A card table has been set up in the corner of the living room with a half-completed jigsaw puzzle.

I look around for Grace, expecting her to bustle out from somewhere, but I can't see her. Isaac has kicked off his shoes and stands in the middle of the living room, looking a little lost. 'Can I have my iPad?'

'Are you allowed to have that now?'

'Yes, I get an hour of screen time when I get home from school.' He blinks at me, so serious.

'Okay, then.' He fetches it from a rattan basket beneath the coffee table and flops onto the sofa.

'Do you know where your mom is?'

'She's probably sleeping.'

That pulls me up short. Probably sleeping? That doesn't sound like Grace. I go through the apartment, looking for her just in case, and also because I'm curious – about her, about the home she's made with Isaac. She's not in the dining room that adjoins the living room, separated by pocket doors that are half-pulled out. The glass table that seated twelve has been replaced by a more modest and kid-friendly table of burnished wood that seats eight. I wonder if they eat there, the two of them, fancy organic meals by candlelight.

I follow the hallway toward the kitchen, where I have never been. It is enormous and elegant, with oak units, marble counters, and a huge fridge. Isaac's cereal bowl is still by the sink, Cheerios stuck to its bottom like cement.

The fridge is covered with schoolwork and pictures he's drawn, kept in place by big, colorful magnets. I pause to examine a spelling test – ninety percent – and a drawing of Steve from Minecraft, done back when he still liked Minecraft, I suppose. I glance at the calendar tacked to a bulletin board – Taekwondo, swimming, and piano every week. So many opportunities, just as I'd once hoped for him.

There is a little room off the kitchen that Grace clearly uses as her office. It's empty, and looks as if she hasn't gone into it in a while. There is a patina of dust on the closed laptop.

I am starting to feel uneasy, like something must be seriously wrong. Is Grace sick? Back in the living room Isaac is absorbed in his game, and hesitantly, almost on tiptoes, I walk toward the bedrooms.

I pause on the threshold of Isaac's bedroom, an ache starting inside me. It's a mess, with Lego pieces scattered everywhere, the bed unmade, his pajamas crumpled on the floor. But it's such a little boy's room, and it feels strangely poignant and bittersweet to realize he'd slept there, grown up there. I step inside and pick up the pajamas, folding them and putting them on top of the dresser. Then I make up the bed, and, feeling I might as well do the rest, I put the Lego pieces back in the bright red bin. Still no sign of Grace.

The bathroom between the two bedrooms is empty, the door ajar; Grace's bedroom door is also slightly open. I push it further open with my fingertips and peer inside.

It's huge, bigger than our entire downstairs, with some kind of exercise machine in front of the window, a separate dressing room and bathroom, and an enormous king-sized bed. Grace is asleep in the middle of the bed, her mouth open, her hair lank, a thin sheen of sweat on her pale face. She looks awful.

Is that why she called me? Because she has the flu or something? Why didn't she just say?

I step back out and close the door, deciding to let her sleep. I don't need to get home right away; the girls can manage for themselves for a bit. I already texted Emma to tell her I'd be out.

I head back to the living room, injecting a bright note into my voice as I say to Isaac, 'So, would you like a snack?'

He looks up from his iPad, blinking warily. I smile back. 'Okay,' he says at last, and it feels like a victory.

'Let's go see what's in the fridge.'

He discards the iPad and follows me into the kitchen. I open the fridge, feeling like a spy or an invader. I survey the contents curiously, expecting expensive, organic foods, things I've never heard of, but actually it's pretty empty: milk, some yogurt, a bag of carrots, some ground beef that looks like it might have gone bad.

Isaac slides onto one of the stools at the big island and watches me silently.

'How about a yogurt?' I suggest, and he shakes his head. 'Carrot sticks?'

'Apple sauce.'

I turn to face him, latching on to that one small detail, something I didn't yet know. 'Do you like apple sauce?'

He nods solemnly. He looks just like Kevin, with his wispy light brown hair and big eyes, those extravagant lashes. Like Kevin used to, when we were young and dreamy.

'Where's the apple sauce?'

Isaac hops off the stool and opens a built-in pantry cupboard that is filled with canned goods. He finds a box of apple sauce snack packs and hands it to me. I break off one, peel back the lid, and hand it to him. Then I open about six drawers before I finally find the silverware, and hand him a spoon.

The kitchen is completely silent as I prop my chin in my hands, my elbows on the island, and watch my son eat his apple sauce. I feel as if I could watch him forever – the way he slides his fingers through his hair, lifting his bangs away from his face, just like Kevin does. His eyes are slightly lighter than Kevin's, more like mine, but he's so obviously from both of us, and I never saw it as clearly as I do now. I never got the chance.

'Do you like school, Isaac?' I ask. I'm eager to know more about him, but he's often so monosyllabic at my house I hardly learn anything. Maybe things will be different here.

'It's okay.'

'What's your favorite subject?'

'Art.'

'Art,' I repeat, rolling this new information around in my mind like a marble, savoring its shape and texture. 'You've got some nice pictures on the fridge.'

He glances at the drawings, hunching one shoulder. 'They're okay.'

'Do you have a favorite game?' He looks wary again, and I suggest lightly, 'Maybe we could play it.'

He thinks for a minute. 'I like Hungry Hippos.'

'I love Hungry Hippos,' I say, even though it's not true. It's a noisy, clacking game, but at least I know it.

Isaac finishes his apple sauce in two bites and then hurries toward the living room. 'I'll go get it,' he calls back.

I clean up the apple sauce and then follow him out; he's already got the game out, and is setting up the colored hippos on the coffee table, having moved an obtrusive sculpture onto the carpet. He must have caught my uncertain look because he assures me, 'It's okay, we always move it when we play games here. Mom doesn't really like it.'

'Doesn't she?' I picture the two of them like we are now, bent over a game, and it feels both good and sad at the same time. I kneel on the carpet next to Isaac while he sets up the game, lining the hippos up with an endearing precision. The object, I know, is to collect as many marbles as possible by opening and closing your hippo's mouth with a lever. Amy used to love this game, and I feel a touch of nostalgia, remembering how I played it with her, how Lucy would always try to take the marbles, and how Emma was too slow, making Amy crow with victory.

Isaac releases the marbles and we begin to play; he's winning easily, even when I try my hardest, as he operates the little plastic lever with intense expertise. When he's concentrating, a furrow appears in the middle of his forehead, just like Kevin and Emma.

We play three games, and he beats me on each one. Isaac has started to relax, laughing and pumping his fist in victory.

'You are trying, aren't you?' he asks suspiciously after the third game, and I laugh and roll my eyes.

'It's kind of insulting that you think I'm not,' I tease. He frowns for a second, and then he figures out what I mean and grins. The sight of his unabashed grin, the ear-to-ear kind, feels like a fist wrapped around my heart. It's almost too much to bear.

I look down, not wanting to show how emotional I am, simply because of a smile. I clear my throat and ask, 'Want to play again?'

Before he can respond there is the sound of a door opening, and then Grace emerges from her bedroom, her arms wrapped around her middle, her step shuffling and slow.

'Grace, hi.' I sit up straight, moving a little bit away from Isaac and the hippos game. I feel a little bit guilty, almost as if I've been caught doing something wrong.

'Heather, thank you so much for getting Isaac.' She leans against the doorway, looking pale and exhausted. 'I really appreciate it. How are you, bud?' she asks, a smile softening her features.

'Okay.'

'Good.'

They share a moment, a kind of silent communication I don't understand but acknowledge is going on. Then Grace's glance flicks to me. 'Thank you, Heather. Really.'

'No problem.' I'm not sure if her words are meant to be a kind of dismissal. I stay where I am.

'Would you like a cup of tea?'

So it wasn't a dismissal. I rise from the floor. Isaac lunges for his iPad. 'Sure.'

We move into the kitchen, leaving Isaac sprawled once more on the sofa. Grace is moving slowly, as if she's an old woman.

'Are you all right?' I ask. 'Do you have the flu or something?'

Grace lets out a humorless laugh and goes to fill up a sleek-looking electric kettle made of chrome that looks like a piece of modern art. She leans against the counter and closes her eyes briefly. I realize she's not going to answer.

'Let me help.' Except I don't know where anything is. Somewhat to my surprise, Grace nods to a cupboard.

'The cups are in there.'

I take two thick pottery mugs in a pretty, iridescent blue and put them on the counter.

'Teabags in that jar,' Grace says with another nod, and I fetch two. I look at her uneasily; she really seems rough.

The kettle clicks off and I pour the water while Grace watches. 'Sorry,' she mutters. 'I'm not up for much right now.'

'It's okay.' I find milk in the fridge. 'Do you…?'

She nods. 'Please.'

It all feels kind of weird, and Grace looks as if she could keel over. She moves slowly to the kitchen table tucked in an alcove and sits in a chair, wincing slightly as if every movement makes her ache.

'Is there anything else I can do for you, Grace?' I ask, because I'm wondering how she's going to make it through the rest of the evening. 'I could make dinner…'

'Oh…' Grace lowers her gaze as she takes a small sip of tea and then shudders.

'Really,' I say. 'You look as if you should go back to bed.'

'I probably should. Today's been a rough day.'

'How long have you been sick?'

'A while.' I wonder why she didn't call me sooner. How has she been managing? 'Actually, Heather…' She looks up, seeming to deliberate whether to say anything more. I wait, feeling tense although I'm not sure why. 'The truth is…' She puts down her mug with shaky hands, and a little tea slops onto the table. She looks at me directly, her expression so bleak something in me both freezes and then recoils. 'I have cancer.'

CHAPTER NINE

GRACE

Heather is looking at me slackly, her mouth open, her expression dazed. Clearly she wasn't expecting that one. I debated whether I should tell her; in my better moments Heather would be the last person I'd want to tell. But I feel the need, the craving, to tell someone, to feel that sense of relief and liberation, the way I did with Eileen, because suffering through this alone is so damn hard. I know I should tell Stella, and I'm working up my courage for it, but it's Heather who was there for me today, who bailed me out. She deserves to know.

'Oh, Grace.' Her lips form the words slowly. She still looks dazed. 'I'm so sorry.'

'It's okay,' I say, even though it's not, not by a mile. But what else can I say? I try to smile, but my mouth wobbles, and suddenly I'm afraid I'm going to cry. And that is something I am not ready to do in front of Heather.

'What kind of cancer?'

'Breast cancer, stage four, invasive,' I answer flatly. 'It's gone into my lymph nodes but no farther. I shouldn't be surprised,' I add, with a bizarre attempt at careless levity. 'My mother died of breast cancer when she was forty-five, and I'm forty-six. I've always checked for lumps.'

'So you found it quickly…?'

'Not quickly enough,' I reply bitterly. I was so diligent about checking; it feels unfair that the cancer had got to fucking stage four before I found it.

'And have you started treatment?'

'Why do you think I look so shit?' I laugh, the sound both hard and hopeless. 'I'm on my second round of chemo, to shrink the tumor so it can be operated on. After that, I'm looking at a double mastectomy.' I haven't even let myself think about that yet, or what comes after. My brain, my soul, can't take anymore.

'And then? I mean…' She trails off, and I know what she is thinking but doesn't feel is polite to ask. *What is my prognosis?*

'I don't know.' It feels awful to admit that. Dr. Stein has given me pep talks, assured me what I'm experiencing now is normal, was perfectly calm when she discovered my tumor hasn't shrunk enough yet. None of it matters. I don't let myself think of that awful what-if, but it hovers on the horizon of my mind, the darkest cloud. 'Hopefully, I'll go back to normal life.' Which feels like the best thing I could hope for. The only thing I want.

'Is there anything I can do?' Heather asks. 'To help?' I know she means it, just as I know she wants to help – not just me, but Isaac. Of course she does. I would be the same in her position.

'Thanks,' I say. I wrap my hands around the warmth of my mug even though I can't stand another sip of tea, bland as it is. My stomach seethes and every joint aches. 'I can't think of anything right now. I have a nanny, Yelena…' I trail off, because suddenly I feel as if I am being cruel. Would I rather Isaac spent time with the mostly indifferent, cold-eyed Yelena, or his anxious, needy birth mother? What a question. What a choice.

'Okay.' Heather nods, acting unconcerned even though I know I've hurt her. I've always known; it's as if we're irritatingly attuned to one another, to each infinitesimal shift in our moods. I can read every flick of her eyelid, every tightening of her lips.

I wonder if she's as attuned to me as I am to her, and I cringe to think that she is, that she might know the petty and ungenerous thoughts that creep into my mind so often.

'Well, let me know,' Heather says. 'If anything comes up…'

'Right. I will.'

We both lapse into silence, and then Heather rises from the table. 'I probably should get back. The girls…'

'Of course.' I realize, with humbling suddenness, how much time and effort she's taken out of her day to help me. 'Thank you so much, Heather.' I sound merely dutiful but I mean it. 'I don't know what I would have done without you. You're a lifesaver.'

'Anytime.' She gives me a crooked smile and then goes to wash her mug in the sink.

'You don't have to—'

'I don't mind.' She leaves the clean mug on the dish drainer and turns around. 'Are you sure there isn't anything else…?'

There are probably a million little things, but I have the weekend to catch up. I need to go food shopping, but I can do it online and it's not as if I'd ask Heather for something like that. Not yet, anyway.

'We're fine,' I assure her. 'Really.'

'I'll just say goodbye to Isaac, then.'

I follow her out to the living room, where Isaac is still absorbed in his game on the iPad. My rules about screen time have gone right out the window, but I can't feel guilty about that now.

Heather turns to me suddenly, a look of alarm on her face. 'Does Isaac…?' she whispers, and I shake my head almost frantically.

'No.'

She nods and then kneels down, resting one hand on Isaac's shoulder, to say goodbye to him. He mutters a farewell without looking up, and I don't have the energy to insist on good manners. Heather grabs her purse and makes for the door. I follow her out.

'I'm so sorry you're going through this, Grace,' she says in a low voice. 'But breast cancer has a good, you know, survival rate, doesn't it?' She looks uncertain, as if she's not sure this is the sort of thing she should say. What is the etiquette for talking to cancer patients?

'Yes, it does,' I say. 'Generally.'

After she's gone I lean against the front door, feeling lonelier than before, already missing the company. The weekend looms ahead of me, three long days to drag myself through, and somehow keep Isaac occupied throughout. I'm too tired to savor the time with him, even though I know how precious it is, and that is another burden, another hurt. I need to cherish every moment, suck the marrow out of it, because who knows how many I have left? Except I hate thinking that way. I'm going to beat this. Of course I am.

Then on Tuesday it all starts again – the chemo, the nausea, the pain. I also have to answer an email from Lenora in HR, who informed me, quite briskly, that I need to give 'sufficient information' for my request to take leave. How much information is sufficient, I don't know. I know I qualify, and can tick the 'serious health condition' box, but will that be enough? Is Lenora going to make me spell it out? And why don't I want to?

Telling Heather was a relief, but it also felt like opening a wound, leaving myself vulnerable. I hate that. For my whole life I've been contained, closed. Even my father, beloved as he was, didn't get the whole me. I've always shown him my best side, Grace the straight A student, Grace the wunderkind at college, Grace the promising Wall Street intern, Grace the successful career woman. Now I'm none of those things. A side effect of cancer that I didn't expect – I no longer know who I am.

At least I am Isaac's mother. I walk slowly toward him. 'Enough screen time, bud.'

He looks up reluctantly, and then surprises me by tossing the iPad aside. 'Do you want to play Hungry Hippos?' he asks.

'Sure,' I say, and I sit gingerly next to him on the floor. As he loads the marbles into the center of the board, I feel a pang of bittersweet longing. Such a simple moment, and yet I want to hold onto it forever, despite the nausea and pain, the fear and uncertainty.

Of course you can't hold onto anything. I know that all too well, but I do my best over the long weekend, managing to find the energy to walk around the Central Park reservoir with Isaac. My steps are slow and he runs ahead, kicking a soccer ball; the sky is so blue it almost hurts to look at it, and everything is in bloom in the park, the buildings of Fifth Avenue soaring above, pointing toward the horizon. The beauty steals my breath and hurts me deep inside, a wound that grows bigger with every passing day.

I'm falling prey to the classic cancer patient shtick of feeling so thankful. A couple of months ago I would have rolled my eyes at it all, at the subtle bragging of a so-called life of gratitude, all the posts on Facebook, *hashtag blessed*, of picnics and presents and gap-toothed children. Now I want to gather all the beauty in my arms, like sheaves of corn, a bounty of blessing I know I possess, despite all the hardships in my life, all the loneliness.

Why did I not see it before? I sit on a park bench while Isaac runs and plays on a stretch of verdant green grass and I practically shake my head in wonder.

Of course that passes too, just like the rest. By the time we get back to the apartment, Isaac having dragged his feet for the last half hour, I am feeling tired and nauseous and decidedly unblessed. I wish there was someone I could call to come over and make dinner, entertain Isaac for a few hours. If Stella were in the city… but she's not, and she still doesn't know. When am I going to tell her? When am I going to admit to myself that every part of my life is going to change? Then I think of Heather; she would come if I called. She would always come.

I end up lying on the sofa, half-dozing, while Isaac watches TV. Eventually I summon the energy to order pizza over the internet from a local place. I fall asleep when the doorbell rings, and then Isaac answers it, shaking me awake.

As he eats three slices of pepperoni pizza and I merely push it around my plate, I wonder if I should tell him the truth about my sickness. Cancer, the word, the concept, is completely off his radar. Does he even know what it is?

I've resisted having one of those serious conversations because my parents had one with me, when I was Isaac's age, and my mother was first diagnosed. I didn't understand the big words; I had no concept of what cancer was. But I remember my father's grave tone, my mother's pale face, the overwhelming seriousness of it all, and how it terrified me. I didn't want that for Isaac, especially when there is no back-up adult to stay reassuringly healthy.

The lack of that backup remains on the fringes of my mind, a niggling worry in case the worst happens. Who will take care of Isaac? It's the first thing I thought of when Dr. Stein told me my diagnosis, and the question continues to torment me now, even though I keep telling myself it's not going to come to that. It just can't.

When I made a will, after I officially adopted Isaac, I made Dorothy his guardian. It seemed sensible, since she was the adult he knew best besides me, and she lived in the city. I have plenty of life insurance, enough savings in trust for Isaac, so while not ideal, it was acceptable. Of course, it's not now.

Dorothy is in Chicago, taking care of her daughter's fractured family. Who can be Isaac's guardian now? It's something I should decide sooner rather than later, and yet my mind flits away from the question, the problem. It's not something I have to think about quite yet, surely, and I have enough to deal with already.

On Tuesday I take Isaac to school, go to my chemo appointment, and then struggle to work by ten. I've already taken two weeks off, and I want to save the other possible ten for when I'm really sick, because that is always at the back of my mind. What if this gets worse? A lot worse?

At work people eye me askance and a few ask me how I am. I tell them I'm fine; what else can I say? While sitting at my desk, catching up on work emails, I run my hand through my hair and stare down at the fistful of strands caught on my fingers.

I thought, with the cold cap, I wouldn't actually lose my hair, but when I inspect myself in the bathroom mirror at the office, I realize how thin it has become. I've just been feeling too crap to notice. I bend my head, and see the pale glint of my scalp through the chestnut-brown strands. There's also a good inch of gray roots, since I've missed my usual six-week cut and color. I look even worse than I realized, which is quite a feat. No wonder people were giving me weird looks as I walked to my office – I looked like something the cat had played with, mangled, and then dragged in through the door.

I once prided myself on how sleek and chic I looked, without ever venturing into sexy or kittenish territory. I was always professional and polished, attractive in a business-like way. That, like so much else, has been stripped away from me. Now I look like a bag lady who bought a rich woman's clothes from a charity shop.

It's no surprise when Bruce stops by my office, acting overly jocular, jangling the change in his pocket.

'Everything all right, Grace?' He doesn't look me in the eye. I don't think he has since Jill Martin stole my partnership from under my nose. Needless to say, we haven't worked out together since then.

'Everything's fine, Bruce.' I rest my hands on my desk and give him my calmest, most professional smile. In the seven years since I was sidelined I've made Harrow and Heath a few good investments. Nothing stellar, but nothing too shabby, either. I've also outed a few investments they thought were solid that I realized weren't. All in all, I don't think I'm quite the embarrassment Bruce acts like I am, out of his own guilt. But now, with this illness, I'm becoming a liability.

'So you took some leave?' He raises his eyebrows, waiting for me to fill in the blanks, but I know how much I have to tell him, or really, how little.

'Yes, I have a health issue that is being resolved.' I smile pleasantly. 'Thanks for asking.'

He makes a bit more useless chitchat and then finally ambles out. When he's gone I wonder if I'm crazy, trying to keep cancer a secret. How can I, when my hair falls out, when I need more time off, when I am so obviously very, very sick?

But I can't escape the bone-deep instinct I have to play my desperate cards close to my chest. I remember the guy on the floor below with Chronic Fatigue Syndrome, how he was cut loose in such a way that he couldn't sue for wrongful dismissal. The company has a very good, very ruthless lawyer on retainer. I don't want to cross him. But of course I don't know how long I'll be able to keep myself under his radar.

I limp through the next week, managing to get to work every day. I also get fitted for a very expensive, very realistic-looking wig. When the stylist puts it on me, I breathe a sigh of both relief and longing. I look more like myself, the self I once knew and took for granted. Isaac notices, catching up the hair, letting it fall through his fingers.

'Is it real hair?' he asks, and I nod.

'Yes, do you think that's gross?' I'm curious, as well as trying to lighten the moment.

'No.' He looks at me assessingly, his gaze sweeping over my new locks. 'You look good, Mom.' I smile, feeling lighter and happier than I have in weeks. I pull him into a quick hug, and he doesn't resist.

'Thanks, bud.'

The next week is my last of chemo, maybe the last ever if the tumor has shrunk enough. It's also Isaac's last week of school, with three whole months stretching ahead of us that I have to fill in.

Stella won't be here either; she's decamping to Provence the day after school gets out. It feels too late to tell her the truth now, and maybe by the time she returns, it will all be over. Maybe by September I'll be getting back to normal.

For Isaac I've patched together some day camps at Asphalt Green and the 92nd Street Y, but when I explain to Yelena about the change in arrangements, she practically throws a tantrum.

'My hours are two to seven.'

'I know, and Isaac gets out of camp at one forty-five,' I say as calmly as I can. 'So it's only fifteen minutes earlier, and you'd start your shift by picking him up.' It doesn't seem all that unreasonable to me, but Yelena shakes her head dramatically, her shiny, dark hair flying around.

'That was not our agreement.'

'It's summer, Yelena. When I interviewed you, you stated that you had some flexibility, which I now need.'

'Some,' she agrees with dark emphasis, and clearly that is a negligible amount. I stare at her, frustration filling me up like water in a well. She glares back at me, her mouth twisted in a knowing smirk. I haven't hidden how desperate I am; I haven't been able to. But am I really that desperate? Is Yelena really going to make me find some other arrangement for Isaac's pick-up so she doesn't have to start one second earlier?

'So. You're saying you can't pick up Isaac at one forty-five from his day camp?' There is a warning note in my voice that Yelena picks up on.

'No, I am not saying that,' she says huffily, as if she hadn't been bitching about that very thing for the last ten minutes. 'Only, it is just, you know, an inconvenience.'

'But one you're willing to put up with.' She gives me a stiff nod. It's a victory, but I have no doubt Yelena will try to make my life hell in some other way. She seems to have a talent for it.

*

The last day of school, Stella invites Isaac and me over for a barbecue on their roof terrace. I haven't seen her in several weeks, and then only briefly, so she hasn't noticed the way my looks have taken a dive off a cliff, hasn't realized how sick I've been. And of course I haven't told her. Now, somewhat to my sorrow, it feels too late.

At least with my wig, some discreet make-up, and a bit more appetite than usual, I am almost feeling like my old self, or what I imagine my old self might have felt like. I've forgotten, really. I am amazed at how quickly that happens.

It's a warm, sultry night in early June, the concrete city far below us. Isaac, Will, and Will's little brother Jamie are playing on a giant checkerboard, with plastic pieces the size of hubcaps. Stella and I are reclining on a wicker sofa; Stella's made up a pitcher of sangria, and while I've avoided alcohol since starting chemo, I decide to splurge tonight and have one glass. I don't feel too nauseous, and Dr. Stein will have the results of my test on Monday, to see if the tumor has shrunk. I'm almost feeling hopeful.

'So do you have exciting summer plans?' Stella asks. 'I know you go to the Cape…' They are off to the south of France for three months on Saturday, their usual exodus to their rented villa, as well as to visit Eric's family in Europe.

'Yes, for a week in August. I love it.' And I really hope I will feel well enough to manage.

'Oh, I love the Cape. You are so lucky.'

I smile, because I know Stella means it, despite her own far more luxurious plans.

'You know,' she says, lowering her voice a little, 'sometimes I feel like it's all overkill. Three months in France? All the lessons? Does a seven-year-old really need to know Mandarin Chinese?'

I laugh, shaking my head. 'You tell me.'

'I admire you, Grace,' Stella says seriously. 'I feel like you have the right balance. Work, motherhood, privilege, reality. It works.'

I glance around the terrace, at the boys having a fun time wheeling the checkers along. 'This feels pretty good to me, actually.'

'It does, right now.' She leans back against the sofa. 'I suppose I just feel guilty sometimes. I know I'm lucky, but do I really know? And are my kids going to grow up spoiled because they have so frigging much?' She grimaces. 'Do you know I grew up in Indiana? I shared a bedroom with two sisters. Seriously, it was a downgrade on *The Brady Bunch*.'

'Your kids will never be spoiled, Stella.' I mean that sincerely. 'You're too down-to-earth for that.' Despite the huge apartment, the endless activities, the summers in France, Stella feels grounded to me, which is one of the many reasons I like her so much.

'I hope so,' Stella says, and for a second I think about telling her about my illness. It seems ridiculous, absurd, that I haven't told basically my best friend that I have *cancer*. She should have been the first person I called. She would have helped me, I know she would. And yet I didn't, and I'm not going to now, because I really don't want our relationship to change, to become defined by my disease, because everything else is.

In any case, right then, relaxing on top of the world, a glass of sangria in my hand, my son playing near me, I can almost pretend I don't have cancer. Or at least that I won't for long.

On Monday I wait in Dr. Stein's office, everything in me tensing, as she comes in with my results. Her manner is brisk, her smile quick. What does that mean?

'Good news, Grace,' she says, cutting to the chase. 'While I would have liked to see the tumor shrink a little more, it's reduced in size enough for me to consider surgery.' Her gaze scans my face. 'That is, if you're still feeling like you want to go ahead with the double mastectomy?'

I gulp. Nod. 'Yes,' I say, feeling jubilant and terrified all at once. 'Yes, I would.'

CHAPTER TEN

HEATHER

When I get back home from Grace's, it's nearly nine at night, thanks to the traffic. The house is a mess, the girls are quarreling, and Kev is in a bad mood. And I have to deal with it all.

'Where have you *been*?' Lucy demands theatrically, hands on her hips, her face tear-stained.

'I had an emergency.'

'An emergency?' Lucy's mouth drop opens. 'What kind of emergency?'

'Nothing, it's dealt with now.' I don't want to get into where I've been with Lucy or anyone yet. I start taking the dirty dishes that are scattered around the living room into the kitchen. My mind is still spinning from what Grace told me.

Cancer, and it sounds serious. What does that even mean for her, for Isaac, for me? Am I awful to think that way already, to wonder *what if…*?

'Has everyone eaten?' I ask as Emma drifts into the kitchen, looking morose.

'I made spaghetti.'

I shoot her quick smile. 'Thanks, Emma.'

'Where were you?'

'Out.' I shrug, feeling strangely guilty. 'Helping a friend.'

Emma looks suspicious, but I don't explain anything more. I don't want to cause ripples by mentioning Grace and Isaac. Not yet, not until I've sorted things out in my mind.

The next hour is spent dealing with all the mess and irritation, and then getting Lucy to bed. Amy is out, and she doesn't come home until after ten, which is against our rules but neither Kevin nor I say anything. At nearly sixteen, she is becoming out of our control, although we haven't said anything about that, either. If we don't say anything, if we don't acknowledge it to each other, perhaps it isn't really happening, or maybe it will at least go away soon.

By eleven I'm getting ready for bed; Kevin is already lying in bed, two pillows stuffed behind his head. He eyes me in a slightly hostile way. 'So what was the deal tonight, you out like that?'

My back is to him as I answer. 'Grace asked me to pick up Isaac.'

'Grace?' He sounds disbelieving. 'In the city?'

'Yes.'

'Why?' Now he sounds even more disbelieving.

I take a deep breath as I shake out my hair. Then I turn around. 'Kev, she has cancer.'

He is silent for a long moment, and I can't tell anything from his expression. 'Is it bad?'

'Bad? Of course it's bad. It's cancer.' But I know what he means. 'She's having chemo now. She looked terrible.'

'Is she going to survive?' Kevin asks baldly, and I flinch a little at the unfeeling starkness of the question, even though I've been wondering the same thing.

'Surely it's way too early to ask something like that. She's only been doing the chemo for a couple of weeks, I think.'

He shrugs. 'Still.'

'Breast cancer has a pretty good survival rate.' I'd Googled it, although why exactly I'm not sure. My feelings are so tangled, and I'm afraid to examine them too closely. Afraid what it will reveal about me.

'Why did she call you, though?'

I stiffen. 'Why not?'

'Come on, Heather. It's not like you and Grace are best buddies. Not by a long shot.'

'I know, but…' I struggle to moderate my tone. I know what he's saying, and even I felt surprised when Grace called me. Asked me. 'I know Isaac.'

'Doesn't she have friends? A nanny?'

'The nanny was out for the day.'

He shakes his head. 'It's just kind of weird.'

'I don't think it's that weird.' I try not to sound defensive as I get into bed.

Kev pats his pillows down as he gets ready to go to sleep. 'Face it, babe, you're the last person Grace would want to ask for a favor.'

That stings, even though I have to agree with him. After I turn out the light I lie in the dark, staring up at the ceiling, wondering why my relationship with Grace has had to be so strained, so antagonistic even as we have always pretended to get along. Was it just because I asked for the adoption to be open, or was there something more, something that was always there, from the moment I first looked at her profile, saw that slightly superior smile, and chose her for the mother of my child? I didn't even know what I was doing back then. I was acting out of a fear that made me so dizzy I couldn't even think. But, looking back, I think there was some sense of superiority that motivated me, along with everything else; I couldn't compete with Grace's money, but she was single. It evened it all up somehow; yet as I think this, I know it's wrong. It's not the way I should have been thinking at all.

Now I wonder, if I'd chosen one of those smug couples, would things have been better – or worse? Would it have felt like less of a competition, a power struggle? And which one of us has made it that way? Maybe we're both guilty, both at fault.

Over the next few weeks I wait for Grace to call. Every time my cell rings I snatch it up, hoping it's her. I've convinced myself that she needs me, but she obviously doesn't. Maybe a pick-up when everyone else is out of town and her nanny is off duty, but real life? The day-to-day? She seems to be managing fine. And then it turns out I'm not.

It starts with the meeting with Lucy's teacher that I forgot about, so it had to be rescheduled. I'm already feeling like a bad mom when her teacher starts our conversation by asking, 'Did you know Lucy has trouble reading?'

Kev's not here, of course. He never comes to meetings like these. 'What do you mean by trouble?'

Mrs. Bryant puts on reading glasses and takes Lucy's test, pinched between two fingers, like it's Exhibit A from some courtroom drama. 'According to the tests I've done this year,' she informs me in a cool tone, 'Lucy has the reading level of a seven-year-old, if that.'

The 'if that' catches me on the raw. She sounds so accusing, so judgmental. 'You weren't aware of this, Mrs. McCleary?'

'No.' My jaw is tight, my hands clenched in my lap. Mrs. Bryant is one of those stern, iron-haired teachers who looks down on pretty much anyone, at least anyone she suspects is stupid. Maybe she knows I didn't finish high school, never mind that I have my GED now. And then there's Kev too, with his straight D average through all four years. Maybe she thinks I don't help Lucy with her homework; that I don't read to her before bedtime. And I don't always. I don't even often. But still, I *care*.

'I'm surprised it wasn't caught earlier—'

'Caught?' She's making it sound as if Lucy has some disorder, some disease. 'What do you mean exactly?'

'I mean the severity of Lucy's learning disability is such that it should, ideally, have been flagged up when she was younger, so she could get the help she needs.'

My mouth is dry. 'And now?'

'Now it's important that we start giving Lucy that help. We have a specialist on staff who has one-on-one sessions with children who are having similar struggles. So, with your permission, I'd like her to start attending these sessions as soon as possible.'

'Okay.' That seems easy enough, but I still feel deficient, as if this is somehow my fault. 'Is there anything I should be doing…?'

Mrs. Bryant proceeds to list all the ways I could and should be helping Lucy – reading to her as much as possible, helping her sound out words, using letter and sight word flashcards, modeling the 'joy of reading' myself. I stare and nod, numbly realizing how little of this I've ever done, or, if I'm honest, will probably do. Who has the time?

'This is important, Mrs. McCleary,' Mrs. Bryant says severely as we both stand. 'Good reading skills equip a person for life. And of course the opposite is true, as well.'

So if I can't help Lucy to read, she's screwed. I nod stiffly and say goodbye.

When I get home things only become worse. Kev and Amy are having a standoff in the living room, and Emma and Lucy are hiding in the kitchen.

'What's going on?' I ask even though I don't really want to know. Amy's body is vibrating with rage and Kev is standing with his fists clenched.

'I caught her stealing money from my wallet,' he states flatly. 'And I told her she's grounded for a week.'

My stomach drops. 'Amy…'

'I was borrowing it,' she sneers, not remotely sorry. My temples start to throb.

'Yeah, right,' Kev sneers right back at her. 'Sure you were.'

'You never believe me,' Amy shrieks. 'You never think anything good about me.'

'That's not true, Amy,' I say tiredly, even though it sort of is. I'm always suspecting her, always afraid, usually powerless. 'But why didn't you ask first?'

'Because he wasn't here—'

'I was here,' Kevin returns in an iron-hard voice. 'I was in the can. You chose your moment well, but not well enough.'

'That's not fair—'

I take a deep breath. 'Amy, if your father says you're grounded, you're grounded.'

She looks wildly between the two of us and then squares her shoulders. 'Oh, whatever,' she snaps. 'I'm not listening to you.' And before Kev and I can so much as blink, she is pushing past us and out of the house.

Kev lets out a roar of anger and springs after her, but he's not fast enough. By the time he gets outside she's already run down the street, hair flying. She tears around the corner and then she's gone.

Kev slams back into the house, and everyone backs away, waiting. 'We're canceling her phone,' he growls. 'What else can we do?'

I shake my head, speechless. I don't know what else we can do for Amy. She defies us at every opportunity, even when she doesn't need to. It's like a challenge for her, either that or a compulsion. Fighting with her only makes it worse.

Kev goes to the fridge for a beer, and I walk into the room Amy shares with Emma. Emma's side is pin-neat, but Amy's is a mess – clothes all over the floor, a spill of make-up across the dresser. I pick my way through the clutter and sit on the edge of her unmade bed.

How did it get like this with her? When did it become so bad? When did mere naughtiness tip over into something darker and more volatile? I gaze disconsolately around the messy room and for a moment I long for those days when my girls were little, three beds crammed into a tiny bedroom, soapy angels in a tub, all elbows and knees. I thought I had problems then, and I did, but these feel more dangerous. I'm scared for Amy, and that feels far worse than being scared for myself.

More out of curiosity than any real suspicion, I open the drawer of her bedside table, hoping for some clue into the complicated mind of my angry teenaged daughter. I blink down at a stash of make-up – expensive stuff, some of it unopened. I pick up a shiny red compact, a gold-plated lipstick. My stomach feels hollow. There's no way Amy could have afforded all this. There are at least a dozen different tubes and bottles and boxes in this drawer – eyeshadow, lipstick, pencils, powders. I barely wear make-up, but even I know all this stuff must cost hundreds of dollars. Amy's only money is from babysitting, and she does that rarely, because Emma is far more reliable. This stuff must be stolen.

Kev appears in the doorway, his beer already half drunk. 'What are you doing?'

'Nothing.' I close the drawer before he sees, not that Kev would know what it all was. But looking as shiny and new as it does, he might realize it has to have been stolen. I'm not quite ready for his explosion when he does.

I rise from the bed and pat him on his arm. 'We'll talk to her when she gets back. Let me make dinner.'

Amy doesn't come home until midnight. Kev has taken his medication – he's still on it, after all these years, for the low-level chronic pain he'll always have – and I wait up alone, curled up on the sofa, the windows open to the spring night. I feel a heavy, dragging sadness about everything – Amy, Lucy, Grace. I meant to read to Lucy before bed tonight, but with Amy and everything else I forgot. I haven't had time even to think of Grace… and of Isaac.

Amy creeps in quietly, and then stops in the doorway as she clocks me. I muster a tired smile, fear outweighing any anger I might feel at her flagrant disobedience.

'Welcome home.'

Amy shrugs off her jacket without replying. I watch her for a moment, her tense body and defiant expression. 'I know,' I say quietly. She still doesn't say anything. 'About the make-up.' I take a deep breath. 'You've been shoplifting, Amy.'

She turns to me, startled for only a second, and then she folds her arms, tilts her chin. 'So?'

'So?' I stare at her, at a loss because she is so unreachable. 'I didn't raise you to be a thief, Amy.' Too late I realize how accusing that sounds, and so I try again. 'Amy, you're better than that—'

'How would you know?'

'Because you're my daughter and I love you.' I hear the tears thickening my voice. 'Don't you want more for your life?'

'Than what?' She's so scornful. 'Anyway, wasn't this about having more?' She turns away.

'Amy, stop.' My voice comes out hard and I press my shaking hands together. 'You're going to return that make-up.'

She stares at me for a long time, her lips pressed together, her eyes narrowed. 'And if I don't?' she asks at last, the same scornful note in her voice. I'm shocked at how cold she seems, how uncaring. Is it an act? Or has she really become that indifferent, that hardened?

'Don't push me, Amy.'

'Why?' Her voice trembles and rises. 'It's a little too late to give me away, isn't it?' And with that parting shot she flounces to her bedroom.

I sit on the sofa, an icy coldness stealing through me. Am I responsible for her rage, or was Amy just doing what she knows so well how to do, and saying what wounds me the most? I can't bear to think that it might be true, that all of this might be my fault. That in trying to hold onto Isaac, I might have pushed away my daughter.

I don't know how long I sit there, feeling so cold inside, my knees gathered to my chest. Eventually I fall into a doze, and when I wake up grey dawn is filtering through the curtains, casting the living room in a shadowy light. My body aches. I drag myself to bed, hoping to sleep for a few hours, but it seems as if only a moment passes before Lucy is shaking me awake, complaining that her stomach hurts. Before I can formulate a reply, she throws up all over me. That's Memorial Day weekend taken care of.

By the time I head back to work on Tuesday I am feeling the strain of everything –Amy, who maintained a huffy silence throughout the weekend; Lucy, who is back at school even though she still looks washed out; Kev, who was grumpy all weekend because of everything; and Grace. Of course Grace.

She is always on the periphery of my thoughts, as is Isaac. I wonder how she is doing, if the chemo is still wringing her right out, if she is lonely or afraid. Kev's remark about me being the last person she'd call twanged a raw nerve, because I know it's true… which means Grace doesn't have anyone else. Anyone at all.

I end up checking my phone constantly to see if she'll call again, knowing I'd drop everything if she asked, for Isaac's sake. And maybe even for hers. I send a couple of texts, asking how she is, trying to keep it light and helpful.

She never replies, and three whole weeks go by without a word. We're coming up to the last Saturday of June, the day of Isaac's visit, but I feel like calling her to ask if they're coming would be insensitive. Still, I want to know, just as much as I want to know how she is doing. How Isaac is doing.

Then, one Wednesday in late June, she finally calls. Her voice sounds tired, although she attempts to inject a bright note into it.

'I'm sorry I haven't been in touch. You've probably been wondering…'

'It's okay,' I say quickly. 'I understand you've had a lot going on. How are you… how are you feeling?'

Grace lets out a shuddery sigh. 'A little better. Well, I still feel like shit, but I've had some good news.'

'Oh? That's great.'

'Relatively speaking, of course. The tumor has shrunk enough so my doctor can operate. I'm scheduled for a double mastectomy next Friday.'

'Oh. Wow.' I'm not sure what to say. *Congratulations* doesn't seem right, even though it's obviously good news, just as Grace said.

'I'll be in the hospital for at least two days,' she continues. 'Recovering. And I was wondering…'

My heart lurches with an awful hope. 'Yes?'

'If you'd be able to stay with Isaac. In my apartment. I know it's a lot to ask, and it would probably be easier for him to come to you, but I want to keep things as normal for him as possible…'

'I understand.' My mind is racing. Two whole days alone with Isaac. With my son. It will be hard on Kevin, on the girls, and I'll have to take time off work, but I don't have to think about it for a minute. Not even for a second. 'Of course, Grace,' I say. 'Of course I'll do it. Anything you want or need, just say.'

CHAPTER ELEVEN

GRACE

The relief I feel when Heather says she can be with Isaac is palpable, a shudder through my body. Something I once would have dreaded has now become my salvation. Because the truth is, I have no one else. Heather is my last resort, my only hope, especially after Yelena went and quit on me with absolutely no notice.

She didn't even have the decency to tell me to my face. She texted me while I was at work, saying she was going to California to be with her boyfriend and wouldn't be able to pick Isaac up from camp that day. I ended up having to take a half-day off work to do it, and then cobble together desperate childcare until my operation. I miss Stella, who left for France a month ago, oblivious to my illness and need. I've thought about calling or emailing her a dozen times, telling her the truth, but I've always held back. I tell myself by the time she gets back, I'll be better. Yet I know she would have jumped to help if she'd been able to, but of course she's four thousand miles away.

After the surgery I'm taking six weeks unpaid leave, to recover. The fact that I'll be watching Isaac while I recover is something I'm trying not to think too hard about yet.

'When is your surgery exactly?' Heather asks.

'Next Friday. I need to be at the hospital at nine.' I'll drop Isaac off at camp beforehand. 'If you could pick Isaac up from camp at one forty-five, that would be perfect.'

'Okay.' Heather pauses, and I can tell she is thinking about saying something else. I wait, hoping she's not going to suggest Isaac go with her to Elizabeth. I don't want him to have to cope with something that is still, even after so many years, unfamiliar.

'Do you want someone to go with you to the hospital?' Heather asks. 'I mean, me?' I'm so surprised I don't say anything and she rushes on, 'Sorry, just say no if you don't. I don't mind. I just thought, you know, it's kind of a hard thing to go through on your own.'

My throat is too tight for me to speak. Yes, it's a hard thing to go through on my own. It feels like the loneliest thing in the world. And I am humbled and honored that Heather is willing to share it with me, even as part of me – a large part – cringes at the thought of her seeing me in such a vulnerable and exposed state. That's not how I've ever lived my life.

'Grace?' Heather asks uncertainly, because I still haven't said anything.

'Sorry.' I clear my throat. 'Sorry, I was just…' I can't think of anything to say, so I decide on the truth, painful as it is to admit. 'That's kind of you, Heather. It… it would be really nice if you came with me. Thank you.'

As soon as I disconnect the call I am already regretting accepting her offer. Heather and I aren't friends. We barely tolerate each other, if we're truthful. If it hadn't been for her insisting on an open adoption, I would have been happy never to see her again seven years ago. I would have been thrilled. And yet she offered, and I accepted, because I'm scared and lonely and right now there literally is no one else.

I spend a couple of weeks trying to get my life in order. Dr. Stein assured me that the surgery isn't too risky, but I've never gone under a general anesthetic before and it pays to be careful. So I spend a morning with my lawyer arranging all my financial affairs, updating my will. The one thing I don't do is change Isaac's guardian; Dorothy might no longer be the most obvious option, but she still feels like the best one. Changing it is an avenue I'm not ready to explore. Not when I finally have a chance at beating this thing and getting my life back.

While I wait for the surgery I also do some odd jobs I hadn't got around to doing, framing photos that had been left in drawers, ones I meant to frame years ago: Isaac as a chubby-cheeked toddler picking apples at an orchard in New Jersey; Isaac at six years old, grinning on the beach at Cape Cod.

I don't think we'll go to the Cape this year. We normally go the first week of August but I'll still be recovering from surgery, and who knows how I'll feel? I hate the thought of missing that week. It tethers me to my old life, my old self, when I took so many simple pleasures for granted. It also would be good for Isaac, a semblance of normalcy amidst all the cancer chaos.

Those two weeks before surgery I also spend a lot of time thinking about my parents – my mother's cancer, my father's last days. I remember how I'd lie next my mom in bed when she was really sick, and she'd rest one hand on my shoulder, as if anchoring me to her. So often I'd wriggle away, impatient to be doing something else, but sometimes I'd stay and listen as my mother spoke in a soft, faraway voice about me as a baby, about her and Dad dating. Giving me memories, I realize now, because she knew she might not be able to give them to me later.

I think of my father in his hospital bed, the way he withered so quickly, but how his smile was still the same. I remember how poignant it was when he made a joke, even though his body was literally decaying, and how upsetting it was when he suddenly became fretful or querulous, so unlike himself, pushing away the Styrofoam bowl of chicken noodle soup I was trying to feed him, or fiddling with the oxygen tubes hooked to his nose. Even then, in the midst of my aching loss and endless love, I sometimes felt impatient with him, and I hated myself for that.

Even now I fight annoyance with Isaac for leaving his sneakers in the middle of the hall, and at the same time I want to grab him into a hug so tight it steals his breath, and never let him go.

A few days before the scheduled surgery I sit down with Isaac to tell him the truth, or at least a version of it. He looks at me worriedly, and I realize I am adopting the same too-serious expression and tone my parents took with me. I try to smile, but everything feels fragile. I'm full of hope, optimistic now that I've made it to the next stage, and Dr. Stein has always been positive, but still. Cancer. My child. The memories are thick.

'What's wrong?' Isaac asks, and his voice wobbles. 'Why are you looking like that?'

'Nothing's wrong,' I say quickly, perhaps too quickly. 'But I need to talk to you for a little bit, Isaac. In a couple of days I'm going to have to go into the hospital overnight.'

His fair brows draw together. 'Why?'

'You know how I haven't been feeling too well?' He nods slowly. 'I need to go to the hospital to help me feel better. It's a good thing, but I've got to stay overnight.'

'By yourself?'

'Yes, I'm afraid so.'

'So who's going to stay with me?' He looks even more anxious. 'Yelena?'

'No, not Yelena. She quit, remember?'

'I didn't like her.'

'I didn't like her either,' I admit. I don't feel guilty tarnishing Yelena's memory. She was a terrible, if competent, nanny, all told. 'No, actually, Heather is going to be staying here with you. Aunt Heather.' The words feel awkward and forced. I never call her Aunt Heather if I can help it, even though she asked, right at the beginning, while she cradled Isaac in her arms.

'Heather?' Isaac wrinkles his nose, and then he nods again, accepting. 'Okay.'

Two days later I am waiting for Heather in front of New York Presbyterian Hospital, having dropped Isaac off at the 92nd Street Y for camp. He clung to me, and I clung back, because as each hour has wound down I've become increasingly terrified.

I've tried to be reasonable about my fears, which is ridiculous, because fear isn't reasonable. I don't even know what it is I'm afraid of, not exactly. The unknown? The pain? The ugliness of the operation? Dr. Stein is hoping to do an immediate breast reconstruction after the surgery, but she won't know if she can until she's opened me up, a fact I find fairly horrifying.

I tell myself this is all progress. After the mastectomy, I'll have several rounds of radiation to zap any lingering cancer cells and keep them from getting ideas. And then, God willing, I'll be well. Healthy and whole, ready to take back my life and live it to the full. Healthy by the time school starts.

The thought is intoxicating, just the possibility of it makes me dizzy: normal again, able to eat, sleep, work, play. When days don't drag by in agonizing minutes, when I can tilt my face up to the sun and simply smile, when Isaac and I will be a team again, ready to take on the world.

I shift on the sidewalk, feeling the heat wafting up from the concrete. It's one of those muggy, stifling days in the city when everyone who possibly can has left. The air shimmers and people walking past me in their business clothes are already sweating through their shirts.

'Grace.'

I turn and see Heather striding toward me, an uncertain look on her face. Her hair is pulled back in a ponytail and she's wearing a t-shirt and stonewashed capri jeans. For a second I recall the time I first met her, standing in the doorway of my apartment, wearing that same uncertain look, it morphing into a smile. It feels as if time is in a kaleidoscope, endlessly twirling.

'Hey.' Her smiles widens as our gazes meet, and then, to my surprise, she envelops me in a hug. Her body is soft and pillowy and she smells like Ivory soap. The contact is shocking; I can't remember the last time I've hugged someone besides Isaac, and I'm usually the one hugging while he twists away. Eileen, maybe, in the hallway.

Hugging Heather feels strange but also deeply comforting in a way I didn't expect. I find myself returning the hug, even clinging for a second, like a child with her mother.

Then we separate, both us seeming a little abashed by the surprising intimacy. 'Hi,' I say, and I brush tears from my eyes, quickly, so she doesn't notice. I am amazed at how undone I've become; I'm so very raw right now, everything exposed. I breathe in and out in an attempt to restore my composure.

'Should we go in?' Heather asks, and I nod.

I've become used to hospitals since that first time, seven years ago, when just walking through the doors sent a shudder of memory through me. I've had to go to ER a couple of times with Isaac for minor injuries and accidents, the bout with pneumonia, and then of course since starting the chemo treatments I've had to get used to hospitals in a whole new way. Now, instead of remembering my father's illness, I am remembering my own.

Heather glances at me, a faint smile creasing her face. 'Okay?' she asks quietly, as if attuned to my feelings and even my memories, and I nod. Gulp.

'We need to go to the Breast Center.'

'Sounds like the right place.'

I'm feeling weirdly disconnected from everything, letting Heather lead me to a place I've been dozens of times already, for the chemo. I don't know why Heather being here has reduced me to this unsettling, child-like status; maybe I've finally reached the end of my fraying rope and I just need someone else to take control. To take care of me. And she is willing.

In the waiting room Heather goes up to the front desk to check me in while I sit on a chair and flip through a magazine, the pictures and words blurring in front of me.

She comes back with a couple of forms that I need to fill out; they never seem to end. Then it's more waiting; we sit side by side, just as we did for Heather's ultrasound, and the memory makes me smile. Heather, noticing, glances at me curiously.

'I was thinking about your ultrasound,' I admit. 'How we were both sitting like this. And how absolutely ignorant I was about everything. Pregnancy, motherhood… I had no clue.'

'I think there's really only one way to learn,' she says with an answering smile.

'Yes… those first few weeks with Isaac…' I shake my head. 'That was a crash course in just about everything.' I don't know why exactly I'm talking about Isaac with Heather now. We've never really talked about him in seven years of this open adoption that I was, until a few months ago, trying to bring to an end.

'You seemed to do okay,' Heather says, and I can't help but arch an eyebrow in disbelief.

'I barely knew how to hold him.'

She winces at the reminder, but I'm past feeling insulted or hurt by that. Way past.

'The first diapers—the first twenty diapers—just fell off.'

'I think everyone feels that way about a newborn baby, especially their first. They're so tiny and scrawny.'

'Yes, he certainly was.' I brought Isaac home when he was only five pounds, one ounce. I could have held him in one hand, if I'd been brave enough. I glance at Heather, whose expression is cautious and I feel compelled to include her in the memories. 'Do you remember?' I ask almost shyly. 'How small he was?'

'Oh, yes.' Heather smiles faintly. 'I remember. He was so tiny and red when he was born. Bright red and wrinkly and scream-ing.' She looks away, and I feel a lurch, as if someone has pushed me off balance, because of course that is a memory I don't have.

Impulsively, perhaps because I am so raw, I touch her hand. Squeeze. 'Thank you,' I say. 'Thank you for giving him to me.'

Heather's face crumples briefly and she gulps a couple of times. I keep my hand on hers, so unlike me, but necessary in this moment. 'You're welcome,' she whispers, and in that moment we are as connected as we were that night long ago when Heather put her hand over mine on her baby bump. We will always be joined by the son we share, no matter how we might have wanted to claim him solely for our own.

'Grace Thomas?' A nurse with a clipboard appears in the doorway. The smile she gives me is kind, too kind. My insides wobble.

'That's me.' My voice sounds scratchy, like a pen on paper, one running out of ink. Heather stands with me, and together we walk toward the door and what awaits us beyond.

We are led to a small room, where there is a clean hospital gown draped over the examining table.

'Change into that, no undergarments please,' the nurse says. 'I'll come back to check your vitals before you're prepped for surgery.'

Prepped, like a piece of meat, rubbed dry and seasoned. I am shaking.

'Shall I give you some privacy?' Heather murmurs and I nod jerkily.

'Thanks.'

She steps out of the room and with hands that tremble I take off my cotton top and navy blue capris, clothes that suddenly seem to belong to another life. Another me.

In the hospital gown, with its gaping back, I feel as if I have been turned into someone anonymous. Patient. That's all I am now. I take off my wig, because I suspect I'll have to at some point, and lay it on top of my folded clothes. Now I am completely exposed, and yet I know there will be more to come.

There is no mirror in the room, and there is probably a good reason for that. I glance at my wavy reflection in the steel basin of the sink, but I can't see much. I pat my hair and feel how wispy it has become. I have not gone completely bald, but I almost wish

I had. The thinning strands and wisps with glaring bald patches feel worse, more depressing.

Taking a deep, even breath, I open the door and beckon Heather in. Her glance takes in my hair, or lack of it, with a flare of surprise; she hasn't seen me without it. I manage a small, wobbly smile.

'Yet another one of the perks of chemo.'

'I'm sorry.' Her voice is soft, heartfelt. 'It must be awful.'

'It is.' I perch on the edge of the table. 'But hopefully I'm on my way up now.' It's just there is a long, long way to climb.

We sit in silence for about twenty minutes, but it's not uncomfortable. I'm glad Heather doesn't feel the need to fill the quiet with banter or meaningless chitchat, because I'm really not in the mood.

The nurse comes in to check my vitals, tick boxes on her chart. Then she tells me Dr. Stein will be here in a few minutes to talk to me before the surgery.

We wait some more, and I feel the tension tautening inside me, like a rope about to snap. Dr. Stein comes in, dressed in surgical scrubs, her manner professional but friendly as always.

'Hello, Grace. How are you feeling this morning?'

'A bit nervous.'

'Understandable.' Her gaze flicks to Heather.

'This is…' A quick breath. 'My friend, Heather.'

'Great. Heather, you can stay with Grace until we wheel her into the operating room, okay? Right up until the last minute.' She flashes a quick smile before adopting a serious expression. She sits on a stool and wheels it closer to me.

'I know we've talked about this before, but I just wanted to have a quick chat about what I'll be doing while you're in surgery.'

'Right.' Although actually I don't want to hear, because the last time she told me the nitty gritty of what a double mastectomy entails, I nearly passed out. Still, I fix a polite and faintly interested smile on my face as Dr. Stein launches into a description of how she's going to cut into my breasts and suction all the tissue out. I glance at Heather and see how pale she looks, and amazingly, I almost laugh. This is definitely not for the faint of heart.

'As for the reconstruction, we're not going to be able to determine whether we have the right conditions for that until during the operation.' Conditions. I think of weather conditions; *it's a little too stormy for that.* I nod.

'Okay, great. Any questions?'

'When… when will I feel better? I mean, enough to call my son and talk to him?'

'The mastectomy takes about two hours, and if we're able to do a reconstruction, that will be another two to three hours. Then you'll be in a recovery room for about three hours, before you're back in your hospital room.' She glanced at her watch. 'It's nearly ten now, so I'd imagine you might be up for making a phone call tonight around nine or ten, but if not, definitely by tomorrow morning.'

'Okay.' Tomorrow morning. I can hang on that long if I need to.

'So all I need to do now is make some marks with my special pen.' She brandishes what looks like a child's marker.

'Do you want me to…?' Heather begins, but I shake my head.

'It's okay.' I feel badly, making her leave the room every time I need privacy, and the truth is, I don't want to go through these moments alone.

'All right.' With brisk movements Dr. Stein slips the hospital gown off my shoulders and I am naked to the waist. I thought she'd be a little more discreet, but obviously discretion went out the window a long time ago.

Dr. Stein asks me to sit up straight while she makes some lines and crosses on my breasts, which look flabby and old, but they're still mine. They're still there. Heather is averting her head, and I appreciate the effort.

'So that's where you're going to cut,' I say, and Dr. Stein nods cheerfully.

'You'll find the incisions will be barely noticeable once we've reconstructed your breasts.'

Which is a sentence that in another situation, another life, might have made me laugh.

'All right.' Dr. Stein helps to pull up my hospital gown. 'I'll see you in surgery in about ten minutes.'

She leaves, and quite suddenly, I am seized by panic. I'm having one of my old panic attacks, like I did right after my father died. I can't breathe; air comes in and out in wheezy gasps and I bend over, my arms wrapped around my waist.

'Grace?' Heather rubs my bare back. 'Grace, it's going to be okay.'

I am gulping for air, sweat prickling across my shoulder blades and pooling between my breasts.

'I'm scared,' I say through chattering teeth. 'I'm so scared.'

'It's all right to be scared.' Heather is still rubbing my back, the way I rub Isaac's after he's had a nightmare. 'Anyone would be scared in this situation. *I'm* scared.'

I laugh, or try to, but it comes out like a sob. I put my hand to my mouth to keep the rest in. Heather puts her arms around me.

'It'll be all right,' she whispers. 'It's going to be all right, Grace.' I close my eyes as I relax into her embrace, the comfort she offers me freely, that I never, ever expected to receive – and yet so desperately need. *Yes, it's going to be all right,* I think, lulled by her words, her motherly tone. *It has to be.*

PART THREE

CHAPTER ONE

HEATHER

I stay in the hospital until long after Grace goes into surgery. I accompanied her into a little room, some kind of pre-operating room, where she lay down on a stretcher and they hooked her up to an IV. Machines were beeping and the number of nurses and doctors bustling around with tubes and needles surprised me; this was clearly a major event.

Grace looked small on the stretcher, her face pale, her poor head with its wispy hair as fragile as an egg. I could have wept for her. The whole experience cut me to the bone, as I sensed the pain and fear she felt. I hadn't expected to feel so much, to ache so much… for Grace.

After they wheel her into the operating room a nurse ushers me out, and I wander down antiseptic corridors before I find a café. I buy a latte and sit at a table, lost in a haze of thought, my coffee forgotten.

I am thinking of Isaac as a baby, Grace under the knife. The way he smelled in those newborn days, when I buried my nose in his neck. The way Grace looked on, anxious and exhausted, while I pretended to know it all. It all seems so unbearably petty now, the deliberate one-upmanship I couldn't keep myself from, even though I knew it didn't do any good for either of us.

Then my thoughts move to my own family – Amy's anger, Emma's confusion, Lucy's needs, Kev's resentment. So much to deal with, day after day after day. And then back to Grace, wondering how she has coped with cancer all by herself, and then considering how much she needs me right now. How much I want to finally be needed. It all drifts through my dazed mind as I sit and stare into space while the hours tick by unnoticed.

Eventually I startle awake, blinking the world back into focus. My muscles are sore from sitting still for so long. It's nearly one, and Grace might still be in surgery for several more hours. I need to pick Isaac up in less than an hour, and so I hurry from the café, stepping through the swinging doors of the hospital into the humid haze of a hot summer's day. Heat boils up from the concrete and the city smells dirty, a whiff of garbage and gasoline in every breath. It hasn't rained for weeks.

I take a deep breath, wanting to focus on Isaac, even though my mind is full of Grace. He's the one who needs me now. I take the First Avenue bus uptown to 92nd Street, resting my head against the window as it lumbers and wheezes up the avenue, stopping every other block to let someone on or off. The trip takes thirty minutes, and by the time I reach the Y on Lexington Avenue it is forty-seven minutes past one, and I am sweaty and out of breath.

As I hurry inside, nannies and a couple of parents march by with their charges. I don't think I'm imagining their superior smiles. In this world – Grace's world – you don't show up two minutes late.

Isaac is waiting by the door of his classroom, backpack on, expression dour. His leader or teacher or whoever is tidying up; she shoots me a quelling look as I hurry in. I feel scolded.

'Sorry, Isaac. The bus took longer than I thought. How was camp?' I reach out to touch his hair but my hand just hovers before I drop it.

Isaac shrugs one bony shoulder. 'It was okay.'

He doesn't look at me as we both walk out of the Y. 'Do you want to walk home?' I ask brightly, even though the heat feels suffocating. Isaac just shrugs. 'Do you and your mom usually walk?'

'We take a cab.'

'Do you want to take a cab, then?' Grace told me she'd left money on her kitchen counter, to pay for anything while I'm taking care of Isaac. I don't know how much it is, but knowing Grace, it will be in the hundreds. We can afford a cab.

Isaac doesn't answer, just steps out onto the curb, one arm raised. Seconds later a cab pulls over. I am impressed and a little unsettled. Seven years old, and he hails a cab without blinking an eye. Even Amy would be unsure, asking me how to do it, and I wouldn't really know.

We slide inside the blissfully cool air-conditioned car, and Isaac scooches over to the window, as far away from me as possible. I tell myself not to mind. I have two or three days with him. I can handle a little awkwardness at the start.

I try not to think of Kev, simmering with silent resentment at being left in charge, or Emma, who will actually do all the work, or Amy, who is likely to spin further out of control without me there, or Lucy, who will certainly whine and cry and be difficult. Two, maybe three days. That's all I've got, and I want to savor them.

I glance at Isaac, whose face is averted from me. It gives me the chance to study him properly, from the sweet, round curve of his cheek to those skinny shoulders and almost concave chest; he really does have Kevin's build. Kevin's eyes and hair, too.

My glance moves down to Isaac's scabbed-over knees, such a little boy, always jumping and running, no doubt. One of his sneakers is untied, and I have to keep myself from reaching down and tying the laces.

The cab pulls up in front of Grace's building, and Isaac slips out without a word, running ahead into the building, as I fumble with crumpled bills to pay.

I follow him into the air-conditioned, potpourri-scented elegance of the building's marble-floored foyer. The doorman greets Isaac with friendly kindness and then raises his eyebrows, waiting for me to declare myself. I know I must look like I don't belong here.

'I'm Heather McCleary,' I say. 'I'm staying with Isaac for a few days. Grace left me a key.'

'Of course,' he answers smoothly, and then produces an envelope from a drawer. I take it with murmured thanks, and then we are in the elevator. The button lights up before I've pushed it, and I realize the doorman must have done it from his station.

'What do you want to do this afternoon?' I ask Isaac. It feels too hot to go to the park, but I don't want to squander our time together with Isaac glued to whatever device is his current favorite.

Isaac gives me a considering look, wondering, I think, how much he can ask for. 'We could go swimming,' he suggests after a moment.

The elevator doors open and I step out into the hall and fit the key in the lock. 'Where do you usually go swimming?'

'Asphalt Green.'

Which is back where we just came from, all the way on York Avenue. The thought of going out into that heat again makes me wilt. 'Maybe we'll do that tomorrow,' I murmur, and as Isaac rushes ahead, I step inside Grace's apartment.

The calm elegance of it washes over me in a soothing tide. Marble floors, plush carpets, soothing colors. The air smells of lavender. Everything is tidy. How does she manage it? I wonder, before I remember she has only one child and undoubtedly a cleaner, as well.

Isaac has curled up in a corner of the sofa, his iPad on his lap. 'Half an hour, Isaac,' I call. 'And then we'll do something else.'

I take his lunch box into the kitchen. I've been here before, of course, recently at that, but it feels different now. I'm in charge. I have sole responsibility for Isaac. I'm even going to sleep in Grace's bed.

I wash out Isaac's lunch box, leaving it to dry upside down on the dish drainer. The fridge holds very little food – just some milk, wine, and cheese. Does Grace never eat? What does she feed Isaac?

I count the money on the counter, crisp bills in an envelope: five hundred dollars. I could shop for good, nourishing food, splurge on organic stuff that I never buy. I could make Isaac a delicious, healthy dinner. I deliberate, unsure what I want to do. How I want to spend this time with my son.

He might turn his nose up at the kind of meal I'm envisioning. I don't want to expend so much effort on something that he won't like – but then how do I fill the time? I finally have what I've always wanted, and I don't know what to do. The irony is not lost on me.

I end up calling the hospital for news of Grace. The nurse tells me she can't say anything about Grace's condition or even if she's out of surgery over the phone.

'But I'm taking care of her son,' I protest. 'She'd want him to know.'

'I'm sorry.' She sounds firm rather than regretful.

It's been forty-five minutes since we got home, and I've basically done nothing. I feel lonely in a way I didn't expect. I've dreamed of this, and yet now I'm uncertain, restless.

I walk back into the living room. 'Hey,' I call lightly. 'Why don't we go out and do something?'

'Swimming?' Isaac asks hopefully.

'I'm afraid I didn't bring my swimsuit.'

'You could borrow my mom's.'

Grace is probably half my size. 'I don't think it would fit. What's the next best thing to do, after swimming?'

Isaac lowers the iPad, his forehead furrowing. 'Can we go to the Central Park Zoo?' he asks at last. 'We have a membership.'

That is something I feel capable of. 'Yes, let's do that.'

Twenty minutes later, both of us slathered in sun tan lotion and with a bottle of water in my bag, we head out. I decide against a cab, wanting Isaac to get a taste of the real city, or what I imagine it is. Besides my times here to see Grace I don't have that much experience of Manhattan life.

We take the bus down Fifth Avenue, the cobblestone sidewalk outside the park filled with nannies and children, strollers and soccer balls. Dappled sunlight filters through the trees and people line up at the ice cream stands that are stationed on every other block. It almost feels like we're in a movie, with the gleaming white spiral shape of The Guggenheim on one side and the park on the other, Manhattan at its sunny best.

We get out at Sixty-Seventh and walk down to the zoo, Isaac leading the way because he knows it better than I do. We stop outside the clock that I recognize from movies and magazines, with the mechanical animals coming to life every fifteen minutes. I'd managed to find Grace's membership pass in a neatly organized drawer in the kitchen; she has memberships to just about everything fun or interesting in the city – Natural History, The Children's Museum, The Met, The MOMA, Asphalt Green, even The Intrepid, the huge battleship permanently parked on the West Side. Sifting through all those laminated cards gave me an almost painful pleasure, that Isaac was experiencing all these things, the kind of things I wanted for him when I first agreed to the adoption. I picture him and Grace wandering through a museum or a park, a sunlit montage of happy mommy-and-me moments.

We line up to get into the zoo, and as soon as we're through the doors Isaac is running off, wanting to see the penguins. I follow him around from exhibit to exhibit, baking in the heat, enjoying the way he hangs on the railing and studies the different animals so carefully and intently.

'What's your favorite animal here?' I ask, and he answers immediately.

'The grizzly bears.'

Later, I watch the two grizzly bears, Betty and Veronica, lumber about, and Isaac chortles at their antics as they try to knock a treat out of a tree. 'Mom always likes the otters best,' he says, glancing at me sideways. 'Because they seem so happy.'

And so we have a look at the otters, watching them glide through the water, slick and dark and graceful. Yes, they do seem happy. I can't help but smile as we watch them, and when Isaac asks for cotton candy, I say yes.

The pink puff of cotton candy is twice as big as his head, and I doubt he'll eat a quarter of it, but I enjoy the sight of him pulling off wispy pieces and popping them into his mouth, savoring the clearly unusual treat. It's been a nice afternoon, a temporary respite from the worries, the unknown.

We are strolling toward the park exit, the concrete still simmering with heat even though the sun has started to sink and there are long shadows cast on the cobblestone pavement, when, out of nowhere, I hear an incredulous voice. '*Isaac?*'

Isaac pulls up short, his face sticky and pink, his mouth dropping open at the sight of the mother and son in front of us.

The woman reminds me a little bit of Grace, with her expertly made-up face, her highlighted hair, a few gold bangles sliding down one super-skinny wrist. She's wearing a pair of hot pink capris that look very expensive and a tight polo shirt in a bright white. She tucks a strand of hair behind her ear as she gives me an appraising look.

'You must be Grace's nanny.'

I hesitate, wondering whether it's easier to just go with it, but Isaac doesn't let me take that option.

'No, she's my birth mom.' He slurs the words together as if they're one word, and I can tell he doesn't really know what they mean. I doubt Grace has spent a lot of time trying to get Isaac to understand what I am to him.

The woman looks at me in surprise, and I can tell she didn't know Isaac was adopted. And why should she? I doubt it's something Grace has ever wanted to advertise.

'I'm Lynne,' she says, holding out one manicured hand, which I shake limply. 'And this is Jasper. He's in Isaac's year at Buckley.'

I nod dutifully at the little boy with the blond hair that looks as if it has been expertly styled, with gel. He's wearing a turquoise-blue polo shirt with a popped collar, khaki shorts, and loafers without socks. And he's seven.

'So do you and Isaac get together very often?' Lynne asks in a trilling voice. 'Where's Grace?' Her eyes dart around, looking for her.

'She's in the hospital,' Isaac says. I have a feeling Grace didn't advertise that, either.

Lynne's eyes go round. 'The hospital?' She reminds me of a shark, greedy for gossip.

'Just a small procedure,' I say briskly, because I think it's what Grace would want me to say. 'Isaac, we should head home now.' I manage a smile at Lynne, who is looking annoyed at being brushed off by someone like me. 'Nice to meet you.'

We walk out of the park, and my back prickles with awareness; I know Lynne is still staring at me. I manage not to look back.

'Mom doesn't really like that lady,' Isaac whispers when we've gone a little bit away. 'And I don't like Jasper.'

Curious, I glance at him. 'Why doesn't she like her?'

Isaac shrugs. 'I heard her telling Will's mom that she was fake.'

'Right.' I'm even more curious now. 'Who is Will?'

Isaac grins. 'My best friend,' he says simply.

A few minutes later he asks to stop at the playground on Sixty-Seventh Street with a big, serpentine slide cut into the rock. I sit on a bench and watch him slide down again and again, laughing at how much pleasure he gets each time.

The shadows are lengthening, the park emptying out. It's after dinnertime, and there is still no food in Grace's fridge. Plus we should get back in case she phones from the hospital.

I call to Isaac and we walk in companionable enough silence to Madison Avenue, where we catch the bus back uptown. We get off in front of the supermarket on Eighty-Seventh Street, and Isaac tags along behind me as I peruse the aisles, luxuriating in not having to count pennies or clip coupons. No EBT card this time, thank God.

'Can we make our own pizzas?' Isaac asks eagerly. 'That's always fun.'

'Sure.' We pick out pizza bases and sauce, grated cheese and a variety of toppings. I add a box of chocolate ice cream bars for dessert, plus orange juice for breakfast and some snacks for Isaac's lunch tomorrow.

As we walk back to the apartment, I play a little fantasy in my head that this is my real life, walking back to my home with my son. Basically, I'm imagining that I'm Grace. I'm not jealous of her, not exactly, but I revel in the simplicity of the moment, how easy everything is, with money and space and opportunity – and my son.

I let Isaac go on his iPad while I set out all the cheese and sauce and toppings for the pizzas. Then we spend a fun few minutes decorating them; Isaac decides to put his toppings on to make a face – black olives for eyes, a red pepper for a mouth. I follow suit, which makes him crack up, a sudden, infectious laugh erupting from him so I am laughing too. I'm happy in that moment – a pure, clean feeling.

After dinner Isaac takes a shower without asking – clearly part of a bedtime routine –and I tidy up. I check my cell phone but there have been no calls. I think of calling Kev or Emma, checking in, but I don't want to hear all the complaints, the note of bitterness that I know will seep in, no matter what. Kev was not happy about my decision to come here. In fact, he fumed.

'This isn't your job,' he said, hands on his hips, while I got out a bag to pack.

'Actually,' I said quietly, 'it is.'

'No,' he returned, spite sharpening his voice. 'You just want it to be.'

I can hear Isaac singing in the shower and it makes me smile. I tidy up his bedroom and then I venture into Grace's room, feeling as if I am trespassing even though she's already told me she put clean sheets on the bed for me. It's a beautiful room, spacious and simple, the pieces of furniture bigger than anything I could fit into my house. I peruse the top of her dresser, run my fingers along a set of enamel boxes that look expensive and hold pieces of jewelry – discreet diamonds and pearls. There is a bottle of lotion by her bed that smells amazing and probably costs more than I spend on a week of groceries.

I peek into Grace's closet and run my hand along the crisp blouses in blue and white, pale pink and pearly gray, skirt suits in various shades of blue, gray, and black, and a couple of cocktail dresses that look gorgeous.

'Heather...?'

From the depths of the closet I hear Isaac's uncertain voice and I hurry out to find him standing in the doorway of Grace's bedroom.

'Sorry,' I say, flushing. I have no ready reason for why I was in his mother's closet.

Isaac's quiet glance takes in the empty bed, newly made-up. 'Did my mom say she'd call...?' he asks in a small voice.

'Yes, she was hoping to.' I glance at the clock; it's already ten past nine. 'Maybe in the morning, though. I'm sure she will then. Have you brushed your teeth?'

He nods, almost dismissively. Of course he has.

'Time for bed, then,' I say, and obediently Isaac turns around and walks to his bedroom. I follow, amazed at the lack of protest or backtalk. Is it because I'm somewhat of a stranger, as much as it pains me to admit it, or is he simply that kind of child? Unfortunately, I don't know.

Isaac slides beneath the navy sheets on his bed, his expression still solemn. 'If she calls, will you wake me up?'

'Yes,' I say firmly, although I'm not sure I will. He needs his sleep.

He nods and turns on his side, tucking his knees up to his chest, one arm wrapped around them. A well-loved, one-eared elephant lies next to him. I rest my hand ever so lightly on his back; I can feel the knobs of his spine beneath my fingers, just as I once did when he was a baby.

'Goodnight, Isaac,' I say softly. He doesn't answer, but he hunches his shoulders a little, and that is response enough.

I leave the room, closing the door quietly behind me. The apartment stretches endlessly around me, oppressively silent. I can't hear the traffic or neighbors or anything. I'm used to people, to the creaks and murmurs of my family, the background of TV or music or even just the whir of the washing machine. Not this incredible *stillness*.

I decide to pour myself a glass of wine from the open bottle in the fridge, even though it feels a little presumptuous and I don't normally drink. It's cold and crisp and somehow soothing. I sit on the sofa as I sip it slowly, and stare out at the darkening night. I wait for Grace to call, but she never does.

CHAPTER TWO

GRACE

The world fades in and out, a hazy blur of color and sound. I wake and try to speak, but my lips are chapped, my tongue dry and thick, feeling too big for my mouth. I sleep again. Someone comes. I feel cool fingers on my hand. I wake.

I don't how long the cycle goes on, only that eventually the cobwebs start to clear from my mind, at least a little bit. It's dark out; I can see the lights of the city from my window. I try to raise my hand to check the bandages I feel on my chest, but I can't manage it. My hand twitches uselessly at my side.

A nurse comes in, after five minutes or an hour, I don't know. 'You're awake,' she says cheerfully, and I blink at her. I open my mouth to speak, but my tongue is still too dry.

'Would you like a sip of water?' she asks, and I nod, or try to. She leaves and comes back a few minutes later with a plastic cup of ice water. With one hand behind my head she helps me to sip from the straw, and those first few gulps are like a little bit of heaven. I close my eyes in relief.

'Easy, now,' the nurse advises. 'Your stomach will still be a little unsettled from the anesthetic.'

There are a thousand questions I want to ask, but I can't verbalize them yet and in any case I doubt this woman knows the answers. Beyond the questions, the need to know, there is a pulsing point to everything: Isaac. I need to call Isaac. I need to tell him I'm okay. But I can't; I can't even manage the words to say to the nurse, and so I subside back onto the pillows and eventually I drift back to sleep.

I wake in the night to sudden, lancing pain through my phantom breasts. My chest throbs. I grope for the call button in the dark, my fingers feeling thick and clumsy. Eventually, after what feels like an age, I find it, and another age later a nurse, a different one, returns.

'Please,' I croak. 'My son. Isaac…'

Sympathy flashes across her face. 'It's the middle of the night. You can call him in the morning.'

I hate the thought of him waiting for me to call, but I know I have no choice. 'Pain…' I gasp out. 'Could I have something for the pain?'

'Let me check.' She consults the clipboard at the end of the bed, and a frown creases her face. 'I'll be right back,' she says, and she returns a short while later with two little red pills. I swallow them without asking what they are. More relief.

I doze on and off; people come in and out. Eventually morning dawns, and with the sunlight streaming through the window I start to feel a little better. A little more alive.

I manage, with a lot of effort, to scoot up in bed. I look down at myself, and see the heavy gauze bandages wrapped around my chest. My breasts are gone, although I can't actually tell from this vantage point. I have no idea if Dr. Stein completed the reconstruction. There are far too many bandages to see.

Another nurse, and then breakfast; I manage to get up and use the bathroom, brush my teeth; both feel like huge victories. I want to call Heather, speak to Isaac, but now that I'm more awake and cognizant something in me hesitates. I want to know more before I make that call. Before Heather, and more importantly, Isaac, ask me questions I need to be ready to answer.

I doze, take pain medication, and then in the late morning Dr. Stein arrives. She looks serious, less cheerful than usual, and a tremor of fear goes through me.

'Hi, Grace. How are you feeling?' Cue the sympathetic smile.

'Well, I've felt better.' I still sound a little croaky.

'I'm sure you have.' She pauses, and I wait, trying to suppress another tremor of fear. Why isn't she chirping about how well it's all gone?

'I've scheduled you for an MRI this afternoon,' she says. 'The surgery flagged a few things for me, and I'd like to check them out.'

I stare at her, my mind spinning. I feel sick and terrified, and yet also weirdly unsurprised. 'Things…?'

'I'll be able to tell you more after the MRI, probably by tomorrow morning. There's no point getting worried before we know all the facts.' She tries for a reassuring smile but it doesn't reach her eyes. Terror seizes me by the throat.

Dr. Stein asks a few more questions about the bandages and my pain management, mentions something about drains that she has inserted into my chest, but which will be taken out at some point. I can barely process what she's saying. All I'm thinking is that I need more tests, that she saw something inside of me that wasn't good.

'Grace.' Dr. Stein puts her hand over mine. 'Try not to worry yet.'

Yet. Because there will be some point in the future when I should worry.

They take me down to the MRI in a wheelchair, because I'm not up for that much walking yet. My chest throbs and I am holding onto my composure by a thread. I feel like bursting into tears, like the frightened child I feel I am in this moment.

A sudden memory pierces me, nearly undoes me – my father's wry smile as he was taken to have a port put in his chest for the chemo drugs and blood transfusions that never worked. I held his hand and tried not to cry, and he made a joke about everyone wanting easy access to him. He smiled through it all, and here I am, struggling not to break down.

Did he have weak moments like this that he didn't let me see? Did my mother? Both struggling with terminal illness, trying to soldier on… I miss them so much; it feels like I can't breathe. It feels like the day of my father's funeral all over again, when I couldn't see how I was going to get through the next few minutes, never mind the rest of my life.

Except maybe that's not going to be as long as I once hoped.

It takes all my strength and self-control not to panic when I'm having the MRI; I feel as if I am being electronically entombed. And then to wait and wait and wait until tomorrow for the results… the seconds tick by slowly, never mind the minutes.

I call Heather in the late afternoon, when I trust myself not to cry.

'Grace.' Her voice is filled with relief. 'I've been so worried. How are you? How are you feeling?'

'Okay. Been better, of course.' My voice wobbles and I take a deep breath. I'm not ready to tell her or anyone about this new, unknown development. 'How have things been? How's Isaac?'

'Good. We went to the zoo after his camp yesterday, and this afternoon we went to that playground by the Met with all the pyramids. Got soaked in the sprinklers.' Such simple things, and yet they make me ache. They feel as distant as the moon, perfect and pure and wholly innocent.

'That sounds fun. Can I talk to Isaac?'

'Of course.' She calls him over, and I don't miss the easy familiarity in her voice that wasn't there before, ever. Then I hear my son.

'Mom?' He sounds uncertain, his breathing heavy.

'Isaac.' Tears sting my eyes. 'How are you, bud?'

'Okay.'

'Are you having fun with Heather? Sounds like you've done some cool stuff.'

'Yeah.' He sounds so uncertain, and it makes me ache. 'When are you coming home?'

'The doctor hasn't told me yet, but hopefully tomorrow.' Although that seems virtually impossible. I can barely walk. But that's what all the literature said: two to three days for a mastectomy. I'm still believing that's what it's going to be like for me.

'Good.'

'I love you, Isaac. I miss you.'

'I miss you, too.' A pause. 'Are you feeling better?'

I smile through my tears, wishing it were so simple. 'Getting there, bud. Getting there.'

We say goodbye and then Heather comes back on the phone, reassuring me that Isaac is doing well, sleeping, eating, bathing and brushing his teeth, all the bases covered. I want to be back in my home so much, curled up on the sofa with my son, that it's like a physical hunger, eating me from the inside out.

When Dr. Stein comes in the next morning, I feel as if I've been waiting forever, and yet as she comes through the door I realize I'd be happy to wait some more. I have a terrible, gut feeling that she is going to give me some really bad news.

I feel that even more when she sits in the chair next to my bed and rests her hand lightly on mine.

'So, I have the results back from the MRI.' Her eyes are dark and sad and I try to swallow, but my mouth is so dry, my heart pounding so hard, I just give a convulsive gulp. 'Grace, I'm so sorry, but the cancer has spread.'

'To my lymph nodes…' I try weakly.

'And to your brain, bones, liver, and kidneys.' I blink, trying to take that in, but it's too much. It's everywhere.

'But…' I want to argue. I want to insist that she's got it wrong, because what about all that damn chemo? The tumor had shrunk, she said. That's why I'm here, with bloody bandages and still so much pain.

'I'm sorry.' Dr. Stein looks near tears, which appalls me.

'But how?' My voice is a plaintive whisper. 'I was having the chemo...' I'm too shocked for tears, too blindsided to realize what this means.

'Sometimes that happens. Tumors shrink even as the cancer is spreading elsewhere. This is metastatic cancer, and we still don't completely understand how it works. It was only when I began the surgery that I realized what we might be dealing with.'

My head feels fuzzy, and I can't think. I know I need to ask questions, important questions, but they don't come, and so I just stare. Dr. Stein smiles at me, her face far too full of sympathy.

'I know this is a lot to take in.'

Somehow I manage to form some words. 'So... I'll need to have more chemo?'

Something flashes across Dr. Stein's face so quickly I can't, in my spinning state, make it out. I realize I've asked a well-*duh* question, because if I've got that much cancer, of course I need to have more chemo. A lot more.

Except I don't.

'Grace...' She swallows and I feel a blind, buzzing panic take over me. 'Of course we can discuss all your options, but if you want my opinion, both as your doctor and a person who could be facing the same situation one day, I don't think it's worth it, to go through more rounds of chemo and feel miserable and sick the whole time. It's... it's not going to help enough. The cancer has spread too far.'

I have no words. I feel empty inside, everything blank. I just stare. And yet some part of me, some hard little kernel, remains unsurprised. Wasn't I afraid of this? Wasn't I expecting it, even?

'We can talk about clinical trials, some new drugs that are being tested, but to be involved in a trial you have to have quite a hospitalized existence, something that you're of course going to want to think about.'

I nod, unable to take it in. Any of it, all of it.

'I'm sorry,' Dr. Stein says quietly.

I try to nod but I'm not sure I pull it off. Everything feels difficult, as if I have to remind myself to breathe, to blink, to be. 'So…' I lick my lips. My voice is a thread. 'So how long… do you think…' I trail off, unable to frame the question, even in my own mind. But of course Dr. Stein knows what I mean.

'It's impossible to say for sure. But with the rate of the cancer's progression, and the number of organs that are now affected…' She pauses, and I feel something wild growing inside me, something that is ready to rage and scream. *Don't say it*, I want to shout at her. *Don't tell me how little time I have left.*

'I would say probably not more than six months,' she says carefully. 'And most likely, more like three.'

I turn my head away from her, needing at least that much privacy. I have probably no more than three months left to live. I almost want to laugh, in that wild, raging way. How can this possibly *be*? My mother lived with breast cancer for six years. Why do I get six months or less?

'We can talk again when you've had time to think and process this. There are some drugs we could try – Kadcyla has been shown to extend life by several months in cases similar to yours, although yours has advanced significantly…' She trails off, and I cannot summon a response. 'I'm sure you'll have more questions, and we can discuss pain management, and, when the time comes, end-of-life care…'

I don't say anything, because I don't trust myself to speak. I don't want to talk about end-of-life care; I don't even want to think about it.

Dr. Stein touches my hand lightly. 'I have a seven-year-old son too,' she says quietly. 'I'm sorry.' She waits a few seconds while I remain motionless, staring at the wall, trying not to blink because then the tears will fall. So many tears. After another agonizing second, she leaves me alone.

The next few hours pass in a haze. I lie in bed and stare at the wall, everything in me numb and blank even as a part of me thinks how this is some of my precious time, and I'm wasting it. Wasting everything.

Three months. That's only October. And I might be dead by then. I fight that bizarre impulse to laugh, because it just seems so impossible. Yes, yes, I know I have cancer. I've felt utterly wretched from the chemo. But underneath the misery and nausea and fear, I honestly thought I was going to beat this. Because I couldn't imagine the alternative.

Eventually my mind drifts, painfully, to Isaac. How will I tell him? And who will take care of him? The answer feels obvious, even as I shrink away from it: Heather. After seven years, Heather will get her son back. It turned out I was only borrowing him, after all.

Dr. Stein discharges me the next day, with a follow-up appointment in a couple of days to check on my bandages and drains, which I have, cringing all the while, been taught how to empty. Hopefully the drains will be removed then, the bandages a few days after, and the sutures and steri-strips next week.

In a normal case – although what is normal about any of this, I don't know – I could go back to work in three weeks. But I don't think I'll go back to work now, ever, yet another thought I can't fully absorb yet.

I feel like an old woman, hobbling into a taxi cab, my body bruised, bloody, aching. Decaying. I look down at my hands, the dark red nail polish on my fingernails. I splurged on a manicure a few days ago, because I wanted some part of me to look pretty.

And my hands do look pretty; I've always liked them. Long fingers, neat nails. They don't look like cancer patient hands. And then I wonder if I will still be wearing this nail polish when I die.

The doorman, Sergei, greets me with his usual restrained enthusiasm as I walk slowly into the building. He takes my roll-along bag and escorts me to the elevator.

'All right, Miss Thomas?' he asks and I manage a weary smile. No, I am not remotely all right, but I'm not about to explain that to him. In any case I know I look terrible. My face is pale, my hair straggly and unwashed – I didn't bother with the wig – and I'm wearing a shapeless black tracksuit. I breathe a sigh of relief when the elevator doors close even as a voice in my head whispers, *another moment gone.* When will I stop thinking that? When I'm dead?

I fumble with my keys, the mechanics of it nearly defeating me, my fingers shaking. Finally the lock turns and I open the door and step into my apartment: I'm home. The relief nearly makes my knees buckle.

'Grace…?' Heather comes around the corner, looking both surprised and hopeful. I see the shock flash across her face briefly, and I know that I must look even more awful than I realize – nearly balding, pale and pasty, swaying on my feet. I'm a complete and utter wreck.

'I'm back.' My lips try to curve but I can't quite manage it. I don't want to cry. Not yet.

'Come and sit down. Can I get you something? Some tea or…?' She's at a loss, but she takes me gently by the elbow and leads me toward the sofa. 'You should have called. I would have come to get you.'

'It's okay. Where's Isaac?' All I want is my son.

'He's in his room. Isaac!' she calls, an urgent note in her voice. 'Isaac, look who's here.'

The situation feels unbearably surreal. Me decrepit on the sofa, Heather hovering over me, beckoning my son over. 'Look,' she says, injecting a bright note in her voice. 'Look, it's your mom.' Words I never thought I'd hear her say.

Isaac stops in front of me, looking uncertain. I don't look like I normally do. I should have put on my wig; he didn't even know I'd lost most of my hair. And I'm hunched over, my chest starting to throb with pain. I need more Vicodin.

'Isaac,' I rasp. 'Come here, buddy.'

He comes slowly, hesitantly, and I do my best to hold out my arms, even though the lymph node removal has made them ache. 'You can hug me,' I say even though I know it will hurt. 'Gently.'

He comes closer and then stands in the circle of my arms. He drapes his arms over my shoulders, barely touching me. I press my cheek to his and close my eyes, breathe in his scent. Memorize him.

Tears sting my eyes and I take a shuddering breath and then ease away. I don't want to freak him out.

'I'm home, Isaac,' I say, and he nods.

'Are you better?' he asks seriously, and I have no answer. I have no answer at all, and so I just manage a smile and a jerky nod, and after another uncertain moment he goes back to his room. He's had enough of sickness. So have I.

I lean my head against the sofa and close my eyes.

'You must be exhausted,' Heather says. 'Do you want to get in bed? Or tea, or soup…? Ice, maybe? A hot water bottle?' She lets out a nervous laugh. 'Sorry, I just want to help.'

'I know.' I open my eyes. 'Thank you.'

'Are you okay, Grace?' she asks, her uncertain gaze searching my face, looking for answers I know I need to give.

I glance toward Isaac's room; his door is partially ajar. I lower my voice, each word dragged from me like a weight. 'No,' I tell her, my nemesis, my friend. 'No, I'm not.'

CHAPTER THREE

HEATHER

I stare at Grace, unsure what to say, whether to ask. She looks awful, even for someone who is recovering from surgery. Her skin is pasty and pale, her hair wispy and flat, but the worst is her eyes. The look in her eyes before she closed them was dark and deadened, like a light has gone out inside her forever.

'Can you please close Isaac's door?' she asks quietly, and my heart flips right over. I go to close it, softly, so he doesn't notice. He's lying sprawled on his floor amidst a spill of Lego, and he doesn't look up. I tiptoe back to Grace; she is still sitting with her head back against the sofa, her eyes closed, like the world is too much for her. And maybe it is.

'Grace…?'

'The cancer has spread.' Her voice is so low I strain to hear the words.

'Spread…?'

'To my brain, liver, kidneys, and bones.' She opens her eyes. 'Everywhere, basically.' She lets out a laugh, the saddest sound I've ever heard.

I sit slowly down on a chair opposite her, my mind spinning emptily. 'What… what does this mean?'

Grace takes a deep breath and then lets it out in a shuddery rush. 'It means I have three to six months to live. Or as my doctor said, closer to three.' Her lips tremble and she presses them together.

'Oh, Grace. *Grace.*' Three months. *October.* I can't even begin to get my mind around it, and for a few seconds all I can feel is a terrible pity and sorrow for Grace, overwhelming, swamping me. Tears sting my eyes and my voice chokes. 'I'm so sorry. So, so sorry.' But right on the heels of that sentiment, deeply as I mean it, is a burning question, essential, urgent. *What about Isaac?*

I can't form the words. Not yet. It feels too callous, too cold, although of course it's the most important issue for both of us. Grace must have some sense of what is in my mind, because suddenly she covers her face with her hand.

'I can't talk about this now,' she says. 'I shouldn't have said anything to you. I'm not ready... to talk... about any of this. I just learned about it myself. Please...'

I feel a lurch of pity for her, and my lips tremble before I press them together. 'Of course. I'm sorry. We don't have to talk about anything.' But I don't feel like I should go. Grace looks terrible, and there is Isaac to think of. 'Let me help,' I say. 'I can make dinner, do laundry, whatever.' Grace looks like she wants to resist, and I say quietly, 'Grace, you're not ready to be alone with Isaac. To take care of him. You're still recovering. We... we don't have to talk or anything, but let me help.'

Her hand is still covering her face. 'I don't mean to sound ungrateful,' she says in a choked voice. 'It's all just so much...'

'Of course. Of course it is.' I put my hand on her shoulder; her bones feel hollow beneath my fingers. 'Why don't you get in bed? Rest for a bit? I'll make you some tea.'

Grace nods slowly. 'Thank you,' she whispers, and a lump forms in my throat.

'It's nothing,' I say, because it is.

She rises from the sofa with my help, taking my hand and clutching it with surprising need. Even now I am still amazed that she wants me here; that she chose me to help. I walk with her into her bedroom, pull back the covers. Thankfully I changed the sheets this morning, in case she came home.

When Grace is settled, I check on Isaac, who is still playing Lego, and then go into the kitchen to make tea and figure out what to do about dinner. Yesterday Isaac and I spent a surprisingly happy few hours in The Food Emporium, stocking up on the kind of food I can never afford to buy – organic vegetables, freshly squeezed juice, a prime cut of beef. He was good company, chattering about camp, remarking on different things in the store – the dead-eyed fish chilling in ice, the bright yellow melon. He's at the age where everything is still interesting, and he wants to tell you about it.

I make a beef and rice casserole for dinner, moving around the kitchen with confidence, knowing where the knives are, the plates and cups and napkins. On the fringes of my mind there buzzes a possibility I can't quite keep from thinking about – that I could get used to this. To having Isaac.

I feel a weird mix of giddiness and grief, and I don't know how to reconcile the two emotions, so I force myself not to think at all. Like Grace said, it's too soon.

I make Grace herbal tea and bring it into her bedroom, but she's already fallen asleep. I put the cup of tea on her bedside table, and then pause to look at her. In sleep she looks younger, more relaxed, despite the harrowing lines of age and illness, the thin, wispy hair. I can't believe she is going to die in mere months. Every time I think it, it shocks me, a cold ripple going through me, a zing of pained surprise.

I hear Isaac stirring in his bedroom and I tiptoe out of the room, closing the door softly behind me.

'Hey, Isaac.' I try for a smile and almost manage it. 'Dinner will be ready in a few minutes.'

'Okay… but where's my mom?'

'Sleeping.' And right then it catches me in the throat, makes me breathless. The grief this little boy is going to experience.

The pain he doesn't know is barreling right toward him, and so *soon*. He's only seven. He's too young. Grace is too young. It's so awful and unfair and there's nothing I can do to stop it. 'Come on,' I clear my throat, force the tears back for Isaac's sake, 'let's set the table.'

We set the table for three, although when I check on Grace, she's still asleep, and so Isaac and I eat alone, and then we play a couple of games of Hungry Hippos before it's time to get ready for bed.

To my surprise he's up for a story; for the last two nights he's politely refused my offer of bedtime reading, choosing instead to study his big solar system book by himself. Tonight, however, he picks a storybook that looks as if it is for much younger children and even lets me sit on the bed next to him, my arm around his shoulders as I read. My heart sings and aches at the same time. None of this feels fair or right, and yet I savor these moments so much, even if it feels a little bit as if I am stealing them from Grace.

After I've tucked Isaac in, I brace myself for a call home. I've only talked to Kev once since coming here, to check in on the girls. I've been gone for three days, three summer days, with the girls home all day while he works shifts and tries to manage meals and bedtime. I know Emma will do most of the work, but still… It's a lot.

The phone switches to voicemail and I'm glad. I'm not ready to talk to Kev; I feel too uncertain and raw. I need to think, and yet I don't want to think. I'm afraid and hopeful and overwhelmed and sad all at once.

I check on Grace again, and she is awake, easing up in bed. Her expression turns a little guarded when she sees me.

'Hey,' I say softly. 'Just wanted to check on you. Is there anything you need?'

'My Vicodin. It's in my bag.'

'Okay.' I find the pills and bring them with a glass of water. Grace swallows them silently, her eyes closed. 'I'll sleep on the sofa,' I venture. 'And leave tomorrow, if you're feeling better…' I know I need to get back. And Grace probably wants me gone. I can't blame her for that; she wants to be alone with her son.

'I'll be better.' Grace sounds determined. 'I've got to be.'

I spend an uncomfortable night on the sofa, and finally drift off to sleep, my mind still full of barely formed thoughts, only to be woken up in the middle of the night by the sound of weeping. I stiffen, and then roll off the bed and tiptoe toward the bedrooms. The crying is so soft and small that I think it must be Isaac, but when I get closer, I realize it isn't. It's Grace.

I stand there for a moment, my hand hovering by the door knob, wondering if I should go in and then knowing I shouldn't. Grace wouldn't want me to see her looking so vulnerable and emotional, and yet the sound of her weeping claws at me. It's a sound of such unending despair, soft, hopeless sobs that make my eyes sting as an answering grief rises within me. After a few minutes I tiptoe back to the sofa, and it takes me a long time to get back to sleep.

The next morning Grace is up before I am, standing by the kitchen counter, sipping a cup of tea. She's showered and changed her clothes, and her wig is in place. She looks a thousand times better than yesterday, and yet there is still something defeated about her. Perhaps there always will be.

'Hi,' I offer. 'You look good.' She gives me a strained smile.

'Hi.' She sounds falsely bright. 'I'm feeling a lot better. Thank you so much for everything you've done, Heather. I can't tell you how much I appreciate it all.' There is a note of farewell in her voice, and I understand why; she needs to be alone with Isaac. Of course she does.

'I'll just gather my things…'

'Have some coffee first.' She nods toward the chrome pot on the counter, and I smile my thanks. We drink in silence for a few minutes, and then I murmur something about getting back home by lunchtime. Fifteen minutes later I'm walking out of the apartment, still feeling dazed by everything.

When I walk into my house, I am hit by the sheer chaos of it all. The living room is a bomb site, with Lucy having taken all the pillows off the sofa and put them on the floor. She's sprawled on top of them, watching TV at full volume to compete with the noise of the techno pop music blaring from Amy's room. There is an old smell of fried food hanging in the air, along with an underlying note of something sour, and as I come in, Lucy scrambles up, squealing, and runs at me at top speed, barreling into my stomach.

'*Oof.*' I step back to take the impact as I put my arms around my daughter.

'I missed you, Mom.' Lucy tilts her head to look up at me; her face is dirty and I don't think her teeth or hair have been brushed since I left, but in that moment I don't care. I don't care that the house is a mess, that Amy is probably throwing a fit or that it looks like Kev isn't even here. This is my home, my family, and I am so grateful for it – for them. I remember seven years ago Grace telling me how lucky I am, and right then I know absolutely that I am. Lucky. Blessed.

'You're back.' Emma emerges from the kitchen with a gusty sigh. 'Finally.'

'Sorry.' I'm not really sure what I'm apologizing for, but I say it anyway. 'Where's Dad?'

Emma rolls her eyes. 'Probably buying cigarettes at CVS.'

'That bad, huh?' I say lightly. Kev hasn't smoked in years. At least, not when I'm around.

'He was a little stressed.' We share a tired and complicit smile. 'Aunt Stacy brought dinner over last night, mac and cheese.'

'That was nice.'

'And she washed the kitchen floor.'

'That sounds like Aunt Stacy.' Determined to do something nice while making me feel inferior for having needed to do it. I unwrap Lucy's arms from around me and take her by the hand toward the kitchen.

'What about Amy?'

This elicits another eye roll from Emma. 'What about her?'

'Dad got really mad at her,' Lucy chimes in. 'He found something in the trash.'

'Don't, Lucy.' Emma silences her with a particularly dark look, and I feel a tremor of foreboding. What on earth could Kev have found in the trash? Drugs? Birth control? I picture dirty syringes and condom wrappers, and suppress a shudder. I can't think about that now.

'Let me sit down,' I say. My gratitude is slipping away, replaced by sheer exhaustion. I think of the quiet, elegant oasis of Grace's apartment, how simple Isaac's needs were, how pleasurable it was for me to meet them, and I feel a pang of longing and homesickness. Resolutely I push it all away.

I sink onto the sofa and Lucy settles in next to me, her elbow burrowing into my stomach as she tries to get closer. I wince as I put my arm around her. Then Kev comes through the door, stopping short when he sees me.

'Okay?' he asks. He looks utterly exhausted, his hair rumpled, his t-shirt stained, purple smudges under his eyes.

'Okay,' I say. I rise from the sofa and go to hug him; his arms close around me in surprise. I breathe in the scent of him – Old Spice and cigarettes. I don't mind.

The gratitude rushes through me again, reminds me of how much I have. Our marriage hasn't always been easy, and me being pregnant seven years ago was one of the hardest things to hit us, but we survived. We got stronger, and I've never doubted that Kev will be there for me, as best as he can. Always.

He rests one hand on my back as he pulls me closer. 'Are you okay?' I ask.

He mutters in my ear, 'We'll talk later.' I know it must be about Amy.

The rest of the day passes in a haze of activity – laundry, grocery shopping, housework. Stacy might have mopped the floor last night but the rest of the house is a mess. Amy stays in her room and Lucy picks a fight with Emma, and it shows how tired Emma is that she responds in kind. I force Amy out of her room for dinner, and she sits at the table, arms folded, a scowl permanently etched into her face, and doesn't eat a bite. Dread seeps into me.

By eleven o'clock Kev and I are in our bedroom, and I'm so tired I can barely peel the clothes from my body. He sits on the edge of the bed, looking just as exhausted as I am.

'So,' he says heavily, 'how did Grace's surgery go?' I know he's asking for my sake. I doubt he really wants to know at this moment.

'Not well.' I take a deep breath. I debated whether I should tell Kev about Grace now, when he's tired and with this unknown thing about Amy heavy between us, but now that we're finally alone I can't not say it. 'The cancer's spread. The doctor saw it when she did the surgery.'

Kev looks up, a flicker of something in his eyes. 'How bad is it?'

'They gave her three months to live, Kev.' I stare at him, my heart beating so hard it hurts. He stares back at me, his expression unchanging and impassive.

'Three months.' He rakes a hand through his hair. 'That's tough.'

'Yes…'

He shakes his head slowly. 'Don't go there, Heather.'

'Go where?'

'You know, Isaac.' He sighs, a long, low release of breath. 'Has Grace said anything?'

'No.' I think of the way she covered her face, her refusal to talk about it any more. 'Not exactly.'

Kev just shakes his head again. I haven't even said anything yet, and already I feel like I've demanded too much. Already he's disappointed me. 'Kev,' I whisper, 'he's our son.'

'Do you really think, after seven years, we can just take him back?'

'The situation has changed.'

'For Grace, yeah, I get that. But don't you think she has someone in mind already to be his guardian or whatever? Someone suitable? She has friends, Heather.'

The assumption being that we're not suitable? I swallow the words. 'I don't think she has someone in mind yet.' Although of course I don't actually know. 'She asked me to help this time, and before, too, when Isaac needed to be picked up from school… she doesn't have any relatives – her parents are dead, no brothers or sisters.'

'So you're the obvious choice.' He sounds sarcastic, but I don't care.

'We are, Kev.' I hear the throb of urgency in my voice. I haven't let myself think this far, hope this much, until now. Until Kev put it into words, and I start tumbling headlong into a fantasy that could finally become real.

But he just shakes his head. Again. 'How would it work?' he asks me tiredly. He sounds defeated. 'How the hell would it work?'

'What do you mean?'

'Isaac comes and lives with us here? Goes to school with our kids?'

'He's in elementary. He'd go to the same one Lucy—'

Kev snorts. 'He'd fit right in there, wouldn't he, huh? Grace would love having him there. Half the kids are on free lunches, and even more than that speak Spanish at home.'

'Kev…'

'What? You turning into the PC police? It's true, Grace would hate having Isaac at a place like that.' Before I can draw a breath he continues, relentless now. 'And where would he sleep? Share with Lucy?'

I try not to flinch or fidget. He's throwing up roadblocks left and right and I don't have the energy to dodge them. 'We'd work it all out.'

'Yeah, how's that going to happen, exactly? Because Isaac doesn't belong here, Heather. He'd hate it, and so would Grace. She can barely stand to be here for three hours on a Saturday. You think she wants her son – yeah, *her* son – living here?'

I blink, absorbing all his words. The terrible truth of them. But I'm not going to just roll over. I can't. 'She has money,' I say. 'I'm sure she's got life insurance or whatever…'

Kev's lip curls. 'So what are you saying?'

'Isaac could go to private school, and her money could pay for it.'

'And what else would her money pay for?' Kev demands. 'Isaac gets new clothes while our kids, the rest of our kids, go in rags?'

'You're exaggerating. It wouldn't be like that—'

'Then how would it be? Because I sure as hell can't see it.' He shakes his head. 'You even think there's a school out here, a private school, that Grace would like?'

I fold my arms. 'Maybe she can't have everything, then.'

'And maybe you can't.' We stare at each other: a standoff.

'Don't you want him, Kev? Our son?' I whisper. 'How can you not want him back?'

Kev stares at me for another few taut seconds, unspeaking. 'You think that's what this is about?' he finally demands in a low voice. 'You think this is about wanting or not wanting my own son?'

'Well, you're sure acting like you don't want him,' I snap. I want to hurt him as he is hurting me because damn it, this isn't fair. I'm so close, we're all so close, to being a family again. It's all I've ever wanted, even if I've never let myself dream of it, six of us under one roof, together. And now it's here, I can practically touch it, and Kev is refusing to go along?

Kev rakes both his hands through his hair, shaking his head as he looks at me with a mixture of resignation and scorn. 'We gave him away seven years ago, Heather. I wish to God things could have been different back then. I wish I'd never hurt my damn back, I wish we hadn't been so damn broke. But that's the way it was and we can't make up for it. I let you have your afternoons because I knew how important they were to you, but hell, if I'm going to let you wreck our family forever because of him. I won't.' His expression settles into something hard and unyielding, something I don't like. 'I swear to you I won't.'

I stare at him, my ears ringing with his awful words, his lethal tone. 'You *let* me?' I finally spit. 'You allowed me? Is that how you've seen it—'

'You know what I mean.'

'You think I want to wreck our family?' I practically shriek, the words scraping my throat raw. 'That's not how it is, Kev. Of course that's not how it is. I want to *restore* it—'

'No.' Kev speaks quietly, firmly now. 'No. This is our family, Heather: you, me, Emma, Amy, Lucy. No more. That's how it has been for seven years; that was the choice we made, even if you could never see it that way.'

'That's not true.' I'm fighting tears, caught between anger and wild grief. 'That's not true.'

'It is true. Do you even realize the toll these visits have taken on the kids you do have? Do you ever see it?' I stare at him, shocked, and he shakes his head. 'You haven't even asked about Amy. You know something's going on but you don't even care.'

'I was going to ask. But this came up first—'

'It always does.'

I spin away, the heels of my hands pressed to my eyes. He's being so unfair. He's twisting everything, making me feel so selfish, when all I've wanted was to do what's right for my kids, *all* my kids. Am I the only one who sees that? 'And what if we are Grace's only choice, Kev?' I ask, my hands still pressed to my eyes. 'Do we walk away from our son then?'

'We can't be her only choice.'

'You don't know—'

'Do you? Or are you just seeing what you want to see? There must be someone, Heather. She doesn't live in some bubble. She has friends.'

I don't answer, because I know we'll just keep going round in circles, neither of us willing to give in. Because I'm not going to give Isaac up that easily – I can't.

'Do you want to know what I found in the trash?' Kev asks quietly. 'About Amy?'

I drop my hands. I don't really want to know, but I know I need to. 'What?' I ask wearily.

'A pregnancy test.'

CHAPTER FOUR

GRACE

Pretty soon I discover I can't live in the 'I'm-about-to-die' mode all the time. It's too exhausting. And so I live day to day, concentrating on the little things that don't actually feel so little – taking care of Isaac, recovering from surgery as best as I can, arranging my affairs. The last is a behemoth of a job, and the most important, and I chip away at it slowly.

I visit Dr. Stein, who takes out the drains, and then the bandages, and then the sutures and steri-strips. The scars are livid and red but they're smaller than I expected. I don't look as cut up as I thought I would; really, I just look deflated. And I feel a bit stronger, even as I know I am getting weaker.

I'm breathless from just getting up from the sofa, and I'm getting more headaches. I'm also numb in my right hand, and sometimes my vision goes blurry. I'm nauseous and I can't eat much, although I force myself to, at least a little. I told Dr. Stein about the symptoms, and she just nodded, unsurprised. It turns out what I thought was a really bad reaction to the chemo was actually the cancer spreading. Silly me.

She offered the experimental drugs again, as well as the Kadcyla that might give me symptoms worse than the ones I already have. I say no to it all. I know false hope when I see it. I can read it in Dr. Stein's eyes. She's got to offer, and I get to say no.

Two weeks slip by far too quickly. Heather calls and leaves messages, and I feel guilty for putting her off, but I need to get my head straight first. I can't just give Isaac to her like a birthday present. I need a plan, a way to ensure his future is secure, that he gets what he needs. I also need to talk to him about the fact that I'm dying, but that is a conversation I'm not ready to have yet, although God knows, I haven't got that long to prepare myself.

I do call Stella, because she's not due back from France for another month and who knows what shape I'll be in then. I feel guilty for not telling her sooner, for not trusting our friendship or maybe just myself. She responds by bursting into tears on the phone and then booking a flight back the next day. I am relieved, but I am also sad. Why didn't I tell her sooner? Why didn't I let her make this journey with me, at least as much as she could? As much as she wanted to? It makes me wonder how many relationships I have consigned to mere acquaintance or colleague when they could have been more if I'd let them. If I'd dared.

Stella comes to my apartment when Isaac is at camp, and when I open the door she hugs me – hard at first, and then more gently.

'I'm sorry, I'm sorry, did that hurt?'

'It's okay.' I step back, trying to smile, moved by the tears trickling down Stella's face and feeling my own crowd in my throat.

'I'm a wreck, sorry. It's just such a shock. *Grace.*' She squeezes my arm. 'How are you coping? What can I do to help?'

'Come inside.' I usher her into the kitchen and make tea while Stella slumps onto a stool.

'I should be making the tea,' she exclaims after a few seconds, springing up, full of panicky guilt. I wave her back down.

'Stella, it's okay. I like to do things while I can. Soon enough I won't be able to.' A tremor enters my voice and I focus on getting out the teabags and mugs. It's been two and a half weeks since my surgery. Since my life started to end.

'I don't know what to say,' Stella blurts as I hand her a mug of tea. 'I'm still in shock. I just can't...' She gulps and shakes her head. 'I'm sorry. Please forgive me if I say the wrong thing, I don't mean to.'

'I know.'

'You seem so calm.'

I shrug. 'Numb, maybe. I'm trying not to think about it too much.' I don't know if that's a good idea; some things have to be thought about. Dealt with.

Stella shakes her head again as she takes a sip of tea. 'I'm feeling so sad for myself,' she admits after a moment. 'How absolutely selfish of me.' She glances up. 'I know you don't have family...'

I wonder what she's trying to ask. 'No, it's always just been me and Isaac.' My voice wobbles and I blink hard. I hate thinking of him alone. But of course he won't be alone if he's with Heather.

'What are you going to do?' Stella asks in a low voice, the question halting. 'I mean, about Isaac?'

'I'm not sure.' That sounds so awful to admit. My son's whole future, and I'm dithering. 'I think I'll probably ask Heather, his birth mother, to be his guardian.'

'I suppose that makes sense.' She releases a shuddery breath. 'You know, if you needed me to... well, anything...' She lets out an uncertain laugh. 'Of course you might not want that.'

I realize what she's suggesting, and I am touched. 'Oh, Stella.' I reach over and squeeze her hand. 'Thank you.'

'But Heather makes sense,' Stella says quickly. 'I understand. So will Isaac move out to New Jersey?' She can't quite keep it from sounding as if I'm consigning him to Antarctica, and that almost makes me smile.

'Yes. I'm not sure how it will work.' I've spent far too much time trying to figure it out, but my mind and heart both keep looping in endless circles. 'I have a very good life insurance policy, and plenty of money in trust for Isaac. He'll be provided for, no matter what.' Heather and her family would have to move to a bigger house, but I've consulted my lawyer about the management of the trust fund, and what it could and couldn't be used for.

It feels a little bit like those good old days, when I was contributing to the household expenses when Heather was pregnant, only on a much bigger level. The McClearys could use my money for a new house, or for anything that would directly benefit Isaac, but my lawyer assures me it can be tightly managed, so no one can take advantage. Not that I think they would… except in my darker moments, I sort of do. I've pictured Kev getting his hands on my money to go to the racetrack, or Amy siphoning it off for God knows what, or Heather justifying using it to pay for some little extras, new shoes for her girls, a vacation for all of them. Then I ask myself if I'd mind. There's enough money, God knows, for stuff like that, and I don't really think Heather and Kevin are going to blow through my life savings. Still, it hurts. It's hard to know after all these years, I'm going to have to hand her everything. The most generous thing I could do is make it a gift.

'And what about school?' Stella asks. 'Will he have to leave Buckley?'

'I'm still trying to figure that one out.' He could stay where he is and the trust could be used for a driver back and forth, but I'm hesitant to do something like that. It will make Isaac seem like even more of a stranger in his community, but maybe there's no avoiding that.

But deep down I know the schools aren't the problem. I know I need to let Heather take care of Isaac, but the truth is that I still don't want him to be *hers*. He's only seven. By the time he's a teenager I'll be a distant, blurry memory. Elizabeth will feel like his home. His sisters will seem like his sisters. And Heather will be his mom.

These are thoughts that should ultimately comfort me, and sometimes they do, but sometimes they don't. Sometimes they just make me feel like I'm losing even more than I thought I was.

'If there's anything I can do…' Stella says. 'I can have Isaac over, you know, whenever. Absolutely whenever.'

I smile. 'How about tomorrow, when I have to see my lawyer?'

The next few weeks pass by all too quickly. Stella steps in, taking care of Isaac whenever I ask, and even arranging a special, cancer-oriented home spa day for me – a facial, massage, the whole works. Heather helps too, calling, texting, always in the background. And still I stall.

Then, the first week of August, I decide I am feeling well enough to go on our annual trip to Cape Cod. I know I'm not well enough, however, to go alone with Isaac. I'm so tired, and my hand is still numb, my vision sometimes blurry. I don't trust myself, and Dr. Stein has warned me that all these lovely symptoms are only going to get worse.

I wish I could spend the week alone with Isaac; it feels so unbearably bittersweet, the last vacation we'll ever have together, but the truth is I know I can't. Stella would offer to go with me; Stella and Will together, and I'm tempted. But I know, deep down, who really needs to go with me. And so I call Heather.

'I have a favor to ask.'

'Of course,' she says quickly. 'Anything.'

'Every year Isaac and I go to Cape Cod…'

'Yes, he's mentioned it. During your visits.'

'Right.' I take a deep breath. 'I want to go this year. I've booked the cottage for next week.'

'Okay…'

'I want you to come with us.' A thunderclap of silence greets this announcement. 'I know it's a lot to ask, a whole week away from your family. But I think it would be good for Isaac…' I pause, because I'm not ready to verbalize why. We can talk about that on the Cape.

'Are you sure?' Heather asks carefully. 'Don't you want to be alone with him…?'

'Yes,' I admit, 'I do. But I can't be. I'm not well enough. I need help, Heather. Your help.'

We are both silent; I can hear her breathing. I know I am asking for a huge favor, just as I know she will do it. Of course she will. One thing I know, one thing I've always known, is that Heather will do whatever she needs to for Isaac.

'I'll need to talk to Kevin,' she says. 'Just to check. But I think I can. I mean, of course I can. I will.'

'Thank you,' I say, and Heather draws a quick, hitched breath.

'Thank *you*,' she answers, her tone heartfelt.

We leave a week later, with Heather driving, me in the passenger seat covered in a blanket because I've been getting cold a lot recently and also I will need to sleep. But I'm going. Dr. Stein waved me off with a smile and a fistful of prescriptions for management of pain and the worst of my symptoms. I'm so drugged up it takes me twenty minutes to get through my pills. I've given Heather a schedule of all the doses, because sometimes I forget. My memory, along with everything else, is starting to slip.

Isaac was nonplussed but accepting about Heather coming with us; I know, over the next week, I'll need to let them spend time together. Logistically it won't be hard, because I sleep so much anyway, and yet emotionally it will be the hardest thing I've ever done. Letting go of my son.

Heather seems tense and nervous as we drive away from my apartment building, the trunk loaded up with suitcases and sand buckets. A lot is weighing on this trip; the air feels heavy with the expectation to make every moment count. I crank up the music, just to lighten the mood.

'This isn't a dirge,' I tell her, knowing Isaac won't know what I mean. 'We're celebrating.'

Heather gives me a quick smile of acknowledgment. 'Okay,' she says, and starts to sing along. By the time we cross the RFK

Bridge, we're all singing at the top of our lungs to Bruno Mars'
'Uptown Funk', even Isaac. And I'm smiling, laughing even;
feeling freer than I have since I can ever remember.

CHAPTER FIVE

HEATHER

As the car eats up the miles my heart gets impossibly lighter. I came into this week desperate to get away from the tension at home and also knowing what a huge price I was paying.

Over the last two weeks things have spiraled down and down, and I have felt helpless to stop it. After Kev blindsided me with the pregnancy test news, I sat slumped on the bed, staring at him.

'Is she…?'

'She refused to tell me.'

I closed my eyes. 'I can't believe it.'

'Just like we were.' There was no humor or lightness in Kev's voice; he sounded grim. 'Except she's two years younger.'

'I didn't even know she had a boyfriend.' I felt faint, sick, all thoughts of Isaac vanished from my mind.

'Maybe she doesn't.'

'Should I talk to her…?'

'Someone needs to.'

It was late, but I knew I wouldn't sleep without knowing, and so I pulled on my bathrobe and went in search of Amy. She was sitting on her bed, knees drawn up to her chest, earbuds in. In the bed next to her Emma was curled up, already asleep.

'Amy,' I whispered. 'Talk to me.' She just shook her head without even taking out her earbuds. 'Please.' Still nothing, but I'd had enough. I crossed the room and stood in front of her, yanking out the earbuds with one quick jerk of the cord. She looked up at me, her eyes narrowed in anger, like a cat about to claw.

'Are you pregnant?' I kept my voice low even though Emma was asleep.

'Do you really care?'

'Of course I do.'

'Because it seems like all you care about is your darling boy Isaac.'

I blinked, trying to absorb that accusation. 'You know that's not true,' I said calmly. 'The reason we gave him up was out of care and concern for you and your sisters.'

'Whatever.'

'Amy.' I put my hand on her shoulder, letting her feel the weight of it. 'Are you pregnant?'

She blew out a breath, not looking at me. 'No.'

Relief poured through me, making me sag. 'Okay.' I tried to marshal my thoughts, figure out my next steps when the truth was I had no idea where I was going. 'Do you... do you have a boyfriend?'

She let out a hard huff of laughter. 'No.'

'Then...'

'Grow up, Mom.' Amy rolled her eyes. 'It's not like how it was with you and Dad, all lovey dovey underneath the bleachers, or whatever.'

I blushed, because even now, nearly nineteen years later, I felt a little bit ashamed of my past. I got knocked up in high school. I did it the wrong way around. And I didn't want that for any of my daughters.

'Who is the boy, Amy?'

'You don't know him.'

I felt like I was battering a brick wall. 'Are you using birth control?' I asked, although that wasn't at all what I wanted to be saying. I wanted to beg her to hold on, to wait for someone she cared about, someone she could love; someone she could count on. I wanted to tell her I was sorry that she didn't feel she could tell me, trust me. I wanted so much more for my daughter than what she had, or even what she wanted for herself.

'Of course I'm using birth control,' Amy said scornfully. 'It was just the one time that I was worried about.' Which made me wonder how many times she's had sex, with how many boys. What kind of life was my little girl leading? I was so sad and swamped by this new information, this new Amy. I'd been closing my eyes to it all, telling myself she was only fifteen; surely she couldn't be getting up to much? And now this.

Things with Amy slumped to a standoff and so I tried to focus on other things. I called Grace several times over the next few weeks, just to check in, but I could sense she was trying to keep me at arm's length, and in truth I didn't mind all that much. Life felt difficult enough without adding our complicated dynamics to it.

As for Isaac… I glance back at him now, curled up in the backseat, gazing out the window. I wonder how much he guesses. Fears. Over the last few weeks I've let myself imagine him in our house, the new, bigger house we'll rent. I've looked up private schools in Elizabeth and have tried to picture how it will work. Somehow the pieces never quite seem to fit. But I can make them fit. Together, if he just gets on board, I know Kev and I can make it work for all four of our children.

We backed out once before, when I was pregnant with Isaac. We said it was too hard, too much. I felt cornered, trapped by life, and I didn't see any other way, but this time it can be different. It will be.

Grace falls asleep as I drive, her head lolling back against her pillow. When she gave me the list of all the pills she has to take, I felt a lurch of panic. It suddenly occurred to me how in charge I was, how much she depended on me – to take care of her as well as Isaac.

We arrive on the Cape in the later afternoon. Grace is asleep, but she stirs as we cross the Bourne Bridge and Isaac shouts in excitement.

'We're almost here!'

I've never been to Cape Cod. I've never been out of the Tri-State area, except for that one trip to Florida. The traffic is a crawl and it gives me time to look around, but all I see is scrubby pines and stores and houses covered in shingle. I'm not quite sure what the attraction is, but whenever Grace has mentioned the Cape, her eyes light up and her expression turns all soft and dreamy.

We drive for another twenty minutes or so before we get to Falmouth, and then Grace directs me down a narrow road that's flanked by trees and houses so I can't see much of anything.

'Turn here,' she instructs, and I pull the car into the drive of a house that is smaller than my own.

'I know it's not much,' she says quickly, as if I'd complain, 'but I love it. My dad took me here every summer since I was six years old.'

'It looks great.' I get out of the car and then help Grace, because I've noticed she struggles with this. She murmurs her thanks but then she gently shakes me off and walks slowly toward the cottage by herself, a pale, thin figure.

The cottage is small and shingled, old and weather-beaten. The shutters need painting and one of them is askew. The grounds are nicely kept though, and as we walk around the house, I see right away why she loves it. There is a stretch of green grass, a couple of Adirondack chairs, and then mere steps to the beach and the ocean – all of it right there, vast and shimmering under a hazy blue sky. Grace walks toward the beach with slow, halting steps.

'Isaac,' she calls. 'Isaac, come here.' He trots up to her and she takes his hand. I stay back, letting them have this moment. Knowing they need it. Grace and Isaac walk hand in hand toward the ocean, the sun making the placid water dance with diamond lights. Isaac kicks off his sandals and Grace, with effort, slips off her pull-on Keds. Then I watch as, hand in hand, they step into the sea.

Isaac starts jumping waves while Grace watches, the surf lapping around her ankles, and after a few moments I leave them to it, and go to empty the car. I call Kev after I've brought everything in, including a lasagna I made last night and brought from home. I pop it into the oven to warm as I listen to his cell ring.

'Heather?'

'We got here okay.'

'Good.'

I feel emotional, for a whole lot of reasons. 'I'm sorry, Kev,' I whisper. 'I know this is hard on you. A whole week…'

'It's hard on you,' he says gruffly.

'She's so sick.' I feel tears start in my eyes. 'It's so hard to see her like that. To know…'

'How's Isaac doing?' He sounds even gruffer, which tells me how much he cares.

'He seems okay, but I'm worried for him. Everything is going to change. No matter what, everything is going to change.'

'I know.' We haven't talked about custody arrangements again. I haven't dared, and Grace hasn't actually said anything. As I turn toward the window and watch Grace and Isaac jumping through the waves, I realize I don't know how I feel about anything any more. It doesn't seem quite so obvious, so simple, right now.

'How's Amy?' I ask, and Kev gives the verbal equivalent of a shrug. I sigh, and a few minutes later, we say goodbye.

Grace comes in a little while later, looking completely worn out, but happy.

'I might have overdone it a bit,' she says as she carefully lowers herself into an armchair in the living room and closes her eyes. Outside Isaac is playing happily on the beach.

'What can I get you?' I ask.

'Just a glass of water, please.'

I fetch one and hand it to her. She looks so pale, her lips bloodless as she slowly sips. I glance around at the cottage; it seems even smaller on the inside – just one main living area with a ratty sofa, two armchairs, and a tiny TV, and a little kitchenette leading off it. The bedrooms are small too – one with a small double and another one with two twins. The bathroom looks like it hasn't been redone since the Avocado Era of the 1970s.

Grace smiles faintly, her eyes still closed. 'This wasn't what you were expecting from me, was it?'

'What do you mean?'

'The house. It's pretty darn shabby.'

'Well.' It's hard to pretend otherwise. 'Yeah.'

'The same lady who owned it when I was a kid owns it now. She only rents to a couple of people. It's a treasure. A hidden gem.' She laughs, the sound raspy. 'I'm glad she hasn't changed it. It helps me remember.' She opens her eyes and looks around at the faded furniture, the dusty seashells on the bookshelf, the local hardware's calendar from 2015 that is still tacked up on the kitchen wall. 'I love this place,' she says softly. 'I've always loved it. When I was a child, it was the only place I felt safe. Where death couldn't touch me.' She glances at me, her expression wry. 'Do you suppose that's true now?'

'What do you mean by that?' I ask. 'That death couldn't touch you?'

'Because when my dad and I came here, we felt safe. Cocooned. My mother came too, for those first few years, but she felt different here. It was almost like it was magic.' She pauses, her gaze faraway. 'I think I've told you about my mom, how she was diagnosed with breast cancer when I was seven, and then died when I was fourteen. It overshadowed my whole childhood. My whole life, really.' She sighs and leans her head back against the chair. 'And here it is, playing out again, except Isaac is so much worse off than I was.' Her voice chokes and she takes a shuddery breath. 'He doesn't have my dad.'

There's so much love and grief in her voice that I feel compelled to say, 'Tell me about him.'

'Oh, Heather.' She sighs, the sound still shuddery. 'He was such an amazing man, so funny and gentle and kind. I know it's easy to memorialize people after they're dead, although God knows who will do that for me.' She shakes her head. 'But in his case it's all true. He took care of me when my mom was sick, and he was my rock after she was gone. We did everything together.'

Her gaze turns distant, thoughtful. 'Sometimes I wonder if he did too much for me. I depended on him so much. And I missed him so much. Maybe if he hadn't been such a huge influence in my life, I would have had more friends. More boyfriends. A husband, even.' She shrugs. 'But who knows? Maybe I wouldn't have, because I've known what it's like to lose someone, and it hurts.' She draws a quick breath. 'I hate that Isaac is going to know that too, and worse than I ever did.' Her expression closes down then, and I wish I could comfort her.

'But he's known love, Grace,' I offer hesitantly. 'Such wonderful and generous love, from you. He won't forget that. It will mark him forever, in a good way, to have known that.'

She looks at me, her eyes bright. 'Thank you.'

'I mean it, you know.' I feel the need to convince her.

'I know you do.' She nods toward the back door that leads to the yard and the beach beyond. 'You should go out there. Check on him. Play with him.'

It feels as if she is bestowing some sort of blessing, and yet right now I am strangely reluctant to accept. 'What about you? You could come out, as well...'

Grace shakes her head. 'I think I'll take a nap.'

'Then let me help you to bed.'

She nods, and I put my hand under her elbow, feeling how sharp and bony it is, as I guide her toward the bedroom, and then turn back the covers. She slips between them, looking pale and slight against the worn sheets. She's lost even more weight than I've realized, since I last saw her. I can see the shape of her skull beneath her skin.

'Go to him,' she says softly, and she closes her eyes.

Outside a breeze is blowing up and the sun is starting its glorious descent to the ocean. Everything shimmers. Isaac is kneeling on the beach, intent on building what looks like an entire city of upended-bucket sandcastles, connected by canals he's dug out and attempted to fill with water, although it keeps seeping back into the sand.

'Wow.' I sit down beside him, stretching my legs out, my hands braced behind me, as I study his creation. 'This looks pretty amazing.'

He gives me one quick, searching glance before looking down, focused on his work, his little hands scooping and patting the sand. 'Where's my mom?'

'Sleeping.'

'She sleeps a lot.'

'Yes.' I know Grace hasn't told Isaac she's dying. I know she is going to have to tell him soon.

Neither of us speak. Isaac continues his work, his expression so intent as he methodically builds his canals and castles. I simply sit and enjoy the sun, the breeze, the beauty of the pristine stretch of beach, the sparkling ocean. It's a far cry from Atlantic City, with its dirty sand and seamy, overbuilt boardwalk, casinos and strip clubs next to arcades and stalls that sell cotton candy and funnel cake. And sitting there in the sunshine, I enjoy my son.

After a while Isaac looks up. His gaze is startlingly direct. 'Will you help me fill the canal?'

'Of course, Isaac.' Even though I know we will never be able to fill it with water. That doesn't matter.

A fun but fruitless hour later, after running back and forth between the water and the beach, the dug-out canals have absorbed all the water, and Isaac's cheeks are reddened by both wind and sun as we walk inside.

The cottage feels dark and quiet after the wide brightness of the beach. Isaac investigates a stash of *Archie* comics that look like they're from the 1970s while I check on Grace, who is still sleeping, and then on dinner.

Grace wakes and comes out of the bedroom as I am putting the lasagna on the tiny table in the kitchen that can realistically only seat two.

'I'll eat on the sofa,' she says as she stretches out. 'More comfortable.' I doubt she'll eat anything, but I make up a plate and bring it to her. She smiles her thanks.

'We'll have to have a bonfire one night,' she says as Isaac and I sit down at the table. She picks up her fork but just toys with her food. 'And roast marshmallows. Remember how we did that last year, Isaac?' He nods. 'And maybe go fishing. We rented a boat one year…' She trails off, as if realizing that might not be possible this year. 'It's always so much fun here,' she murmurs. When I look at her again, she has fallen asleep, the plate dangling from her finger-tips, the untouched piece of lasagna nearly sliding onto the floor.

I rescue it, and I catch Isaac's gaze as I put the plate on the counter.

'My mom is really sick, isn't she?' he says, his voice trembling a little.

'She is sick, Isaac.' My heart feels as if it is, quite literally, breaking. Splintering into shattered pieces. I return to the table, trying to smile. 'She'll talk to you about it if you want. Answer any questions…'

'When will she feel better?' I stare at him helplessly, and he must see something in my face, feel it in the air, because he shakes his head quickly. 'Never mind. It doesn't matter.' Yet nothing matters more.

Grace rouses herself a little while later to play a game of Connect Four with Isaac while I wash the dinner dishes. I watch them, a warm feeling blooming inside me, along with the ever-present ache. For the first time perhaps in my whole life, I am enjoying the sight of Grace and Isaac together, the pleasure untainted by any envy or dissatisfaction on my part. I watch the quiet, easy interplay between the two of them: Grace's loving smile, Isaac's quick grins. It almost feels as if I'm intruding, and yet I feel like I could watch them forever, mother and son, a team of two.

The night has turned chilly, and Isaac asks if we can have a fire in the little wood stove. When I gather the wood from the little lean-to outside, I tilt my head up to the sky, amazed at how many stars I can see. The sky is spangled with them, endless clusters and constellations, like clouds of diamonds, distant and sparkling. Isaac comes outside, and I beckon to him.

'Like your bedroom ceiling,' I say, and point upwards. He tilts his head up too, and we stand there together, gazing at the galaxies, silent and amazed. After a second he slips his cold little hand in mine, and as I stare up at the stars, I squeeze my eyes shut, overwhelmed by this tiny gesture, borne, I know, out of fear as well as affection or even love.

When we go back inside, Grace has fallen asleep again.

The days pass, endlessly slow in some ways and yet slipping by far too fast. Grace's health limits what we do, and although she tries to shoo Isaac and me off to go for a walk or a swim by ourselves, I am reluctant to leave her alone. She fades a little more every day, even as I shake out the pills and make sure she's getting all the different medications she needs just to stay alive a little bit longer, a little more with us.

I find myself encouraging Isaac to be with her, not me, because I know he will keep these memories forever, and I want to make sure they make them together. So I bring a chair out for Grace to sit on the beach, and I put out all the shovels and pails and sit a little bit apart as she, painstakingly, makes a castle with him. I set up Connect Four on the table by the fire and when she is too tired even to lift the pieces and slot them in, I do it for her, letting her instruct me where they go.

At first, Isaac seems a bit uncertain about these arrangements, glancing between me and Grace as if he is not sure whom to look to, or even how to feel. But then he starts to accept it – the three of us, a unit, a team, working in sweet, silent harmony. At last.

Four days into the trip, Grace finally talks to me. Isaac has gone to bed, and she beckons me outside, even though the night is turning chilly. She has a blanket draped around her painfully thin shoulders and she curls up in an Adirondack chair, gazing out into the starry night.

'I wanted to tell you,' she says slowly, choosing each word with care, 'that I think you should have Isaac when I'm gone.'

I knew it was coming; of course I did. And yet it still surprises me, leaves me with an ache of longing, a well of sorrow. I've thought of little else for days, weeks, and yet I'm still not ready for this moment.

'I think,' I reply, just as slowly, just as carefully, 'that I thought I should have had Isaac for the last seven years.'

Grace turns to give me a sharp look. She doesn't say anything, just waits.

'But I shouldn't have,' I continue, each word lancing through me. 'I shouldn't have had him. I shouldn't have even thought it. He's yours, Grace. He's always been yours. And you're a great mom.' My chest tightens as I think of all she will lose. All Isaac will lose. And yes, all I will lose. 'Such a great mom.'

She gives a sad little laugh and leans her head back against the chair. 'How I've always wanted to hear you say that.' This surprises me; I didn't think she wanted or needed anything from me, except maybe to back off. 'Whenever I came to visit,' she continues, 'I felt like I didn't know what I was doing. Like I'd never know what I was doing as a mother, and you always did.'

I flinch with guilt. 'I'm sorry.' I'd been meaning to make her feel that way, at least a little bit; I just never thought I'd succeeded.

'It was as much my insecurity as anything else,' she says, straightening a little. 'Everything was so new and strange. When I held him as a baby I felt like I was holding a very precious yet also rather inconvenient parcel, and yet I would die if I broke it.' I laugh a little, recognizing the mother's truth of those words. A newborn takes over your life, your identity. You feel like you're drowning, but you wouldn't have it any other way.

'I felt the same with Emma. It was as if someone had handed me a grenade.'

'Exactly.' She shakes her head. 'It was so hard at first, and yet so wonderful. And now... now I can't imagine life without him. And of course I won't have to.' Her voice wavers and then grows stronger. 'But he'll have to imagine life without me.' She takes a deep breath, lets it out slowly. 'So. I need to prepare him for that.' Her look is direct and unflinching. 'You can have him, Heather. You can finally have him back.' There's no bitterness in her tone, only a dignified sorrow.

I stare out into the night, the ocean no more than a soft, whooshing sound in the darkness. I haven't even let myself dream of this moment, not truly, not fully, and yet now it is here. There is so much swirling around in my mind – so much longing and sadness and fear. And joy, too, that we've arrived at this moment at all. That Isaac could be mine again, that Grace wants me to take care of him. That we've managed to reach this bittersweet yet wonderful point of friendship and understanding. And that makes what I know I have to do next feel harder than ever.

'Heather?' Grace's voice sharpens. 'Say something.'

'You know I love Isaac,' I say slowly.

'Yes,' Grace answers. 'I know that.'

I drag a heavy breath into my lungs. I know what I have to say, but it doesn't make it any easier to say it. 'The truth is, Grace, I'm... I'm not sure it's best for Isaac to be with me. With us. Best for him, I mean.' Tears crowd my throat and eyes. This is even harder than I thought. Grace is silent, staring, waiting, yet I'm not sure I can say anything more.

'I can't believe you're saying that,' she says at last.

Another breath. 'Surely you can see it's true?'

'I have my doubts and concerns, certainly, but it doesn't seem right or fair to let those be the deciding factor.' She pauses, seeming to draw upon some hidden strength. 'You're his mother, Heather.'

I close my eyes, take a deep breath. 'No, Grace,' I say. 'You are.'

She shakes her head, impatient now as well as tearful. 'This is a wonderful Hallmark moment, but let's get serious here, Heather. You want Isaac to be with you. You've always wanted that—'

'I have, but it's been a selfish want.' It hurts to admit it, but also good in a strange and healing way. 'And now I want to do what's best for Isaac. Having him yanked away from everything he knows, everyone he knows... living in a completely different kind of community... that would be so hard for him. And the truth is, he doesn't know me like a mother. He never has. We can't manufacture that relationship out of a lifetime of Saturday afternoons.' Saying it so starkly is another wound. Then, just in case she thinks I'm being a complete martyr, I add, 'and I want to do what's best for my family. Because Amy is off the rails and Lucy has some learning difficulties and Emma just gets lost in the shuffle. I don't want to shortchange any of them, or Isaac. And I know if he came to live with us, I'd spend all my energy making sure he was okay, seeing him through this, and I'd neglect my girls more than I already have.'

'You haven't neglected—'

'I think I have,' I admit painfully. That hurts as much as anything else. 'I really think I have.'

We are both silent, absorbing it all, thinking about the repercussions that spread out like endless ripples in water. 'Is there someone else…?' I ask tentatively, half-wanting there not to be, even now.

Grace is silent for a long moment. 'Yes, I think so.'

'If there wasn't… then of course we'd step up. Of course we would, no question.'

'Thank you.'

We're both quiet, listening to the sound of the tide coming and going, coming and going. 'Then…?' I finally ask.

Grace lets out a huff of sound that is something close to a laugh. 'I never imagined this happening.'

'I know.'

'I thought you'd jump on it, to be honest. I was so sure you would. I'd already looked into how my lawyer would manage Isaac's trust fund, and I was thinking about whether he should continue at school or not, commuting from New Jersey…'

'I'm sorry,' I say. 'I know this is unexpected. And truthfully, I was picturing how it could work. I had this image in my head, but it never seemed to fit, for anyone. I just wanted it to.' I sniff, trying to hold back the dam of emotion. 'Of course I'd always want to be there for Isaac. If he ever wanted to see me, or visit, anything…' I can hardly believe I'm saying the words. No more monthly visits. No more precious Saturdays.

'Of course,' Grace says. She still sounds disbelieving, and no wonder. After all these years.

'This is killing me,' I admit with a ragged laugh that's halfway to a sob. Then I realize what I've said. 'Oh no, Grace. I'm sorry…'

She laughs, and it sounds like tears too. 'Trust me, I know what you mean.'

I stare out into the darkness, and part of me, a huge, painful part, wants to take it all back. I want to say, *forget everything, I've changed my mind, I want him. I want him, I want him, I want him.* The words work their way up my throat, crowd my mouth, bursting to get out. I have to bite my lips to keep from saying something I know I'll regret.

Because no matter how much it hurts now, no matter how wrong it feels, I know I'm doing the right thing. The hardest thing. Just like before.

CHAPTER SIX

GRACE

After all that. After all that, Heather doesn't want him. Except I know she does, terribly, and that's what makes what she said, what she's choosing, all the more unbelievable – and admirable. In a different way, she's giving him to me all over again, and I am humbled by her offer. Her sacrifice.

That night I lie in bed, my mind hazy and already starting to drift from the heavy meds I'm on, thinking about what Heather said. What she's willing to give up. When she asked if there was someone else, my mind leapt to Stella. Stella, who had already half-offered, whose son was Isaac's best friend. It made so much sense, and yet I hadn't let myself think of it because of Heather. Because of what I felt I owed her, after all these years.

I picture Isaac living there, with his best friend and his family, amidst the happy, privileged chaos of their lives. I think he'll be happy. At least, I hope he will, that he could be, with time.

But is Stella willing to take him on? I know what she offered before, but it was in the spur of an emotional moment. I can't take it for granted. And the real question that burrows right down into my soul is should Heather still have him?

She's his mother. She's connected to him by blood and bone and deep, instinctual love. Her three girls are his sisters, not step or half or anything other than total and complete. The six of them could be a family again, the family I know she's always wanted to have. And they could be comfortable financially, thanks to my life insurance. I'd have to put some checks and balances in place, yes, fine, but they would definitely be better off than they are now. Why isn't she jumping all over that? Should I have made it more clear, what I was willing to provide? To give not just to Isaac, but to Heather and her family? Isaac's family. I fall asleep before I can think about it any more, much less come up with any answers.

I wake up the next morning and my vision is so blurry I can barely make out my hand in front of my face. My stomach heaves and my mind spins when I try to rise from the bed. I take a few minutes, keep my breathing even; try not to feel terrified. Every time I think I've become used to this slow, or not-so-slow, descent, I realize I haven't. Not at all. And losing my sight is not something I feel remotely ready for.

My vision clears enough for me to be able to get dressed, but it takes forever just to do the simplest tasks – put on yoga pants, brush my teeth. I look in the mirror and I can make out new hair growing on my scalp, a light brown fuzz, like a baby's. It amazes me that even as my body shuts down, new life grows. There's hope in that, somewhere, but all I can think is that my hair follicles have not got the memo about what's happening.

This new raft of symptoms makes me realize I can't put off any longer the one thing I've truly been dreading to do: telling Isaac.

Late that afternoon, after a nap to restore what little strength I have left, I walk with him out to the beach. It's a perfect day, blue skies, lemon-yellow sun, endless sand and sea. I want to soak it all up but I'm dreading this too much to do more than notice.

We sit for a while as he makes one of his enormous creations – towers and walls and canals he scoops out with his hands. I could watch him forever. If the rest of my life was just sitting here on the sand with him, I would be happy. An eternity of this.

He looks up at me, a slight frown furrowing his forehead. 'Mom?'

My son is smart. He knows something is up. Of course he does. He's known for a while, even if he doesn't want to guess or to be told the truth, any more than I want to tell it.

'Isaac,' I say, my throat already aching, 'I need to talk to you about something. Something important.'

He puts down his shovel and waits. He knows it's serious. He *knows*.

I take a deep breath, blink it all back. 'Isaac, do you remember when I went to the hospital?' He nods. 'I went there to get better, and I thought I would, but the truth is, I didn't.' I stare at him, willing him to understand even as I wish he didn't have to. He's only seven years old. 'I didn't get better, Isaac.'

He blinks at me, his face so serious, so young. 'So will you have to go back to the hospital again?'

'Yes, I probably will.' I know that's where my last days will probably be. 'But…' How can I say this? How can I break his heart and shatter his world? 'The truth is, Isaac…' I reach out and slide my hand through his hair, needing to touch him. And it's a testament to this moment that he doesn't pull away. He just closes his eyes, accepting my little caress, needing it, just as I do. 'The truth, Isaac,' I say quietly, 'is I'm not going to get better. Ever.' I let those words sink in for a moment as I stare out at the ocean, trying desperately to hold onto my composure. 'The truth is, I'm going to die.'

Isaac is silent, his head lowered, his face hidden. I squeeze his shoulder. 'Do you understand what I'm saying?' He nods, and we both stay silent for a few moments, struggling. Struggling on and on, until the end. 'I'm sorry,' I finally whisper. 'I wish… oh, I wish so much I could be healthy and well. That I could be there for you. I want to see you…' I stop, because I can't burden him with my own sorrows, all the things I won't be here to see. Third grade. Losing his front teeth. Graduation, girlfriends, becoming an adult, finding his way. Everything. I'm going to miss absolutely everything.

Sometimes I wonder how much Isaac will even remember me, ten or twenty years from now, when he's been living somewhere else, loving other people, but I can't bear to think that way. I can't stand the thought that one day I will be a faded, fuzzy memory, and nothing more.

Isaac is still silent, but I watch as a tear plops onto the sand, making a damp, dark circle. My brave little boy. I pull him into a hug, hold him as tightly as I can, even though everything in me aches and my heart, my heart has already broken in pieces. It broke the first time I saw him, but now it's shattered completely and there will be no putting it together again. I can live with that. I won't have to for long.

'I love you, Isaac,' I whisper, my voice fierce. I want to imbue him with the words; I want him to always, always remember them, to count on them, as sure as the sun blazing in a cloudless sky. 'I love you so very much.'

His skinny little arms come around me as he burrows into my chest. 'I love you, too.' Then, a ragged whisper. 'I don't want you to go.'

Oh Isaac, I think. *Oh Isaac, if I could stay, I would.* I would do anything, endure anything, to be able to stay. To live. But I just hold him, because that's all I can do now. He will have questions, I know, questions I will need to answer about who he will live with, who will love him and keep him safe. Because his future is the most important thing now. It's the only thing left in my control.

We have three more days on the Cape: warm, golden-soaked days, lying on the sand, playing in the waves. I mostly sleep, whether it's in the cottage or on the beach. The meds I'm on are making me dreamy, distant from myself, which can be pleasant sometimes but also disconcerting. I feel like I've already cut loose and am drifting.

Often I find an hour or even two have passed and I have no idea what I've been doing. Have I been sleeping? Staring? My mind is a dreamscape of memories – my father, my mother, my childhood, Isaac, all of it jumbled together, passing through my consciousness. I suddenly remember absurdly small things – my mother braiding my hair when she had none of her own, the smell of my father's sweaters when I sat next to him as a child, watching TV.

Sometimes I have moments of crystalline clarity, playing Connect Four with Isaac, laughing with Heather, sitting on the sand and staring at the ocean, reveling in the simplicity of it. I am here. *I am here.*

Those moments anchor me in a reality that feels too painful to bear, and yet I don't want to give them up. I will hold onto them until the last. At least I will try.

By the time we leave the Cape, Heather packing everything up, I know I need to go home. I am far weaker than I was a week ago, and my vision is getting worse, so sometimes I bump into things unless Heather steers me right. My right arm is numb to the elbow. Breathing is hard.

The end is closing in. I can see it in the distance, a finish line I want to ignore, a flag waving, and yet it still feels impossible. It's been a month since my mastectomy, since my world began to end. Just one month. I thought I'd have more time. I thought the end would come suddenly, three months and then boom, not this gradual wearing away, the crumbling and the shrinking.

In the end, and it really is the end, I have three more good weeks. Right into mid-September, when the days are crisp and golden and the leaves begin to turn, my favorite time of year. How can anyone not like September, when everything feels new? I'm not going back to school; I'm not going back to work, either, but I feel the urge to sharpen pencils, to buy new notebooks and smooth my hands over the clean pages, to make fresh starts and well-intentioned resolutions.

When we got back from the Cape I called Stella and asked her to come over. She came right away, no questions, and while Isaac was out with Heather – I don't know how I managed without her, now – I asked Stella if she would take care of my son. If she would love him.

Her eyes went huge and tears spilled down her cheeks. 'Oh, Grace. I can't believe we're having this conversation.'

'I know.' I was half-sitting, half-lying on the sofa, a blanket wrapped around me even though it was ninety degrees outside, the middle of August. I'd withered away to skin and bone; even my yoga pants practically slid off me. When I looked in the mirror I genuinely didn't recognize myself, which was the oddest feeling.

'I love Isaac so much. You know that. And you know I wanted to offer… before you mentioned Heather…' She waited uncertainly.

'I thought Heather was the right person to take care of Isaac, but in the end she didn't feel she could, or should. She will, though, if she needs to, but… she wanted Isaac to be in a place, a home, where he feels comfortable, with the least amount of disruption. And I think that's with you.'

'That's so…' Stella shook her head, sniffing, tears spilling over. 'Wow. I mean, that's just…' She dashed at her eyes. 'Sorry. That's amazing of her. And of course we'll take Isaac. We'll love him as our own. Of course we will.'

'It's a big decision,' I felt compelled to warn, even though I know Stella means every word she says. 'Don't jump into it just because you want to be the nice guy here.' I tried to smile. 'Think about it. A lot. For you, as well as for Isaac.'

She nodded, looking serious. 'Of course we will.'

'But,' I said, trying to joke, 'don't think about it too long.'

Stella burst into tears then, and I tried to comfort her, but I couldn't get up from the sofa. 'Sorry,' she said, as she wiped tears and snot from her face. 'Sorry, sorry, sorry.'

'It's okay, Stella.' I smiled, or tried to. I had to think of other people now; I was already slipping away. I was nearly gone.

The next day Stella called me to say she'd talked to Eric and he felt the same way she did. They would be happy and honored to be guardians for my son. The day after, in what felt like a Herculean effort for me, the three of us went to my lawyer and hammered out the details of Isaac's trust fund, how he would be taken care of financially, forever.

I nearly fell asleep in the middle of the meeting, but we got there in the end. Signed and sealed. I could rest easy now. I could die.

A couple of days later I went to Dr. Stein and asked what I'm sure every terminal patient asks for at some point or another – more time.

'I'm not asking for a miracle,' I told her, trying to smile. 'I just want a little more time. Weeks, even. Anything to spin it out a bit longer, because every day I'm feeling worse. Weaker.'

Dr. Stein looked shaken. She's taken my case hard, I think, maybe because our sons are the same age. 'I wish I had that power, Grace, I really do…'

'There must be some experimental drug,' I persisted. A few months ago I thought I didn't want to go down that route of desperate hope. Now I know I do. Anything, anything, to let me have a little longer with Isaac. 'You mentioned Kadcyla…'

'Yes.' Dr. Stein took off her glasses and rubbed her eyes. 'If your cancer hadn't been so aggressive and spread so quickly, I might have prescribed it. But at this stage, Grace…' She looked at me sadly. 'I can manage your pain, and make you as comfortable as possible. Quality of life is an important part of palliative care.'

I looked away, hating her words, knowing they were true. I felt a sudden spurt of rage, surprising me. I'd taken this all on the chin, more or less, but right then I wanted to hurt things. I wanted to scream and rage and shake Dr. Stein's shoulders, asking her why I should have this happen to me. Haven't I lost enough in life?

'I'm sorry, Grace.'

I swallowed it all down, knowing I didn't have the luxury of indulging in that kind of anger. I certainly didn't have the energy. 'Thanks,' I murmured, and then I waited, feeling numb inside, while she wrote a bunch of prescriptions to help with the ever-increasing pain.

Three weeks is not very long. Three weeks slips away like a moment, a second, when it's all you have. Heather came a lot, and so did Stella and Eric, with Will and Jamie. I told Isaac he would live with Stella and Eric when I was gone, and he bit his lip and nodded, trying hard not to cry. I wished he would cry, because then I could comfort him. Instead it will be Stella's arms around him, Stella's shoulders that will feel the weight of his cheek, the dampness of his tears.

One day in mid-September, about a week after Isaac started school, when I am feeling so weak that I end up needing to use the wheelchair Dr. Stein had ordered for me to go outside, Heather, Stella, Isaac, and I all head to the Central Park reservoir. It's a gorgeous day, the sky hard and bright and blue, the leaves only just starting to turn, glimpses of crimson and yellow amidst the green. Isaac skips ahead with Stella, light-hearted for once, while Heather pushes me and I try to soak it all in, right into my skin, because everything about that moment is perfect.

The air smells clean. The trees are in technicolor. I hear Isaac laugh. We walk all the way around the reservoir, the water sparkling under the sunlight as if it is strewn with diamonds. I doze off and on as Heather pushes me, the wheelchair jolting over the rougher parts of the path, but it doesn't bother me. Nothing does, that day. I think some part of me knows it is my last, the last day when I can feel like I am still living, and not just dying.

We don't talk, even when I'm awake, because there is no need for words or sentiment, not when there is sunlight and breeze and the sound of Isaac's laughter. Those are all the things I need.

Heather watches Stella and Isaac together, and I see her smile. It feels like a blessing. It all feels good and right in a way I don't think any of us ever expected.

That night, I have a seizure. I don't know that's what I'm having, not at the time. It's Isaac who finds me, who stares at me in terror as I jerk and twitch, who has the presence of mind to call 911.

I don't remember the rest – the blur of paramedics, sirens, a hospital room. My first thought when I come to is for my son. I try to jerk upright, but my body feels as if it is tied to hundred-pound weights. Moving is near impossible.

'Isaac,' I gasp out, and then, like a miracle, Heather is there. She looks tired and pale and strained, but she smiles and touches my hand. I grab onto her, or try to. I feel so powerless, like I'm drowning in a bed. 'Isaac,' I say again.

'He's at Stella's, Grace. He's fine.'

'How…'

'The paramedics called Stella, and Stella called me. The numbers were written by your bed.'

I'd forgotten I'd done that, just in case. I'd thought I was being so thorough, but I had no idea. No idea whatsoever what it would feel like when the time came, when everything felt as if it was screaming to a halt and careening off a cliff at the same time.

I close my eyes, my grip relaxing on Heather's. 'What happened?' I ask after a few moments. My voice is thin, like a thread.

'You had a seizure. The tumor is putting pressure on your brain, which is what caused it.'

'You've seen Dr. Stein?'

'Yes, she came by.' Heather sits in the chair next to my bed, her hand still touching mine. 'Would you like to see Isaac?'

The way she says it, her voice so soft and sad, floods me with fear. I turn to look at her. 'Is this it?' I ask in disbelief. Despite everything, I can't believe I'm here. Already. 'Is this the end?'

Heather's eyes fill with tears. 'Oh Grace, I don't know. But Dr. Stein seemed… serious. She's coming back soon.'

'Okay.' My mind is spinning. I look out the window, and all I can see is sky, a whitish-gray. A cloudy day in September, and it might be my last day on earth. Does it happen that fast? I remember that last endless week with my father, the long, agonizing days as we both waited for him to die. Is that all that's left for me, the *waiting*?

'I want to see Isaac,' I tell Heather. 'Before…' She nods. She understands.

Dr. Stein comes by a little while later, I don't know how long. Minutes and hours pass with equal speed for me now, everything dazed and distant. Dr. Stein sits by my bed, where Heather sat, and smiles at me, her face full of sympathy and sadness.

'How are you feeling, Grace?'

'Is this it?' I just want to know. 'Am I going to leave the hospital? Ever?'

'That's up to you.'

That doesn't sound good. 'What do you mean by that?'

'We've done some tests, Grace, and the cancer is continuing to spread. Your organs can't take much more stress, I'm afraid.'

This shouldn't be a surprise, and yet it is. Every bit of bad news shocks me all over again. 'So…?'

'So we can arrange for you to go home, and be as comfortable as possible. Or you can stay here, if you'd feel safer with the hospital staff nearby.'

Safer? What is safe about death? It's the most dangerous, frightening thing ever, and yet it's coming for me. I shake my head, at a loss, trying not to cry, because the truth is I'm scared. I'm scared to die, and die alone; I'm scared about what it will feel like, and I'm also scared for Isaac, for the pain I know he'll feel, the pain I can't spare him from. 'I want to see my son.'

'I know, and I believe Heather is going to get him for you.'

This can't be it, I keep thinking. I don't want this to be it. It feels so sudden, so *pedestrian*. A hospital bed, anonymous nurses, that awful beeping of machines. What if I die alone? I am suddenly seized by a choking terror. I don't want my last moments on earth to be alone. I've been lonely for so long, but God knows, I need someone now.

I try to focus on Dr. Stein even though I am screaming, shrieking inside, everything resisting. 'I'll stay here,' I say. If I went back home I'd need someone, most likely Heather, to stay with me twenty-four hours a day, and I can't ask that of her, not after everything she's already done. I also don't want Isaac to see me at the end. He's too young to bear the weight of that memory.

'How much longer?' I ask Dr. Stein, as if she could tell me the date and time, as if she knows.

'I don't know.' She draws a quick, ragged breath and pats my hand. 'A few days, maybe a week.'

I nod slowly. So now I know. And strangely, that brings its own sorrowful peace. There will be no more striving, no more savoring, no more eking out another precious moment. Now is the time for goodbyes, and amazingly, my body relaxes. The screaming inside me stops, forever silenced.

Heather brings Isaac to me that night. I am doped up on a morphine drip, the world going hazy at the edges. But I see my son in full clarity. It will be the last time I see him. I want his memories of me to be good ones, strong ones, building sandcastles on Cape Cod, not withering away here.

His face is pale, his eyes huge and dark as he stands by my bed. Heather quietly leaves the room, and I try to smile. 'Hey, bud.'

'Mom.' His voice wobbles, and his lips tremble. I reach for his hand.

'It's all right,' I say, stroking his fingers, memorizing the feel of him. His skin is so soft. 'You can cry. It will always be all right to cry.'

And he does, the tears spilling down his cheeks, and strangely I'm glad. Now is my chance to comfort him, to give him the last of my strength. I reach my arms up, scrawny, skeletal arms, bone-white, that don't look as if they belong to me, and I hold my son.

I press my cheek against his and close my eyes as I breathe him in, the smell of sun and soap and little boy sweat. In my mind he is a newborn, squalling and perfect, a baby, chubby and red-cheeked, a toddler, a gap-toothed six-year-old.

And then, with my cheek pressed to his and my eyes tightly closed, he is a cocky ten-year-old, a moody teenager. He is learning to drive, graduating, going to college. I see him as an adult, comfortable in his own skin, finding his place. I see his arm around his wife's shoulders as they laugh together. I see my grandchildren, a whole handful, boys and girls, grinning and laughing, the family I never got to have. My family.

I see it all in that hug, I feel it and I believe it with everything I have left, and I hold onto it even as I let Isaac go.

CHAPTER SEVEN

HEATHER

For three days and nights I stay by Grace's bed. Isaac is at Stella's, which is where he should be. And I know, with every instinct I've ever possessed, that this is where I need to be.

I've never seen someone die. I hope I'll be strong enough. I sit by Grace's bed as I watch her sleep. I watch her eyelids flicker open; sometimes the world comes into focus and sometimes it doesn't. Nurses come and go quietly; they up the morphine, check her vitals. Dr. Stein visits and gives me sympathetic smiles, talks to Grace if she's awake and lucid, which isn't very often.

But sometimes she is. Sometimes her eyes open and she smiles at me, and a memory comes to her, unbidden, spilling from her lips.

'My dad was just in here,' she says with a shake of the head. 'By the door. He had a fishing rod. He loved to go fishing. I always pretended I didn't mind the worms.' And then she closes her eyes, murmuring about how strange it is to see him again. A few minutes later she opens her eyes again. 'I thought my dad was here. It's so odd… I can't tell what's real any more.'

'Maybe it's all real,' I offer, and she smiles.

'That would be nice. I think I'd like that, although…' Her eyes close as a faint smile curves her mouth. 'A little while ago I thought I saw spiders scuttling all over the floor. Like *Raiders of the Lost Ark*. I hope that's not real.'

'Don't worry, only the good things are.'

'Yes,' she murmurs as she falls back asleep. 'Only the good things.'

I call Stella when Grace's asleep. We've developed a strangely intimate relationship over the last few days, conducted through texts and phone calls, pictures she sends for me to show to Grace, while I give her halting, grief-ridden updates. I hear the warmth in her voice when she talks of Isaac and her children, and it comforts me. There's not a single pang of envy or shard of regret in me when I hear her voice, and I recognize the love she already has for Grace's son.

Then I call Kevin. When I had told him I needed to stay with Grace, he didn't offer one word of protest. He just said 'Of course.' I loved him all the more for it.

He is my rock now; taking time off work, talking me through it all, helping me to be strong, knowing how important this is. How beautiful, in its own painful way. Because this is painful, all of it, even as it feels right to be here, to be a part of it. And Kevin is a part of it, as well. When I told him I'd said no to Grace, that we wouldn't take Isaac back, he just hugged me. He offered me comfort, because he knew how much I was hurting. Just as he does now.

'How's Amy?' I ask Kev on the second night, my body aching with tiredness, my eyes gritty. Grace is dozing fitfully, twitching, her eyes fluttering open before she sinks back into sleep. She hasn't eaten anything in nearly eighteen hours.

'She's all right. Quiet. She hasn't gone anywhere. Out, I mean.'

'Is she going to be okay?' I ask Kev, as if he can tell me. As if he knows.

'She'll get there. We all will. It's just going to take some time.' And I decide to believe him, because I need to believe in my family, the family I chose seven years ago, and am choosing now.

Later, when Grace has lapsed into a deeper sleep, Dr. Stein comes in and checks on her. Her forehead is furrowed as she reads the notes clipped to the end of the bed and then checks Grace's pulse, scans her face. I hold my breath.

Dr. Stein gives me a quick, sympathetic look. 'Not long now,' she murmurs, and I am jolted, as if by electricity.

'You mean…?'

'I'd say no more than twelve hours.' She pats my hand and leaves. I stare at Grace, fighting an urge to shake her awake, to somehow make these last hours count. I think of Isaac, and my chest hurts. Everything does.

Outside dusk is falling, the sun sinking below the buildings, making the dozens of windows shimmer like gold. I pace the little room, stretch my legs. Wait.

My mind starts to reel back, a montage of what-if moments. When I first saw Grace's profile on the internet. When I first mentioned her to Tina. When I first met her. I had no idea back then how our lives would become so intertwined, so intimate.

And then, of course, seven years of visits. Of silent, crackling tension and quick, sharp looks. A world of conversation in pointed glances, suppressed sighs, thinned lips. What if we'd hammered out our objections, admitted our fears, back when Isaac was a baby? Would things have been different? Could we have become friends a long time ago, instead of now, when it feels so late? But not quite too late.

Maybe we needed everything to happen the way it did, messy and complicated and unplanned, so we could be where we are now. Where we need to be.

Grace opens her eyes. They look bright, almost green, and her mouth curves in a faint smile. My heart turns over and I sit down next to her.

'Can I get you something?'

She licks her lips and shakes her head. 'I thought Isaac was here. He was a baby, sitting on the floor, smiling up at me. At us.' She closes her eyes briefly. 'I know it's not true, but it's so strange.'

'I'm sure it is.'

'I'm losing it, aren't I?'

'It's the morphine, Grace.'

'I know.' She opens her eyes. 'My father was the same.' She looks at me, maybe taking in how bedraggled I must look after spending two days and nights on the hospital floor. 'Have you been here long?'

I know she doesn't really have any sense of time. 'Not very long.'

She falls back asleep, and at some point I do too. When I wake up something feels different, it's almost as if the air has changed. I jerk upright and check on Grace; she's still breathing, but more slowly, her head tilted to one side, her body slack. It's as if something vital has left her, something I didn't even realize she still had to lose. My heart starts to race.

A couple of hours pass and no one comes in. It's as if we've been forgotten, as if we've entered some Twilight Zone of reality, of life, a hovering between one thing and the next.

She stirs, twitching restlessly, and I take her hand and clasp it between mine. Her bones feel hollow, her skin dry and papery. Everything so light.

Autumn sunshine pours through the windows. It's a beautiful September day, the kind of day when you feel like starting something new; going on a jog or making something fancy for dinner. Breathing life in deep.

A nurse comes in, checks the morphine. Smiles at me. I stay where I am, stroking Grace's fingers, sometimes murmuring something, I don't even know what. I just want her to hear a voice.

She opens her eyes a few times, but doesn't seem to focus. 'It's all right, Grace,' I say as I stroke her hand. 'It's all right.'

Then, when it feels like I've been sitting there forever, as if I always will be, she opens her eyes and this time she sees me. We stay suspended for a moment, staring at each other, and then her gaze moves down to our hands.

A smile curves Grace's mouth, and lightly, so lightly, her fingers squeeze mine. She leans her head back against the pillows. 'Thank you,' she whispers, 'for holding my hand.'

Those are the last words she ever says.

Death feels sudden, even when you've been laboring toward it for hours, days. It feels like the moment in musical chairs when the music stops, and you're left looking around, wondering where to go.

After Grace dies I sit there for a moment, simply because I don't want to begin the next part. But then her skin starts to cool and I don't like seeing her so still, so I get up and tell a nurse. Half an hour later, having filled out some forms and called Stella, both of us fighting tears, I drive home.

Walking into the house feels strange, like stepping through a gauzy veil, from one reality to another. It's four o'clock in the afternoon, and Amy and Lucy are at home; Emma is still out at the community college where she's training to be a nursing assistant.

'Mom?' Lucy looks up from the TV, instantly anxious. I try to smile. Then Amy opens the door of her bedroom.

'Is she dead?' she asks bluntly, as only Amy can, and all I manage is a nod.

Lucy looks nonplussed and Amy goes back into her bedroom. I sit down on the sofa, feeling as if I am a hundred years old.

'Will we ever see Isaac again?' Lucy asks, and I turn to look at her. I can't tell anything from her tone; she sounds merely curious.

'Yes,' I say. 'Yes, I think we will.'

Later, when the girls are in bed and we are alone in our room, Kevin holds me and I cry. I didn't realize I had so much sadness inside me as the sobs wrack my body and my breath shudders through me. Kevin strokes my hair and my back and keeps his arms around me. He doesn't say anything; I don't want his words. I just need his body next to mine, the thud of his heart, anchoring us to this moment.

The next morning, I wake up early, the light still grayish as I make coffee in the kitchen. I feel like I've been away from my normal life for a lifetime, first with Grace's surgery, and then the trip to Cape Cod, and then the weeks after, when I took unpaid leave to help her live, and then to help her die.

I need to go to work, if not today, then tomorrow. Get back to living my own life, making money, making dinner. Life with all its little trials and errands. I can't imagine it yet. Even just standing here feels like an effort. It's hard.

I am just sitting down at the table with a cup of coffee when to my surprise Amy appears in the doorway. Her hair is rumpled, her face pale. I lower my coffee cup.

'Amy…?'

'Can I talk to you?'

'Of course.'

She hovers in the doorway, pleating the bottom of her t-shirt with her fingers. She looks nervous, which is something Amy never is.

'Amy…?'

'When I told you that thing before… it wasn't true.' My mind is racing, trying to figure out what she means. The make-up? The boyfriend, or lack of one? 'The pregnancy test,' she whispers, and realization slams into me.

'You mean you're pregnant?' She nods and I try to keep my expression neutral rather than shocked or appalled, both of which I feel, even though I, of all people, shouldn't be either. I wasn't that much older than Amy when I was pregnant with Emma. 'How far along…?'

Amy shrugs. 'I don't know. A couple of months.'

I sit back, reeling. 'And the father…?'

She doesn't look at me as she answers. 'I don't know who it is.'

The words fall into the stillness like stones. I have no words. *Amy.* My little girl. It takes everything in me not to look horrified. Not to cry. And then Amy does.

'I'm sorry, Mom,' she says, her face crumpling as tears streak down her face. Amy, who never cries. Somehow this makes everything simpler; my choice is clear.

'Oh, Amy. Amy. Come here, sweetheart.' I fold her in my arms, hugging her for the first time in years, while she cries and trembles. I stroke her hair and tell her it's going to be okay, even though I have no idea if it is or not. She's fifteen years old and pregnant, no father in sight. But we can talk about all of that later. Right now all she needs to know is that I am not going to walk away from her now, or ever.

The next few days pass in a blur of grief and activity; I go back to work, I tell Kev about Amy. He is stoic and accepting, as I knew he'd be. We arrange for a visit to the doctor. I sit with her in the examining room, both of us pale and tense as the doctor confirms her pregnancy and says she is about sixteen weeks along.

Sixteen weeks. Already in the second trimester, nearly halfway through, and she still looks so slim. She could find out if it's a boy or girl soon. Feel it kick.

I hold her hand as we walk out of the doctor's office and then sit in the car. Rain drums against the windows; the weather has turned. Amy stares into space, dazed.

'Amy?' I ask gently. 'Have you thought about what you want to do?' She shakes her head. I rest my hands on the steering wheel and take a deep breath. 'Sixteen weeks is pretty far along. You'll feel it kick soon.' Her lips tremble and she presses them together.

'I guess… I guess I should give it up for adoption.' She glances at me swiftly, searchingly, without bitterness or accusation. 'Like you did.'

Does my daughter finally have a glimmer of the difficulty of the choice I made, have lived out every day since? 'You have time to think about it,' I say. 'To decide what is right and best for you as well as the baby. You don't need to say for sure right now.'

She nods, and I take another deep breath, let it out slowly. Then I start to drive home.

Three days later we all dress in our somber best for Grace's funeral. Stella organized it all, and called me to let me know when and where

– a big, beautiful church on Fifth Avenue. We file in quietly, sit in the back. There are more people there than I expected – neighbors, parents from school, colleagues from work, or so I assume. A whole life I never knew about, people who care, and yet I was the one who was there in the end. It feels like an honor now, a privilege.

We watch silently as Stella and Eric come in, their two boys behind them, and then Isaac. He looks so small in his dark suit, his face pale, his eyes serious. My heart squeezes with love and pain and I want to reach out to him so much my fingers twitch. Kev reaches for my hand and holds it tightly.

I don't remember much of the service. A priest, a prayer, a poem. Thoughtful silences, singing, kneeling. The words blur by as I stare at Grace's coffin, shrouded in white, a single wreath of white roses on top. *Grace.* I miss her. I miss her more than I ever expected to, and I know I will feel that ache for a long time.

After the service, we circulate with cups of coffee and paper-thin sandwiches cut into triangles, the girls sneaking looks on their phones as we smile and nod, exchange bland greetings with strangers. I know it's hard for them. We don't quite fit here, and yet we belong.

Then Stella comes up to me and Kev, taking both of my hands in hers. 'How are you?' she asks. She looks gaunt and grief-stricken, dressed in an unobtrusive black suit. 'I've been thinking about you so much, Heather…'

'I've been thinking about you, too. And Isaac.'

'He seems okay.' She tries to smile, but sniffs instead. 'I know it will be a very long road, and it's all so hard, but it's good. If that makes sense.'

'It does.'

She squeezes my hands. 'You shouldn't have sat in the back. We'd saved a pew for you all, up front…'

'It's okay.' I squeeze her hands back before slipping mine from hers. 'But thank you.'

'It's you I should thank. For being there for Grace, and for Isaac...' She pauses uncertainly, and I know what she is trying to say. She is thanking me for giving up Isaac. For letting go of my son. 'Do you want to see him? Talk to him, privately, I mean?'

Kev and I exchange looks. 'You go,' he says softly, and I gulp. Nod.

I find Isaac half-hiding by the trays of sandwiches, scuffing his shoes – they look shiny and new – on the floor. I smile at him.

'Hey, Isaac.' I touch his shoulder. 'I wanted to see how you were doing.' He blinks at me uncertainly. 'Shall we go somewhere a little quieter?' He nods, and I take him by the hand and lead him outside to the foyer of the church, and then to a dim little room off the side with dusty chairs and piles of old hymnals. It smells of incense and candle wax. We perch on the chairs and I smile at him, or try to.

'How are you?' I ask quietly, and he hunches his shoulders. 'It's hard, I know. It will be hard for a while. A long while.' I wish I had more words, words that would help and heal, but all I can offer is this. 'I just want you to know that I'll always be here for you, Isaac,' I say, trying to keep my voice steady. 'No matter what. If you ever want to call or email or visit, whatever, all you have to do is tell Stella and I'll be there.' I squeeze his shoulder lightly. 'I'll be there, Isaac. I promise. Always.' He nods slowly, unblinking.

Gently I draw him into my arms, and he rests his head against my shoulder. I close my eyes as I memorize the feel of him; he fits under my chin. His skinny arms wrap around my waist. We stay like that for a few seconds, and then Isaac starts to wriggle away. I let him go.

He smiles at me, a funny, lopsided smile, just like Kevin's, and I smile back. 'I love you,' I say, and I realize it's the first time I've ever said it to him. He nods, silently accepting, and then I rise from the chair and we head back to the crowd.

A few moments later, with Isaac running back to Stella, I find Kev and take his hand. He squeezes my hand and I nod. I'm okay. Amazingly, I'm okay.

We find the girls, gather them up. Lucy clings to my hand as Amy and Emma murmur together. My family. I say goodbye to Stella, and she grabs my hand. 'You know, if you want to see him, anytime… I mean…'

I nod. I know what she means. 'You know where to find me,' I say. And so does Isaac.

For a few moments I let myself imagine a future where I'm involved in Isaac's life. We all are. Where Isaac stops by just to say hi, or we have Thanksgiving dinner together, a family of sorts. When we share the little moments as well as the milestones. Maybe, in this new, unexpected world, grief-touched but still wondrous, it could happen. Maybe it will. I will let myself hope.

Holding Kev's hand, the girls walking along beside us, I step out of the church and into the sunshine.

A LETTER FROM KATE

Dear Reader,

Thank you so much for taking the time to read *A Mother's Goodbye*. I am so pleased that you did and I really hope you enjoyed it. If you did, and want to keep up-to-date with all my latest releases, just sign up at the following link. Your email address will never be shared and you can unsubscribe at any time.

www.bookouture.com/kate-hewitt

As a mother myself, I am always fascinated and intrigued by the complexities and challenges of modern motherhood, and the genesis of this story came originally from a snippet of a newspaper article I read on the difficulties and benefits of open adoptions. However, the characters of Grace and Heather are entirely my own, and I think there is a bit of me in each of them! I enjoy writing stories where there are no villains or heroines, just real people facing real issues, as Grace and Heather do.

If you enjoyed *A Mother's Goodbye*, I would be so grateful if you could spare a couple of minutes to write a review. You can also get in touch via my Facebook page or Twitter account, or join my Facebook page 'Kate's Reads' where we discuss all sorts of books. I always am grateful to be in touch with readers; social media can feel like a lifeline to a writer working on her own!

I am currently working on my next book, and am looking forward to sharing it with you.

Thanks again for reading!

Best wishes
Kate

katehewitt.blogspot.co.uk

@katehewitt1

@katehewittauthor

ACKNOWLEDGEMENTS

There are always so many people involved in the writing of a book; it really does feel like a group effort sometimes! I'd like to thank my agent, Helen Breitwieser, for seeing the promise in the manuscript, as well as Peta Nightingale, Isobel Akenhead, and all the team at Bookouture for their hard work in helping me to make this story the best it could be. I'd also like to thank my dear writing friend, Jenna Ness, for cheering me on as I wrote to manic deadlines of my own making, and to my husband Cliff and my five forbearing children, Caroline, Ellen, Teddy, Anna, and Charlotte, for being patient with a mother who often seemed to only be half in this world. I'm all yours now!

Made in the USA
Lexington, KY
07 July 2018